TORTURED ECHOES

TORTURED ECHOES

CODY SISCO

Resonant Earth Publishing

Resonant Earth Publishing
P.O. BOX 50785
Los Angeles, CA 90050

Library of Congress Control Number: 2017902183
ISBN: 978-0-9970348-4-4

Book cover design by Novak Illustration
Editing by Lindsey Alexander and Beth Wright

Author photo by Nate Jensen

www.codysisco.com

First Edition

For truth seekers everywhere

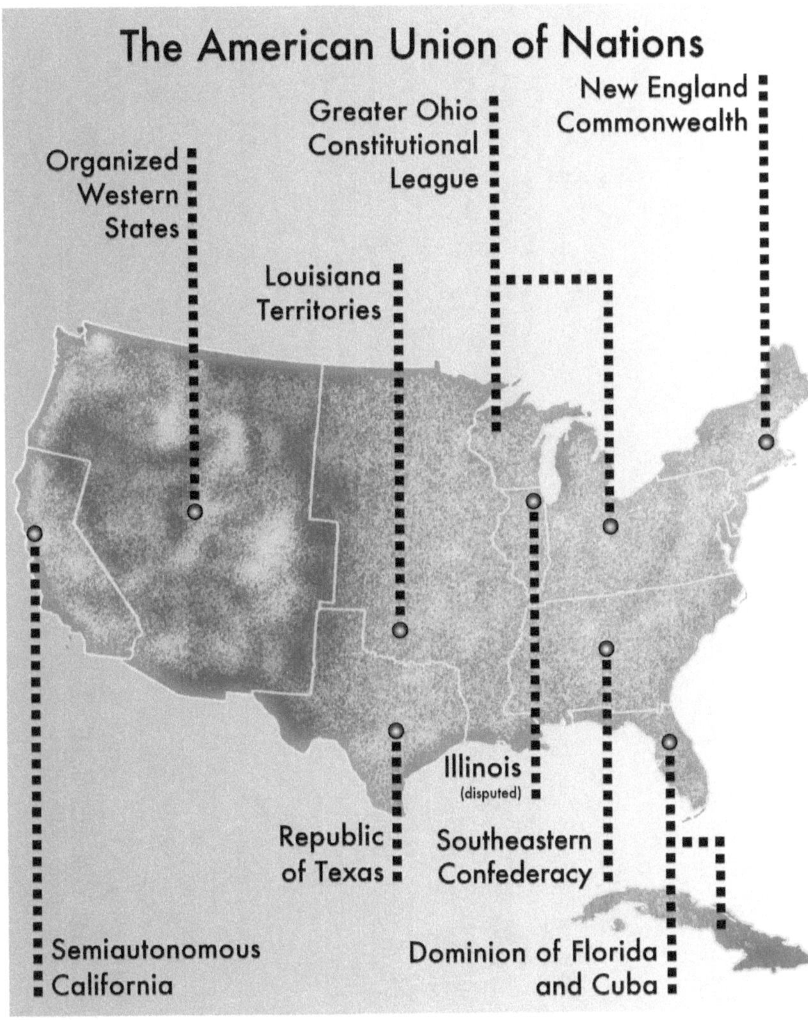
The American Union of Nations
New England
Commonwealth
Greater Ohio
Constitutional
League
Organized
Western
States
Louisiana
Territories
Illinois
(disputed)
Republic
of Texas
Southeastern
Confederacy
Semiautonomous
California
Dominion of Florida
and Cuba

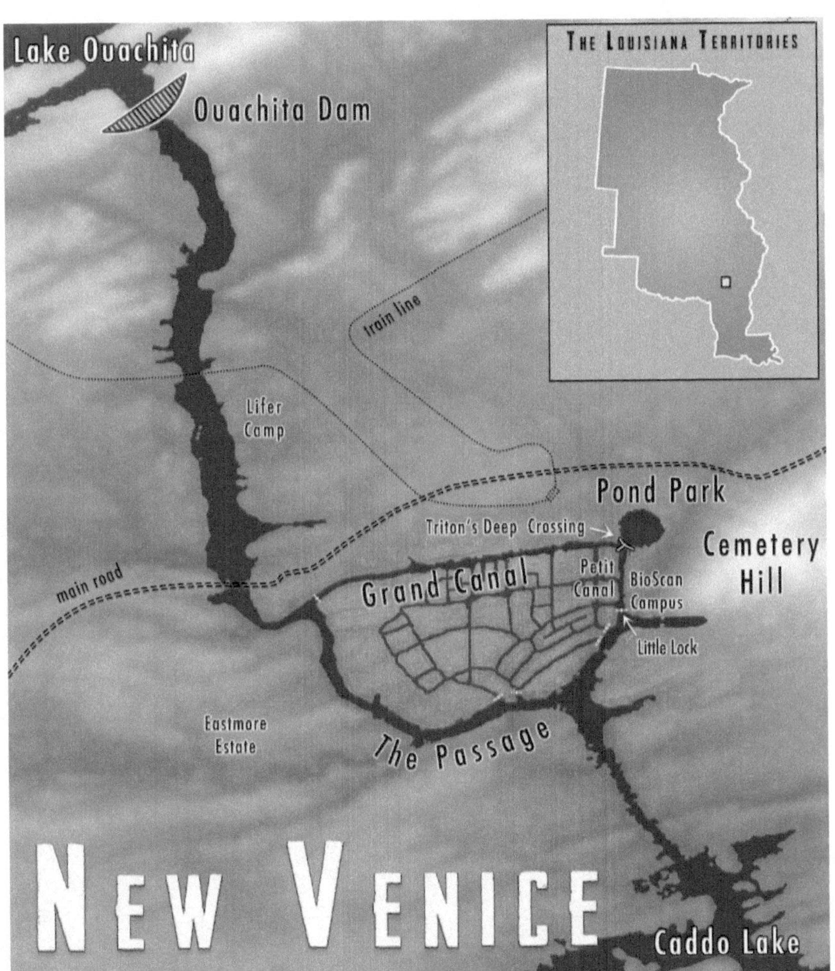

Lake Ouachita
Ouachita Dam
The Louisiana Territories
train line
Lifer Camp
Pond Park
Triton's Deep Crossing
Cemetery Hill
main road
Grand Canal
Petit Canal
BioScan Campus
Little Lock
Eastmore Estate
The Passage
New Venice
Caddo Lake

Mirror Resonance Syndrome:

A degenerative brain disorder associated with electrochemical imbalances within mirror-neuron networks. These structures enable individuals to understand and interpret others' intentions and emotions. Symptoms of mirror resonance syndrome (MRS) can be severe, vary widely, and usually include habitual aggression and violence.

Many people with MRS experience extreme emotional transference. The syndrome is linked to a genetic variation in less than 1 percent of the population.

Emotional hyper-reactivity over an extended period, including these progressively worsening symptoms:

1. Abnormally strong physiological and emotional reactions to physical or mental stimuli, including synesthesia and hallucinations

2. Subjective experience of being controlled, lacking autonomy, following a predetermined course, or reliving events (e.g., episodes of déjà vu lasting hours or days)

3. Persistent, immersive fantasies to the exclusion of reality and maladaptive daydreaming

4. Depersonalization, loss of emotional vividness, motor-body disorientation, dissociative states, or extreme variability in self-image

5. Episodes of "brain blankness," i.e., dreamlike fugue states and sleepwalking

6. Addiction to resonant-class narcotics [new criterion]

—*Diagnostic Criteria for Mental Disorders,*
Semiautonomous California Health Board,
Third (Revised) Edition

1

My honeymoon should have been the happiest week of my life. Claudio's too. We were supposed to spend it relaxing, making love in the afternoon, enjoying sunsets and crickets and music. Instead I saw horrors.

Memories of the people we've lost disappear faster the more fiercely we hold onto them. They fossilize, hardening into unsatisfactory substitutes. One crystalized poignant reflection—a realpic of lovers spooning gelato into each other's mouths—can erase a lifetime of less precious moments, even the beautiful ones.

Our dead can never delight, disappoint, or surprise us again. Death is painful certainty. Death is dully unsurprising. And death is a cruel comfort in an uncertain world.

—Interview with Mía Barrias in *Five Years After Carmichael* (1976)

5 May 1991
Oakland & Bayshore, Semiautonomous California

Two Classification nurses in blue coveralls brought Samuel Miller onstage. He moved in a kind of lurching hobble, his wrists and ankles shackled with carbon fiber cables. His eyes gazed forward, witless. The Personil had had the intended effect.

A quiet murmur threaded through the crowd that had assembled in the National Theater as the nurses led Samuel into a steel-barred cage.

Mía Barrias stood offstage next to the folds of a gold-and-blue striped curtain, watching the nurses affix a biometric lock joining the cable to an eye bolt protruding from the stage. They checked his restraints again.

"You don't need to be gentle," Mía said into the small voicecap pinned to her collar. "He can't feel a thing."

The nurses' sonobulbs relayed her comments to their ears. One of the nurses glanced her way and gave a fingerburst of acknowledgment.

Samuel Miller's arms hung limply at his sides. To a casual observer, he would have resembled a wax figure in a museum of the macabre. *Come look at the madman of SeCa. Gaze in astonishment and revile him.*

The nurses left the cage and locked the door. A loud clang resounded though the theater. The crowd was silent for a moment, seemed to draw a collective breath, and then erupted in shouts, shrieks, and catcalls of obscenities.

Their howling wasn't a surprise, but its strength startled Mía. Thirty years after the Carmichael Massacre and the people of Semiautonomous California still picked at their scabs. She didn't blame them. Samuel had been the source of so much of her own anguish that even now, decades later, her mouth filled with venom on seeing him. He was older and wrinkled now, blank eyes reflecting a blank mind, but the monster who'd killed her husband on their honeymoon, and hundreds of others, was still in there somewhere. She knew it.

The ruckus went on for some time, survivors and victims' families making themselves heard with force and energy. Mía waited for them to calm down before giving her remarks. This was their good-bye, a final send-off, and it shouldn't be rushed. Samuel Miller's custody was being remanded from SeCa's Classification Commission to BioScan. Soon he would be moved to a facility in the Louisiana Territories, where the research into mirror resonance syndrome that had been on hold for two decades could begin again. Everyone would benefit.

She checked that no one was looking and pulled a tiny pliable flask like a jellyfish from her boot. Bourbon. If there was one consolation prize for moving to the LTs to supervise

Samuel's care, it was being closer to the source of her favorite medication. She swigged what was left, wiped her mouth, tucked the flask back in her boot, and walked onstage.

Like a switch had been flipped, the crowd's jeers transformed into cheers and applause. She waved to the audience as she approached the cage, then turned to stare into Samuel's dark brown eyes from a few paces away. Nothing going on in there, thanks to a quadruple dose of Personil. He looked younger than his fifty-something years close up. Though his eyes were open and he blinked every few seconds, she didn't see a single spark of consciousness, exactly as the Commission board had agreed—they weren't putting him in front of a SeCa audience with anything less than total cognitive suspension.

Still, she knew this wasn't entirely true. Somewhere, deep in his brain, sensations were registering, although they would most likely fade without becoming memories. Maybe later he would wonder why his wrists hurt. Not now.

She turned to face the crowd. The cheers intensified. She was their hero. The woman who'd escaped Carmichael—and returned with help. No. The terrified woman who'd run away. She'd tried to correct them countless times, but no one would hear of it. She'd made investigating Samuel Miller and others with mirror resonance syndrome her life's work, created the Classification Commission, and put a stop to the bloodshed. She was their hero.

Mía stood at the podium and spoke. The lines were the same as always, her canned speech that for decades had functioned like a healing ritual. *What happened to me in Carmichael. How I escaped. What I vowed to do.* Men and women in the audience were crying, faces upturned.

Now she came to the pivot point, a new line. An untested one.

"Today marks a new era for SeCa. We have healed. We are ready to move on."

Lately she'd been wondering if, after all that had happened, she'd led SeCa down the wrong path. The Classification Commission had been designed to protect the populace, to make them feel secure, and to return them to a society free from violence. But if the people's pain persisted after so much time, perhaps they hadn't been healing. Perhaps instead their rituals normalized victimhood and fetishized the stigmatization of Broken Mirrors.

"The people of SeCa are unfortunately familiar with the dangers of mirror resonance syndrome," Mía said, "and they have worked diligently to create a society free from fear. I'm here to tell you today: we no longer need to carry our burden alone. Samuel Miller and a portion of our MRS patients will be transferred to the Louisiana Territories, where they will remain in the custody of BioScan. For this, we are grateful."

As Mía wrapped up her remarks, she noticed that the survivors and victims' families were lining up on a wooden ramp that led from the hall to the stage. The first five in line were in wheelchairs.

She had gotten to know all of them over the years. The woman whose sister had died in the gazebo. The mother of the boy whose house had been obliterated in front of Mía's eyes. The brother and sister who'd lost their parents to rampaging autocabs.

As Mía watched, the first several groups approached the cage and leered at Samuel. A few even spat through the bars. Broken Mirrors in SeCa had always created a spectacle—providing people with an outlet for their fear and anger served a specific purpose after Carmichael. Now she wondered whether the people of SeCa could move on. Was today helping? The Classification Commission couldn't just whisk Samuel away. They'd decided that the people needed closure. One last ritual.

Mía wished Jefferson Eastmore was here to assuage her doubts. He would have cleared his calendar to attend if he were still alive. Oddly, today there were no Eastmores in the audience, but then, they would have added a gloss to the event that wouldn't have entirely been welcome. This was about healing and moving on, and the Eastmores somehow always attracted attention, even when they didn't seek it out.

A commotion in the audience drew her gaze. Security officers in black-and-green uniforms surrounded someone in the queue. The stage manager's voice whispered through the sonobulb in her ear, “They confiscated a shockstick. The man is demanding they let him continue anyway.”

“Fine, let him approach—but with an escort,” she said.

Are our enemies our own creations? was a question Mía hadn’t thought to ask until it was too late. Worse, what if your enemies were powerless—guiltless even—and yet you punished them all the same?

Samuel deserved every insult heaped on him. But what about the rest? They needed a fresh start. That’s what she was working toward, why today mattered so much. A fresh start for her and for people with MRS everywhere.

“Murderer!” The shout came from a woman standing in front of the cage, her hands gripping the bars, shaking so hard, Mía was surprised the whole apparatus didn’t rattle.

Samuel stood there, shackled, medicated. His mouth opened, and a low moan escaped.

Mía hurried to the cage, leaned into the steel bars, and looked closely. Samuel’s gaze met hers as another moan, a long rolling O, came out. He was coming to.

“Get him offstage,” Mía said into her voicecap.

The people in line started to bunch up, rushing the cage, reaching through the bars.

“He’s awake!” someone cried. “The bastard can hear us!”

“Ghosts,” Samuel said, his voice ragged and gurgling.

“Sicko Samuel,” a woman yelled, and the crowd took up the chant. “Sicko Samuel! Sicko Samuel!”

“Ghosts! You’re all ghosts!” Samuel shouted. He lunged forward and fell, pulled up short by the restraints.

Security officers were pouring onstage from the wings, holding back the crowd so the nurses could remove Samuel from the cage. The stage manager bounded over to Mía, pony tail bucking, and escorted her offstage. She resisted. “Turn up my volume,” she said. He did.

“Please remain calm,” she pleaded.

No one seemed to hear her. People started pelting Samuel, the nurses, the security officers with objects: MeshBits, bottles of nail polish, keys, whatever they could pull from their pockets.

"Shut the whole thing down," she told the stage manager. But he was no longer in charge. Security officers were trying to push people back down the ramp. Trinkets and trash flew onto the stage. Mía ripped off her sonobulb and voicecap, found a door marked "Emergency Exit," and hustled down a hallway to another door. Then she was outside, catching her breath.

The fog had already rolled in, and the air was filled with the sounds of engines, people shouting. She rounded the corner and stopped, dumbstruck.

Thousands of people were assembled at the steps to the National Theater, their disparate chants rising and falling. Police in riot gear were struggling to establish a barricade. She checked—this was not getting Mesh coverage. Sirens came from the direction of City Lake, echoing through the canyons of skyscrapers. The sea of people in front of the theater surged against the barricades. Mía walked closer, approaching the battle lines from an odd angle.

A policewoman stopped her.

"What do they want?" Mía asked.

"Blood."

The officer pointed to a statue of Jefferson Eastmore at the center of a plaza across the street. The statue's hands held a DNA molecule styled to resemble Hermes's serpent-entwined Rod of Caduceus. At its base was a platform of wooden pallets. A noose swung from the rod several meters over the pavement.

The policewoman's mouth twisted in derision. "Can't say I blame them." She looked at Mía and seemed to recognize her. She blanched, opened her mouth: "Excuse me, I'm so sorry. I didn't realize who you—I'm so sorry."

Mía thought to ask if the crowd would be a problem, if she should do something to secure Samuel's passage out of the city. Had they gotten him offstage?

The crowd's plaintive cries washed over her.

"Don't let the murderer escape!"

"Justice before mercy!"

"Death to Broken Mirrors!"

Mía's throat burned. Tear gas somewhere nearby.

Her MeshBit vibrated. *Prisoner secured*, the message read.

She shook her head, turned away. She'd done enough to make SeCa what it was. She could do no more. It was time to start over somewhere else. She would do better this time.

2

> European overlords! Why do you 'deny rumors that any MeshSats strayed from their designated orbits'? WE TOOK YOUR SATELLITES AND THEN WE GAVE THEM BACK. YOU COULD AT LEAST SAY THANK YOU.
>
> —BrAiNhAcKeR Collective

7 May 1991
New Venice, The Louisiana Territories

Take a look and let's talk at noon, Ozie's message read, *away from snoops.*

For the fifth time, Victor Eastmore watched the hacked vid-feed Ozie had sent that showed Samuel Miller standing blank and shackled as a parade of angry SeCans yelled at, taunted, and spit on him. Ozie had to know exactly how much seeing the footage would bother Victor. Over many years of friendship and intimacy stretching back to their time at university together, they'd both struggled with MRS, offering each other tips to regulate their wayward brains, and they'd endured years of abuse along the way. Ozie had finally escaped SeCa, and years later he'd helped Victor do the same.

When the vidscreen showed two nurses hustling Samuel Miller offstage, Victor rolled up the Handy 1000 and jammed it in his pocket, disgusted, though not quite sure why. Before Samuel had become the Man from Nightmareland, he'd been a teaching assistant at Victor's GoodStart school. He was always showing the kids neat tricks on his MeshBit, like pixelated cartoons of cats and other animals chasing each other. The teachers praised Samuel's intelligence and creativity and told the students they could do worse than to grow up to be like him. None of the teachers survived the massacre; they were at the top of Samuel's kill list.

Victor walked on to Pond Park, where he borrowed a kayak, let the weak current take him down the Petit Canal, passed through Little Lock, and paddled into the Passage, leaving behind the construction noise that had turned the east side of New Venice into an aural hazard zone. A casino paddle boat churned the water alongside him, rocking his kayak in its wake. Then it turned to follow the tourist circuit that would take it up the Passage, past the entertainment district, and into the Grand Canal. Wind heavy with mud and rot dragged across the water.

When Victor was halfway to the opposite shore, he hooked the shaft of the kayak's paddle into its clamps, took his cigar-shaped Handy 1000 from his pocket, and double-tapped one end. It unfurled to show a vidscreen the size of two palms side-by-side. He tried raising a vidfeed with Ozie. No response. Ozie was less punctual now that he was homeless and on the run from the Diamond King's hired Corps.

Victor put the Handy 1000 on his lap, unclipped the paddle, dipped a blade into the water, and pointed the kayak upstream. He paddled unnecessarily hard. The current in the Passage was minimal. Beyond the stone buildings and parkland along New Venice's western shores, Victor could just make out the sweeping curve of the massive Ouachita Dam upstream. Somewhere behind him, downstream, Qaddo Lake Dam held back the waters that filled New Venice's canals.

A visionary achievement. An engineering marvel. The soul of the LTs. New Venice was called all these things. Hundreds of kilometers upstream from the tarnished jewel of New Orleans and its half-drowned archipelago of neighborhoods, the Eastmores had transformed a small, pointless town into the most prominent tourist destination in the nation. Their wealth, along with LT Repartition Bonds, had financed the dredging, quarrying, and engineering of the canals and dams, back in the 1930s. Victor's personal wealth owed as much to the return on that investment as to the profits from Grandfather Jefferson's subsequent business successes. In a way, the town was partly his, and yet he felt as much out of place here as he had in SeCa. But at least no one here could lock him up for having mirror resonance syndrome. Not yet anyway.

Victor touched the data egg in his pocket through the fabric of his pants. It was still there, helping to keep his brain from going into overdrive, Jefferson's secrets locked inside it, along with, perhaps, the answer to who had murdered him.

To the west, hidden by an earthen levee, a few kilometers distant and tucked amid rolling hills and forests was the Eastmore Estate where his great-granma Florence lived. He hadn't seen her since the last family reunion a decade ago. She'd not been well enough to travel to Jefferson's funeral and, besides, she'd long ago sworn never to set foot in SeCa. Victor knew he should visit her. The problem was he didn't trust himself not to tell Florence how Jefferson, her son, had really died even as the killer remained a mystery.

The Handy 1000 chimed.

Connection pending . . .

Ozie's face appeared on the vidscreen. "Hello, fuckface," he said.

Victor didn't bother with a greeting. "What's going on in SeCa? What did I just watch?"

"MeshNews feed, classified for officials only. BioScan is moving Samuel Miller to New Venice in two days."

Victor felt suddenly out of breath and grew quiet.

"You knew about this," Ozie said. "Don't let it rattle you."

"I just didn't think it would happen so soon."

"They're making a big deal out of it in SeCa," Ozie said, "but as far as I can tell, there's been nothing about it anywhere else in the American Union, including the Louisiana Territories, but that's not surprising. You know how the Mesh works. Its info flows are more dammed up than the Oauchita watershed." He paused a moment. "The crowd would have torn him apart if they could."

"I don't want to think about it," Victor said. "Where are you?"

"Off grid and on the move. I haven't been outside the van in six days." Ozie swung the vidlens around to show off the interior of his mobile hacking station and home. Racks of blinking electronic equipment lined the walls, blankets were pushed into a pile in one corner, and Victor spotted a box that looked suspiciously like a chemical toilet.

"Come to New Venice. You can stay with me."

"In a BioScan-rented suite? No thanks. There are things I have to take care of here."

"Where is here? Or can you not say?"

"Somewhere in the Organized Western States. I see road ahead and road behind," Ozie said.

"You really can't tell me? This is a secure feed, isn't it?"

"Secure is the easy part," Ozie grumbled. "Staying untraceable is harder, but not much."

Victor could tell Ozie was anxious despite his boasting. It couldn't be easy living that way. Ozie couldn't go back to the Springboard Café. Not after the Diamond King had sent his Corps mercenaries there looking for the person who'd stolen gobs of data from the Institute for Applied Biological Sciences in Las Vegas.

Ozie removed his glasses, rubbed his eyes with his shirt sleeve, and put them back on, blinking. "Therein lies the problem," he said, as if responding to Victor rather than continuing whatever private conversation was running through his MRS-affected mind.

"Problem?"

"No hack is satisfying after you've moved a fleet of satellites around the world."

"Come to New Venice and crack the data egg. It'll lift your spirits. That's what it's doing for me, right?" Victor noticed the kayak had drifted toward the muddy shore. He unhooked the paddle, dipped into the water, and pulled, swinging around so he was facing the Petit Canal.

"That is not technically what the data egg is doing and you know it. It's attenuating your resonant episodes like my braincap. Doesn't do anything for depression. Wait, why is your feed all wobbly? Are you on a boat? Don't tell me you actually have the data egg with you on a boat! What if you drop it? Victor, you need to keep it secure. I've told you that a thousand times."

Victor shrugged. "I have to keep it with me. That's as safe as I can make it." The data egg was in his pocket, close by and keeping his brain from running away with itself.

"I have a better idea." Ozie paused for dramatic effect. He loved pregnant silences. Victor rolled his eyes, making sure the Handy was close enough to convey the expression.

"Implantation," Ozie said, emphasizing each syllable.

"Huh? You want me—"

"It's not that big. Plenty of room in your belly. Under the skin right about here." Ozie lifted his shirt and gestured to his midsection, which had grown a little flabbier since Victor had last seen him at the Springboard Café.

Victor jammed the paddle into the hooks. "No. I'm not doing that. End of story."

"Beats dropping the damn thing in the water, but whatever. So . . . Why hasn't Karine or Circe looped you into the Samuel thing?"

Karine LaTour, Victor's boss, rarely ever told Victor anything except to get something in return. Not to mention Victor had accused her of killing his grandfather and still thought she might have done it. So they weren't that close. And Circe, his auntie, always seemed to think she was protecting him by withholding information.

"It's kind of an open secret at BioScan," he explained to Ozie. "The public isn't supposed to know, and MeshNews hasn't made a story of it yet. The thing is, today I saw a woman rowing down the Grand Canal with a big sign that said, 'Murderers Go Home. No Madmen in New Venice.'"

"So word is out."

"No kidding."

"Yeeps. Yet another reason for me to stay away. Besides, I'm chasing a hot lead on where the polonium came from."

Victor brought the Handy 1000 close to his face to get a better look. Ozie wore a manic smile as he fiddled with a piece of equipment in the van. "Literally chasing?" Victor asked.

Ozie looked up, his smile gone. "Don't worry about me. I've got something for you in the meantime. Terabytes of data I scraped from Karine's traces on the Mesh. I'm sending you the access protocol now."

"What's in it?"

"No idea. Maybe a clue as to whether she killed Jefferson."

"No idea what's in terabytes of data?" Victor repeated. "Ozie! How am I supposed to go through that much information on my own?"

"Sorry, my plate is full as it is. Too bad you didn't get what you wanted when you tied her to a chair."

"Tosh tied her to a chair. I stopped him and Elena from killing her."

"Yeah, about Tosh, I'm keeping my eyes peeled. We're going to get that piece of Jefferson's tongue back from him," Ozie said.

"Yeah, let's do that," Victor said meekly. He was reluctant to do anything to get on Tosh's radar again. They'd had no contact since Victor came to New Venice, and he was fine with that. "But let's do it in a way that doesn't get us killed."

Ozie said, "What a smart idea. I've got to go. Talk soon."

Victor was about to tell him to stay safe, but Ozie had already terminated the feed. Great. Ozie had always liked alone time, said it helped him keep on the level. But this seemed different.

They'd often joked that MRS could be like walking a tightrope in a hurricane. Now the winds seemed to be blowing hard in Ozie's van. Victor hoped his friend's brainhacking gear was up to the challenge.

Victor paddled toward New Venice. Cold moisture rose from the water, making him shiver. MeshNews said the unseasonable cold spell was supposed to end soon, perhaps as early as tomorrow. As he neared the esplanade, bustling cafés, bistros, and bars came into view. The strip of buildings directly facing the southern bend of the Passage held hundreds of revelers who were drinking, dancing, and gambling.

He waited in Little Lock, where the Petit Canal emptied into the Passage. The lock's stone walls surrounded him, looming. It was like floating at the bottom of a stone-walled grave. Water gushed from holes in both sides; soon his kayak rose to the top, and the gates swung open. He maneuvered around a clueless tourist couple whose rowboat was going in circles while they laughed and blamed each other.

The streets along the Petit Canal rose several meters above the water in this part of town. The walls seemed to descend as he slid north, so that by the time he neared the Pond the streetscape was almost level with the water. He passed under Triton's Deep Crossing, a three-pronged bridge with steps that looked like stone but were actually made of fungus grown over an aluminum scaffold.

Victor reached a dock, climbed out, and dragged the kayak onto the pebbled shore, where city employees who were paid to keep things tidy could pick it up. He climbed the steps of Triton's Deep Crossing to take in the spectacular view.

New Venice prospered because Old Venice was now mostly underwater, save for glittering glass towers, floating walkways, and aquarium corridors that allowed submerged glimpses of the former merchant republic. Everyone said it was a shame the old city had been lost but at least the water quality had improved enough to enable submarine tourism, thanks to some cleverly engineered zooplankton.

Tourists came to New Venice for a taste of the old life, whether it was real or not.

When Victor reached the highest point of the bridge, with the sweeping curve of Ouachita Dam visible above the stone houses lining the Grand Canal's north side, he checked to see that no one was looking at him. Then he took the data egg out and held it to his head. By the law of inverse squares, whatever radiation it was emitting should be much stronger and have a greater effect the closer it was to his brain. Unless it could sense its distance and vary its power level. Victor put the data egg in his pocket again. He'd repeated this same sequence of actions countless times. Data egg to head, wondering how it worked, questioning its effectiveness, then returning it to his pocket. Over and over again. Doing this had almost replaced his mantra—*the wise owl listens before he asks who*.

Victor leaned over the railing, exhaled, and listened. Construction had finally ceased for the day. He heard water lapping against the canal walls, ducks quacking to each other, the drone of traffic from the highway north of town, and, oddly, voices chanting. The chanting seemed to be coming from the western edge of Pond Park. He descended to investigate.

Assembled in the park with their backs to the pond was a group of a dozen or so people dressed in dark pants and white robes. They wore thick, gaudy, multicolored belts that might have been Qaddo designs. Some normally dressed folk stood nearby and seemed to be debating whether to join the gathering. The chanting evolved into a strident call and response. Perhaps it was a political protest; Victor was too far away to make out the words.

A bonfire with flames as tall as a man's shoulders burned at the edge of the grass. One man poured a bucketful of water around the fire's perimeter and returned to the pond to refill it. A woman tossed planks in. Sparks spiraled up.

Fire glow warmed the faces of the gathered people. Every few minutes, a robed member of the crowd, and less frequently an unrobed person, would approach the fire and toss an object into the flames.

Victor approached cautiously. When the next verse of call and response rang out, he heard the words clearly.

"Who are we in this universe?"

"We are unique, we are sacred, we are human."

"What is our role in this fallen world?"

"We must preserve, we must protect, we must prevail."

"What must we do in the name of our sanctity?"

"We must be pure, we must be human."

The chanting faded, and a short, plump man with gray hair fringing his bald head stepped to one side of the fire while the crowd shifted opposite him.

The man said, "In the beginning, we lived as beasts. We picked berries and roots of the forest. We hunted boar, stag, and buffalo. And we were human. We planted fields, we raised cows and chickens, we lived and died on the land. And we were human. We created the steam engine, the coal power plant, the Mesh, and virtual entertainment. And we were human. But we have been led astray. We are injecting poisons. We are consuming degradations. We are becoming monsters. Yet we resolve together: We will remain human. Give up your poisons! Set yourself free! Human life! Human life! Human life! Human life!"

The crowd energetically took up the chant. More people stepped forward and tossed their possessions into the flames: pill bottles, tubes of liquid, syringes, and cream containers melted in the fire. A few also flung electronic components in. Victor thought he spotted a braincap. Along the periphery of the crowd, a few onlookers accepted white robes and put them on.

Victor maintained a distance of several meters and gripped the data egg in his pocket. He had never seen a religious ceremony in public before. Semiautonomous California was one of the most secular societies in the world, despite having been settled by Cathars. Adherents to religions worshipped in private, quietly. They rarely inflicted it on others. Even the Puros in the Republic of Texas were more focused on building a sober community than they were in proselytizing.

The ceremony confused Victor—there didn't seem to be a metaphysical logic to it; there was no deity invoked, no reference to established religions. There was an odd animation to their faces: tight, shiny, luminescent. Some were holding their hands close to the fire, yelping in pain, but at the same time smiling, exultant.

A young woman in a robe saw Victor and began to approach him. She had pale skin, wide oval eyes, a full mouth, and a button nose. She held out her arms wide, palms up, and smiled at him, a broad, toothy expression that made him smile back. She had freckles, an endearing flaw.

"Welcome," she said. "Don't be shy. Or be shy, that's fine too. No matter who you are, you're perfect already. My faith name is Wonderment. Wonda for short."

Victor guffawed, but then he realized his name was also a noun.

She giggled. "You don't know what to make of us, do you?"
"You're all human, I hear."

She giggled again. Victor loved the sound. It tasted sweet, like a drop of syrup. He wanted to sit close with her by the fire and see what would happen when the embers cooled, how they might keep each other warm.

"And maybe you're all suffering from buyers' remorse?" he said.

More people were tossing their possessions into the flames. The good feeling drained out of him. The medicines they were throwing in the fire were probably made by Eastmores. Would they prefer to live in caves and die of common and easily curable diseases? They were just like the Puros, only worse.

She reached for his hand. He jumped back with a sudden yelp.

"It's okay," she said.

Victor said, "I don't like being touched."

She frowned, concerned. "You don't have to choose sadness."

Sourness like green lemons flooded his mouth. "It chose me a long time ago," he replied.

"I'm sorry," she said.

"I get it, you know. I took Personil for years. It was like living in a plastic bag. Nothing touched me. I know what it's like to hate a handful of pills, to really hate them."

"You don't take them anymore?"

"That's not the point. They probably saved my life. They kept me sane, and they kept me free."

"And now you're free of them too," she said. "Shouldn't everyone have that chance?"

"I'm free, but I'm not easily fooled. What you're telling people is medieval. Sorry, but it's true. Good night, Wonda."

As he turned and left, he kept his gaze on the reflection of flames in the water and repeated the owl mantra a dozen times: *The wise owl listens before he asks who*.

Victor took a direct route toward the center of town. His steps clanged on large steel slabs partially covering a ditch full of pipes and electrical conduits. As he walked across, the edges of his vision shimmered—synesthesia, a symptom of mirror resonance syndrome. A tingle in his groin and a weightless sensation throughout his body signaled that blankness was close.

He had been doing better recently. A combination of fumewort and bitter grass tinctures helped him manage most aspects of his condition. He hadn't gone blank since he'd stood in front of the Lone Star Kennel, hovering at the edge of blankspace, seeing shapes moving across his vision and feeling that there was something inside the blankness, as if he'd glimpsed a secret world.

Blankspace had felt oddly *full.*

The vision had shaken his understanding of himself, his brain, and mirror resonance syndrome. He'd managed to retreat from the blankness, to stave off a blankout for the first time, which caused the data egg to open and divulge his granfa's message.

Granfa Jefferson had said the data egg held both Victor's and Samuel's neurograms in it, that the data egg would help both of them, and that Victor should spend time with Samuel, implying the data egg would open again when they were together.

What could he have been thinking? Victor wondered.

Close to the inn where he rented a small room, Victor found a quiet self-serve restaurant. From the buffet line he assembled an unremarkable plate of meat, vegetables, and starches, and found a table by himself in a corner. He tried not to think about Ozie eating, shitting, and sleeping in his van. After he ate, on his walk home, his Handy 1000 beeped. Karine's data. He stopped for a faux-café at one of the kiosks facing the Grand Canal. It was going to be a long night.

3

European authorities continue to investigate whether the SatSwarm bug poses an ongoing threat. Tens of millions of Mesh users in Europe were affected by the bug last month. Officials maintain that the Mesh crashed due to a spike in demand related to the Global Games. Although Mesh coverage has been fully restored, operators may face claims from user groups whose computing time was impacted by the bug.

—MeshNews dispatch

8 May 1991
New Venice, The Louisiana Territories

Victor woke the next day in a bad mood. Karine's data trove—the little of it he'd been able to go through, less than .01 percent of the total—contained a confusing jumble of message logs, data transfers, and clones of databases, much of it related to BioScan, little of it personal. The data would take weeks to sift through, and much longer if he were to read every word.

Karine was almost certainly the culprit in Granfa Jefferson's death. After all, she had taken Jefferson's place on SeCa's Classification Commission, and when the Eastmore family's Holistic Healing Network had acquired Gene-Us and renamed itself BioScan, Karine had become second in command after Auntie Circe. When Victor started looking into his grandfather's death, Karine hired two inept thugs to track Victor. They'd chased him throughout SeCa, the Organized Western

States, and the Republic of Texas until Victor had turned the tables on them.

If only he had evidence now. He had to figure out a way to sift through the data.

Thanks to little sleep, the first half of his work day was spent in a daze, applying a software patch so BioScan's new Cogitron Exelus machines could store their data more efficiently.

A message from Auntie Circe came through on his Handy 1000 in the afternoon.

Samuel's transfer delayed. Negotiations between SeCa and the LTs complicated. More soon.

So she was keeping him informed after all. That was something, at least.

He told himself everything would be okay, but a squirmy ball of uneasiness gurgled in his stomach. He'd been doing so well, better than he could remember in a long time. What if seeing Samuel again pushed Victor back over the edge?

At noon, Victor got up from his desk and navigated through hallways crowded with people, boxes, and equipment that had been displaced by the ongoing renovations. He crossed the administration building's atrium. Pallets of construction materials and new equipment were stacked high, almost to the ceiling.

Victor made his way to a narrow meeting room with a long table made of real, red-stained pine and five white synth-leather chairs on each side. Stuffy air recirculated. Members of the BioScan New Venice executive team entered and sat talking quietly to one another.

Victor avoided getting absorbed into a conversation and stood off to the side, rolling the data egg in his hands, wondering how he could open it again. Something in his brain, something in the way his condition worked could unlock it. Out the window, he spotted earth-movers carving a flat area next to the sheer cliffs of Cemetery Hill, where a pair of twelve-story buildings would rise and provide research space for hundreds of lab directors and clinicians. The bulky machines beeped and rumbled as they loaded up their cargo, shuddered into motion, and carried heaps of dirt down the slopes to a staging area at the water's edge. From there, barges would carry the waste downstream and dump it on the western shore of Qaddo Lake. The dirt would reinforce decades-old levees that kept the low-lying countryside safe from New Venice's waters.

Someday Victor would work in a top-floor office in one of the towers with a spectacular view of New Venice. The canals would look like lines drawn by a rake in wet soil. He might even be able to see the Eastmore Estate on the other side of the Passage. In the meantime, he had to make do in this cramped room with mid-level executives and blaring lightstrips.

Karine entered with a loud, "Good morning."

He glanced over, and his breath locked up in his chest.

Standing behind Karine was Mía Barrias. Victor hadn't seen her face-to-face since the Carmichael Massacre. She'd reached out a few times over the years, and he'd rebuffed her—how could she think he wanted talk to her? She was the one who'd made people with mirror resonance syndrome pariahs. She was the one who'd created the Classification Commission. Now here she was, her salt-and-pepper hair hanging over her shoulders, wearing a flower-patterned dress in blobby blues and yellows.

Next to Mía, shorter and wearing a royal-violet business suit, was Ming Pearl, his herbalist, who had been missing for weeks. Her usually frizzy gray hair was dyed coal-black and plastered to her head. She winked at Victor.

"Let's get started," Karine said. "Please have a seat everyone." She sat at the head of the table flanked by Victor and Blair, one of the executives.

Victor blinked at Karine. *What the laws was going on?*

Pearl shot him a wry smile as she took the seat next to him. Mía sat at the opposite end of the table and stared at Victor with eyes that appeared flat and hard. She nodded at him after a long moment.

Karine said, "I'm bringing in additional staff to ramp up our capabilities. I want to introduce Mía Barrias. She'll be our liaison with the public and with MeshNews. She'll also help us manage the psychological impact of bringing Samuel Miller to this campus and publicizing his history."

Karine paused. A few executives murmured welcomes and good-to-have-yous. Victor watched Mía say thank you and offer a weak, close-lipped smile to the people in the room. Then she turned to stare at him again, and he felt as if she was seeing a four-year-old boy rather than a twenty-five-year-old man. Hot smoke burned his lungs, and his eyes watered—memories from Carmichael. Bodies lying in the street. Smoke billowing up. Waiting for the Man from Nightmareland to find him.

A pressure on his arm jolted him back to the present. Pearl was squeezing his wrist and pointing at Karine, who had asked Victor a question.

"Sorry," he said. "I missed that."

"I said, you'll be working closely with Mía going forward. Understood?"

Victor gulped and nodded.

Karine turned to the executives and said, "I also want to introduce Ming Pearl, an herbalist. You're all aware that commercializing natural remedies has become a core part of our research agenda. She'll be consulting with the team in charge of mirror resonance patients and substance abusers."

"It is most pleasurable to meet with you," Pearl said in a thick accent that Victor knew was 100 percent performance. She snuck him another wink, and he smiled to himself. It was good to see her again.

Pearl had been kidnapped by the same thugs as Victor. She'd paid them and regained her freedom only to be forced to leave SeCa when the authorities cracked down on her illicit brainhacking distributorship. After that, she'd gone silent, perhaps sneaking across the AU to wind up at BioScan.

Looking at Pearl, Victor couldn't stop thinking that she didn't belong here, dressed like a corporate lackey.

Karine went on, "Circe called from Cologne this morning. She's pleased with our progress and will be here in a few days. I'll be booking her meetings so you might hear from me about that. Now, department updates. Let's start with finance."

The meeting steamrolled onward. On Karine's other side, Blair, who'd never given Victor the time of day, swiveled in his chair, flashing an insincere smile. Victor tried to listen as Blair spoke about BioScan going on a buying spree, but he didn't recognize any of the company names. His mind wandered.

When Blair was done, Marilyn, a woman in her forties, leaned forward and gave an update on the construction of the research towers up the hill. Then she relaxed into her chair, delicately fingering the collar of her blouse. "The one question I have is how we're going to integrate our new sequencing capacity into our health care protocols. What data do we collect, and what do we do with it?"

This was Victor's area of expertise. He sat up, but Karine silenced him with a shake of her head. Laws, he wanted to rip her hair out.

No, he told himself. The wise owl listens.

"Thank you, Marilyn," Karine said. "You raise an excellent point. Many of you may be unfamiliar with the sequencing capabilities we've acquired along with Gene-Us. Victor Eastmore is going to review those capabilities for us. He has a special relationship with our work, and no one knows genomic analysis better."

The executives exchanged glances. Blair cleared his throat. Marilyn smiled and scratched at the corner of her mouth.

What did she mean by special relationship? Victor wondered. Because he was a Broken Mirror? It would have been a laughable euphemism if it wasn't an insult.

"Victor, when you're ready, walk us through your summary."

"Certainly," he said, unable to dull the hard edge in his voice. His instinct that it had been his turn to speak had been correct, but grandstanding Karine had wanted to make an insulting introduction. Everything she did aggravated him. He wanted to scream at her. Instead he used the type-pad to load the presentation he'd shown her last week.

"This is the way it worked at Gene-Us until 1990," Victor said. "Outdated technology, inefficient processes, and unskilled staff." A diagram swam to the surface of the vidscreen on the wall showing boxes connected by lines to indicate each step in the sequencing process. It was a high-level summary. He'd dumbed it down for the audience.

He advanced the presentation to the next image showing a black and white checkerboard of blobs.

Victor said, "Until recently, we used electrophoresis to compare the reference sample with potential matches. Each sample started with the full genetic copy of each donor. But useful information was wasted early in the process. We were only looking at a few tiny portions of their genomes."

Blair interrupted, "In other words, we got the job done efficiently. We didn't need to do more." He looked around the room for support, and a few heads nodded quietly.

Blair had argued against investment in new sequencing equipment. Apparently he still hadn't come around, but it wasn't Victor's job to change his mind.

Victor moved on to his next point without responding.

Blair piped up again, "Hold on there. Risk reports for insurance companies are still the most profitable sales channel for us. That's the market. We only need to analyze a few key sequences to know if someone has MRS or not, am I right?"

Victor saw that Karine was watching him carefully. An anxious sweat oozed down his back. He knew, in the midst of these polished and poised executives, that he had a lot to prove.

Victor flashed an insincere but passable smile at Blair and said, "You're not wrong. Gene-Us made most of its money identifying people with the mirror resonance gene. You're saying, why bother with more useful genomics?"

"That is not what I'm saying," Blair said.

"What about demonstrating the efficacy of gene therapy?" Victor asked. "Or conducting ecological genomics studies? Or microbiome characterization? Or a dozen other applications?"

Karine knocked lightly on the table. "Let's get back on track. Victor, calm down and show them what we're doing to improve our sequencing operations."

Victor ground his teeth. He didn't need Karine's chiding. "We now have five next-generation automated sequencing machines from Prolexa. They sequence at a rate of ten trillion base pairs per day, about a thousand-fold increase. We can capture the full genome of every patient. We could learn a lot more about them—get the big picture—than we do now."

Marilyn looked as tightly wound as the bun at the back of her head. "Before we can sequence our patients' genomes, we have to get consent, don't we? Our clinics and our affiliates will be very concerned about a system-wide effort to gather genetic information from our patients without it."

Karine swept her hand across the table. "The chief attorney of the Louisiana Territories reassured us that the genetic information we obtain from samples using our own technology is our property, not our clients' or patients'."

Karine looked at Victor and said, "Wrap this up."

He stopped himself from yelling, "Shock you!" and managed to say in a controlled voice, "Going forward, the main problem will be sample preparation. It takes time and lab staff to change a few drops of saliva into a sample that can be fed into the sequencer. We're still working out the process."

Karine looked at each executive in turn. "It goes without saying that we'll need your cooperation and input. That's all for now. Mía and Pearl, you'll stay please. Victor, you too."

Karine stood, smiled stiffly, and nodded at the executives as they filed out of the conference room. When they were gone, she shut the door and motioned for Mía to come sit closer. The four of them sat at one end of the conference table.

Victor took the data egg out of his pocket. He rolled it between his palms and breathed on it at intervals. He should be in Karine's place right now, he thought.

Karine looked in turn at Mía and Pearl. "Stim addiction is spreading quickly across the AU. We here at BioScan are the best equipped company in the world to address both mirror resonance syndrome and addiction to resonant-class narcotics. We're relying on your expertise to help us reach our goal."

Pearl wore a tight, skeptical smile on her face. "I'd like to meet the patients this afternoon if possible, one at a time. Some may be more interested in herbal supplements than others. Also, I've reviewed the files, and I believe the psychological profiles have significant gaps in them."

What does Pearl know about psychological profiles? Victor wondered.

Karine said, "Very well. That should be doable for the addicts, at least. As you know, Victor is our only MRS reference case until Samuel Miller and the other patients arrive. I want the three of you to join a special task force to manage Samuel's treatment. You'll also liaise with MeshNews to tell our story. Speaking of which, Mía, Victor will make a better face for the Classification System than Samuel Miller, so factor that into your plans."

Victor's lips felt parched. The face of the Classification System? A vein throbbed on his forehead.

"Karine, what are you talking about?" he asked.

"You'll be talking to policymakers, the media, and the public as we work toward passing the Classification Act in the LTs," Karine responded. "Don't worry, we'll give you coaching. It's nothing you can't handle—at least that's what Circe thinks."

He opened his mouth, gasped. It felt like the air had been sucked out of the room. "I won't do it," he said with labored breath, staring into her cold eyes. "Why would I ever help you sell a system as corrupt and unfair as the one you created in SeCa?"

He turned a withering gaze toward Mía. She withstood his scorn stoically, her face emotionless, an empty echo.

Bile crawled up Victor's throat as he looked again at Karine. He said, "Haven't you done enough to ruin Broken Mirrors' lives? Granfa Jeff wasn't enough?" Victor slammed a fist on the table. "I know what you did to him."

Pearl put her hand on his. "Softly, little owl."

"That rubbish? Still?!" Karine said, her voice a serpent's hiss. "If I breathed a word of this to Circe—" She stopped herself. "If you can't control yourself in private—"

She closed her eyes. Victor sensed that she was fighting to contain an anger as deep crimson as his own.

Karine turned to Pearl. "I need you to keep him sane and stable. No more outbursts. No more crazy talk. That's priority number one."

Pearl patted his hand. Her fingertips were smooth and soothing. His synesthesia painted her face a cold indigo. "Don't worry, my little owl. Plenty of room for an herb garden. We can start digging tomorrow."

Something in her voice made him look closer. Pearl's expression was mirthful and reassuring, but false. Underneath, in the flare of magenta tension around her eyes and a thick purple haze surrounding her lips, Victor saw lethal intent.

"Karine, Pearl, could you give us a moment?" Mía asked. She sat with her hands palms up on the table, fingers curled in, studying them as if looking for answers.

Karine bowed her head at Pearl and waited for her to leave before following with one hard glance back at Victor.

When Karine was gone, Mía looked up and said, "It's been a long time, Victor."

He clenched his jaw. This wasn't a good time for a trip down memory lane. "You can't convince me the Classification System is just. I'm not going to help."

Amazingly, she nodded. "I know. Believe me. If I had known . . . It got out of hand. But now I can fix it."

"You can't fix it! The only thing you can do is stop it. Don't let your experience with Samuel Miller—"

The look that passed across her face shut him up fast. It was as if darkness radiated from her eyes. The room seemed to dim.

Mía said, "He's irrelevant. This is for you, for the others. I'm seeing clearly now. It's why I asked for us to work together."

"You did?" Victor said. He'd assumed it was Karine's idea.

"Victor, I'm worried about you now that Jefferson is gone."

He straightened. "I can take care of myself."

Mía smiled. Victor felt like he was glimpsing her face in the past, decades ago, before Samuel Miller had killed her husband and set her on a sadder path. "You sound like him," she said. "He always had faith in you."

Victor gripped the data egg. She didn't know anything about Jefferson.

Mía glanced around the room. "We need to talk. Not here, though." She reached into her pocket, pulled out a MeshBit, and fiddled with it. His Handy 1000 chimed to announce that her details arrived in his feed.

"Come find me later." She raised a hand to his face and laid it on his cheek. It felt cool and smooth, like a stone at the base of a waterfall.

Victor felt warmth in his chest, attraction. How was that possible? She was old enough to be his mother. He rushed past her and out of the building into a wall of warm air. His peripheral vision blurred. He had to find Pearl.

The wise owl listens. But Victor didn't have time to listen. Blankspace was encroaching. He jogged toward the clinic, despite the heat. Pearl would give him tinctures and help him recover his calm. If not, he'd ask her to lock him in a room until his mind returned.

4

I saw four new ghosts today, surrounded by their primal auras. The ghosts work at the school with me. Now they're on the list and their time is almost up. I will help them cross over.

—Samuel Miller's *The Carmichael Journals* (1971)

8 May 1991
New Venice, The Louisiana Territories

As Victor stepped outside, jackhammering rattled his skull. Warm, sticky air carried the tang of red dirt and plaster dust. Every building on BioScan's New Venice campus was shrouded in scaffolding and plywood tunnels, shielding employees from tripping hazards and falling debris. Victor covered his ears to block out the *rat tat tat* and navigated through twists and turns to emerge at the edge of the Petit Canal.

Victor could handle the noise and chaos of construction on the BioScan campus. He could handle the stares of the townspeople, who surely recognized him as an Eastmore. He could even handle Karine. These were all bumps in the road as far as he was concerned.

But becoming the face of a system designed to control people like him? He would be a hypocrite and a spectacle.

Samuel had killed hundreds of people to satisfy his delusions. Most of Carmichael's population had fallen to rampaging self-driving cars, explosions, and Samuel's lethal shockstick. Victor, only four years old at the time, had hidden in his home, terrified by the man he'd seen in his dreams for weeks prior to the rampage. Samuel Miller, the Man from Nightmareland.

To prevent violence by people like Samuel was the entire reason the Classification Commission existed in SeCa. Once Samuel arrived in New Venice, people would look at Victor differently. Victor had left SeCa to escape the stigma and persecution that went along with being a Broken Mirror. But could he ever really get away?

Banging from somewhere uphill sounded like the earth was cracking open, and Victor's teeth ground against each other. How could any of the clinic's patients hope to recover from their addictions with all that racket? The mind-rending cacophony of bulldozers, earth pounders, tugboat engines, and trucks backing up with high-pitched beeps made Victor's skin itch.

Jefferson's message had implied that the data egg would open if Victor was physically close to Samuel Miller. So he had to make that happen. But looming in Victor's mind was the fear that Samuel would somehow infect him, cause him to lose control of his condition, and drive him headlong into blankness. It was an irrational fear, and nothing Victor did could extinguish it.

How long would he keep his sanity once the monster arrived? Days? Weeks?

The drug huts lay scattered on the hillside. Each had a wraparound deck that began on the uphill side and hung over the downhill side with flat-earth views of the Passage and Qaddo Lake further downstream.

Victor found Pearl on the uphill deck of one of the huts talking to a clinician.

"We need to talk," he said. "About Jefferson. When the data egg opened—"

"Not now, little owl," she said.

"You don't understand! They want me to—"

Pearl put a finger on Victor's lips. Waves of tingling pleasure rippled from his face to his toes. The world seemed to be made of fabric whipped by the wind, undulating drunkenly. His skin felt like a balloon stretching bigger and tighter, bright and hot, like sunlight at the beach. He tried to speak but vomited a white fog, blocking out the world. He was too stunned to fight—the blankness took him.

The world reformed from blank white haze into shapes with color, depth, and meaning. Victor found himself sitting on a shaded park bench overlooking barges moored to the new harbor's quay. Elena sat next to him. Reflections off a nearby artificial pond shimmered in her hair, which was long, brown, and draped loosely off one shoulder.

His mind moved with gummed-up slowness. Pearl hadn't wanted to talk. He remembered nothing after that.

"Did you follow me here?" he asked hesitantly.

Elena said, "You were yelling at Pearl, and then you got that look. I led you here by the arm. I don't think anybody noticed you were blank."

"Thank you," he said. "I owe you one."

"Yeah. One or two. You okay now?" Elena asked.

"When have I ever been okay?" Victor tugged at his shirt collar to waft air onto his sweaty chest. A truck rumbled along the waterfront and stopped next to a barge. Hydraulic jacks lifted one side of the bin, and dirt and rocks tumbled into the barge's container, filling it up.

Victor sensed that Elena had something else to say. Though she was guarding her feelings closely, he saw black fearful murk around her eyes.

"What is it?" he asked.

Her lips pressed together in a taut line.

Victor remembered another time—it seemed like years ago, though it was only a month or two—when he and Elena sat on a bench outside a cabin in the Sierra Nevada mountains and she confessed her stim addiction. He'd been shocked. That's when he started to think of Elena as broken like him.

It was fitting they had come to New Venice while it was being remade. The land east of the Petit Canal was a vast construction site for BioScan's "Evolving Together" initiative. The company's investment in a new treatment and research center would revolutionize treatment for sufferers of mirror resonance syndrome as well as curtail stim addiction. Victor hoped the ripples of change lapping on the town's shores and sloshing against its canal walls would transform both him and Elena and mend their brokenness.

"Tell me," he said. He'd do whatever he could to help her. And she would help him stay sane. That was the sum total of their relationship.

Elena sighed. "My therapist thinks I should take a break—from you."

Victor thought he'd misheard her. "A break?" Where was this coming from? They weren't a couple. What would a break even mean?

Elena said, "I told her what happened in Amarillo."

Victor jumped to his feet. His chest heaved as if his organs were battling each other, kidney versus kidney, lung versus lung, spleen and liver punching it out in his ribcage. White blankness feathered the edges of his vision.

"That's—that's—You told her?" His heart hammered in his chest.

Elena hauled him back to sitting. "Not everything. I told her about leaving SeCa with you and the fighting between the Corps and the Puros in the ROT I didn't say anything about Jefferson being murdered or what happened in the lodge."

That should be a relief. Too bad his body was off to the races. Elena was watching him. He patted her hand. "Give me a minute," he said.

He clasped his palms, closed his eyes, and murmured the owl mantra to himself. When he felt in control, he opened his eyes. The barges sat lower in the water as the dirt piles in the holds grew. Two earth movers were queued at the bottom of a dirt track, waiting for a truck to pass so they could return up the hill. He looked beyond the barges downstream. Murky, muddy water undulated in the breeze.

Victor was torn. On the one hand, he wanted Elena to tell him exactly what she'd told the therapist. On the other hand, he didn't want to remember anything about the Republic of Texas. He never wanted to return there, not in real life, and not in his memories.

There was one problem, however, a problem not even Elena knew about: Victor was certain that Jefferson had done something to the Lone Star Kennel dogs, something that had to do with a cure for mirror resonance syndrome.

Elena's fa, Hector, had admitted to knowing something about it, but he had refused to give specifics. At some point Victor would need Elena's help to get her fa to talk. Of course, even Victor was sane enough to know that this wasn't the right time to bring it up. And he was cowardly enough to avoid making any plans to return to Amarillo.

Elena said, "You and I've been through some stuff together."

He almost laughed. "That's an understatement." He realized with relief that the blankness was receding.

"Shocks, yes!" Elena smiled. He chuckled, and she went on, "The therapist says that I'm in the habit of transferring my goals and emotions onto you, that I need to focus on me, figure out who I am, and a bunch of other bullshit."

"Do you agree with her?" he asked.

Elena looked at her hands. "Not really. I'm going to give it a shot anyway. She says addiction is what fills the empty spaces in our psyches, and I need to learn to live without my addictions. All my addictions. You understand, right?"

Victor caught a loose strand of Elena's hair and tucked it behind her ear. Therapists had a way of extracting the truth bit by bit. Could he trust Elena to keep his secrets?

He said, "I want the best for you."

"Same," she said. "Things are going well here for me. So many new addicts arrive every day that I'm like the matron of the place. I don't feel pulled to stims. I don't even really think about them. I have to make new habits, the therapist says, a new mindset. For when I get out. She won't say when that'll be . . ." A bitter look crossed Elena's face. "I'm under the impression I might get out sooner if I follow her advice. Then I'll be free of this chip." She rubbed her shin.

Victor didn't want their daily talks to stop. They needed each other. However, he knew better than to try to change her mind.

"I'll do whatever you think best," he said, "but please be careful. Before Granfa Jeff and I found Dr. Tammet, we tried out half a dozen therapists. Granfa warned me not to trust anyone who takes power away from the patient. Those kind of people isolate you and mess you up even more."

"Thank you," she said. "I agree: I'm messed up enough as it is."

"That's not what I meant."

Elena patted his knee. "I'm kidding, silly. Anyway, I'm going to give her advice a chance. Don't hate me."

"I couldn't," he said, leaning over to hug her. She was the only person whose touch didn't bother him, now that Granfa Jeff was gone.

"How are you really doing?" she asked. "You seemed better before."

"I was. I hadn't had a blankout since I got to New Venice. But I didn't sleep last night because Ozie sent a few terabytes of Karine's data to dig through. I've got to find proof of what she did—"

"What she might have done."

"Right. Might have done."

"You told me to remind you."

"I know. Thanks."

Elena was right. Granfa Jefferson's message had said, "I've been murdered," but he hadn't said by whom. He claimed that it was too dangerous to let Victor in on the secret. *Thanks, Granfa.*

Elena reached into Victor's hair and pulled out a fluffy pod with a seed at its center. She tossed it into the air, and it floated toward the water.

Elena sighed and looked toward tiers of rose bushes lining a trail that switchbacked up the hill. "Look at me, getting drawn in again. I have to go. But there's one more thing."

Victor shivered. Her voice felt like cold water running down his back. "What is it?"

"Samuel Miller," Elena said.

His pulse spiked. He gulped, then asked, "What about him?"

"What's the news?" Elena asked. "When does he arrive? Is there a date set?"

"Not yet."

Elena let out a string of curses: "Laws!" "Shocks!" and a few Victor didn't recognize that she must have picked up from the Puros in the Republic of Texas.

"So it's true. This place is a disaster! A disgusting shit pool of a town and now *he's* coming," she said.

Elena liked to badmouth the clinic's cramped rooms, the therapy sessions, and the other addicts, and she had a special loathing for tourists. Victor knew her complaints were mostly out of boredom and that she was happily committed to recovery. It was ironic. Victor had a dark sludge of feelings about Samuel Miller. By contrast, Elena's anger was white-hot and effervescent.

Victor said, "I only know what Auntie shares with me. MeshNews isn't covering it yet. They're probably debating how to introduce the story to the Louisiana Territories without causing panic. The Carmichael Massacre was never a big story outside SeCa. Too gruesome."

"Rumor is he's going to be housed here, in the drug huts."

Victor cleared his throat. "Yes, that's looking likely."

Elena poked his arm, hard. "If they put him anywhere near me, I'll choke the life out of him."

Victor couldn't blame her.

"Find somewhere else to keep him," she said.

"Where? There aren't many options, other than a hole in the ground . . ." Victor waved his hand at the construction pockmarking the slopes below Cemetery Hill.

"Get him an apartment. Put him on the Qaddo reserve. Give him a houseboat. Anywhere but here. Say you'll try, please? Victor, I—"

"Okay. I'll talk to Karine about it. Or Auntie, if I can get a hold of her. Can I ask you something? I ran into some Human Life people last night. I'm not sure why they bothered me so much."

"Forget them," she said. "They're Puros on steroids."

"They didn't seem crazy. They seemed—"

"They're cuckoo crazy. All of them."

"They seemed calm. Like they've figured out something I haven't."

"They can rant about drugs until they're blue in the face. You don't have the luxury of throwing away your pills."

"But I did."

"Aren't you still chugging tinctures like they're candy shots?"

Victor blushed. "They're helping."

Elena raised her hands. "It's not my place to say. Gotta run." She stood and hugged him. "Stay away from those people. You don't need more crazy in your life. And make sure you're here when I get out. I mean it!"

He grasped her hand. "I'll be here. Promise."

5

> Celebrity is an advantage, of course, but it's also a burden. The high cost of public life is felt most by our families and loved ones. We must carefully guard against the false choice between loyalty and duty.
>
> —Circe Eastmore's *Race to the Top* (1991)

9 May 1991
New Venice, The Louisiana Territories

Circe arrived the next morning and called a meeting of the task force on the treatment of Samuel Miller that afternoon. From the moment Victor entered the penthouse apartment, he felt a terrible premonition, a feeling that the next hour would determine not just his fate but the fate of the world, as if the balance of history would be tipped definitively toward devastation. Through a pair of glass doors that led onto a roof deck, Victor saw a deep blue sky with faint orange painting the horizon. Like flames burning the edge of the world. He pictured floodwaters rising to drown New Venice, hot springs bubbling over with sulfurous fumes that poisoned the survivors, and Cemetery Hill erupting to bury the land in mud and ash.

Auntie Circe wore jangling gold bracelets, and her black curls were gathered at her neck. She circulated between the room's real leather couches, stuffed velour love seats, and retro modern swivel chairs, checking on each guest and asking if there was anything she could do to make them more comfortable. How does one relax when planning for the arrival of a mass murderer? With mulled wine, ample bourbon, and classic cocktails, apparently. Victor abstained, though he had two vials of calming fumewort tincture in his pocket—just in case.

Pearl sat in a clear plastic swivel seat, feet on the floor, knees together, in an electric-blue suit. She read from a MeshBit and only looked up when someone spoke directly to her. Her composure probably appeared natural and effortless to everyone else. Victor didn't buy it. He could see the tension in her vibrating yellow-green aura.

Mía stood at the window, looking down on the Passage. They were on the top floor of the Newtonian, a hotel built before the canals, which had attained new prominence when it became the only building on its own island. An offshoot of the Eastmore clan had purchased the building and all the land on the island, preventing any other construction, save for elaborate gardens, a private marina, stables, and guest houses. Circe had reserved the penthouse suite, a more relaxed setting than the cramped rooms of the clinic's administration building. But no one appeared relaxed, least of all Mía. She stood stiffly, preserving an unnatural though familiar detachment. Victor hadn't seen her move in over five minutes. She hadn't said a word to him.

The emotions moving across the gathered faces threatened to overwhelm Victor. Dr. Tammet's mantra, the untruncated version, played in his head. *The wise owl listens before he asks who. The dark forest hides the loudest cuckoo*. He breathed deeply and slowly. He blinked his eyes with the regularity of a metronome.

Karine arrived with a young woman whose black hair poked out of a colorful headscarf. She had olive skin and deep brown irises, the same color as Elena's, but without the hint of green that made Elena's so special. She made the rounds introducing herself with the same phrase, "Dr. Alia Effendi, neurological imaging specialist."

Alia approached Auntie Circe and chatted with her over a few nibbles. Victor was tempted to join them, but he knew he'd never get a word out of his mouth. Auntie Circe was intimidating when alone, despite her short stature. In the company of an intelligent and beautiful woman—nope, he'd just embarrass himself.

Looking around, Victor realized he was the only man in a room full of women, the youngest by almost a decade except for Alia, and that he suffered from the same problem as the subject of their discussion. Every time they mentioned Samuel Miller or mirror resonance syndrome, whether they meant to or not, they'd be talking about Victor. He wanted to sink into the couch and disappear.

"Sorry," Karine said, "we got cornered on our way out the door. Is everybody here?" she asked, looking around.

Auntie Circe nodded and motioned for everyone to take a seat in the lounge. Karine sat on the same sofa as Victor, with Marilyn between them as a buffer. *Marilyn, my new best friend*, Victor said to himself. Mía sat next to Pearl, and Alia sat primly on a straight-backed chair that didn't fit the decor—a loaner, perhaps.

Circe perched on the arm of the love seat. Victor wondered if the effect of having the highest perch in the room, a subtle reminder of her authority, was lost on anyone else. He doubted it.

"Thank you, everyone, for coming," Circe said. "I want to say at the outset that I know this is going to be a difficult conversation. We all have strong emotions. I encourage you to express them. We must be open and honest in our dealings, especially given how sensitive the topic is. Nothing we say here leaves this room. Do you all accept these terms?"

Circe looked to each guest to confirm, eliciting a chorus of yeses and of courses. Pearl only nodded.

"Good. I'll get right to it. Samuel Miller arrives tomorrow. He will be our patient and our responsibility. A security detail from an approved contractor will be stationed at Building E, where he will be housed. We'll have him under constant surveillance.

"Let me remind everyone. He is not our prisoner. He is our patient. However you feel about him or his crimes, we must respect his rights. I should note that he has consented to all of these terms."

"What a relief," Pearl deadpanned.

Her joke didn't provoke any laughs, though Marilyn and Karine exchanged amused looks. Circe's face was a stern mask.

Alia smoothed her hair and said in a clear voice, "I'm not as familiar with his history as most of you. I looked up what I could on the Mesh, but it seems the story wasn't covered here like it was in SeCa, and I don't have the access privileges."

"You wouldn't find much," Mía said. "Pretty much everything has been classified or destroyed." She shot a look at Circe.

Alia said, "I have to ask, based on what I do know: How competent is Samuel Miller to agree to anything? The mere fact of his transfer from a public health agency to the care of a private company raises a lot of red flags for me."

Auntie Circe smiled, a mixture of compassion with a hint of condescension. She seemed to appreciate assertive women, which explained why Karine had done so well as her associate.

"There are many aspects of Samuel Miller's situation that aren't available to the public, including his competence. Karine, why don't you review those now?"

Karine nodded, opened her briefcase, and pulled out a stack of paper. She distributed one sheet to each person. Victor took the paper and skimmed it. A summary of Samuel Miller's psych evaluations over the past two decades since Carmichael. Karine hit the highlights.

"Samuel Miller was apprehended in Carmichael in the middle of a blank episode. We believe the incomplete implementation of his plan—"

"Mass murder is not a plan!" Pearl shouted. She sat stock still in her seat, except for the rise and fall of her chest.

"No, it's not," Karine agreed. "I'm sorry. I'm never sure what words to use when talking about his—"

"Atrocity?" Mía offered. "Destructive rampage? Any of those will do."

"Please," Circe interjected, "we're not here to rehash the past. We're here to make plans for the future. Karine, please continue."

Mía rose in a huff and moved to the window.

Did Karine know that Pearl had lost relatives in the Carmichael Massacre? Victor doubted Pearl had told her. She kept secrets better than anyone he knew. He was pretty sure she knew more about Jefferson's assassination than she'd told him. Pearl's truth would come out when she was ready. He'd learned that lesson well enough.

Karine said, "The short version is that Samuel Miller was catatonic for months. When he came to, his conception of what he'd done was fractured. He believed that Carmichael never happened. He spoke of parallel worlds and that he was on the wrong one. Over the years, through medication and therapy, doctors worked toward reintegrating his personality. I'm telling some of you what you already know." She smiled apologetically at Pearl, Mía, and Circe in turn. "Two years ago he took responsibility for his actions and disavowed his fantasies. In SeCa's Classification Commission parlance, he was reclassified from a One to a Two."

"What?" Victor said loudly, involuntarily. Everyone in the room looked at him. "I didn't know that was possible."

Mía answered, "It's rare. No patient has ever received as much focused care and attention as Samuel Miller."

Victor felt her words on his tongue as briny sour slime.

"How?" Victor asked. "What worked?"

Circe and Karine exchanged a look, concern and anxiety on their faces.

Mía saw this and shook her head.

Circe stood. "We know that Personil is effective in attenuating mirror resonance episodes."

"Because it attenuates *all* higher functions," Mía said. "Personil swats a fly with a mallet. It didn't help him."

"Is that your medical opinion?" Karine asked.

Mía retorted, "I may not be a clinician, but I'm as close to this case as it gets. Personil is not a cure, end of story. His disavowal wasn't genuine."

Circe cut in smoothly as if she'd been in the middle of a speech: "Of course Personil is not a cure. However, we've learned that it can be helpful in extreme cases."

"Extreme cases? I was Class Three! Why was I taking it?" Victor asked.

Mía said, "That's what I was trying to tell you. The Classification System is not perfect."

"We all want a cure, Victor," Karine said. "Until we find one—"

Victor interrupted her: "We'll just lock everyone up or sedate them!"

Circe caught Victor's gaze. She said something in a quiet voice that didn't rise above the argument crisscrossing the room, yet he heard her words distinctly. "You were traumatized at an early age. When you were diagnosed—how old were you? eleven? twelve?—Jefferson arranged your prescription. It was an aggressive treatment option, but he was adamant. Not even I could persuade him to change his mind."

It felt like a slap in the face. Victor didn't have a chance to question his auntie about it.

Alia asked, "So what worked for Samuel if not Personil?"

Mía said, "Who knows? Ask each person involved in his case, and it's a different story. Pearl thinks it was her herbs."

Pearl stiffened. "Perhaps they did the second time we tried them. I am not responsible for what happened before."

Victor got up and paced in the dining area. More secrets and lies—he could read the deception on everyone's faces. There was something huge in the past they weren't telling him. "The second time?"

"Drop it," Circe said.

Alia said, "If I could access the patient's complete records—"

Mía cut her off. "We don't have answers for you, Victor. I'm sorry."

Karine cleared her throat. "That's the case history. Should we move onto research, Alia?"

Alia stood and smoothed her rumpled coat. "We're bringing Samuel Miller here to study what works in treating mirror resonance syndrome. The question is: What constitutes good treatment? What constitutes a good outcome? We know which gene is responsible for mirror resonance syndrome, and we have some idea of the neurological underpinnings of the disorder. However, based on the research I've reviewed, there's hasn't been a comprehensive study of neural activity associated with the disorder. We have a new model of the Cogitron Exelus. It will allow us to make realtime recordings of someone's brain activity with an astounding resolution. We'll be able to see exactly how a resonant episode in the brain starts and evolves, which should give us some ideas for how we can treat it. I'd like to get started as soon as possible taking baseline measurements of Samuel Miller and all the other patients." She looked at Victor then blushed. "The substance abuse ones too, since stim addiction and MRS have similar cognitive impacts. I put together a schedule. We should have the baselines completed within a week."

Pearl raised an eyebrow and asked, "Could someone explain in English what she just said?"

Victor said, "She has an expensive toy for looking inside people's heads. Mine, for instance."

Circe stood in the center of the room and said, "We need to make the most of our resources. Samuel Miller is coming here, and his brain is coming with him. We're going to get to the bottom of his perceptions—"

"Don't you mean *delusions*?" Pearl asked. She looked at Circe with open hostility and then turned and shook her head.

What was that about? Victor wondered.

Circe continued, "We're not going to stop until we understand mirror resonance syndrome and its effects as well as we understand cancer. That is our mission."

"Fine," Mía said, "Let's just skip to the point. All this effort is for naught if it's not put into practice. You've asked me to work with Victor to build public support for bringing the Classification System to the Louisiana Territories. Well, I want everyone to hear me now. We're not going to do that. We need something new."

6

I dream about Mía finding me at home in Carmichael. Instead of leaving to go get help, she tries to open the back door. She asks me to unlock it.

I reach up and notice that my hand is small, a toddler's, and I realize I'm in a dream.

I don't want to unlock the door because I know what will happen. I know that Samuel visited our house weeks before and planted an explosive below the back steps along with a quantum trigger.

Mía begs me to open the door, and when I do, Samuel's quantum trigger activates. Each second counts another superposition collapsing, from both/and to either/or. He believed we would cross over, we would live on in some other world, and our ghost bodies would be reunited with our primal essences. But in this one, in the real world—the "real world" of my dream(!?!)—we are consumed by flames.

—Victor Eastmore's dreambook

9 May 1991
New Venice, The Louisiana Territories

Mía said she wanted to talk to Victor before making a proposal for amendments to the Classification Act. Soon after her announcement, the task force adjourned.

After a brief walk, Mía led Victor to a Repartition-Era building overlooking the Grand Canal, and they took the elevator to her furnished corporate apartment on the top. He should have stopped by his apartment to get food and more tinctures now that Pearl was in town and he didn't need to ration them so strictly. For someone who thrived on routine—who needed it to stay sane—he had gotten far too lax about his schedule.

While Victor waited in the sitting room, Mía changed into a two-piece synthsilk leisure suit—a gray unfitted sack, essentially. She was attractive for a fifty-something woman, with severe eyebrows and deep lines on her face that somehow added to her allure. He hadn't seriously contemplated sex with anyone since the incident with the prostitute in Las Vegas, and he was once again surprised by how appealing she was to him. *Why her?*

Why couldn't they have talked at BioScan, during the day, without the claustrophobic privacy of her rooms? Victor swallowed when Mía invited him to sit with her on a synthleather sofa. His heartbeat thundered in his chest. He should be interrogating her about his granfa, not getting butterflies in his stomach. There was no reason to think she'd invited him for sex, and yet somehow his mind wouldn't let go of the idea.

"It's awkward between us," Mía said. "I know our history is complicated."

"Complicated," he echoed. "You saved my life in Carmichael, and then you ruined it. Yes, awkward and complicated sums it up."

"I meant what I said about reforms . . . Well, I'll get to that. First, I want to explain myself." She retrieved two glasses from a niche in the coffee table and reached down again to pull out a bottle of LT brand bourbon. "Drink?"

Victor nodded. Not as good as a tincture, but it would do.

She poured them two belts each. He picked up his glass and held it up, expecting the customary gesture of clinking to good health.

She ignored him, staring out the window. She took a drink, draining half her glass, exhaled, and began speaking.

"I changed that day in Carmichael. I became someone I didn't recognize when I looked in the mirror. Every vital part of me was burned away, except for my desire for revenge. I thought I was doing the right thing, preventing another

Samuel Miller from coming along and wiping another town off the map. We were doing what was best for SeCa: the Classification Commission was a necessary step to protect our citizens, and the cost was worth the pain. But deep down, I wanted more than revenge. I wanted restitution."

Mía drained her glass and refilled it.

She said, "An impossible desire has a way of corrupting everything it touches."

Victor realized he'd been holding his glass out, hand shaking, the liquid churning and splashing over the side—a tempest in a tumbler, Granma Cynthia would have said. Mía didn't seem to notice. He put the glass down.

"I built the Classification System," Mía continued. "I'm responsible. At every step, I was there pushing it forward: the diagnostic tests, the treatment protocols, the budgeting, the legislative battles, the constant drip of propaganda fed to the SeCa masses to maintain support.

"I might not ever have seen the truth if not for Jefferson. He was patient. He was kind. He was brilliant. And he changed me. I became a person again, instead of some soulless, hungry ghost. My biggest regret is that I couldn't help him when he needed it. I wasn't seeing clearly. Not yet. And now . . ."

Mía fixed her gaze on Victor, and he saw so much hurt that it felt like hands around his neck, squeezing. It hurt to hear her confess what she'd done—she ruined Victor's life and the lives of everyone like him in SeCa.

But wouldn't he have done the same in her place? She hadn't mentioned her husband, killed the night of her honeymoon by a shockstick to the head, one of Samuel Miller's many victims that day. Wouldn't Victor have been as twisted, as aggrieved, if he'd lived her life? He blamed her, and yet she was blameless, cast in a role she couldn't step out of and playing it through to the bitter end, same as he was. Except now she was saying she'd changed.

Victor put a hand on her knee, though he couldn't meet her eyes again, the pain was too raw, too cutting. He said, "I—" His voice caught in his throat, and he coughed. "Mía, do you want me to forgive you?"

She jumped to her feet, her arm moving in an arc toward the window. Her bourbon glass shattered and fell to the floor. Liquid streaked the window below a starburst crack.

Victor sat on the couch—still, mute, and confused.

Mía strode to the dining room table and leaned on it with both hands. She appeared to be searching for words. Then Victor realized she was crying. He got up and approached.

She held out a warding finger. "Don't. I'm sorry. I need a minute."

Victor needed to leave. The sight of her in pain twisted his stomach in knots.

"I don't want your forgiveness," Mía said, squeezing each bitter word from her heaving chest. "I want your help." She straightened. Her voice took on a strident quality that Victor had heard many times on MeshNews feeds. "The system needs reform. The LTs can't just replicate SeCa's Classification Act and expect better results here. You need to help me shape the amendments."

Victor searched in the kitchen, found some disposable synthsilk towels, a dustpan, and a brush, and began to clean the mess. Mía stared out the window, or maybe she was watching her reflection.

She wanted reform? The Classification System ought to be dismantled. At the very least, it had to stop at SeCa.

He said, "I'm going to find a cure. When that happens, we won't need a Classification System. And in the meantime people like me don't deserve to be locked up. You understand that, right? You said yourself it's wrong."

"There are bigger forces at work, Victor. It's not just Broken Mirrors anymore. We have to consider the impact of stims too. The patient population is growing. That in itself is a huge incentive we're fighting against. The number of new health care jobs alone could end thirty years of stagnant economic development in the American Union."

"I'm not interested in economic development," he said. "It's the patients, people like me—they're what matters. I'm going to find a cure."

Victor wiped his forehead and felt a stinging scratch. A sliver of glass must have cut him. He went to the sink and washed his hands, gently wiping his forehead. Mía hadn't changed, not really. It was an illusion she needed to believe because the truth was unbearable. The good in her had died in Carmichael—just as she said—and this was an angry ghost inflicting its hurt on the world again and again, finding different ways to torment the living.

She said, "We need reform first. Jefferson thought so too, and that's why . . ."

Victor turned toward the door, then hesitated. Something in her voice caught his attention. "What? What were you going to say?"

"Never mind. Now that he's gone, there's no stopping the expansion. The best thing we can do is direct its evolution. Listen, Victor, if you help me, I can do something for you."

"What?" he asked.

Mía said, "You need someone to look out for you."

Flickering light out the window caught Victor's attention. It looked like a fire across the Grand Canal in the direction of Pond Park. The taste of soot filled his mouth.

Mía glanced to the window, following Victor's gaze, and then turned back. "I wonder about Jefferson's death too, you know."

Victor gripped the door handle. She'd known his granfa well. So why did Victor feel a hollow chill in his chest and an urge to plug his ears? There was a time not long ago when anyone who acknowledged Victor's suspicions had earned an instant loyalty. Toward Mía he could only muster sad disdain.

"What about it?" Victor asked in a tired voice.

"Jefferson was stubborn, autocratic. He didn't like his decisions being challenged. He made a lot of enemies. You need to be careful about who you trust. Take Pearl, for instance. I saw the way you looked at her during the meeting."

"Granfa Jeff trusted her."

"Look what that got him."

"How do you know so much about Pearl?"

"He didn't tell you? We brought Pearl in once before. She almost killed Samuel Miller."

"Would that have bothered you?"

Mía didn't answer, then straightened her shoulders. "If someone killed Jefferson—"

"He died of heart failure," Victor lied, feeling on the verge of vertigo for twisting a truth he'd worked so hard to uncover. He had to get fresh air. The energy between him and Mía wasn't sexual; it was twisted remorse and bitter atonement so thick it suffocated.

He said, "I wonder sometimes if he was a Broken Mirror too. Not that he would have told you. He didn't trust anyone."

7

The universal wave function never collapses. It never does! I found this fact on the dark grid. Hugh Everett III proved it. Which means there are infinite worlds like ours where the paths of atoms and energy, the meanderings of history, they're all bent. They're twisted out of joint compared to our own.

That's the reason the primals are calling desperately. I hear them. I hear them pleading to me for help.

I think it's possible to help the ghosts cross over. That's why I conceived The Plan.

—Samuel Miller's *The Carmichael Journals* (1971)

9 May 1991
New Venice, The Louisiana Territories

As Victor exited Mía's building, a huddle of people on the canal promenade looked up from a device they were sharing. Some of them gave him a curious glance.

A slight aftertaste of LT bourbon lingered on his tongue. Stupid Human Life nonsense phrases repeated in his head. He walked to his favorite bar, feeling the urge to drink an ocean. Lightstrips reflecting in the canal water caused blobs of floating colors to move across Victor's field of vision. He cursed the beautiful mirage silently. He felt penned in and trapped in his body, in this place, with a broken mind and a legacy he didn't choose. Now, when he pictured Mía's face, the blankness threatened to return, and he had no choice except to put all thoughts of her out of his mind.

Inside The Flock and Waddle, Victor got a beer, settled onto a padded bench, rested his beer stein on a tiny oak slab table, and watched the other patrons. The alcove Victor sat in was often empty and easily overlooked. Patrons sometimes stumbled into the table and made lengthy apologies when they recognized him as an Eastmore. The alcove was illuminated by yellow-tinged light from his Handy 1000 as he returned to the data Ozie had scraped from Karine. It was overwhelming and disturbingly intimate. Financial records, utility bills, search histories, a cache of documents that would take Victor much too long to read through. He needed to narrow his efforts somehow.

A group of young women from the local college were playing a game at one of the round tables between the entrance and the bar. They teased each other; their voices ricocheted playfully around the room. He overheard them dare each other to go up to him—he was the youngest man in the bar and apparently a sufficiently handsome target. He ignored them while sucking down his second drink, an LT vodka, through a translucent blue straw. Eventually their taunts about him withered, perhaps from his neglect, and they left.

A few minutes later, he was interrupted by a woman in her thirties wearing an ankle-length swirly fuchsia dress. She sat down at the other end of his bench, plopping a grass-green synthleather bag between them.

"Gorgeous evening," she said. "The cold snap is finally over." Her fingers wrapped loosely around a long-stemmed glass of bubbly. She took a long sip, appraising him. "Wait a minute, I recognize you."

Her tone was cloying, aroused, intimate. By the way she looked at him, Victor figured he was the most interesting thing to happen to her in a while. Examining her face, he noticed high cheekbones, a thick layer of skin-smoothing cream around her eyes, and deep blue lipstick that made it look as if she'd just come in from the cold. Her dress clung tightly, showing off her trim and curvaceous figure. He rolled up the Handy 1000 and put it in his pocket. What was the point of moving to a new place if not to meet new people?

"Call me Vic."

"I'm Lisabella. Mind if I sit here?" she asked as she scooted closer.

Her breasts stretched the fibers of her dress. Either a subtle rose pattern was woven into the fabric, or it was a trick of his perception. He tried not to stare. "Please do," he said.

"New Venice is such a small town. I'm sure people recognize you all the time."

"I don't know," he said, "I've only been here a few weeks. Work keeps me busy."

"You work for BioScan?"

The hairs rose on his arms. She'd inflected her voice like a question. Steel blue certainty on her face told a different story. Victor took a sip of his beer.

"Sorry," she said, "I didn't mean to put you off. What do you think of all the construction?" She nodded toward the door.

The Flock and Waddle sat at the corner of the Petit Canal and a "C-grade" canal, one of the wider watery thoroughfares. The BioScan construction on the east side of the Petit Canal could be heard in half of town. People spoke with awe and pride about the millions of AUD flowing in, thanks to the Eastmore family's roots in the area, which extended deeper and further back in time than New Venice's famous canals. Surely the family knew what was best, and if they didn't, too bad. The town was stuck with them.

In the few weeks since Victor had arrived, hundreds of employees and contract workers had moved in, snapping up apartments along the canals and filling all the tables at local restaurants long before the start of the summer tourist season, which would swell the population even further.

"It's loud," Victor said.

"Ha!" Her laugh sounded like the high-pitched cry of a mockingbird. "Isn't it, though?" She smiled again. Victor felt his lips stretch in response, though he was starting to feel that she was forcing her emotions on him, trying to get him to warm to her.

Lisabella ran her fingers through her hair. "It seems like there's a layer of dust on everything in town." She looked at him with a raised eyebrow. It reminded him of the way Dr. Tammet would silently encourage him to answer her questions on days when he was feeling mute. Usually the expression preceded more insistent pressure. He gripped his beer thinking of what he could say to excuse himself without seeming odd or rude. It was a small town. He was sure to run into Lisabella again.

"What it's like to come back to your family's town? Is it much different than SeCa?"

Different? She couldn't be that naive, could she? "Sure, it's different. I can't be locked up here for being what I am." Hardness had crept into his voice. He took a deep breath.

Lisabella smiled, a deep purple overlay of satisfaction that sparkled with a specific shade of red. It was familiar, but he couldn't quite place it on the emotional spectrum. Confidence? A hunter's thrill?

"It's interesting you mention SeCa's Classification System," she said, her voice crackling with charged urgency. "People have been wondering about Samuel Miller's legal status when he comes to the Louisiana Territories."

Victor sat back. Her gaze flicked down to a brooch on her jacket and quickly returned to his face. She smiled to reassure him. He glanced at her brooch, a blue butterfly. Its black marble head reflected his face. A vidcapper.

"I do not consent to this recording," Victor said.

She smiled sadly and also with a bit of pride. She reached into her green bag and flashed a MeshNews badge. His objection was powerless. MeshNews agents could record anything they wanted if they deemed it newsworthy. They had only their senior editors in Europe to answer to. "What's the first thing you'll say to Samuel Miller when you see him again?"

Victor crossed his arms and watched the bartender pour a flight of beer shots for a group of guys at the bar.

"Have you seen him since the Carmichael incident?" Lisabella asked. Her voice was a chisel trying to chip away the truth.

Victor picked up his beer stein and raised it as if he were toasting her. "You want me to make a statement?"

Lisabella leaned forward eagerly.

Victor got up, chugged the remainder of his beer, slammed it on the table, and walked out of the bar without a word.

More alcohol seemed like the best thing. It would lead to a different kind of blankness that would be comfortingly obliterating, render him safely unconscious and reliably immobile. The next bar he entered, The Diligent Badger, resembled any other in New Venice: it sagged under the weight of its age and smelled of canal muck and spilled spirits. A few townie-looking middle-aged men sagged on barstools and alternated between insights on the nature of life, sips of their drinks, and demands for another.

Victor sat at one end of the bar and pointed to a dark liquid in a clear bottle. The young bartender, an attractive man with black skin and a sexy sweat-sheen that reflected the lightstrips, served him a double with a wink, and Victor took the shot in one gulp. It burned down his throat and hit his stomach, a hot surge of calm spreading.

A beautiful picture formed in his mind: a DNA double-spiral, the sequence of genes responsible for mirror resonance syndrome. His program had deciphered it with a bit of help from Ozie. Now Victor needed to get the sequence from Ozie and start synthesizing proteins, growing neural tissue, and looking at how it all worked.

The MRS mutation in his DNA tweaked the way a protein in his neurons folded, which weakened the cells responsible for dampening neural activity and made his brain hyperactive. He took out the data egg and held it to his forehead. He wondered how alcohol affected the way the data egg worked. His granfa never had access to Victor's inebriated brain. Maybe the egg could sober him up? He returned it to his pocket and made a fingerburst at the bartender to order another. As his fingers spread out, his perspective warped—the room appeared to bulge and rebound, as if instead of air the room were filled with clear gelatin shaking in an earthquake. Not his favorite synesthetic effect. Victor brushed his hair back from his face and tried to picture his DNA again. Instead, he could only picture Karine's face smugly announcing her plans to make BioScan a great company, which were in fact Circe's plans. Karine liked to take credit everywhere she could.

Victor, she'd said, *you'll be an advocate for the expansion of the Broken Mirror Classification System.*

Oh, really? Not me. No, ma'am. That's as likely as me drinking a bucket of horse piss. You're the insane one to think I would help you.

The offer from Mía, however, was tempting. Evolve the Classification System in SeCa, in the LTs, and across the AU into something new, something more humane. Maybe it was possible.

On Victor's sixth or seventh drink, the bartender suggested that he pay up and move on. Victor refused. But somehow his thumb found the type-pad, almost on its own, and authorized the deduction to pay his bill. He lurched from the bar. Good riddance to liquor. He banged into an empty table. What good are empty tables? Good luck staying in business if you kick out your paying customers. He flung himself outside, where neon lights hummed their disapproval. He hissed back.

Lisabella's questions rang in Victor's ears and left a foul taste in his mouth as he walked south past storefronts selling shirts, belts, and hats with colorful beaded Qaddo patterns sewn into them. A fumewort tincture would go down well right about now. He had to get more from Pearl soon.

He was halfway home when his Handy 1000 buzzed. He stopped, took it out, and unfurled it. Ozie's face stared up at him, looking flushed and nervous, eyes swimming fearfully behind his thick-rimmed glasses.

"Where have you been?" Victor's shout echoed down a canyon of stone masonry houses.

"Long story," Ozie said. Sweat pebbled on his forehead. His black skin glowed yellow from his own Mesh device. "I don't have much time. The Diamond King wants to talk."

The Diamond King? Victor blinked. Ozie had stolen from the him. He should be hiding, not seeking him out.

Ozie said, "I'm going to see him now. You need to—"

The feed cut off. Victor tried calling Ozie back, fumbling with the type-pad. No response. The feed was blocked. Victor used the Handy's ping function to try to locate his friend. No luck. Ozie must have gone off grid again. Wherever he was, he'd have to fend for himself.

The stones flowed unsteadily beneath Victor's feet. Trying and failing to walk a straight line, he tried instead to walk a narrowly meandering path, rather than the wildly disjointed vectors by which his feet wanted to carry him forward, toward his room, toward the blissful feel of a pillow and darkness. First he had to turn left before the Grand Canal, a couple hundred more yards down a quiet canal-side street in a stupid town, to sleep soon—

Footsteps clacked behind him.

Victor turned to look.

Pain greeted him, an explosion of light and aching on the side of his head. He reeled toward the railing. Blam! Something hit him again. Agony in his skull. His vision went black, something slammed into his chest, and he felt weightless, spinning—*uh oh, I've got the spins*—then water surrounded him, burbling, cold wetting his clothes, dirty canal water soaking in. He gasped for breath, his lungs filling with water, and everything went dark.

8

Swirling white. Falling—that feeling in your gut the moment before you hit the ground. Glowing blurs, a flare across your field of vision that fades. Insubstantial, this place, perhaps a memory of blankness. Pain moving to different parts of the body, especially the back and left side of the head. The light beyond eyelids becoming less bright, less hot.

Victor opened his eyes, and the world took on shape, weight, and color. A sharp ache cascaded through his skull. When he moved, the pain was too great. He lay still, asking himself, *What the laws is going on?*

He wore a yellow synthsilk patient's gown, and he was lying in a hospital bed surrounded by palm plants and a gentle artificial light reflecting off the walls. A large window faced a construction site. After a moment, Victor recognized the dirt pits that would be replaced by BioScan towers.

He searched for a mechanism to call for help, trying not to move his head too much but failing, setting off waves of pain and nausea.

There was something he was supposed to remember, something vital he'd forgotten. What? He couldn't think through the pain.

Victor reached out for a type-pad on one of the biometric monitors, pressed it, and fell back, waiting, willing the pain to pass through him like neutrino particles passing unhindered through the Earth. He watched the door.

After a knock, the door opened, and Alia entered, wearing a sand-colored uniform that fit as loosely as men's pajamas. "How are you feeling?" she asked with a voice that burbled like a mountain spring.

"Are you my doctor?"

"No. Circe asked me to be here when you woke up."

Victor would have been uncomfortable in the presence of such a beautiful woman if he felt halfway human. "My head is pounding. I can barely think."

"You have a head wound and a concussion," she explained.

"Concussion?" Victor had fallen and knocked his head while blank before, and a doctor at Oak Knoll Hospital had explained how they determined the severity. He asked, "What grade?"

She was silent for a moment and looked at him quizzically. "Are you familiar with the Hamburg scale for mild traumatic brain injury?" she asked.

Victor put a hand gently on his forehead and pressed, slightly relieving the pain. "If I can remember, it's not as accurate as it purports to be."

She smiled. Perhaps his knowledge impressed her. "We still use it as a benchmark. My conclusion is that you experienced a Grade D2 concussion: loss of consciousness and bruising of the skull with some residual compression. I haven't observed any transcranial hematoma or anomalous vital signs, aside from the fact that you've been unconscious for sixteen hours. As soon as you feel up for it, we'll peek inside your head."

A D2 concussion and being knocked unconscious. This was serious. There could be lasting effects. Now his brain was more screwed up than ever.

Victor closed his eyes. What was he forgetting? He said, "Have you brain scanned someone with MRS before?"

"I don't expect any surprises." Her voice soothed the pain in his head, and he wished she would keep talking until he fell asleep. "Then again, you're no ordinary patient. Victor Eastmore, twenty-five. A risk taker. An advocate for the disenfranchised. Not scared of taking on Corps thugs or corporate fascists."

His eyes popped open. She wore a wry smirk. For a moment, Victor thought he had hallucinated what she said. He ran his palms over the bedsheets and gripped them. Was he going blank? She continued to look at him. Blankness felt far away, and the room felt real. He asked, "You got all that while I was unconscious?"

"I've been brainscanning our addiction patients, including your friend Elena. She can't stop telling everyone how brave you are. It made the procedure quite a chore."

He groaned. Elena needed a muzzle for her big mouth. She shouldn't be telling people about their past. There was still a murderer on the loose. But it didn't feel bad to have someone say something nice about him for a change, and coming from her it meant the world.

Alia approached the bed and spoke softly. "The blow to your head might cause dizziness, sensitivity to light, or more subtle changes to your emotional and cognitive functions. We'll run some tests to see what we're up against." Alia gestured to his head. "Do you feel up for a trip to the Cogitron Exelus now, or should we wait?"

Victor began to pull himself forward. Pain rose again and crashed against him like a storm surge breaking through a levee. He fell back on the mattress. "Wait."

"That bad? I'll get something for you. Don't go anywhere." She walked into the hall.

Victor lay still and tried to recall what happened after he left Mía's apartment. He didn't remember feeling on the verge of blankness. Drunk, yes, and sloppy from it, but not blank.

Flashes of memory began to return. He hadn't noticed anything or anyone remarkable at the bar. The college girls catcalled him. The bartender kicked him out. He passed very few people during his drunk walk through town. Ozie had called to say something about talking to the Diamond King before the feed cut out.

Then Victor had heard footsteps. The attacker must have snuck up the stairs from the path beside the canal and struck him. Victor placed his palm on his head. Two areas were raised and inflamed—a rare case of his favorite number two being a decidedly bad thing. The weapon had probably been a nightstick. Anything with a more complex shape would have created deeper, more irregular, and scabbier wounds.

He'd stumbled over the railing and fallen into the water. Someone must have pulled him from the water quickly, or he would have drowned. His assailant maybe? Why?

Alia returned with several pills and a cup of water. He washed down the pills. Maybe the heaviness in his chest was from inhaling canal water. He'd have to take a look at his chart, a slab of e-paper in a holder at the foot of his bed, to make sure they'd dosed him with antibiotics. He didn't feel as if he had a fever, so that was good.

"What did you give me?" he asked. "Pain relievers? Sedatives?"

"Both. You're going on a little journey. We'll be here when you return."

"I was attacked," he told her. "I want to file a police report to find who did this to me."

She looked surprised. "Are you sure you didn't just have one too many and take a spill? Paramedics found you lying next to the canal, stinking of alcohol, and sopping wet."

"I was hit twice in the head." Two—the best number there is, an inner voice chimed. His obsession with the number two dated from his childhood. He would shake his head to clear it, but that would be too painful. "Yes, I was drunk, so drunk I couldn't have pulled myself out of the canal. Whoever attacked me may have also saved my life. I want to file a report. Please."

She hesitated. "I could call the sheriff's office. He might not be . . . Never mind. I'm sure he'll send someone to talk to you."

She walked out. Eventually the pills began to take effect. Rather than masking the pain, they seemed to make other sensations fade. Victor moved into the pain, cozied up inside it, and made it his world, unnoticed because it was everything, everywhere around him, as unremarkable as air.

When he woke a few hours later, the pain returned, an angry knitter needling him in ferocious bursts. Despite the pangs, he was able to slip back to sleep again. Toward late afternoon, he awoke when Alia returned. She helped him take a few steps to the bathroom, waited for him to relieve his bladder, then helped him back into bed. An attendant, male, brought a plate of cold bland food, gave him a few doses of pain reliever, and left him on his own again.

Then Karine showed up and said, "I'd fire you right now if I could."

9

> There can be no periphery without a core, but I contend it depends on your vantage point. Common wisdom says that Europe is the political and financial center, dictating world affairs. I take a different vantage point. Where will the center be in fifty years? One hundred? The core is the place closest to our future. The periphery is saddled by the past.
>
> —Circe Eastmore's *Race to the Top* (1991)

11 May 1991
New Venice, The Louisiana Territories

Karine swept into Victor's room accompanied by a crackling nervous energy. "Look at you! This is unacceptable. What do you have to say for yourself?" Her gaze never rested on his face. She flitted around, her frantic gestures transforming the room into a stage for her own emotions.

"I'm so glad you're here," Victor said with a dose of sarcasm. Karine sickened him. She was a manipulative and gloating player of games who didn't care whom she trampled during her rise to the top. He bet she'd hired someone to attack him. First Jefferson, now Victor. Auntie Circe was probably on her hit list too.

Karine sighed. "It's my job to know what happens to my employees and to make sure they are safe. I take it we need to add alcohol abuse to the list of your challenges."

"Drinking isn't my problem. I was attacked! Maybe you already knew that."

Her eyebrows narrowed. "Attacked? You don't believe that, do you? The fantasies you come up with could fill a book. I wanted to give you a chance to prove your value to the company. Then this . . ."

Victor looked at the ceiling. Rather than lightstrips, each ceiling tile glowed. The default setting was soft white light. He found the type-pad controller by his bed and played with it until a light orange suffused the room.

When he tuned in again, Victor heard Karine saying, "I can't believe you passed out drunk and fell into a canal."

"That's not what happened," he said. Anger clawed up his throat. "Like I said, I was attacked."

"No, you weren't. It's yet another delusion, like thinking I'm responsible for Jefferson's death. If you can't recognize when your imagination has gone off the rails, I'm not sure we can trust anything you say."

"The feeling is mutual," he said bitterly.

"Then we're at an impasse. I'll talk to Circe about your termination."

Victor felt as if he'd been plunged into ice-cold water. Without his job, he wouldn't have access to Samuel Miller, and he'd never get the data egg to open again.

The data egg! That's what he'd been trying to remember. He looked around the room but didn't see it.

Karine said, "Or you could do what you should have already done and resign."

"Wait," he said, stalling for time. "Give me one more chance." A note of desperation entered into his voice. "It was all the noise and construction. I'll wear earplugs. No more outbursts, no more crazy talk. I promise. My head is on straight, now that it's been banged around."

Karine laughed. "To a fault, I am far more tolerant than I get credit for. You want to make this right? You have to talk to MeshNews. They're already reporting on your injury. I told them there's an informal investigation when there's no such thing. Tell them you hit your head during a blank episode.

That'll generate sympathy. 'The Classification Commission is for our own protection,' is what you'll say. Agreed?" Karine asked, one eyebrow raised high.

Victor did his best to keep his voice calm. "Yes, I'll do it."

"I'll set it up," Karine said.

After she left the room, Victor groaned. He'd lost the data egg. If making a mess of everything was his job, he deserved a promotion.

He'd also just agreed to do a MeshNews interview claiming he'd bumped his head while the deputy was coming to take his statement about being attacked. He couldn't mix things up worse, could he?

Victor climbed down from the bed, careful not to move too quickly and set his head to aching, and searched the room. His clothes were nowhere to be found. The data egg could still be in his pants pocket. Or maybe in the canal—or his attacker could have it.

If Ozie were here, he could program a search matrix using local Mesh resources, scout around town with his van looking for anomalous spectrum relay signals, or rig up a dozen other techie widgets that Victor would think were slightly magical. Ozie would find the data egg. Maybe Pearl could get in touch with him somehow.

Victor was bending over, searching beneath the hospital bed, when he heard a cough behind him. Then he noticed how cold his butt was. He straightened and spun around, holding the gown closed. Alia looked to the floor, a smile on her lips. "The deputy is here, if you're ready to see him."

"No! I mean, wait," he said. "First, could you get a message to Pearl and tell her I need to see her as soon as possible? My Handy 1000 is gone."

"Sure," Alia said and tapped on her MeshBit. She looked at his patient gown and flashed a smile. "Ready?"

Victor blushed and nodded.

Alia turned and faced someone in the hallway. "Come on in."

The deputy entered the room. He was short, his dark black skin contrasting with his tan uniform. Victor thought he looked more like a park ranger than a policeman. A miniature park ranger at that: his hat reached only as high as the top of Alia's headscarf.

"Chris Spaulding, sheriff's deputy," the man said. "Alia tells me you want to file a report of an assault." He hooked his thumbs in his belt. Insecurity smoldered behind his scowl.

"I'm not sure," Victor said. "Maybe not . . ." He hesitated. What was the likelihood the deputy could actually find the data egg? Zilch, probably. And Karine would go ballistic if he reported an attack. She might really fire him, or at least turn his auntie against him.

Let her try, Victor thought. He was tired of half-truths and full-out lies. Jefferson's secrets got him into trouble. Victor wouldn't handle his own situation the same way.

"I was attacked on my walk home," he said. "You need to find out who did it."

"Whoa, whoa, back up," the deputy said in a high-pitched yet unhurried voice. Each word twirled with musical diphthongs. "We have a procedure for filing crime reports. First we have to suspect one has been committed. Alia says the most likely explanation is that you got drunk and fell into the canal."

Alia looked at the deputy with scorn and then said to Victor, "I told him that's only what I thought at first, before I heard your side of it."

Deputy Spaulding said, "It wouldn't be the first or the last time someone lost their head and took a dip. A fool on stims fell off Triton's last month—jumped probably. It's happening more and more."

"I didn't jump," Victor said.

"I know who you are, Mr. Eastmore, and I know what you are. I'm not going to trust what a Broken Mirror says without proof."

Victor flinched. *Broken Mirror*. Even people here were calling him that now. Maybe this was MeshNews's doing. He should give up, tell the deputy to forget about it, and lie his way out of trouble.

Spaulding stared at him hard. Victor guessed that he'd been a bullied child who grew up to be a bully himself. No way would Victor give in to him.

Victor ran his hands across the sheets, smoothing them, feeling their rough texture on his palms. "My condition is irrelevant. You have no reason to trust my story. You have no reason to doubt it, either. I'm telling you, I was attacked. Someone out there"—he pointed to the window—"nearly bashed my brains in, and I want to find out why. Would you please take my statement now?"

Spaulding grimaced and took a MeshBit the size of a small paperback book from a holster hanging from his belt. "State your full name, date of birth, and transnational identification number."

Then the deputy rattled off questions in a disinterested voice.

"State your residence. What brings you to New Venice? Tell me about the events leading up to the assault."

Victor provided the information while leaning against the bed. Alia stayed and listened, appearing to give close attention to Victor's answers.

The deputy asked about Victor's past, his interests, and his involvement in any organizations.

"Do you have any enemies or people who would have reason to harm you?"

"Other than people who hate Broken Mirrors, you mean?" He did mention how valuable the data egg and his Handy 1000 would be on the tech black market.

"Can you tell me anything about who attacked you?"

Victor shook his head. "I didn't see anything."

The deputy crossed his arms. "Let me summarize what I'm hearing. A young man is attacked in the street. There is no description of the suspect and no hope of developing a useful profile. I can tell you this case is going nowhere fast. I'll file the report, but don't expect us to waste time chasing shadows."

"Thanks for your help," Victor said, struggling to keep his composure.

"Do you have anything to add?" the deputy asked Alia.

"I'll send you the file describing Victor's injuries and the logs from the paramedics. For the record, I believe Victor, so perhaps you could ask the other deputies to keep their eyes open? Is there anything Torsten could do?"

"Let me do my job. I know your fiancé wants to find some hot-button issue to add to his campaign, but if he wants our support, he better not try to make something up out of thin air."

"This has nothing to do with support for his campaign, Chris. If there's someone out there attacking people in New Venice, law enforcement needs to address it."

"Maybe what we need to address is *special* people," Spaulding replied with a sneer. "You both have a wonderful day."

After he left, Victor said, "Yeeps. I'd love to be a criminal here."

Alia shook her head. "I'm sorry about Chris. Not many people here know about MRS."

"Not yet."

The conversation left Victor feeling drained. He put a hand on the bed to steady himself and a long full-body yawn swayed him on his feet.

Alia asked, "Do you need help getting back in bed?"

"No, but maybe some privacy?"

She turned away, and he climbed into bed, trying not to flash his backside. Not that she would look. She had a fiancé, Torsten. *What's Torsten running for?* Victor wondered. *Luckiest guy in New Venice?*

As Victor settled into the bed, Alia typed something on his chart and said, "Let me know if you need anything. We'll start scanning your brain tomorrow if you feel up for it."

"I think I will be," he said.

There was a knock on the door frame. Pearl peeked in, saying, "I'm here, little owl. I bring you some tinctures."

10

My ambitions were undimmed by the failure to quickly find a cure for mirror resonance syndrome. My efforts were unflagging. Ingenuity and perseverance would be more than enough to unravel the disorder's secrets, I believed. The ban on research meant only that I would need to be more creative.

—Jefferson Eastmore's *The Wheel of Progress* (1989)

11 May 1991
New Venice, The Louisiana Territories

Victor told Pearl to enter the room.

Alia smiled and said, "I've got to see my other patients. Ms. Pearl, I'd love to have tea with you sometime, if that's something you do."

"Of course, my peach blossom."

Alia pointed at Victor. "Let's take a look at your brain tomorrow."

Pearl bowed as Alia left the room and then turned to Victor. "Here, I give you tincture. Fumewort and bitter grass," she said, continuing her heavy put-on accent. She handed him a bag, which clinked with the reassuring sound of glass vials knocking against each other. It soothed Victor immediately. He breathed easier.

"You're a life saver." He removed a vial, popped its cap, and downed the tincture, feeling a pleasant burn along his throat and down his gullet. "Between this and the pain meds, I'll be feeling great."

"That's good," she said, cooing. "I let you rest." She turned to go.

"Wait! I need to ask you—"

"It will be so good to speak with you." Then she mouthed the word, "later." She put a finger to her lips and shook her head sadly.

He glanced around the room. There could easily be a vidlens or a sonobulb hidden in the room with a transmitter to beam their conversation to eavesdroppers. Then again, maybe she was being paranoid. And why did she keep putting on the heavy accent? Did she really think anyone was convinced by it?

She made a pitying face and approached the bed, gesturing for him to lean forward. Victor sat up while she fluffed a pillow. Pearl showed him a small grey cylindrical piece of metal, squeezed it, and said, "We have only two minutes. The bugs can't hear us."

"You really think someone is listening?" Victor whispered.

"Better careful than careless," she said.

"I lost the data egg. Can you get in touch with Ozie? He might be able to find it."

"It'll turn up. Listen, little owl, Ozie went to the Diamond King because he traced the polonium back to Las Vegas. He's trying to trade info."

"But that means the King might have killed Jefferson, doesn't it? Isn't Ozie in danger?"

"Neck deep, but that's how he likes it. He thinks he can make himself valuable to the King. It's a dangerous bargain. I'm waiting to hear more. In the meantime, I have you to take care of."

She squeezed his hand. The skin around her eyes crinkled, and Victor felt teary eyed with gratitude. He wished he'd known Pearl while his grandfather was still alive. It would have been nice to see them together.

"Mía said that I shouldn't trust you."

"She has her reasons." Pearl moved on to fluffing another pillow. "We have one more minute to talk freely." She put a hand on his shoulder and gently pushed him back against firm pillows. "Mía never liked anyone who disagreed with her, including Jefferson, but she respected him. When he and I became friends, I don't think she approved. It's a long story. When you get out, we'll take gondolas on the Grand Canal. I have many stories to share. How would you like me to bring you more herbs?" She leaned over him and whispered, "I don't think Karine did what you think she did. Keep your eyes open, and take care of yourself."

Victor hissed, "Do you know who did?"

She backed away. Her mouth puckered, as if sucking on a hard candy. "I don't *know* anything. I observe. I wait. And when the moment is right, I act. Or not." Pearl chuckled. "Others have expressed that thought more eloquently. I must go. Samuel is here." She sounded reluctant to leave.

Victor gulped. So it had finally happened.

"I hope he's okay," he said sarcastically.

"He's alive," Pearl responded. "For now."

The next morning, there was a knock at the door.

"Come in," Victor said.

Alia entered. A bright yellow and black tiger-striped headscarf covered her hair. "How's your head?" she asked.

"Getting better."

"That's good," she said. "Let's do those tests now."

She helped him clamber down from his bed. He shooed away the wheelchair when she offered it. Eventually, though, he yielded to her firm, unswerving persistence and sat in it. She pushed him through the halls unhurriedly.

"Tell me about your family," she said. "They're legendary here."

"I don't know many stories."

"What about Florence? She's your great-granma, right? I've never met her myself. The whole town talks about her. She's a treasure, our oldest resident. Also, Charlene, her caretaker, helps out at the clinic a few days a week when she's not calling on Florence."

"I should go see her when I get out. It's been—I've been busy."

"I'd say, 'Never be too busy for family,' but that would make me a hypocrite."

"Spaulding mentioned your fiancé," Victor said as casually as he could.

"Torsten Lund. He's a city council member, and he's running for a seat in the national legislature."

They emerged into daylight as they exited the main building. She pushed him along several switchbacked inclines up a landscaped slope.

"Let me give you the campus tour."

He chose not to remind her that his family owned everything in front of them.

BioScan New Venice consisted of a handful of buildings arrayed on the southwestern face of Cemetery Hill directly across from the entertainment district at the southern entrance to the Petit Canal. It had long served as a treatment center for cuts, breaks, pains, strains, and pathologies in New Venice and the surrounding communities, but it would soon become far more important, Alia noted with pride. Farther up the hill, a flat area had been scraped into the hillside where the research towers would rise.

They reached a two-story building shaded by tall elm trees. Alia took Victor through a set of double doors, down a hallway, and into a room holding three machines: Cogitron Exeluses, curving plastic boxes each the size of a large garden shed. A patient berth protruded like a tongue from the center of each one.

She said, "Welcome to NANA, our Neurology and Neuropathology Annex. First we'll run baseline scans. Then we'll scan you again while we ask you a set of questions to test your memory, logic, muscle control, imagination, and other functions."

Victor climbed on top of the slab and lay back. The machine's tongue retracted, and Victor entered the mouth of the Cogitron Exelus. It thrummed to life around him as giant magnets began exciting particles in Victor's brain and taking readings to map the structure and firing patterns of his neurons.

A small speaker set near his ear carried Alia's voice as she explained the calibration and imaging procedure, though in much less detail than the manuals he'd studied. In a few moments, they moved on to the diagnostic phase. She provided a series of commands and statements: imagine a flock of geese flying in the sky, list the prime numbers in sequence up to fifty, recall what you were doing on your most recent birthday, think of a time and place when you were most happy, recall the events of the last twenty-four hours, and so on for many minutes.

Eventually, Alia expressed satisfaction at the amount of data she had collected and released Victor from the machine. They sat together in front of large screens that showed the patterns of Victor's brain in slow-motion three-dimensional color frames—his neurograms. He called out timestamps while she cross-referenced the questions that she'd asked. They annotated the feed, adding observations based on the different concentrations of oxygen and other compounds that signaled intense neural activity during and following each question and response.

"Do you have any copies of your neurograms?" Alia asked. "We could compare the patterns and see if you've been affected by the concussion."

"They're not available."

She turned her chair toward him. "What do you mean?"

"They're gone. I lost a data egg full of them." She looked at him for a moment, then turned to the screens. Victor asked, "How do you know so much about MRS?"

"I accessed all the files, but . . . I expected there to be more research, more data."

"From what I've been told," Victor said, "there was a comprehensive research program in SeCa after Carmichael, but it was quashed sometime before I was diagnosed. The research my grandfather continued afterward was probably skirting the rules, but he was on the Commission so he got away with it."

"I see. Scientists everywhere are always running up against politics. It's too bad."

Victor studied the display carefully, advancing and reversing the feed, and cross-referencing the audio log of her questions. He pointed to very subtle surges of color in the ventrolateral prefrontal cortex, an area of the brain involved in top-down control of emotions. "Fascinating," he said, mainly to himself, "a lot's going on there."

The light from the screens flickered on Alia's hand as she pointed out several areas of Victor's brain with subdued activity. "That's unusual. I would have expected stronger blood flow."

"What do you think it means?"

"There may be some effect from the concussion evident in several distinct neural subsystems, including"—she pointed to several areas on the screen—"the cerebral cortex, the limbic lobe, and the basal ganglia."

He highlighted another sequence where clouds of light swirled like eddies in a stream and rechecked what questions she'd asked him. "What does it mean that this region lit up when you asked me to imagine standing on my tiptoes?"

She looked closely at the image. "That area involves spatial-temporal reasoning. Distances. Motion and speeds. Intervals of time."

"But look here," he said, pointing to another area. "And here. These regions went dark. This is visual, kinesthetic, and here, mathematical reasoning. Is that right? You would expect some activity between all of these locations at the same time, but these are delayed and then"—he advanced the series a few more frames—"Boom! The spatial-temporal area lights up like a sparkler."

"Hmm. The timing is strange. Let's take a look at the other questions that would impact these areas."

They cross-referenced the question set and pulled up feeds of Victor's brain activity for several seconds before and after each relevant question to look for patterns.

"It's not very clear what's going on," Alia worried. "I don't have even the beginnings of a hypothesis." She tapped her fingers on the point of her chin. "There's some congruence in these regions, but it's not consistent across all of the regions each time. We'll need—"

"A larger data set," Victor interrupted. "We should have been brainscanning me all along."

"The machines only arrived—"

"Do you remember the data egg I mentioned before?"

Alia nodded.

"It contains my neurograms from before. If I could find it and get it open, we'd be able to compare it to these readings."

"Hopefully, it'll turn up. In the meantime, I'll track down more questions related to spatial-temporal reasoning, motion detection, and some of these other areas. We can run you through the machine again tomorrow."

"Okay. I assume you'll want to keep me in bed for the next day or so." He meant it innocently, but when she looked at him strangely his face reddened.

Wryly, she said, "You'll enjoy a couple days in our care. Victor, this has been instructive. I look forward to working on your brain again soon."

That evening he searched through every room, cupboard, and box in the clinic where his data egg might have ended up. He also searched the ambulance while two paramedics watched him clambering around inside. He found nothing.

Back in his room, he downed two fumewort tinctures, a vial of bitter grass tincture, and the pain medication and sedatives a nurse had dispensed with his dinner.

He dreamed he was trapped in a pitch black room. He stretched out his arms and felt the walls curving around him. Then he was jostled as a giant hand shook the room and a voice screamed at him to give up his secrets. It would have been amusing—he realized it was a dream, bitter grass helped in that regard—but someone was with him in the egg, a dangerous presence, breathing, stalking him, moving closer in the dark, preparing to strike: the Man from Nightmareland.

11

To everyone's surprise, a cult of nostalgia never formed around the ruins of the United States of America. The nations of the American Union were too busy moving on and fighting to secure the benefits of Repartition. Perhaps some of the elder generation looked back and wondered if we'd lost something in the process. But the young accepted the new state of affairs despite diminished horizons.

—Robbie Eastmore's *A Study of Alternate Histories*

13 May 1991
New Venice, The Louisiana Territories

The soft, gray cocoon of Victor's morning slumber was interrupted by a crescendo of knocking, accomplishing what shafts of sunlight, birds chirping, and street traffic could not: Victor escaped the binding fibers of sleep.

A voice he didn't recognize called through the door, "Mr. Eastmore, there's someone here to see you."

"I'm awake. Give me a minute." He could hear murmurs on the other side of the door, but it was too early and Victor's mind was too foggy to speculate about who it might be. He rolled over the bed railing and stood groggily for a moment, yawning and shaking the sleep out of his head.

When Victor opened the door, he found an oversized hulk of a man looming in the hallway. It was Tosh.

Trouble, Victor thought. From the moment he'd run into Tosh's gas traps at Oak Knoll Hospital, the man had caused

Victor nothing but trouble. For some reason, Jefferson had put his trust into a violent, unpredictable bully, saying Tosh would look out for Victor. Was it "looking out" to force Victor to have sex with a prostitute to try to open the data egg? Was it "looking out" to steal the piece of Jefferson's tongue from Ozie and turn it over to the Diamond King? Was it "looking out" to try to persuade Victor to kill Karine?

"No," Victor said. He blinked, surprised he'd spoken aloud.

Tosh smiled, flashing his teeth, making Victor's stomach clench. Trouble was here. Victor took in a deep breath. Tosh had introduced himself back in Oakland as Táshah, the Qaddo word for wolf. He was a wolf in sheep's clothing, certainly.

"Looking good, Vic. More like Jeff every day."

Tosh's angular, high-cheekboned face looked rougher than Victor remembered, though his gaze was piercing as always. He wore a green canvas jacket, a white V-neck shirt, and tight black pants tucked into buckled-up shin-high boots. A shopping bag sat on the floor next to him.

"What are you doing here?" Victor asked.

"Nobody passes through New Venice by accident." Tosh seemed to scrutinize Victor as if he were a damaged credenza at an estate sale. "Feeling all right?"

Understanding flooded Victor's brain. "You took the data egg!" he said. "You gave me a concussion!"

Tosh grabbed Victor by the shoulder and leaned in, lowering his voice. "You should have told me the data egg opened. Put something on, and let's go someplace to talk." He gestured to the shopping bag, which was full of clothes.

Victor traded his hospital gown for the outfit Tosh had brought him. Tosh tugged on Victor's arm. "Outside."

At the end of the hallway, Alia stood at the nurse's station, using a type-pad. "Victor, where are you going?"

"He's checking out," Tosh said.

"Who are you?"

"This is Tosh," Victor said. "We've got to go. I'll explain later."

Alia looked alarmed. "I don't think you should be up and around like this, and you certainly shouldn't leave."

"We'll take that under advisement," Tosh said, clearly implying no such thing. "We're going now," Tosh said. His grip on Victor's arm tightened painfully.

"I'll come back for the tests," Victor said. "I promise. There's no harm in me leaving."

"I can't stop you, and I'm too busy to argue," Alia said sadly. "Enjoy your jailbreak."

Tosh led Victor silently through town to a footpath bordering bird-flocked marshes along a quiet stretch of the Passage. Under the sun's glare, the buzz of insects whirred around them. Tosh stopped at a bench and sat down. Victor's stomach churned from hunger and anxiety. He stood awkwardly, not sure what to do. After a moment, Tosh told him to sit, and Victor obeyed.

Victor said, "Do what you came here to do, and let's get it over with."

Tosh swept his hand in front of him, as if the grasses, the water, and the blue sky were somehow going to speak for him. The occasional tourist paddleboat scooted along below them. They overlooked the Circle Route, which brought tourists from the opening of the Grand Canal, downstream along the curve of the Passage, and along the entertainment district before heading up the Petit Canal and back into town.

"What do you hope to accomplish with your life, Victor?"

It wasn't a comfortable question, and Victor felt he was being challenged in a game he hadn't agreed to play. Expectations were low for someone with MRS—the condition was degenerative, or so it had been thought. When Victor had told Dr. Tammet that he wanted to be an astronaut and go live on the moon, she had frowned and lectured Victor about setting reasonable goals: perhaps Victor might one day live on his own, in his own apartment, and hold down a job part-time.

The one thing he really wanted from life was a cure to his condition, but Tosh didn't deserve that kind of intimate honesty.

"What does that have to do with anything?" Victor said.

"Well, what do you want in life? Be honest. What drives you?"

Figuring out what the hell I am, for starters. "I don't know," Victor said. "It doesn't matter."

Tosh smiled wolfishly. "Some people don't have trouble answering that particular question. They say, 'I want a good job.' Or 'I want to start a family.' Some people set their sights on seemingly impossible goals. They want to travel every continent. They want to run an empire. The point is: you have to identify that one thing that makes your gut burn, that keeps you up at night, and then go after it with everything you've got. First you have to choose."

The words and tone reminded Victor of Granfa Jefferson, but they sounded pompous coming out of Tosh's mouth.

"Good thing you're here to help me out," Victor said.

"You're up to your eyeballs in trouble, Victor, and you don't even see it."

"Uh, I'm well aware there's a shit storm crapping on me daily. What do you want, Tosh? You already took the data egg."

Tosh nodded. "That's true." He leaned over and patted Victor's bandaged head. Victor grunted and recoiled. "Why didn't you tell me it opened?"

"It's been a rough couple of weeks," Victor said, lamely. He'd dreamed up a dozen excuses, but they'd vanished. *Typical me brain, gone when it's needed most.* "Were you able to listen to Jeff's message?"

"We're working on it."

"You and the King?" Victor asked.

"Here," Tosh said, "I've got something for you." He pulled out a device from his jacket. It was Victor's Handy 1000.

Victor took it, eyeing Tosh suspiciously. "Thanks. Do I get the egg back too?"

"Maybe . . . eventually. Depends on how helpful you are and how helpful Ozie is."

The colors swirling on Tosh's face were black, red, and gold—doom, rage, and pride all mixed together. Victor's stomach flipped.

"You're going to be very helpful to me, you know why?" Tosh said, taking a small plastic container out of his pocket.

Victor looked at the container with curiosity and a twinge of dread. Maybe it wasn't anything bad. Maybe it was the piece of Granfa Jefferson's tongue Tosh had stolen from Ozie.

Tosh pointed at the Handy 1000. "Does that thing read fingerprints?" At Victor's slow nod, he continued, "Go ahead and bring up the program."

Victor did as he was told with a growing ball of fear in his stomach. He opened the container.

Inside was a black-skinned severed finger. It had been scrubbed clean of blood and looked thoroughly dry, like an artifact in a museum. Tosh snatched the finger and scanned the tip against Victor's device.

The screen read: Osirus Abraham Smythe.

Ozie.

"Shocks," Victor whispered. The sight of bone and flesh at the cut end made Victor's eyes water. He imagined Ozie, screaming in pain, while Tosh pressed a glinting cleaver down through the bone, snapping with a sickening thunk, parting Ozie's finger from his hand.

Victor set the container down on the bench, leaned over, and puked in the grass. His head throbbed, and his body felt filled with buoyant gas. He stood up, doubled over, and dry heaved.

Tosh said, "The King does not tolerate people who don't get the job done. Now, both you and your friend are going to be 100 percent cooperative, or you're going to find yourselves less than 100 percent. Understand?" Tosh pointed Ozie's severed finger at Victor, jabbing it toward him.

Victor blinked. The world seemed to be receding, leaving him to rattle in a hollow shell. He wandered away, following the path, barely feeling the ground beneath his feet. He looked up, expecting to see that he was rising toward the sun, face sweating in the blazing heat. Dizziness swayed him from left to right and back again.

Why not run? What's the worst he could do to me? Throw me in a canal again?

The image of Ozie's finger rose in front his eyes, and his stomach spasmed, but this time he breathed deep and didn't vomit. The path led to a street that descended to lower ground. He caught glimpses of the Grand Canal between some houses to his left.

Tosh caught up to Victor as he was crossing a bridge. The man wrapped his arm around Victor's shoulders and held him steady. They faced a railing and the water below. Victor thought about wrestling away from Tosh and jumping in, feeling the cold mucky water on his skin.

"What do you want from me?" Victor asked.

"I've already got what I want," Tosh said, "your attention."

12

The world is made by great thinkers, not small minds.

—Jefferson Eastmore's *The Wheel of Progress* (1989)

13 May 1991
New Venice, The Louisiana Territories

Victor stared at his hands. Eight fingers and two thumbs—two is the best.

Poor Ozie. He had two thumbs, but only seven fingers remaining. It was his own fault though, wasn't it? Making bargains with the Diamond King was like grabbing a knife by the blade.

Victor looked at Tosh's long, severe face and into his unreadable dark eyes. "What do you want me to do?" he asked.

"What I say, when I say it."

"But what?"

"Something big. Something the King wants. You don't have to worry about it yet."

Victor shrugged away from Tosh and rushed across the bridge, muttering and cursing. *"Something big." Be more vague, you garbage human.*

Why couldn't people just say what they meant? Secrets and double talk never helped anyone. His feet thundered on the concrete—a hallucination surely, he thought, as he startled leisurely strollers who weren't used to anyone rushing on Main Street. Pedestrians in Victor's path stepped aside. When he glanced back, he could see Tosh following, an amused and curious grin plastered on his face. Maybe he'd never seen Victor on the verge of going blank before and he was enjoying the show. Maybe he planned to take advantage of him while he couldn't resist.

Victor ground his teeth. He didn't know where he was going. He just needed to stay away from Tosh and keep the blankness at bay. He shouldn't have left the hospital without his tinctures.

When he reached a plaza adjacent to the Grand Canal, he found Human Life protesters squatting on stairs that led down to a waterfront promenade. They'd also formed a human chain stretching from the railing to the opposite side of the plaza. Townies and tourists had to detour around them. Victor considered ramming the blockade, the way kids had played Navy in grade school. No. The thought of touching them, even to knock them on their asses, made his skin itch.

He turned away and saw Tosh nearby scrutinizing the crowd. "What's all this?" he asked Victor. "Are these your Broken Mirror friends?"

Victor stood still, breathed, and repeated the owl mantra, congratulating himself on his self-control. He wouldn't go blank, and he wouldn't be baited into aggression—that's how much he'd grown over the past few months.

Chanting behind him interrupted the mantra in his head. The Human Lifers were spouting some nonsense about Emergence.

"Embrace the eternal present!"

"Abandon your poisons!"

"Free your shackled potential!"

Fail to receive the cancer cure, Victor added silently. *Die of uncontrolled tumors.*

"Broken Mirrors are people too!" someone shouted.

Victor snorted at the irony of these fools using a slur to defend his rights.

Someone broke away from the human chain and approached Victor. He recognized Wonda, who smiled at him goofily.

"Hello, Victor. It's good to see you again," she said. She moved close but didn't touch him.

Beautiful Wonda, smelling of floral perfume. Unwelcome figures from his past were converging on New Venice, demanding things of him, and this fresh-faced girl didn't care, didn't want anything from him except maybe affection. Maybe her touch wouldn't be so bad.

Wonda was followed closely by the rotund preacher from the protest in Pond Park. The preacher smiled and extended his hand. Victor hesitated then shook it. The preacher's face was round, unlined, uncomplicated. He looked as if he couldn't hide a lie even if he wanted to.

"My faith name is Deliberation," he said. "Call me Del, please. Florence Eastmore is one of my idols, and I met your grandfather a few times too. An incredible man."

Wonda thrust out her hand to Victor, smiling. "We can shake too, can't we? I didn't know who you were before." They shook, and he felt a warm pulse travel up his arm. "Pleased to meet you, Victor Eastmore," she said. "May your Seeking unfold magnificently."

Tosh stood a few paces from them, his expression neutral, but Victor imagined the wheels turning in his head, evaluating whether Wonda and Del were friends or foes, people he could exploit or pick on, or irrelevant to his egocentric goals. If Victor could toss Tosh in a canal and be done with him, he would.

Del wrapped an arm around Wonda. "Don't mind her enthusiasm. Wonda forgets that we seem like fanatics to the pluripotent." Del must have noticed Victor's eyebrows raise because he laughed at himself. "Sorry, our terminology is unfamiliar, I know."

"Is this your friend?" Wonda asked, looking toward Tosh.

"Come on over—don't be shy," Del said to Tosh. "I'm Del. This is Wonda. What's your name, my friend? Come chat with us."

Tosh executed a half bow, though he still wore a wary expression. "My pleasure," he said grumpily as he linked arms with Victor. It felt like the opposite of a protective gesture.

The protesters' chanting had quieted into low murmurs like water lapping on the canal walls. Wonda stared at Victor, which normally would have made him twitch, but her face was so open, ebullient, and joyful that he smiled. These people were the exact opposite of Karine and her troop of condescending executives or Tosh and his aggression. They lacked deceit, ulterior motives, and contempt for broken people. Their attention was a warm breeze after a summer shower's clouds passed. So what if they wanted to tell him about their silly cult? Victor wasn't afraid of being converted.

"Let's have a squat talk." Del abruptly bent his knees and squatted there in the middle of the plaza. Wonda winked at Victor and squatted too. Tosh lowered himself with surprising grace for a man who was all muscle. Victor looked around. There were at least three benches nearby. They must prefer this odd squatting, or maybe their belief system required it. He joined them in the squat, feeling foolish.

Del said, "We are the New Venetian and Qaddoan Lands Potentiate. We are stewards of the pluripotent."

"Why do you keep saying pluripotent?" Victor asked. "It doesn't make any sense."

Tosh said, "White people talking about the Qaddo without respect could find a world of trouble."

"All respect due, of course," Del said earnestly, brow wrinkled, eyebrows high.

"Skin is skin," Victor said harshly to Tosh and turned to Del. "Pluripotency describes stem cells' capabilities to transform into different types of tissue. But I'm sure that's not what you meant."

"Ah, I understand the confusion," Del said, chuckling. "For us, the pluripotent are those who've not yet found their calling. The purpose of joining a potentiate like ours is to change and grow, to seek and to set our feet on the path to purity." He held up a hand as if he was going to place it on Victor's head. The hand remained upraised. "May the road you travel turn toward purity and happiness." Del's smile and voice harmonized emotionally. Victor read only good intentions on his face and relaxed.

Wonda gave Del a look that reminded Victor of a dog who'd been promised a treat. "Del promised not to recruit you," Wonda said. "I made no such vow. I'll win you over eventually." She turned to Tosh. "You too," she added.

Del smiled apologetically at Victor. "As an organization, we don't push our beliefs on anyone. However, individual potentiates like Wonda are free to take it on themselves to find people who need our help, like you, for example. Those we call 'seekers' are free to participate in our potentiate. If they want to join and become a Path Treader, we'll consider it. Most take a different path, and we accept that."

"Anyone can join?" Victor asked, throwing a poison look at Tosh.

"We welcome everyone who is willing to follow the Principles of Emergence." Del cleared his throat and spoke hesitantly. "Our rules are strict. Anyone on medication or taking alcohol, stims, or other drugs would need to give them up."

Victor's face flushed hot. He couldn't stand when people made assumptions about him or his condition. "I don't want to join. Besides, you wouldn't let me. I don't take Personil anymore," he said, wondering why he felt the need to explain himself, "but I take herbs, natural medicine. A Chinese woman. She arrived with a woman who saved my life when I was four . . ." He was babbling. He tried to focus and talk his way out of it. "You've probably heard about Samuel Miller and the Carmichael Massacre already."

Both Del and Wonda looked at him curiously.

Wonda's brow creased. "Victor, if you take herbs as medicine . . ." She looked at Del.

He patted Victor's shoulder. "This warrants a careful study of the rules. I'm called Deliberation for good reason. Come by our camp some time and we can discuss it." Del stood, reached into his pocket, and handed Victor a card.

"Why here?" Tosh asked. "Why New Venice?"

Del said, "This is where we can do the most good. The future is emerging, and we want a hand in shaping it." He looked suggestively toward the BioScan campus.

The guarded expression Tosh had been wearing vanished under a wide, tooth-filled smile. "I'm sure you will."

Like a shark, Victor thought, but worse because this shark is good at fooling people.

His Handy 1000 chimed. It was a message from Karine: *Why haven't you responded to my messages? Where are you? MeshNews is here to interview you!*

Victor rose from squatting. Del looked at him with a kind, soft expression. He couldn't leave the man in Tosh's grip.

"Run along, Victor," Tosh said. "It looks like you've got somewhere to be. I'll catch up with you later. In the meantime . . ." He turned toward Wonda and said, "I'd love to learn more about the potentiate."

"Bye, Victor," Wonda said with affection in her voice.

Victor left them with one glance back at Tosh. He would pay for what he'd done to Ozie. Somehow Victor would make sure of it.

13

Can you hear the voices? They are calling out for answers hidden in a memory. Do you remember? Once in louder days, we hollered from the mountain tops. Now we curl in hidden valleys, gathering our treasures close to our breasts, waiting for a light that will not shine in the quiet dark.

—Estrella Burgos's *Theories of Emergence* (1906)

13 May 1991
New Venice, The Louisiana Territories

Victor arrived at Karine's apartment, and she ushered him inside. She wore a tight smile, dark eyeliner, and a puffed-up hairdo. She shut the door behind him.

Expansive windows and glass-walled balconies overlooked the east side of town. The sun hid behind a layer of clouds. The apartment was spacious. The kitchen, dining area, and living room were all visible, occupying and defining their own space in the wide-open floor plan. His gaze was drawn to a raised corner nook with a curved bay window where Lisabella sat.

"Hello, Victor," Lisabella called, without rising to greet him. "Please have a seat. And thank you for talking with me." She wore a tight-fitting dress that showed little skin, only her hands and head, yet it revealed every curve of her hips and bust.

He crossed the room, climbed the steps, and sat facing her, his gaze drawn to colorful boats moored in the canal six stories below.

Karine cleared her throat. "I've been over this with both of you already, but I'll say it again. This is a sympathy piece. We show why it's important that people with mirror resonance syndrome are acknowledged by the government and get treatment. We're lucky not to have experienced anything like what happened in SeCa here. Victor, you're a model patient"—He was surprised she didn't choke on those words. He supposed she was putting her best foot forward for Lisabella's sake—"and you're proof that therapy and medication work."

She thrust a bottle of Personil into his hand.

He looked at it and said, "I'm not—"

"It's not only about you," Karine said, talking over him. "It's about the people in the LTs who don't know they're suffering. They have no access to treatment, no validation that what they're going through is real. Mention the suicide rate, how we think we can bring that down. But try to stay focused on your own story. And make sure we get the truth about how you knocked your head. We don't want any more rumors."

Rumors were said to be a second currency in the American Union. The official story came only from MeshNews. Everything else was imaginative fiction. The footage Lisabella gathered in the interview would be chopped up into digestible pieces, reframed, spun into an evolving narrative, and distributed to MeshNews users in the Louisiana Territories over the next few weeks. Victor had never been interviewed before, but every other member of his family had, including his cousin Robbie, who treated media relations as an art of war and liked to lecture Victor on how unsuited he was to the spotlight.

Shock you, Robbie, I've got this.

"Karine, please," Lisabella said. She smiled apologetically at Victor. "I'm sorry about the deception before. I hadn't quite received permission yet from the suits upstairs. Everything's now on the up and up."

Victor asked, "Are you proud to bring Samuel Miller's story to everyone in the nation?"

Lisabella maintained her smile. Victor envied her. Most people in SeCa would flinch when they heard that name.

Karine said, "Let Lisabella ask the questions, Victor. Shall we start? Just pretend I'm not here." She sat on an ottoman in the living area, watching them closely.

Lisabella checked her sono and vid feeds, gave Victor a thumbs-up, and leaned forward. "You let me know at any time if we need to redirect or pause. I want to make this as easy as possible."

"Thank you," Victor said.

"Let's start with something I've been curious about. We're dealing with a stim addiction epidemic in the LTs. I've read about your condition, and I've spoken to many of the stim addicts in New Venice. I understand they feel something akin to what you experience when you have a resonant episode. Can you tell me in your own words what it feels like?"

Victor blinked. It had been a long time since anyone asked about that. Years maybe. Dr. Tammet had quizzed him all the time. The only other person who asked was Elena.

He said, "I can feel an episode coming on, usually. They're not always the same. Sometimes it's like losing my balance, like I'm falling. Other times it can be . . ."

"What?"

"Sometimes I feel weightless and . . . It feels good."

"Good how?" she asked.

He met her eyes briefly. Dark blue sympathy colored her face. Her curiosity wasn't predatory; it was understanding. She simply wanted to know. He breathed more freely. This was going well.

He answered, "Blissful. Sexual sometimes."

"Interesting," she said. She licked her lips. He was sure she wasn't even aware she'd done it. Her fingertips brushed her cheek and smoothed her hair back. "And when you're blank?" she asked.

Victor frowned. "I'm gone. I'm not there anymore. I've seen vidfeeds of my episodes, and it's like watching someone else. I don't remember any of it after. It feels—" He stopped himself. This was the worst part. The embarrassment and shame so thick it was like a second skin.

"Please go on," Lisabella said.

He cleared his throat. "I feel vulnerable when I'm not in control. If it happens at the wrong time . . ." He looked down at his shoes. "People used to make me do things at school. I woke up once with no clothes on. It was a big joke to them."

Victor looked up. Lisabella's mouth was open, shocked. He glanced at Karine. She stared at him, stone still. He couldn't tell what she thought of his confession.

He continued, "When someone with MRS is blank, they're highly suggestible. Malleable. Lowered inhibition. That sort of thing." He put a finger to his temple. "We hear and understand, but there's no one in charge. That's why we need protection, not just from ourselves but from others too."

Karine was nodding vigorously. She made a fingerburst of approval.

Victor sat up straight. "I want to make sure that things are done differently in the Louisiana Territories than they were in Semiautonomous California. I want to help Bro—to help people with mirror resonance syndrome without stigmatizing them."

"Speaking of helping people," Lisabella said, "what signs should someone look out for? How can people recognize when their friends and family members need a checkup?"

"If I may?" Karine said and continued without pausing. "We'll be implementing a comprehensive screening and testing procedure. The public won't need to be worried about helping make diagnoses."

Victor glanced at Karine, surprised. She was saying the right thing for once.

Lisabella looked down at her MeshBit, poked at it. Her lips moved, repeating something. Victor thought maybe she was trying to get back into the flow of her interview.

After a moment, she looked at Victor again and gave a small smile. "You're doing great. I want to ask: Are you happy with the treatment you've received?" Lisabella asked. "Medical treatment, I mean. Your therapy and medication, specifically."

Karine pointed to the pill bottle in his lap.

Victor stared at Lisabella, ignored Karine, and said, "I credit many years of therapy for helping me cope."

"Don't forget many years of medication," Karine said.

"I don't take Personil anymore," he snapped.

"But you would if your condition worsened," Karine said. "If you had delusions, say, or if you found yourself going blank."

"I'd consider it," Victor said through gritted teeth.

"Are there downsides to medication?" Lisabella asked.

Victor nodded. "It's like living in a thick fog. I almost didn't recognize that my grandfather was—" Karine was shaking her head. "I wasn't going to say anything about that!" Victor said to her. "I was going to say that he was sick!" He turned to Lisabella, "I almost didn't recognize myself. On Personil, I'm not much fun to be around."

"I want to make one thing clear to the LT public," Karine said. "Personil is an effective treatment for cutting down resonant episodes. It acts on the emotions and leaves higher reasoning function intact. Victor produced exceptionally complex and sophisticated computer models for Gene-Us Enterprises when I was chief and while he was taking Personil. Intellectually, he was not at all affected by his medication."

"That's a fair point," he said bitterly. "I was the best emotionless human computer that ever worked for Karine."

Lisabella laughed, and no small portion of it was at Karine's expense, Victor thought.

"'Personil takes the person out of you,'" Victor said. "It's what another Class Three and I joked about those few times we were lucid."

Karine smoothed the fabric of her dress, running her hands along her thighs. She said, "I'd like to clear up a misconception. Personil was originally named for its green coloring, based on a derivative of parsley, which in French is *persil*."

"What I find puzzling," Lisabella said, looking down at Karine, "is that the drug wasn't renamed after Broken Mirrors became stigmatized in SeCa. Wouldn't that have been the compassionate thing to do?"

Karine waved a hand in front of her face as if she were shooing a bad odor.

"Let me ask you now about Samuel Miller," Lisabella said, turning back to Victor.

"Fine," he said, steeling himself.

"What will you say when you see him?"

Victor touched his pocket, remembered that the Diamond King had the data egg. He hopefully wouldn't have to speak to Samuel until he got it back. "I honestly don't know."

Lisabella looked down at her MeshBit. "That's all the questions I have for you, Victor."

Karine said, "We still need to touch on Victor's injury."

Lisabella regarded him, waiting for his comment.

He gestured to the bandage on his head. "Look what can happen. Just another reason we need protection."

Karine said, "But—"

"That's all I'm going to say about it," he said. "I do want to say something about the Classification Commission, though."

"I don't think now is a good time," Karine said.

Lisabella leaned forward. "I'm listening."

"I want the citizens of the Louisiana Territories to know they have a choice to make. In Semiautonomous California, people with mirror resonance syndrome are treated like criminals. That must not happen here. Our symptoms get worse not because the disease's progression is inevitable, but because we are ostracized and locked up. The facilities and camps were a mistake. I'm opposed to any attempt to recreate the Classification Commission here without significant reforms to how people like me are treated. Our rights must be respected. We deserve better. The Louisiana Territories and all its people deserve better."

"I see," Lisabella said. "That doesn't quite align with BioScan's official position. Care to comment, Karine?"

Karine sniffed and said to Lisabella, "As Circe worked out with your suits in advance, we'll be reviewing your footage carefully before it goes live. We're all on the same page, or we will be by the time it reaches the feeds." She glared at Victor and then turned a fake smile toward the reporter.

"Of course," Lisabella said. "I do have one more question for you, though, Karine. It's about a death at Oak Knoll Hospital."

"I'm sorry?" Karine looked confused.

"The death at Oak Knoll. A suicide."

Victor froze.

Karine said, "Are you—are you asking me about Jefferson Eastmore?"

"No," Lisabella said.

Victor heard the sound of an eagle shrieking before it dove at its prey. He was almost entirely sure the sound was only in his head.

"I'm referring to Dario Sanchez, the nurse who killed himself after caring for Samuel Miller. Given the circumstances of his death, how will you prevent more suicides here in New Venice?"

14

All citizens are classified by their level of Mesh access, whether they are aware of it or not. At the top are the system administrators and content consultants who have unrestricted access. Then there are those like me who can hack their way to knowledge. Then there are seekers, who delve one layer at a time at great expense, worming their way toward the truth. And then there's everyone else, the blissfully, contentedly ignorant who accept whatever comes through their Mesh feeds.

—Osirus Smythe's "Data Isn't Free," an unpublished term paper

13 May 1991
New Venice, The Louisiana Territories

"I can't answer that question," Karine said slowly as if she were tiptoeing out of a cave, fearful of waking sleeping bats.

Lisabella stared at Karine, waiting, looking unsatisfied.

"I wasn't there, need I remind you?" Karine's voice hitched and sounded almost like a child's.

"Surely you're aware of the suicide, though," Lisabella said. "You're second to the chief of the company bringing Samuel Miller to New Venice. I looked through the SeCa MeshNews records, reported and unreported. Surely you've discussed the history of mass hysteria and hallucinations around Samuel Miller, and you've a plan to protect your staff and the public?"

“Do you want to create a panic?” Karine asked. Hardness gave her voice a hammer’s heft. She and Lisabella were sizing each other up. Lisabella maintained her relaxed posture, seated, though she’d turned toward Karine, who was standing and seemed to be struggling to maintain her composure. If she’d been holding anything in her hands, Victor thought, it would have already been shaken to pieces.

“There is no risk,” Karine went on. “I don’t see any reason why we would need to cause undue alarm.”

Lisabella frowned and stood. “I see I’ll have to take this question up with Ms. Eastmore.”

“I’ll let her know you’ll try,” Karine said.

“Thank you, Victor,” Lisabella said. “You did admirably.”

Victor stuttered a response. The tension in the room could power a generator, and he wasn’t sure what it was all about. A suicide at Oak Knoll? When?

Lisabella left the apartment without another word. As soon as she was gone, Karine cursed, “Laws,” grabbed a pillow on the couch and squeezed it with both hands, fingers digging into the soft material, and then threw it down. She crossed to a table where her purse was resting, took out a MeshBit, and started speaking. “Circe, this is Karine. Our reporter just launched a sneak attack named Dario Sanchez. MeshNews is going to fuck us hard if they run this. The LTs will come down harder on Broken Mirrors than SeCa ever did. Hang on.” Karine breathed, held a hand to her forehead, started speaking again. “She’s a fame-hungry bottom feeder, but she’s not going to rattle us. Nothing bad has happened here in the LTs. No matter how they try to play it, we’re talking about an event that’s decades old in a country no one here cares about. It’s probably a bit of colorful fluff to raise curiosity. Still, we really need to know what angle they’re taking. Talk to your friend and get back to me.”

Karine hung up. She seemed unaware that Victor was sitting in the elevated nook. Her anxiety left him feeling oddly calm. Perhaps he’d so demonized her that he wasn’t at all tuned in to her emotions. Or maybe the relief he felt was a confessional afterglow, the benefit of speaking truthfully to

Lisabella without reservation. And he hadn't had to lie about being attacked. Not a bad day after all.

When he stood up, Karine looked at him and grudgingly said, "Not bad. Then again, I'd say she went easy on you."

"What was she talking about? Mass hallucinations?"

"Not now. Alia wants to run another scan on you."

"But—"

"I promise we'll fill you in. This is more Circe's area than mine. I wasn't there. Go on."

Victor walked past Karine and left her apartment. He rode the elevator to the ground floor and made his way to the BioScan campus, pelted by rain and feeling buoyant but not in a blank way, in a things-are-going-great kind of way.

He pinged Alia, and she sent a message back that something had come up with a patient and they should meet later. He went to his desk and returned to the data he had on Karine, focusing so hard his head throbbed. He drank a vial of fumewort and carried on.

He heard a chime and saw that a message had come through on his screen.

Cogitron Exelus, now.

Oddly, there was no sender listed. Maybe Alia had a problem with her MeshBit.

Victor jumped from his chair, trying to ignore the pain in his head, rushed out of the room, almost ran into an employee in the hall, apologized, never slackened his pace, and rocketed into the blazing outdoors. The storm had passed, leaving in its wake the scent of rain on pavement and wet grass.

Late spring in the Louisiana Territories was hot, though not quite swamp-gross hot. New Venice lay hundreds of kilometers upstream from where the Mississippi disgorged into the Gulf of the Americas, so there was always a hint of dryness inside the insufferable humidity, suggesting that the situation could be worse, that it could be even wetter and stickier than it already was, and people should be happy it wasn't.

Victor stripped off his shirt, arranged it to cover his head—there was nothing so stupefyingly hot as a head full of sunbaked curly hair—and headed uphill. By the time he reached the annex, sweat dripped down his chest and back. He wiped himself with his shirt, and as he did, he swayed, a rush of woozy pleasure moving through him. Victor's skin, glistening like the upper reaches of Lake Qaddo, almost matched the mud in color, its muted brownness, like pale bluish clay smeared thinly over a darker, richer coffee-ground layer of healthy soil.

He'd been standing for a minute or so, looking at his skin and the landscape, trying to figure out whether the similarities were an illusion or an accurate representation of reality, when he heard someone call his name.

Victor blushed, realizing that he was standing naked from the waist up where anyone could see him, adding to the eccentric Eastmore rumors that were no doubt already circulating.

"Victor!" the voice called again, and this time he recognized it.

Ozie was walking up the hill, looking somewhat winded. He wore gray pants, a navy windbreaker, and two black gloves. Sweat covered his face.

"I was worried about you," Victor said.

"Put your shirt on, and stop showing off. No one wants to see that." Ozie patted his stomach with his right gloved hand, an oddly stiff and halting movement. His belly lacked the washboard firmness of their college days. Ozie said with a grin, "I need to start eating whatever you're eating."

Victor looked at Ozie's glove and remembered. "I'm so sorry," he said. "Your finger . . ."

"What about it?" Ozie asked.

"Tosh showed it to me! I scanned the fingerprint."

"He what? You—ohhh . . ." Ozie shook his head, wearing an expression of rueful admiration.

Ozie's right shoulder was lower than his left, as if he were carrying a heavy weight. He saw Victor looking at him and smiled. "You want to see?" His grin was playful and sly.

A memory of one of the few times they'd stripped naked and wrestled came unbidden to Victor. A brief sexual phase of their relationship had been fun at first. Then it had turned weird. One or both of them would usually go blank during the act. Neither liked the idea of getting it on with a mindless version of the other, and the sexual attraction they felt toward each other had quickly dissipated.

Ozie raised his hand. The dark gray glove covering it was large and loose, a giant's glove on a child's hand. He pulled the glove off and showed Victor the most bizarre prosthesis he'd ever seen.

Flesh the clear snot color of a pale jellyfish surrounded chrome metal bones and red and blue tubes that looked like optic cables and liquid pulsing capillaries. The hand flexed and made a fist, its inner pieces shifting smoothly.

"How far up does it go?" Victor asked.

Ozie gestured with his human hand to his upper arm where the curve of his shoulder ended.

Victor shivered. He'd never thought about this type of enhancement. Chemicals and brainhacking were one thing. This was replacing a part of yourself with something foreign, alien.

"Why?" he asked.

"Why not?" Ozie grinned. "In all seriousness, you're looking at the most sophisticated, high-powered mobile computing device in the Louisiana Territories. And it's impossible to lose or have stolen." He reached into his pocket and pulled something out. Cupped in the palm of his translucent hand was the data egg, a black oblong on the oceanic blob of his prosthetic hand.

Victor took the data egg, pressed it briefly to his forehead, then stuffed it in his pocket. "Care to explain?"

"It was the King's idea to see if I could fully open the egg once you'd cracked the initial message. I couldn't. Though I now have a good idea what it'll take to unlock it again. I didn't know Tosh was going to bash your head in to get it. Sorry about that."

Victor punched Ozie in the shoulder hard.

"Ow!" they both said at once.

"Thanks a lot, asshole!" Victor said, flexing his bruised hand. "So you were never hurt? Your finger?"

"Tosh must have pulled it from the trash bin. The King and I have an understanding. I'm on his payroll now. Tosh isn't as tight with the King as he claims to be."

"And you are?"

"No one is! He doesn't ever meet you in person. He's a talking head on a vidscreen, a ridiculous avatar that looks just like a playing card. I'm serious! But he's got more money than pretty much anyone. He's paying me as a security consultant. He knows about that data we stole from the Institute and BioScan, but not about the MeshSats. That's worth at least five million AUD."

"And the polonium? What did you find out?"

Ozie wiped his prosthetic hand across his forehead. "Can we get out of this heat?"

They walked up the hill. Air-conditioned air blasted from an over-door chiller as they entered the research building.

"Shocks," Ozie cursed. His glasses were steamed up. He tried to wipe them with his windbreaker. His robot hand fumbled, and he lost his grip on the glasses.

Victor grabbed them mid-air and wiped them on his shirt. "Looks like you need some fine-tuning of the interface," he said, looking pointedly at Ozie's arm.

"It works fine when it's not snagging on clothing." He carefully removed a tissue from his pocket, pinching one corner delicately with his artificial fingers, and wiped his forehead. "The Diamond King procured the polonium and shipped it to Oak Knoll Hospital. He says he thought he was dealing with Jefferson Eastmore."

"Impossible," Victor said. "I don't believe Granfa Jeff killed himself."

"Neither do I. He very much wanted to live. When it became clear that he couldn't counteract the poison, he reached out to me, to Pearl, and to Tosh. We were supposed to help you overcome MRS symptoms and find a cure."

"The question is: who at Oak Knoll got their hands on the polonium? and how did they administer it?"

"The answer is in the data egg," Ozie said. "Do you want to open it or not? I hear there's a Cogitron Exelus here. And a doctor named Alia Effendi you find very attractive."

"How do you know I think that?"

"Your voice. It goes deeper. Like this," he said in a baritone.

"My voice?" Victor stopped mid-stride and laughed. "You bugged my hospital room? Pearl was worried that someone was listening. It was you, wasn't it?"

Ozie wrapped his synthetic arm around Victor's shoulder before he could squirm away. The arm rested there heavily, more like a thick cable than a limb. Ozie said, "She and I already caught up." They walked to the scanning room together. Victor was surprised that Alia wasn't there waiting for him.

"Wait, I forgot," Victor said. "Dario Sanchez, a nurse who killed himself the first year after Samuel was captured. Did you know about him?"

Ozie didn't answer. He pulled up his sleeve. A square of skin on the inside of his wrist glowed with red characters. It looked like the menu on a MeshBit, numbers and brief snippets of text, and while Victor watched, the characters changed.

Victor asked, "How are you—"

"Shh," Ozie said. "It takes concentration. There's no mention of him in public records, not even birth and death dates, which is weird, because there should be records for other Dario Sanchezes, right? Let me dig deeper. Okay, I'm in classified records now, everything I've scraped together from HHN. Here! A pay stub, the last one is dated June 1971. You say he killed himself?"

"That's what the reporter said."

"It would have taken a lot of digging at high-up access levels to uncover this. That means someone with lots of Mesh privileges is taking an interest in this. No sweat. I'm on it." Ozie grinned. Victor knew he liked a challenge.

The glowing characters on Ozie's wrist faded. He pulled down his cuff, then gestured to the Cogitron Exelus. "Let's get started!"

"So how is this going to work?" Victor asked.

Ozie explained, "I helped Jefferson put your neurograms in the data egg. And now we know your ability to control your blank episodes is what triggered it to open. We also know that it'll open next when it's near both you and Samuel Miller. But what we don't know is what specifically will happen to trigger it."

"Jefferson said he wanted me to spend time with Samuel Miller. That the data egg would help him as well. 'You must prove that alternative treatments are effective,' he said."

"Exactly," Ozie said. His gaze wandered to the Cogitron Exelus machine.

"What are you thinking?"

"It's a crap shoot that we'll be able to rehabilitate Samuel. I know Jefferson thought it was possible, but I'm not so sure. But what if we could trick the data egg into opening?"

Victor looked at the machines, the most detailed brain scanners in existence. "How?"

"Just get in and let me poke around with the controls."

"Really?"

"I learn by doing."

"What's the harm?" Victor said.

After several minutes of pecking at the type-pad, Ozie looked up, smiled, and gave an almost lifelike fingerburst with his jellied hand. Victor moved to climb into the machine.

"Hold it!" Ozie held up his robot arm. "I can't believe I have to point this out to you. You know what kind of machine this is? What it does?"

"Yes, it uses magnetic fields to—oh." Ozie's arm had far too much metal in it. "You'll have to wait outside."

"I didn't get a big hunk of magnetizable metal fused to my arm bone, but I am definitely putting off enough interference to screw with the readings."

"What do we do?"

"I seem to recall there's another expert on campus who can help us. Am I right?" Ozie smiled slyly and turned to the door as if he expected someone to walk through it.

No one did.

Victor waited a minute or so, sitting on the lip of the scanning bed. "Well?" he asked. "I only have an hour and then—"

Alia walked through the open door. "Victor, I don't appreciate that kind of sexually explicit message. You do not have permission to speak to me that way. Understood?"

15

Organized Western States???? What a joke!!!! The OWS should stand for Oppressive Withering Slavery. OWS citizens are chips the Diamond King cashes in whenever he sees a chance for profit.

—BrAiNhAcKeR Collective

13 May 1991
New Venice, The Louisiana Territories

Ozie waved at Alia with his robot arm, hidden by his windbreaker and glove. The gesture was somehow stiff and fey at the same time.

Victor wiped a hand down the front of his face. "I'm sorry, Alia. You can thank my friend Ozie for the message. What did it say?"

"Don't ask," she said.

"Pleasure to meet you, my ravishing lady. Victor hasn't said a word about you, though I'm sure you've been in his thoughts." Ozie smiled broadly and turned to Victor. "I didn't expect such an exotic beauty here in New Venice." He turned back to her. "We need your help."

Alia folded her arms.

"Please, Alia!" Victor showed her the data egg. "Look what I got back."

Her eyebrows rose. "Interesting. May I?" He nodded. She took the data egg and held it in two fingers, its black oblong shape featureless except for the red ring around it.

Ozie said, "We need you to bring this into the room while he gets scanned. I'll be monitoring from outside, adjusting the scanner to compensate for interference from the data egg. We're trying to gauge how it interacts with Victor's brain."

"And if we can get it to open," Victor said, "I'll find out who murdered my grandfather, and you'll have access to both my neurograms and Samuel's."

"Murder?" Alia looked alarmed.

"Afraid so," Ozie said. He told her about the polonium he'd been tracing.

"The neurograms would be useful," Alia said. Victor couldn't tell if she believed everything they'd told her. "You want me to bring it in the room and take it over to Victor?"

"That's right," Ozie said.

"Should I walk smoothly forward? Should I pause at certain distances? If this thing works on electromagnetic radiation, the signal should become stronger as I get closer, yes? So . . ."

"Yes, of course, you're right, I—" Ozie cleared his throat. "I hadn't actually thought about that. Other things were on my mind. Yes, move slowly. Stop every meter or so for thirty seconds, and then move forward again. Stop when you reach the scanner. Victor, don't you move. This whole time I want you stable, immobile, thinking about puppies or something."

"You don't want me to try to go blank?" Victor asked.

"Not this time," Ozie said. "We'll do one run through totally calm, and the next we'll get you excited. Everyone ready?"

Alia moved to the doorway. Victor lay back in the chair, eyes closed, picturing the little owl in the forest, claws gripping a branch, silently staring through the trees. From the hall, he heard Ozie say, "Here we go."

The scanner began to hum. Other than that, he didn't feel anything strange.

Alia said, "I want you to picture a smiling baby. Now think of the sound of the ocean. Visualize making a fist. What's eight times six? Where is the northernmost point of the American Union?" She continued with questions and instructions. Her voice grew louder. He could smell her, faintly soapy with a subtle floral perfume and some spice. A pressure began to build in his pants.

He called out, more loudly than he intended, "Should I be feeling anything weird? I mean, when I was in Dr. Santos's chair, it was like there were bees and smoke in the room. Right now I feel fine."

Ozie said from the doorway, "That's because I'm making adjustments. Do you want to feel what's it's like if I don't mess with the settings?"

"No, thank you," Victor said.

The scanner's hum diminished and went silent.

"Is that it?" Victor was eager to leave the scanning bay.

Ozie came back into the room. "We should do it at least once more. With the egg in there with him. Can you run him through the same questions?" he asked Alia.

"I can," Alia said, "but they're not novel anymore."

"Hmm, that means they'll trigger the memory part of his brain. MRS isn't known to affect memory necessarily."

"This is all pretty much a stab in the dark," Alia said, "isn't it? I'll ask the same questions. Let me prepare." She reviewed the data they'd collected and made some notes on a piece of paper. "Ready," she said.

"From the top!" Ozie said.

They ran through the experiment again. Victor felt calm and grateful. It was good to have friends to help. During a final repetition of the experiment, Victor brought the blankness close, like wrapping himself in a blanket, then pushed it away when it was over.

After Alia had run through the questions and prompts, she asked, "I can see you in there. What are you smiling about?"

He opened his eyes and raised his head. Her face, a beautiful composition of delicate features and kindness, just outside of the scanning bay, made him smile even more broadly. "I appreciate your help," he said. "Sorry Ozie tricked you."

She touched the type-pad, and the scanning bed rolled along its track, freeing Victor from the bay.

"It's a worthy cause," Alia said. "I'm as curious as you are about what's inside." At first he thought she meant the data egg, but then she pointed to his head.

"Don't think I'm awful just because he is," Victor said.

Her smile dipped at one corner, becoming more sardonic. "You boys will have to take it from here. I need to get back. Tell your friend if he needs my help, he should ask nicely next time."

She left, and Victor caught a glimpse of Ozie bowing dramatically in the hallway as he watched her leave.

Ozie laughed as he stepped into the room. "A hot doctor who knows all about MRS. I have a major hard-on for her."

"She's engaged."

Ozie mimed choking himself with his robot hand and for a second Victor was worried he might actually hurt himself, but it was just a face. Ozie had always been good at clowning.

"How about a beer?" Ozie said.

"Sure, there's a bar called the Flock and Waddle. A Mesh-News agent has been hanging around. She'll want to talk. Maybe you can hack her feeds."

Ozie smiled, the excitement of a hunter flashing in his eyes. "Let's go."

Victor glanced at the scanning bay and frowned, feeling as if he'd seen movement out of the corner of his eyes.

"What's wrong?" Ozie asked.

"Nothing. I just realized that if this doesn't work, I won't have any choice but to see Samuel."

16

Progress is made of innumerable and individually insignificant moments of transformation, from this to that, from a to b, from hypothesis to result. Revolution occurs, not spontaneously, but because the accumulating weight of incipient change overcomes the inertia of the status quo.

I don't believe in the spark of invention. The creative gestalt is a myth. Without steady advancement, without a carefully cultivated field, the future cannot grow. We can believe that something emerges from nothing only by closing our eyes to what the past has wrought.

—Jefferson Eastmore's *The Wheel of Progress* (1989)

13 May 1991
New Venice, The Louisiana Territories

Freedom, release, graduation—Elena's big day. She was officially freed from her stim addiction, and she could leave BioScan feeling whole. She could enjoy the sunshine, budding flowers, fresh green shoots in the garden, and a gentle afternoon breeze caressing her hair. She could almost ignore all the construction equipment buzzing on the hillside. Victor would meet her soon, they'd have a nice meal somewhere in town overlooking a canal, and she wouldn't worry too much about what she was going to do next. No need to rush things. Time would pass the same no matter what.

Alia walked next to Elena, a final send-off from the treatment program. It was a nice touch to have one of her doctors there. Elena liked Alia much more than her therapist.

Alia asked, "Are you nervous?"

"No," Elena replied, "I'm . . ."

What was she? Free? Whole? Nah. She was a person with enough scar tissue inside her to soak up a vat of scartoo ink.

"I'm good," she said. "You don't have to see me out."

"I want to. I try to meet with everyone when they're—"

"Released into the wild?"

Alia smiled and gestured to the bridge over the Petit Canal. "I think you're crossing over to a new adventure."

Elena's mouth soured. Crossing over. Words made famous in SeCa by Samuel Miller. The man had tainted all their lives, so that even an innocent-sounding phrase carried bitter echoes now.

Elena checked her watch. Victor was already ten minutes late. He'd promised to be here and to be on time, but things were a bit slower paced in the Louisiana Territories. She wouldn't begrudge him a few minutes. She looked out at the city, poised above the water, windows opened for air.

Alia said, "All of New Venice shrank back under the scrutinizing gaze of the lioness."

A grin tugged at Elena's mouth. "Lioness, eh?"

"You're strong," Alia said. "The things you've been through would have broken most people."

Elena said, "I think most people are broken. It's the strong ones who figure out how to heal. Like Victor."

Alia nodded, then bit her lip.

"What's wrong?" Elena asked.

Alia shook her head and put her arm in Elena's. Elena stopped, feet rooted to the ground, and slipped her arm free. "You don't have to wait with me. I'm meeting Victor here."

"I don't think he's coming," Alia said.

Elena held her breath, hurt. He'd promised. "Why not?" she asked.

"He and Ozie—"

"Ozie's here? The two of them together are like . . . like . . ." Elena struggled for words. "Two heads that are worse than one."

"They're trying to get the data egg open."

A wave of pessimism crashed down on her. Same old Victor. Desperately seeking. Willing to sacrifice his peace of mind for a destabilizing truth. His quest for answers would send him over the edge again if he wasn't careful.

Elena let out a long sigh. So Victor had found a way to ruin her big day. She was finally kicking stims, and not only was he not there to congratulate her as he'd promised, he was scratching an old itch that had scarred him time and time again.

Alia said, "I know he cares a great deal for you."

Elena looked out at Qaddo Lake. Haze hid its distant stretches. Victor's business wasn't Elena's business anymore.

During therapy, Elena had come to understand that her addictions stemmed from a hole inside her, which finally felt, if not full, then at least only half empty. She'd latched onto Victor in high school because his attention and his problems felt bigger than hers. When she was with him, she didn't think as much about herself and her feelings.

That was then. Today, she was determined she wouldn't let him take center stage in her life anymore. She wouldn't let his moods and his issues control her feelings anymore. There was no room anymore for a Victor-sized, attention-seeking, problem-addled plug in her heart.

Elena stared out at New Venice. Memories that were still painful now lacked the power to make her run from them. The shunning after her parents were kicked out of the SeCa trade union, the move to the Republic of Texas, the pain of Victor abandoning their friendship, stim addiction, the Puros. She might have made mistakes, but she could no longer hold onto shame. She had to move forward.

And, in truth, the Puros weren't on the list of problems in her life. They were good people with a good cause. They'd helped her. They'd done their best. They'd always had her back.

Shocks to you, Victor. Enough is enough.

Alia seemed to sense Elena's thoughts, her resolve. She gave Elena's shoulder a squeeze, then turned and walked back into the construction chaos of the BioScan campus.

At the crosswalk, Elena hailed an autocab. It arrived within a minute, wound through tiny streets to the main road that bent through town, and whisked her to the train station. Amarillo was her next step, and she was better off to go it alone without a messy good-bye dump of Victor's feelings onto hers. It was time to live without him, and good riddance.

17

The primals are beautiful, like colorful, vibrating clouds of particles shaped like humans walking, moving, gesticulating, and then disappearing again. They are the essence of spirit yet they are incomplete. Their corporeal forms—what I call ghosts, the people I grew up with, all the forsaken of Carmichael—are trapped in this reality. I hear the primals pleading to be reunited, for me to help their ghosts cross over. It is my calling to help them.

—Samuel Miller's *The Carmichael Journals* (1971)

14 May 1991
New Venice, The Louisiana Territories

Victor hiked up the slope to the drug huts, watching his feet take measured steps on the asphalt path, knowing each one took him closer to his nemesis. He wasn't afraid, wasn't anxious. The last few weeks had been filled with dread, and now that the day had arrived when he would see Samuel Miller, Victor felt he was made of stone.

He did regret one thing: he'd failed Elena yesterday, maybe for the last time. She'd asked him repeatedly to be there when she finished the program. He knew it was important to her. Yet he'd been too preoccupied with his own problems, too obsessed with the data egg, too narcissistically focused on what was special about his brain, too pleased to see Ozie again and grateful for his company. Now that she was gone, he realized how much he wanted to speak to her, how she was the only person who made him feel normal.

The wooden deck of one of the drug huts loomed over him. Spindly stilts held it aloft. How much force would it take to snap them and send the building careening down the hillside?

When Victor reached the path to the front door, a pair of iridescent green hummingbirds darted past, vibrating and tweeting in high-pitched bursts. They dodged and weaved, fought over a bright yellow flower with narrow curling petals, and sped away like sentient missiles.

Victor knocked on the front door, his heart thumping and palms sweaty. It swung open, and a tall man in a navy jumpsuit greeted him, demanded his MeshID. The name Perry was in white thread woven into the garment at chest level. Victor showed Perry the ID screen on his Handy 1000 and was ushered inside. Another man, Velasquez, according to his embroidered name, was shorter and stockier than Perry and stood outside the door to a sitting room. When Velasquez saw Victor, he motioned for him to head inside.

The sitting room was a square box. Its cream-colored walls bore countless dark marks and scuffs and few decorations. A drawing in black pencil of three trees covered the entirety of one wall. Opposite the drawings, Samuel Miller sat on a sagging green-and-blue-striped couch, staring forward. The face was the same as Victor remembered, a long rectangular shape, sunken cheekbones, wide-spaced eyes, and thin lips. Time had worn grooves into his skin. Bags under his eyes looked pregnant with purple fluid. His salt-and-pepper hair was slicked back, nothing like the wild rat's nest Victor remembered him having in Carmichael.

He didn't seem to notice Victor at first. Karine sat primly on a folding chair next to the couch. She had been speaking quietly to Samuel. She stopped and looked up at Victor. Her expression was calm and controlled as she gestured to a line of folded chairs leaning against the wall.

Victor felt the weight of the data egg in his pocket, breathed deep, retrieved a chair, and sat, all without looking too closely at Samuel. He stared into Karine's eyes, hoping without reason that the data egg would begin to vibrate and divulge Jefferson's next message and implicate her in his death.

"Samuel and I are discussing what will be expected of him when speaking with MeshNews agents," Karine said. She turned to Samuel. "Victor was interviewed already, and I think he did quite well."

Victor peered into Samuel's eyes. They were dead calm. It was as if there were no one there.

"When both of you are ready," Karine said, "we'll start hosting small events on campus with cherry-picked attendees. City council members. Law enforcement. Our goal is to introduce you gradually to dispel any myths and prejudices about mirror resonance syndrome and to win allies to help us advocate for change."

Samuel looked at Karine while she was speaking, appearing to listen, but Victor couldn't tell what, if anything, the Man from Nightmareland was feeling.

Victor swallowed and addressed Samuel while gripping the data egg in his pocket. "We're not going to duplicate what was done in SeCa. We want a fairer system. One that isn't built on fear."

Samuel blankly looked at Victor, the same way he'd looked at Karine—not blankly like being in the midst of a resonant episode. This was a strange, matte-dull kind of empty. Like a pigeon watching a person who didn't have any breadcrumbs—detached and uninterested.

"You understand what I'm saying?" Victor asked.

"Yes, Victor. I understand." His voice was flat and soft, making the hair on Victor's arms stand up.

Had Victor sounded like that when he was on Personil? A robot's voice held more emotion.

Victor stood, looming over the nothing-there man on the couch. "People are afraid of you. You know that?"

Samuel blinked, looked at Karine, and then said to Victor, "I understand. I caused many g-go—I caused many deaths a long time ago."

The way Samuel stuttered gave Victor pause. Had he wanted to use a different word?

Ghosts?

Victor felt an intense need to provoke Samuel, to crack his calm facade. He said, "I understand. You thought you were helping ghosts cross over."

Samuel sat very still, almost a statue, though Victor might have seen a twitch move across his face.

"I did," Samuel said with conviction, without a hint of regret about the people he'd murdered.

Victor smacked Samuel in the face, knocking him onto his side.

"Victor!" Karine jumped to her feet. She ran to the door and called to the security detail, "Get in here!"

Samuel lay on his side on the couch and slowly raised himself. There was no rage, no resentment on his face. Victor wondered, not for the first time, what was going through the man's head, what could go though a mind neutered by Personil, the way Victor himself had been before he'd broken free.

Victor's hand gripped the data egg hard, straining the muscles in his wrist. He relaxed. Forget it, he told himself, Samuel's mind is mush. Whatever signal the data egg is supposed to recognize is too weak, too attenuated. Neither the data egg nor the Cogitron Exelus was going to get what Victor needed from Samuel while he was like this.

Victor moved to the door.

"Where are you going?" Karine asked. The two security staff blocking his way looked at her questioningly. "It's all right. Please wait outside."

They stepped out of the room with mechanical efficiency. Victor wondered exactly what they'd been told about him, what limits to his freedom Karine and Circe had imposed.

Samuel sat, staring forward. He might as well have been a statue.

"Look at him," Victor said. "He's useless like this."

"You need to be patient."

"He's a lump. There's nothing going on in there. Not really. Not while he's on Personil."

"Come now," Karine said. "You led a full life on Personil."

"I lived in a bubble on Personil, and you know it. If you really want to understand mirror resonance syndrome, you need to alter his treatment."

"Laws, protect us from the consequences," Karine said as Victor left the room.

Alone, Samuel Miller blinked in the silent room. He looked out the window. A breeze pushed tree branches to and fro. There were guards around him all day. They slept next door after locking him in at sundown. The windows had special locks. The balcony outside was wrapped by a transplastic bubble. He was sealed in. He'd be trapped and might burn to death if there was a fire. There was no use to dying like that, he reminded himself.

Crossing over. It had been so long since he'd thought about it. Why had he forgotten?

Samuel looked out the window, noticing stone buildings and a wide stretch of water that curved around them. He wasn't in SeCa anymore, and this wasn't a facility or a ranch. He was in the Louisiana Territories.

There were no other Broken Mirrors.

Except . . . someone had just visited him. Karine LaTour and the other one. Victor Eastmore. He was a Broken Mirror. He remembered his full name now; he hadn't when she'd mentioned it earlier. Victor Eastmore. Age four. The bright one who attended kindergarten even though he was younger than the other students. Victor hadn't been on the list—Samuel had never seen his primal.

Primals. How could he have forgotten? He couldn't remember the last time he'd seen one.

He looked around for a pen and paper.

He would start a new list.

18

> A delicate tea leaf that trembled in the breeze
> drowns in my teacup, boiled and limp,
> as I stare at my garden. My fingers itch.
> Tomorrow I'll plant beans.
>
> —Ming Pearl's *Now Blossom* (1973)

16 May 1991
New Venice, The Louisiana Territories

A couple days later, at his request, Pearl met Victor in Pond Park under the shade of a jacaranda tree. Pink and lavender flames blossomed above them.

"Let's go out on the water," Pearl said.

Victor selected a gondola that looked well-maintained. Its black-lacquered hull bore a high-gloss finish. Inside, red paint was smoothly applied without any nicks or worn-away edges.

"You thought I'd want this Asian one?" she asked, then winked and climbed carefully aboard the gondola while he steadied it.

Victor stepped in, bracing himself with the long pole and shifting his feet to a wide stance. He pushed them away from the dock and poled the bottom of the lake every few seconds to propel them toward the canals.

"I want you to help me get Samuel Miller off Personil," he said when they cleared Triton's Deep Crossing and began heading up the Grand Canal. "I need a way to reach him when he's unmedicated."

As they neared a bridge, sheriff's officers surrounded a woman who stood at the railing, laughing and looking down. Her face had a sheen of sweat. Her mouth stretched in an ecstatic smile, blood tricking from her lips. The noises coming from her sounded sexual. A stimhead, it looked like.

A juggler standing a few paces away held up one of his balls toward the police. "She stole my ball and tried to cram it in her mouth."

Between cackles and sexual moans, the woman squealed, "I want to eat until I'm full. I'll swallow the world!"

An officer approached the woman, restraints held up in one hand. "We'll feed you everything if you put these on."

Their boat slid past the bridge and left the scene behind. After a long moment of silence, Pearl said, "Do you believe in Emergence, Victor?"

Victor shrugged, knowing Pearl would take him on a winding journey before getting to the point. He shifted the pole to an opposite grip, turned the gondola ninety degrees to the left, and moved them toward a side canal that headed south through the main shopping area. The boat traffic moved slowly, but there was less current here, and up ahead more canals branched off to quieter parts of the islands.

"I don't know," he said. "It depends how you define it, I guess."

Emergence was a popular dinner table topic, and probably had been for the last sixty years. It happened to be the best way Victor knew to reveal whether people believed in logic and science or not. Emergence could mean one hundred different things to ten different people. For some, it was a period of time that began after the end of the Great Asian War when Europe became a global superpower. Others had a more religious interpretation, believing that the weakening of the old religions of the Middle East created space for new beliefs and organizations to grow. In North America, it was was a political philosophy that was characterized by decentralized decision-making and ad hoc collaboration.

Victor thought, and science supported his view, that Emergence meant seemingly separate and distinct phenomena spontaneously combining and adding up to more than the sum of their parts, like the way his brain cells became overexcited and produced MRS symptoms, including blankness.

They reached an intersection where the canals branching off narrowed and traffic became one way. The pole he held was longer than this canal was wide. He moved them forward carefully, slowly, listening to the sounds of splashing water echoing off the narrow stone canyon.

He glanced back at Pearl, who sat upright with her chin raised, blinking at him through large round lenses the color of morning urine.

She said, "I believe Emergence is the unfolding process of time moving forward. Seeds of the past bloom, turn into flowers: our future. Emergence is the present moment, always becoming, forever being, itself existing whole and eternal. Emergence is now. Cause and effect are illusions. We look to the past for hints of what may be, and we imagine the future as the result of our actions today. Emergence is the truth behind this veil of lies, seeking to be free. We must open our minds to perceive it."

"Thanks for the tip," Victor said glibly.

Pearl laughed, a gutsy gust of mirth. She was a wholehearted believer in Emergence—an eternal now, the great truth behind the world's illusions—and, as he considered this, his concept of her began to sour. She didn't want to help him get what he wanted. She had her own agenda. The walls of the canal closed in. He looked behind, wondering if they could back out, but another gondola followed, one of the town's gondoliers in a stupid tricornered hat was pushing a middle-aged couple forward. Both passengers had white hair, mixed-brown skin, and flowing synthsilk jumpsuits. They looked happy, as if they'd never heard of Emergence.

"Here's the plain talk, which I know you like," she said. "Don't worry so much about the past that it blinds you to what's happening now. Let the truth emerge."

"I worry about the past because it's a threat," he said. "Granfa Jeff was murdered. The people he said I should trust—you, Ozie, and Tosh—aren't really helping me. You keep saying 'shush' and 'later,' but I don't have time. I need to get the data egg open, and to do that I need to convince Auntie that getting Samuel off Personil is safe. How can I do that if you won't tell me what you know?"

"It didn't work before," Pearl said in a hard, flat voice. "We tried other medications. There were complications." She stared at the bottom of the boat.

"You mean Dario Sanchez?" Victor asked.

Pearl looked up at him, shocked.

"Lisabella, the MeshNews agent, said he killed himself. Why haven't I heard of him before?"

Pearl's hands, which had been fidgeting in her lap, gripped the gondola seat. "Everyone panicked. Before then, MRS research had been a public affair. After Dario killed himself, everyone was afraid that the madness was spreading, like it was an infection. People started to riot, the worst of it in the Asian slums, thanks to a false story about Dario being half Filipino. MeshNews started censoring everything, which probably caused greater alarm. Mía started talking about euthanasia, which caused the medical staff to walk out, and I . . ." Pearl leveled a hard gaze at Victor. "I found enough sedative to knock down a horse. Was prepping the syringe while Samuel was in one of his blankouts. Jefferson found me, convinced me not to do it. But I was this close." Pearl pressed her palms together, almost in prayer. "Since that time, the story of MRS in SeCa has been a carefully crafted tale without the inconvenience of facts and truth."

Victor jammed his pole into the mud at the bottom of the canal, stopping their progress. "You didn't try again to kill him?"

"I try not to regret my failure. I didn't have the will. I resigned, started my little shop of herbs, kept in touch with Jefferson over the years."

The gondolier behind them yelled to clear the way. Victor ignored him. "What's going to happen when Samuel goes off

Personil?" he asked. "Will your herbs keep him in check, like they did me?"

"It's dangerous to assume that," Pearl said, frowning in a way that wrinkled her face and made her look old and tired. "You were young when you started medication and therapy. You never had the type of break with reality that he did."

Victor poled the boat forward, navigating in silence until he could pull alongside a quay and allow the boat behind them to pass. When they were alone, he asked, "Exactly what did Granfa Jeff want you to do with me?"

Pearl took off her glasses and rubbed them with the tip of her neckerchief. "Jefferson asked me to help you come off Personil and manage your symptoms. He thought your example—an Eastmore living an upstanding life despite being a Class Three—could change the political climate in SeCa. He also wanted me and Ozie to help you work with Samuel Miller to fix him and use his recovery to overcome stigma against people with MRS. He believed that reform of the Classification Commission in SeCa was vital and it had to precede research for a cure. He was adamant about that, though I never understood why. We were all supposed to work toward that goal in Carmichael. It was an impossible task and doomed to failure, but I owed it to him to try.

"Now we find ourselves here instead. I will help you. The present unfolds as it must."

19

The key to business success is vision. You have to have a clear destination in mind and knowledge of the path to get there. Of course, there will be twists and turns, and you might be assailed by bandits along the way. It takes fortitude and foresight to walk through the dark forest of an uncertain future, but the mountaintop awaits.

—Circe Eastmore's *Race to the Top* (1991)

16 May 1991
New Venice, The Louisiana Territories

Victor returned to work, distracted by everything Pearl had said, unable to focus on his vidscreen. An hour passed, then his Handy 1000 chimed. Auntie Circe had finally agreed to chat. Could he meet in ten minutes at the bottom of Cemetery Hill?

He rushed outside. The heat was a blanket smothering everything. Walking along the east side of the Petit Canal, he felt trapped between the sun high above and the bulk of rock and dirt looming to his right. He passed Pond Park and reached the cemetery, where large trees provided delicious cooling shade. Sweat stains spread along his chest and back. He wiped his wet brow.

Circe was waiting at the cemetery's entrance overshadowed by one of the stone pillars holding up a massive wrought-iron gate. When she saw him, she waved, tapped the silver bracelet on her wrist—a fashionable MeshBit she'd likely picked up in a trendy European tech boutique—and started up the trail. He hustled to catch up.

They skirted the high cemetery wall. Its crenellations were topped by gargoyles with large goofy eyes that made them appear childlike and innocent, almost cherubic, if he ignored their finger-length teeth. The wall provided a cool strip of shade lush with grass and jumping bugs.

Victor walked in the shade a meter or so behind his aunt, knowing that she wouldn't slacken her pace for him and that she preferred exercise to talking. She never indulged in the languid let's-chat-and-stroll relaxation that both Granfa and Granma had liked. Circe always chased the next idea, trying to get ahead in a world that had the habit of running amok, and Victor admired her for it.

When they left the cemetery behind, the trail baked in the full glare of the sun. Red dirt was hot as embers, and pale stones poked out like the unsettled bones of an ancient civilization. The trail switched back and forth across the slope, rising higher with each turn, sometimes with views of town to the west or sometimes looking out at the highway to the north and, beyond it, the sweeping arc of the dam holding back the waters of Lake Ouachita. More rarely they glimpsed the Qaddo mud flats to the south.

Sulfur tingled in Victor's nostrils. For a moment, he worried a resonant episode was on its way. Exercise could trigger one, though rarely. Over the long term, physical activity was good for Victor, especially hiking over rough ground, which provided varying physical and mental stimulus. He'd been told physical inactivity was to be avoided, as were repetitive activities like treadmill running.

The sulfur blew with the wind, and he nearly smacked himself in the head for forgetting the hot springs. The hills and valleys to the east of town were geothermal hotspots. Springs, pools, and geysers of mineral-rich water could be found throughout the Qaddo lands, including on Cemetery Hill. He sniffed then wrinkled his nose. New Venice was lucky the winds were usually blowing east.

The peak was marked by a circle of boulders. Circe walked to the center, touched her palms to her head, and then raised them. Victor didn't ask what she was doing, and she didn't bother to explain. They both knew he preferred the real world to her fantasies and whatever religious expression she chose to explore this week.

"Water?" She unstrapped a bottle that hung from her belt and held it out to him. He took it and drank thirstily.

"Your parents asked me to speak with you about the restructuring of rights for the Eastmore holdings. Father left us with a tangled mess. Some of it looks deliberately obfuscated—"

She stopped when she glanced at Victor. He could feel his shoulders tensed around his ears and his hands clenching and unclenching. "Here," she said, leading him to a rock in the shade of a stand of trees and gesturing for him to sit. "Try to relax."

He nodded and repeated the owl mantra. *The wise owl listens. The wise owl does not flinch at every creaking branch. The wise owl stays cool.*

"I'm not going to candy-coat it for you, Victor. Part of you maturing is realizing that we play the cards we're dealt and there's no asking for a reshuffle. There's no hiding from the truth. Father messed things up. We have to unfuck our finances, to put it bluntly. There will be some paperwork for you to sign."

"That's fine. I don't really care about all that."

"Good. Stretch?"

They sat on the ground. The soles of their shoes pressed together, legs and torsos making L-shapes, as had been their habit since he was young and he became intrigued by her practicing yoga in the mansion. She took his hands and pulled. He felt his hamstrings grow taut, and he breathed, trying to relax. If there was ever a time to bring up a difficult topic, this was it, while his body was physically forced to unwind.

"Auntie, I saw Samuel Miller. He's basically a vegetable on Personil. We're not going to get what we need from his brain while he's like that."

They straightened. She said, "You're not wrong. But we've got to wean him from Personil carefully. It didn't go well for you, remember."

"That was a difficult time for me," Victor said. He almost laughed at how stupid he sounded.

She squeezed his hands, and he gently pulled. As she doubled over, her arms and torso seemed to lengthen as if she were adding space between each body part.

They straightened again, and she pulled him forward. His body was not nearly as limber as hers. He softened his knees and rounded his back. Instead of stretching, he focused on letting go. His head lowered a fraction toward the ground.

"That's it," she said. "That's good. We should enroll you in a yoga class."

Blood crowded his face. He was glad she couldn't see his expression. He was tired of people telling him what was good for him, even Auntie Circe.

He came up, let go of her hands, and stood. "At the meeting the other day you said Granfa Jeff made the doctors prescribe Personil even though I was only Class Three."

She stood, balanced on one leg, and grabbed her other foot to stretch her quad. He mirrored her, holding his impatience in.

"A sad bit of manipulation that. Father had an extraordinary ability to motivate his employees. He pushed them to accomplish great things while simultaneously eroding their confidence in themselves. Part of the trick was his temper. Hardly anyone dared disagree with him. I can't believe Dr. Tammet lasted as long as she did, but he seemed to respect her opinion even as he overrode it in your case. I can't blame him. He was worried about deterioration of your inhibitory neurons. Every time you have an episode, your ability to fight off the next one is weakened."

"But Karine shared the studies with me. They said that catatonia wasn't inevitable."

"In most circumstances, that's true. The ones who fared the best were patients in rural locations with strong family support networks. They fared well before Classification, I mean.

I don't know how to say this without sounding prejudiced." She cleared her throat. "Some Cathar families seemed to do exceptionally well in caring for family members with mirror resonance syndrome. The times the Classification Commission stepped in and imposed treatment—the results were tragic. In your case, after what happened to you in Carmichael, there was a concern that you would slide more quickly toward Class One status. It's a testament to your fortitude that you've done so well for yourself. I admit, Victor, we're flailing. Until we find a cure, I'm afraid there are no good options."

"If the Classification System is making things worse, why can't we get rid of it?"

"It's not that simple. Now that stims—"

"Forget stims. I don't know why we care about them. It was a data leak. Who cares! Why is it so hard to admit mistakes and fix what's broken!"

Circe stood tall, looking up at his face, hands on her hips. "We made mistakes, yes. Not this time. I reviewed the Mesh-News footage, which we're starting to share with the public, by the way." She looked closely at Victor. "You never knew about Dario Sanchez, did you? Did anyone ever tell you what really happened the first year after Carmichael? Did Father?"

Gooseflesh rippled on Victor's arms. Pearl had only told him today. Why was Auntie Circe asking him about it now?

"Not really," he said.

Fear hovered around Auntie's face, as well as a kind of sentimental astonishment, and he had the feeling that she was about to say something that would change him forever.

But Auntie Circe didn't say anything. She walked toward a steep slope overlooking New Venice. He followed. The sun glinted off the water. The canals were a bright grid outshining the stone buildings. A breeze blew over them, and Victor smelled sulfur and also char that evoked the smoke that day in Carmichael. He pulled a tincture from his pocket and drank it. Auntie Circe seemed to have forgotten he was there, absorbed in her own memories.

Eventually she turned and said, "Father called it a mass hallucination. The stress, he said, played tricks on people, on their ability to reason. This was before Personil, when we had in our hospital a man who had killed hundreds of people and who spoke of other worlds and crossing over and patently impossible things."

The derision in her voice made Victor gulp. He was curious: Was she mocking Samuel Miller or someone else?

Circe kept going without a glance at Victor. "The problem was he was convincing. One of the nurses, Dario Sanchez, killed himself by following Samuel's instructions for 'quantum suicide.' And then everyone was talking about another world that was almost like this one, about primals and ghosts, all the imaginings that Mía found in Samuel's journal. She exposed them to show how absurd they were. But people started to believe them instead. People started to think MRS was infectious. A psychic infection, if you will."

Victor stood, sun relentlessly bombarding him with heat and radiation. He felt pressurized, a shell filled with gas growing hotter until one day he would catch fire. Memories of the burning dreams returned.

"That's insane. Isn't it?"

"The Classification System, the tests, the treatments, the classes—all of it was informed by that experience. Even Father believed that we needed protection, if only from our willingness to believe in delusions." She said the word with exactly the cadence and emphasis Jefferson had used.

Victor knew how easy it was for him to slip into delusion. But he was different from normal people. The staff working at Oak Knoll shouldn't have been as susceptible. Yet Auntie Circe was saying that they had been. He took out the data egg and held it to his forehead.

Circe looked at it curiously. He remembered the last time he'd shown it to her, right after the funeral, before his life had gone further off the rails.

She began, "Is that—"

"It opened. Not all the way, but a little bit. I know what's in it now. Jefferson's messages. And some clever brainhackery that helps keep blankness at bay. Granfa spoke to me. He wants me to reform the Classification Commission, thinks that I should be in Carmichael. But he never told me any of this." Victor shook his head, lowered the egg.

A sensation like being watched settled over him. Like a mouse at night when an owl stops hooting. He looked up. There was no one else there, just him and Circe, but the air felt full. Maybe he was going to go blank. He hoped it would be one of those pleasurable orgasmic times. Maybe he should just let it happen.

Circe was looking at him. Her shining eyes reflected sunlight, swollen with tears that hadn't yet fallen. Sadness painted her face like the sky when dusk turns to night, and perhaps—unless his mind was playing tricks on him—a green shade of guilt.

She said, "I'm so sorry. Forgive me."

Victor felt the crushing ache of her regret, more than he could bear. In his mind, he was flattened by it, like a huge stone rolling over him. Floating, he existed somewhere in the circuit of emotion between Circe and himself, less himself and more like his reflection in her sad eyes. An inner voice screamed something wordlessly, but he smothered it quickly.

"Why?" he asked, feeling tears trace cool tracks down his cheeks.

Her face hardened, her features like obsidian. She stared at him. Strong Circe again. She wasn't one to dwell in her emotion. She was always moving forward.

"I—I'm envious," she said in a quivering voice that grew steadier with each word. "You got to hear Jefferson's final words. I hope they were comforting."

A cool dark certainty began to solidify in Victor's belly. The data egg wasn't ever going to be comforting. He couldn't ever be sure it held the truth. It was one distorted shard of it, a sliver of understanding that was filtered through Jefferson's mind, skewed by his lifetime of experience and passed on to Victor through tortuous detective work. It wouldn't answer all his questions. It would only poke him in the eye.

"I'd like to listen sometime," she said. "I'd like to hear his voice again."

"I talked to Pearl," Victor said. "With her herbs and this data egg, I think we can help Samuel. There won't be any hysteria. We're prepared this time."

She grabbed his shoulder and squeezed hard. "You inspire me, Victor. You never stop trying. All right. I'll let Karine know. I want the truth as much as you do. I hope we find it together."

20

I suppose we must ask ourselves, "When a large institution crumbles, what replaces it?"

After the United States of America devolved, Europe decided to take an active interest in the nine new nations of the American Union.

What filled the spiritual void created by the Catholic Church's implosion? Have we yet glimpsed the next development, or is it still beneath the horizon and we must venture beyond the rim of our world to see the future?

—Robbie Eastmore's *A Study of Alternate Histories*

16 May 1991
New Venice, The Louisiana Territories

Victor descended Cemetery Hill, grateful that Circe had chosen a more circuitous route down while he retraced their steps. He tried to go over their conversation again, but he couldn't concentrate. Instead, he felt surrounded by flames, burning from the bottom of his feet to his head, living the fire dream while he was awake. He worried it was a new side effect of the bitter grass that somehow allowed his brain to put a lucid dream overlay on his waking-state consciousness. Why the fire dream now? Because he was overheating in the humid air? He stripped off his shirt, used it to mop up his sweat and careened down the hill clumsily, on the verge of falling, or maybe on the precipice of blankness.

When he reached Pond Park, he rushed to the water, waded thigh deep and splashed himself, wetting his hair, his torso, clapping the water to his face, knowing that it was polluted by duck shit but failing to care. The fire dream faded. He pictured Circe's face, tears wetting her cheeks, and wondered why she'd been so affected. A cold spike chilled his spine. The blankness, hovering close, promised deliciously frigid catatonia.

That's when he noticed he had an audience. Wonda, Del, Tosh, and a group of Human Lifers, standing in a circle as if they'd just risen from a squat talk, were watching him. Wonda approached with the others following closely behind. They stopped at the water's edge. She looked at him. Awe filled her eyes to the brim and flooded him. Her hands clasped together to keep from shaking.

"We saw you on the Mesh with Lisabella," she said. She smiled exultingly and stepped forward into the water, gingerly at first, then splashing and laughing, her voice tinkling like chimes. "Let's celebrate!"

He took a step back. "My skin feels like it's on fire."

She cocked her head. "Let me help." Bending down, she ran her hands through the water, stepped close, and placed them on his cheeks. A flash of irritation at being touched coursed through his body but then immediately transformed into an icy hot sexual heat. Drops of water traced luxurious tracks down Victor's back. Waves of tingling warmth pulsed with each heartbeat. Every cell cried out for contact. He pulled Wonda close, couldn't let her go. The air surrounding him vibrated, felt as if it were part of him. There was no such thing as stillness, as boundaries—the world and his body, his mind, were intertwined, one. Her body pressed into his, heat rebounding between them. He tilted his face down and kissed her deeply. She grasped his shoulders and held him close. Someone's arms embraced him from the side, curling around them both. Tosh's scent, a deep musk, and Del's now too, a soapy gentle odor. Victor removed his lips from Wonda's. Feeling tightly held, loved by three people he'd never felt close with, he nearly choked, his throat swollen by unfamiliar feelings.

After several long moments, their grip on him loosened, and he stood, staring back at the three of them.

"What just happened?" Victor asked.

"You amaze me," Wonda said. If a lower lip could be proud, hers stood at attention.

"I don't understand."

She said, "I believe when you feel something strongly, and you can't explain it, that's the universe talking to you."

Tosh looked at Victor with an odd expression, part respect, part hunger, and part shame. A sliver of confusion shadowed his face.

"We heard about the Classification Act, and we want you to speak to our potentiate," Del said. "I don't care if you denounce us all as loonies. They need to hear what a struggle you've had with medication. To see how you're standing up now. It will inspire them."

Looking into Tosh's brown eyes, the way his irises seemed to whirl, it was as if Victor understood him for the first time. Tosh didn't really know what he was doing or what he was looking for. He was making it up as he went along, like the rest of them. "You didn't hurt Ozie," Victor said.

"No, I didn't," Tosh replied. His fists curled and relaxed then curled again.

"Why do you think you're here?" Victor asked.

Tosh seemed to struggle for words. "Like I said, sometimes you have to go after what you want with everything you have."

"You want to help me?"

Tosh returned a curt nod that seemed to say there was more to talk about but now wasn't the time.

Victor turned to Wonda and Del. "I need a minute with Tosh."

They left him and returned to the other Human Lifers, who had been keeping their distance while watching Victor.

His skin was nearly dry, though his hair still dripped onto his shoulders. "Tell me what the King really wants," Victor demanded. There was a force to his words that sounded unfamiliar to his ears.

Tosh avoided Victor's gaze, a puzzled expression on his face as he spoke haltingly. "He wants to stop the Classification Act. He's the one selling stims throughout the American Union. I don't know why I'm telling you this. I can't—I can't seem to stop. What are you doing to me?" He sounded puzzled and fearful.

"Did he have Jefferson killed?"

"I don't think so. Are you making me talk like this? Please stop."

"Why not?" Victor said. He felt woozy, drained.

Tosh said, "Because I think he wants the truth as much as you do. I'm sure of that. And . . ."

"What?"

"I think he feels guilty about the polonium. He had the tongue tested. It's the same radiological signature as what he provided to Oak Knoll."

Knowledge like a dark raven snapped at Victor's consciousness, but he pushed it away. How could he have doubted the importance of the data egg? Minutes before he'd been telling himself it was a skewed truth, Jefferson's slanted version. That type of thinking was madness.

"We're going to get it open," Victor said, his voice hoarse. "We're going to do this. If you want to help, you keep us safe. Let's hope the truth doesn't get us killed."

21

People say they can't see the primals. They're either lying or someone has figured out a way to block the signals. Maybe the Mesh Towers are interfering. I can see the primals. I can hear them. I would never ignore them.

—Samuel Miller's *The Carmichael Journals* (1971)

23 May 1991
New Venice, The Louisiana Territories

Victor stood with Pearl on the drug hut's deck, fighting the urge to jump at every creak and groan of the boards beneath his feet. A transparent, flexible sheath sealed the deck. It looked like a giant soap bubble had come to rest.

Towering thunderclouds moved east, their shadows preceding them as they darkened the muddy Passage waters, gray stones of New Venetian townhouses, and rustling greenery on Cemetery Hill. Sunlight broke out on the slope, heating Victor like an oven element. A cloud moved overhead, dropped pellets of rain, and moved on.

Change had come to New Venice, but he couldn't tell whether the world had transformed or if it was all in his head. It seemed that he was finally getting answers to his questions and people were being truthful when they never had been before. The flowering of truth felt like something more than coincidence.

“You think the Personil is gone from his system?” Victor asked.

Pearl stood at the railing. She looked out of place. Her pale blue business suit rustled as she folded her arms. “It’s been a week. He’s taking fumewort, bitter grass, and a few other herbs for good measure. Ozie’s been fussing with his braincap every other hour. This is exactly the type of aggressive treatment we had planned for you.”

Victor knew exactly what she was implying—if he hadn’t intuited Jefferson’s murder and started investigating on his own, the plan wouldn’t have gone so far off the rails. Then again, they’d all planned to take their sweet time in contacting clueless Victor.

“If you had told me when I first came to your shop . . .” He didn’t finish his thought. This wasn’t a fight that mattered. She herself had said he should let the past go. “Never mind.”

Victor brushed past Pearl and entered the hut, noticing how there was no glass in the building, nothing sharp or breakable, all plastic edges, cloth, and stuffing, which was fine, better that Samuel Miller didn’t have easy access to anything that could be used as a weapon. But it made Victor think of all the other ways to kill someone. To suffocate with a pillow. To rip fabric from the couch and wrap it around someone’s neck. To bludgeon with fists unceasingly.

To the guard outside the sitting room, Victor said, “Don’t let anyone interrupt us. Not even Karine. Especially her.”

The guard, Velasquez, shifted on his feet. “She’s the second chief.”

“And my auntie is the chief, and I’m an Eastmore—I own this company. I’m telling you don’t let anyone in or I’ll have you fired. I mean it.”

Velasquez nodded.

Victor took a deep breath. It was too late for second guessing, too late to go back and let sleeping dogs lie. He opened the door.

Samuel Miller was painting the walls with blood.

Victor blinked, looked twice, then realized the walls were streaked with rusty-red paint from a tube. The shapes decorating the room were vaguely humanoid, fuzzy limbs stretching from blurry torsos, heads suggested only by circular whirls above the rest. Samuel was painting a red layer on top of other layers, stacks of colors, all streaky and blurry.

Samuel didn't stop when Victor entered. He moved frenetically, sometimes using a brush, sometimes his finger or the side of his hand. Stepping into the room was like stepping into a resonant episode. The owl mantra silently passed Victor's lips.

"Samuel," Victor said after a moment, "we need to talk."

Without halting his painting, Samuel said, "Talk, yes, and more, an exchange of vibrations, not just speech, emotions as well." He straightened, became still. "I remember you now, Victor."

"We're going on a walk to another building. When we get there, we're going to use a brain scanner to see inside your head."

Samuel ignored him, working on his paintings, weird primal visions of beings in other worlds. They looked familiar. With a slow creeping dread, Victor realized they didn't look so different from the auras and colors of his synesthesia that he'd learned to interpret as emotions. In that respect, he and Samuel weren't so dissimilar.

Victor took out the data egg and set it on the table with enough force to make a knocking sound. Samuel turned, gaze intersecting with the data egg.

"Have you seen this before?" Victor demanded.

"In my dreams," he said. Then he laughed, a soft hollow sound like stones landing on dirt at the bottom of a dry well.

Samuel squeezed and emptied the tube of paint, held a gob of red in one hand, smacked both hands together, and then smeared the wall. "I've been hearing the voices again, not so clearly as the first time, they were never clear, but now they're like faded echoes. The primals are back."

"You're hallucinating," Victor said.

Samuel stopped and looked at Victor, a smirk twisting one side of his wide mouth. "You think it's all in my head? It's in yours too. Our minds sieve the universe together. We're barely solid." He began painting the wall again. A life-size figure like a red upright shadow took shape. "I kept calm in Carmichael for the most part. I listened. I tried to record the voices and make sense of them. I applied myself to finding a scientific explanation. Ours is not the only universe, you know. There must be other worlds floating on a quantum foam of probability. Must be. So many angels dancing on the head of a pin. The same angel really. Time itself. How many paths does a waveform follow? How many paths to the future? This fork branches; that fork stubs. I realized, instead of a dead end, we could cross over. And the primals were calling to me for help."

Victor's heart beat faster with each word tumbling out of Samuel's mouth. The appeal of a manic state was that it felt true and right. Delusions were more comforting than uncertainty, the exhilarating rush like a drug.

"I thought I had dreams of you before the massacre and knew what you were planning," Victor said. "I was wrong."

Samuel froze, put one arm up against the wall, rested his head on it. "I wish you had. Dreams. Voices. Electrochemical pathways activating, reacting to stimuli, cogitating. The multiverse hacks our brains."

Then Samuel was silent for so long that Victor thought he might be asleep standing up. Victor looked at the data egg. It sat on the table, motionless, black, looking inert. Was it helping Samuel? It didn't seem to be.

Victor muttered, "The wise owl listens before it asks who."

Samuel spun around, eyes wide, mouth open, outraged, and then he moved so quickly Victor had no time to react. Paint-smeared hands grabbed Victor's shirt, shaking him.

"I didn't know whose voice it was!" Samuel's eyes moved back and forth, accusing. "It was you!"

The walls of the room began to dissolve, and blankness filled the void. Smoke seemed to fill the air, to swirl in the whites of Samuel's eyes. Victor grasped Samuel's shoulders. "You're going to sit down and repeat the mantra with me. *The wise owl listens before he asks who.* Say it!"

"Oh, he listens. The wise owl listens," Samuel repeated in a pained voice. "Yes, he listens. I listened. I did!" He sat on the couch, palms together between his knees, rocking forward and back.

Victor pulled a chair over. He cupped the data egg in his hands and grasped Samuel's so they held it together.

"Quietly," Victor said. "Softly. We're going to push the blankness away and then head over to the brain scanner. Have you seen this before? Did Jefferson speak to you about it?" Everything felt insubstantial, as if he and Samuel, the room, and the air were made of light, ephemeral, barely there.

Samuel looked up, brow wrinkled, confused. "Nothing. He never spoke. Only looked at me. I probably wouldn't have remembered anyway. They doped me, made the primals disappear."

"He came to you with a plan, didn't he? He must have."

Samuel rocked, shimmied, and shied away like a chained mongoose in a fight with a viper. The room dissolved, then returned. "Victor, your voice—it echoes. I didn't know it was you. I could have stopped it. Shocks! Shocks! Shocks! I heard it. I could have stopped it."

Samuel yanked his hands away. The data egg dropped to the floor and rolled under the couch.

Victor scrambled onto his hands and knees, reached under, fingers swiping across the floor. It felt like his hand was dipping into a cold well of outer space.

He heard a smacking sound, looked up, saw Samuel hitting himself, hard flat palm striking his face, repeatedly.

"Stop it," Victor said, pulling himself up, grabbing Samuel by the shoulders, coaxing him to standing too. "Calm. Focused. Repeat the words! Calm. Focused."

Samuel closed his eyes. "Calm. Focused. That voice!" His voice was panicked, high and wavering.

"Breathe," Victor said.

Knocks on the door made Victor jump, though they sounded muffled, from another plane of existence. "Is everything all right?" Karine's voice asked.

"We're fine!" he yelled. "Give us some time."

"Time!" Samuel repeated. His eyes popped open, dark brown irises appearing nearly black. "Space. Blankspace."

Victor felt the ground drop from beneath his feet, and then he and Samuel were floating. Whiteness all around them. "No," he said, digging his fingers into Samuel's shoulders. The room's outlines, grayish areas fighting with the blankness, shimmered into view.

"Help me cross over," Samuel said. His voice was calm, neutral, persuasive.

Why shouldn't I? Victor thought, picturing his hands closing around Samuel's neck.

Vertigo like a wrecking ball slammed into Victor like the entire weight of the universe, then ricocheted away. There was nothing to see, white blankspace all around.

"No," Victor whispered, his own voice small and ragged. "I'm not going." He flexed his fingers, felt the material of Samuel's shirt, smelled paint wafting. "We're staying right here. Now."

The room was back. Victor was back.

Samuel blinked at him with the near blank passivity of a resonant episode. On the cusp. Victor had to bring him back too.

"I gave you an owl," Victor said. "Do you remember? The first day you worked in the preschool classroom. I drew an owl and gave it to you and said you were supposed to keep it and listen."

"A little owl. A drawing. A missed connection. I never saw your primal."

Victor looked at the blurry painted figures on the wall, Samuel's primals, representations of the halos he saw around people he was supposed to help cross over. Victor shuddered.

Samuel said, "You wanted them to cross over. I listened."

"No. The voice wasn't real. That's the past anyway. This is now. We're in a room at the BioScan clinic in New Venice. Me and you. The primals aren't real. I see crazy stuff all the time, and it feels real. It's hard to tell the difference, but you can do it."

Samuel's jaw stiffened; his eyes began to focus.

"Look at me," Victor said. "I'm going to help you. Without drugs. You're going to be okay."

"Help me cross over?"

"No. We have the same problem in our brains. We're going to fix it." Victor grabbed Samuel by the chin.

Samuel's gaze snapped back into focus. He shrugged away. "I don't like to be touched," he said. He put a hand on the wall, looked down at himself, raised his hands, staring at the paint. "I need to clean myself up."

Something rattled by the wall. Victor turned and saw a glow, as if one of Samuel's painted primals was pulsing. He got closer. The light changed. Victor pushed the sofa to the side and uncovered the data egg. It was shining white now. Then opalescent colors whirled across its surface—magenta, electric blue, green like specks in Elena's eyes.

The data egg was opening again.

Victor grabbed it and sat with his back to the door to block it.

The hologram of Jefferson Eastmore's head appeared and opened its mouth.

Samuel, so eager to see primals, apparently didn't like this manifestation and cowered in the corner.

"Tell me, Granfa," Victor whispered. "Tell me who killed you."

22

Never regret hard choices. The world needs them, whether it knows it or not.

—Jefferson Eastmore's *The Wheel of Progress* (1989)

23 May 1991
New Venice, The Louisiana Territories

The hologram showing Jefferson Eastmore's face looked like the shining head of a statue had come to life monochromatically. The resolution wasn't fine enough to create realistic eyes. It looked like a blind white bodiless ghost.

"Victor, if you're listening to me now, you've triggered my second message by helping Samuel Miller moderate a resonant episode. I'm so proud that my faith in you has been proved justified. By now it's reasonable to assume you're having an impact in Carmichael, helping Semiautonomous Californians rethink their relationships with their fellow citizens who battle mirror resonance syndrome every day. I trust you'll continue to be an inspiration.

"Now that you've achieved mental stability and clarity, it's time for me to level with you. I haven't always been forthcoming about my aims and methods. Helping people who suffer maladies has always been my north star, but sometimes my path took me into dark places."

The Jefferson head shrunk as if he'd sat back from the vidcapper. A moment later when it moved forward again,

Victor noticed his granfa's hair was thinning, his face starting to look blotchy, signs the radioactive poison he'd been dosed with was having an effect.

"Tell me," Victor whispered. "Come on, Granfa, tell me."

Jefferson continued, "The ban on research into mirror resonance syndrome was a mistake. The worst in a series of mistakes we made after Carmichael. It was sold to me as a temporary measure. I would never have agreed to a permanent ban. The atmosphere post-Carmichael was toxic, and we made mistakes. Yes, I'll admit it, we didn't take all the precautions we might have, but we were in such a rush to find answers. When that poor nurse killed himself, people blamed Samuel, and all hell broke loose. Mía was on the warpath and wielded more influence than I anticipated. She got the ban passed—for everyone's protection, she said.

"If only your friend Ozie could fix up some magical machine to send messages to me in the past, and tell me how to fix my mistakes before I made them."

Jefferson smiled sadly, a smile Victor couldn't help but mirror.

"Listen to me sounding foolish when I should be telling you the truth. The truth is hard, Victor. That's a lesson that keeps coming round.

"I was responsible for the data breaches at both the Holistic Healing Network and Gene-Us Enterprises. For the latter, you unwittingly helped me. I'm glad no one learned the truth about that, not even you. I'm sorry to have used you that way.

"Working with the Diamond King and his techies, I leaked the genetic sequence for mirror resonance syndrome to bypass the restrictions on research in SeCa. The idea was to run a research program in the Organized Western States to develop more effective treatments."

Jefferson's expression hardened, a crease forming between his eyebrows, a dark *V*, a sparse photonic emotion—frustration—appearing on a face made of light.

"I was duped. The King never wanted a cure. He wanted a narcotic. The stims we're having such a problem controlling came from that bad decision on my part. The wheel of progress turned backwards, I fear, and the scourge of addiction haunts us.

"Circe found out what I did. She must have thought by poisoning me little by little she was dispensing justice for the addicts. Who can blame her? We've never had a normal relationship. I wasn't a good father to her. I was too strict, too determined that she would follow in my footsteps. When someone has been pushed too far, it should not be a surprise when they push back. Of course I'm angry, and I feel betrayed. But I understand.

"I'm telling you this because now you've seen Samuel. You understand that he's delusional, that his ideas are nonsense. I needed you sane enough to recognize that. You see, Circe does not. She believes him in his lunacy."

Victor couldn't move, couldn't blink, couldn't breathe. Time moved on around him, but, inside, everything had stopped.

"I'm relying on you. I fear not just for you but for—Laws, I don't know how to say this without sounding melodramatic—Circe has plans far darker, far more twisted than Samuel Miller ever did. And with the resources she has at her disposal, frankly I fear for humanity.

"In my last message, I warned you about people with mystical beliefs, who believe in other worlds and crossing over. I was warning you about her. Do not cross her. Do not engage with her.

"The data egg is open for you now. It has all my research on the cure, what little I could accomplish under the radar, at least, and it will point you to a useful tool I managed to conceal at the Lone Star Kennel in the Republic of Texas. Use it wisely.

"Be safe, Victor. And remember. Trust in science. Trust in logic. Trust in the real world. Everything else is fantasy. I love you. I'm sorry."

23

> We each play a role. Mine has been to seek and foster excellence in the people around me. I do not do this because I lack an ego but because I believe firmly that together we are greater than the sum of our parts.
>
> —Circe Eastmore's *Race to the Top* (1991)

23 May 1991
New Venice, The Louisiana Territories

The primals seemed to shimmer on the walls. The paint was still wet, scattering photons through dust particles that swirled in the drug hut's stuffy sitting room. Green streaks like blades of grass formed a halo around one of the figures.

"She believes," Samuel said. He sat in the corner, feet flat on the floor, hands gripping his knees. "She believes me." He started to rock, weeping. "She'll help me."

An unbidden intuition intruded on Victor's mind: What if these figures represented the primals of actual people? What if Samuel was recreating his list here, right on the wall for Victor to see, of people he intended to help cross over? Deep in Victor's mind, he knew he should warn someone about it, but the blankness was too inviting to stay with that thought for long.

Victor stood, shoved the data egg—black now with two red rings around it—in his pocket, and wobbled a bit, feeling woozy. He lurched to the door, opened it. Footsteps pounded on the floor boards behind him. He was turning slowly, was shoved to the side. He gripped the door frame as Samuel burst past him into the living room.

Samuel banged on the door to the balcony, demanding to be let out, while the two guards tried to pull him back, having little success. One searched through his utility belt for a sedative. Karine stood by, watching them closely. For a moment, Victor felt drawn to go up to her and apologize. Instead, he let himself out the front door.

A cool breeze moved through the vegetation. Trees shed cottony seeds with every gust, clouding the air as competently as fog. The low horn of one of the barges sounded down the hill at the new harbor.

A feeling of unreality washed over Victor. He couldn't really be seeing all this. He must be somewhere else. And then he was gone.

And he was back again, crossing a bridge over the Petit Canal, smelling algae atop the water and barbecue from one of the street vendors, ribs on a grill, sweet and smoky.

Then he remembered Carmichael, the smoke floating over the houses, a low black ceiling over the town, smelling of char.

Blankness was preferable to knowing what he couldn't now unknow. Victor let it surge through him, a tingling warmth that started in his groin and spread throughout his body. Better to feel this good for as long as possible.

He came to, half-conscious, outside of Ozie's van, in a gravel parking lot not far from the highway north of town. His hand pressed against a metal plate, warm from the day's sun, and the door swung open. Ozie wasn't inside, but his smell was, a musk Victor associated with flannel shirts and white briefs and rooms dimly lit by the green-on-black glow of idle vidscreens.

Without thinking much about it, Victor's hands searched through bins of electronic gear, pulling headcaps from their hooks, tossing aside circuit boards and coming back tangled with cables that flexed of their own accord like eels.

He found what he was looking for: a plastic box, black but not as black as the data egg, with gold thread woven through it reminding him of expensive marble countertops in an Oakland & Bayshore bank that was the gateway to much of his personal wealth. He'd never had unfettered access to it. First he was a minor; then he was a Class Three Broken Mirror, and he'd only had permission to withdraw a certain amount per week for basic living expenses. Funds to buy a MeshBit, like the one Ozie had confiscated back in the Springboard Café, had required a visit to the bank with the black-and-gold countertops along with his mother, who cosigned for the amount.

Auntie Circe on the hike to the top of Cemetery Hill had said she wanted him to sign some papers. He supposed that was better than killing him for his portion of the family's estate. On thinking that, he felt blankness surge through him, a kind of thick, pervasive weight like meters of water pressing down on him.

He was no longer in the van. Grasses rustled. His feet were ankle deep in muddy water. Across a stretch of the Passage, he saw the Western Embankment, the levees that kept the countryside dry and isolated from the murky New Venice floodwaters, the inundation that had never receded.

The blankness moved with him now. He was transitioning in and out of it, like going from room to room in a large house. He supposed he was lucky to not find himself in actual water, drowning, though he might in fact be able to tread water and even swim while blank. His mind's self-preservation instinct was likely that strong on autopilot.

Feeling in his pockets, he found a plastic box. He opened it, saw the data egg, closed it. The box, a Faraday cage that would block all transmissions from the egg, needed a home.

The Eastmore estate was located to the west of New Venice, across the Passage. Victor walked to the edge of town. Grassy banks surrounded three sides of an inlet that led to one of the minor canals. A tiny wooden dock, big enough for only one or two people to stand on, floated on the still water.

As he approached the dock, he saw that it was actually a raft. Two square meters of wood covered an inflated rubber honeycomb with a central plinth to hold the structure together. A boy around ten years old was standing on a bench around the plinth.

"Can you take me across the Passage?" Victor asked.

"Climb on board," the boy said.

Victor stepped on gingerly. The raft settled and stabilized in the water, and the boy was soon poling them away from shore.

"You owe me five AUD for this trip. Another five per hour if you want me to wait to ferry you back." The boy spoke without feeling, laying out the terms of his service.

"It's a one-way trip." Victor authorized the transaction on his Handy 1000.

"Where ya from?" the boy asked.

Victor didn't answer.

The boy stopped poling and used a MeshBit to activate a propeller below the plinth, and they accelerated into the Passage.

It was sunny and cool, with a brisk wind blowing puffy clouds eastward. Shadows of the clouds formed a patchwork of light and dark across the water.

At the far shore, Victor disembarked and ignored the boy, who ignored him back. He climbed a set of stone steps set into the steep grassy slope. He reached the top. Cultivated fields, wild meadows, and stands of trees stretched forward across gently rolling hills. Victor walked for two kilometers due west, then cut south on a small, meandering dirt road that crossed two creeks until he found the road leading to the entrance of the Eastmore estate.

He arrived at a large gate. Fences three meters tall ran left and right, rising along raised ground for a long way before turning and continuing along the other edges of the big family plot.

Victor pressed his thumb into the type-pad next to the gate. The gate swung open, and Victor proceeded through. It closed behind him.

The land was well chosen. Rich brown dirt and vegetation covered the small valley, which rose toward a plateau where the mansion and several other buildings were clustered. Regularly spaced pine trees topped the ridge on the side of the road and cast bands of shadows across Victor's path. He followed the road for several minutes, watching the mansion grow as he drew closer.

The house served as both a home and a monument to the Eastmore family. He wondered about his ancestors' history, where they had been before New Venice, why they'd come here. He'd never listened closely to the stories; it had all seemed too distant and disconnected, rootless. Now, a curiosity to understand their history began to grow. Who they were, how they had lived, what they had worked toward during their lives. Had they been as awful as their descendants were?

Voices drew his attention to the front porch. Behind the balustrade, deep in the shadows that sat heavily there at this time of day, two people on the porch reclined on a low wicker couch piled with pillows. Stepping closer across the gravel yard, he saw the porch dwellers had been watching him, likely for some time, so he raised his hand and greeted them with a "good afternoon."

A weak, trembling voice asked, "Who is it, Charlene?"

Victor took a few steps up the porch. The voice belonged to an ancient woman with thinning white hair and an oval face that may have once been firm and beautiful, but now was wrinkled and furrowed like a knitted sweater. His great-granma Florence.

Her companion, a woman in her fifties or sixties, had thin, curly blond hair framing a round face. Her beady eyes swam behind thick round glasses with a slightly tinted quality that Victor associated with the decade when he was born.

"Flo's hearing ain't so good. Can't see very well either. Come closer so she can get a look at you," Charlene said.

"I asked you a question," Florence said. "Rude bitch."

Victor took some steps forward. "I'm Victor, your great-grandson."

"Linus's boy. I remember. Great-grandson. Well, that's good. Good to have one of everything, I always said."

Charlene clucked. "You have more than one, Flo. Circe's boy, Robbie."

"Circe!" Florence spat from her dry and puckered mouth. "Never know with her. Might be her son, might be some devil she raised from the pit of hell. Forget her! Victor, give me a kiss on the cheek and take a seat."

Victor leaned over and kissed her, being careful to do it in a way that, if he fell, he wouldn't crush her. He pulled a nearby chair closer and sat.

"Would you like some iced tea, Victor?" Charlene asked.

He shook his head. "I'm—I'm not entirely here."

"Neither here nor there, eh?" Florence said. "Me too. Victor, I want you to tell Cynthia and your parents that I will never, ever forgive them for keeping Jeff in California."

Charlene hushed her, but Florence continued. "He should be here."

"He's dead," Victor said.

"I know that," she snapped.

Charlene leaned toward Victor. "She's angry because she didn't sleep well last night and her hip is paining her."

Florence turned her head and shifted against the sofa. "When do I ever sleep well? I haven't slept in years." She reached for her drink, and Charlene brought it closer and held it under her mouth so Florence could use the straw. "I've lived longer than all my children. That's the world we live in."

"I have some bad news," he said, for a moment thinking he should tell her who killed her son.

She raised a hand and pointed at him. "I got all the news I need. Saw you with the lady on the Mesh. It's all horseshit."

"She's swearing again. I think it's nap time, sweetie," Charlene suggested.

"You don't look at peace, Victor," Florence said.

Victor couldn't tell if her eyes were teary from emotion, biology, or both. He said, "I don't think there's peace to be found anywhere."

"You're not the dumbest Eastmore," Florence said approvingly. She brought her hand to his face. It felt as soft and delicate as a rose petal. "Did you know, the Eastmores have always attracted more than our share of pain? Has anyone ever told you about Zoë Eastmore?"

"I'm sorry?"

"Some other time."

Charlene said, "You go along, Victor. I'll take her to bed. We have a routine, and it's easier without distractions. You go on."

He climbed down from the porch. "I want to go away," he said, though the words seemed external to him, like something from a sonobulb somewhere nearby.

Around the side of the house was an abandoned garden, tomato plants and beans withered and dry, grasses overgrown. He dug a hole big enough for the Faraday box and buried it.

His task completed, he dove headlong into blankness.

His butt was damp, his hands muddy. Victor looked around. It was evening. The canal water reflected light posts lining the street above. He was sitting, back to the canal wall, on a ledge just wide enough for him to sit on. Someone called his name. Across the canal, at street level, Wonda leaned over the railing and asked if he was all right.

He started to move his mouth, stopped, realizing his throat was jammed full of so many emotions that if he opened it to speak, he might scream. She vanished from the railing. He felt a sudden anxiousness, checked his pockets, found them empty, and relaxed, wondering why that would be so.

Wonda came over to him.

"Are you okay?" she asked.

Victor stared into her eyes, blue-violet in the evening light, like one of the flowers on the yam bushes in Granma Cynthia's garden back in Oakland. A calm, soothing chill spread across his chest.

"Are you blank? Can you hear me?"

He tried to shake his head, but it wouldn't move. His lips felt parched, throat dry. Everything felt numb, and he couldn't say anything, do anything. The blankness was near. He knew he could call it closer and lose himself to it.

"I'll take care of you," she said, and she grabbed his hand, tugged gently. His feet and legs moved of their own accord, lifted him to standing, and followed as Wonda took short, slow steps toward the stairs that led up to street level.

He felt her hand, strongly gripping his own, felt safe, and let himself go blank again.

24

> I allowed myself to disappear. No, that's a lie. I sought out self-nullification and I got more than I bargained for.
>
> —Victor Eastmore's *Apology*

29 May 1991
Amarillo, The Republic of Texas

Elena drove along Amarillo's dusty streets, keeping an eye out for Corps while a rock ballad blasted from her car's speakers. She sang along.

"Get out of my way. It's only temporary. Don't you want to see me happy? Maybe I'll come back someday."

She drove slowly past the town's central plaza and waved at one of the Puros working the vegetable stand, a volunteer, strictly secular, meaning he wouldn't be much use in a street fight.

The conflict across the Republic of Texas was as bad as it had ever been. Everybody knew the Corps were winning. They were better armed and their numbers were bolstered by fresh faces from the Organized Western States, courtesy of the Diamond King.

Worse was the fact that the Puros counted on popular support, and people had started to say they just wished the conflict would go away, let them have their way, and it's an unwinnable fight, so why not give up?

Elena thought all that was nonsense. If they let the Corps have their way . . . Doom and gloom didn't begin to describe how bad the situation could get. Stims were appearing in more and more products: soft drinks, edibles, little vapor-filled tubes you stuck in your mouth and then sucked to get a dose of stims direct to your lungs without the hassle of smoking from a pipe. Pretty soon half the town would be hooked with no one the wiser. Sure they could read the ingredients on product labels. It was an open secret. But nobody seemed to *care*, except the Puros. Regular folk should be vigilant, they should be concerned, but they weren't.

The lessons of the Communion Crisis—singed so deep into the collective unconscious of the Republic of Texas—when the people rose up against the church's mind-controlling poisons and won—seemed to be fading. That was natural, Elena supposed, since no one alive had lived through it. It seemed odd, though, that in the few years since she'd lived in Amarillo there had been such an about-face. This was different, people said. The church was controlling us, tricking us. No one was to blame for stims except the people who decided to do them or who couldn't be bothered to pay attention.

But they're addictive, she would say.

You beat them, didn't you?

I had help.

People find help if they want it.

And on and on and back and forth, and no one changed their minds, and the problem got worse and worse.

Elena parked in the driveway of the Baldwin Street house. As she walked to the front door, she pushed back her shoulders and lifted her chin. She had quit stims, and now she would fight to help other people get off them too. No matter how difficult the situation, she had the right idea, and she was following through on it. The Corps couldn't take away her pride.

She opened the door and stepped into the hallway. Xavi, the Amarillo Puros' chief, sat in the dining room, talking to a burly man. She recognized him instantly. They were both leaning back in their chairs, which weren't made of wood—they were plastic or some other material grown from algae. It was weird she was thinking about that, but she supposed it was better than thinking about why the man sitting at the dinner table, looking at her with eyes like sharp little arrowheads, was Tosh.

"Hi there, tough girl," Tosh said.

Elena pointed at Tosh and then pointed at the front door. "Out!"

He rose smoothly, face grave, cracked his knuckles theatrically, and tossed a bemused expression at Xavi. "See you again soon," he said.

She watched as Tosh moved slowly around the dining table, pressing her buttons with his faux-calm demeanor. He held the front door open for her. "How about a walk?"

She balled her fists, ready to shout for him to get the shocks out.

He said, "It's about your fa."

She breathed out, deflated. Tosh was good at those gut punches. After a moment, she walked past him down the steps and into the front yard, once again outmaneuvered.

Elena removed a couple hairpins, smoothed her hair, and let it fall across her shoulders to hide the orange diamond tattoo she'd just had inked. It throbbed like a bad sunburn. She'd gone in to get a scartoo inked where the MeshTracker had been removed from her calf and, while she waited for the artist to finish a guy who wept and cursed while getting a rose around his nipple inked, she decided that she needed something more to mark her fresh start. The back of the neck was the perfect spot, visible when it didn't matter, hidden when it needed to be. The diamond represented the four points of purity—humility, resilience, hope, and determination. To the Corps, the same diamond looked like a bull's-eye.

"Are we not safe walking here?" he asked, waving at the two-story homes lining the street with their fenced-in yards and barred windows.

"Safe as anywhere." The streets lacked sidewalks, one of a dozen signs they were farther from civilization than it might first appear. The culverts, clogged with dirt and leaves, created fertile berms for grasses and shrubs. Though rain was scarce, when a big storm did roll through, often the yards would flood and take a day or two to dry out. Many homeowners had dug little moats around their properties. It was nothing like the large-scale, precision hydrological engineering of New Venice, but it worked in a bootstrap kind of way, a desperate yet practical homespun innovation.

Tosh didn't say anything as they walked, so Elena had to try to coax his lies and exaggerations free. "Tell me what you came here to tell me and then leave me alone."

He smiled broadly and said, "You sound just like Victor."

His teeth, white and straight and likely artificial, gleamed. Elena wished she knew how to defuse the aggressive pleasure he derived from annoying her.

"You know, a lot has happened since you left New Venice," Tosh said. "Victor finally got the data egg open again."

She halted mid-step. "Say what?" If he'd actually found proof that Karine poisoned Jefferson, there was no telling what Victor would do.

"The cat is out of the bag. He's taking it well. Only goes blank for a week at a time. I don't mind. He's so agreeable when his mind's not there." Tosh smiled again. There was no mistaking the sexual innuendo in his voice.

"You're a pig," she said.

"Guilty." He sounded delighted with himself.

"Was it Karine?" Elena asked.

Tosh winked at her, then began strolling forward. Elena hustled to catch up.

"Well?" she asked.

"You should ask him yourself. He's full of secrets. He's not blabbing much to anyone else, even when he's blank, but I've been persuasive. One of the little gems he'd kept to himself is what's hidden in that kennel."

Elena remembered the long journey to Amarillo, how Victor had come up empty in his search of the Lone Star Kennel. He'd stopped there again on their way out of town, though she'd barely noticed—she'd been such a mess, stim withdrawal making her squirm and lash out. What did Victor know about the kennel that he hadn't told her? Her fa still worked there—was he in danger?

They reached a small park at the end of the street, a patchwork of green shoots and reddish dirt. A hoard of ants scurried on the ground underneath a picnic table, swarming over what looked like a chicken bone.

She wouldn't give Tosh the satisfaction of begging for information. He'd come here to tell her something. He'd get to it eventually, whether she groveled or not.

Tosh grinned. "Tough girl. I like it," he said, sitting on the picnic table. "Now if you'll recall, the mercs that showed up to guard the kennel were working for BioScan. They were Corps. Not anymore. Working for BioScan, yes, but these new mercs are independent. Karine made a mistake that has now been corrected. Unfortunately, the swap limits my access."

Access, that's what Tosh wanted. Elena's father could help. But that was sure to lead to trouble. The question was, what kind? "What does Karine want with the kennel?"

"I don't think she knows. I don't think Circe knows. Neither of them knows what Victor knows."

"Stop riddling me to death! Is my fa in danger?"

"Not if you cooperate. Not if he cooperates."

"You know, Tosh, for someone who says he's a fan of cooperation, you're really difficult to work with."

"I like my work to be fun."

"You like the sound of your own voice."

His cheeks, so high on his face, hardened, and his eyes glinted. She smiled to herself—she'd found his button after all.

He said, "Your fa needs to tell us what's going on in there."

She'd seen her fa once for dinner to celebrate her kicking stims. He'd seemed proud but reserved, like something was weighing on his mind. But that could have been anything. Life in Amarillo was hard for many reasons. It probably had nothing to do with the kennel. "He doesn't know anything."

"Victor thinks he's hiding something. Thinks your fa is scared. Maybe he should be."

Elena resisted the urge to smack Tosh in the face.

"I understand," he said, "that you don't want to make problems for your fa, especially when he's already so deep in trouble. So here's a suggestion: find out what he knows.

He tells you, you tell me, I do my best to make sure he's not collateral damage. Alternatively . . ."

His eyebrows narrowed, but not in anger. It seemed as if he were genuinely considering a new idea.

"What?" Elena asked.

"Here's another possibility. Get someone into the kennel who can get the full story. Someone who can watch and listen, and put our devices where they need to be to figure out what the laws is going on there."

"A plant," she said. "I get it. I do that, and you leave my fa out of it. Deal?"

"Honor swear. Though I can't really promise he won't get hurt as long as he works there. I can hold off any fireworks until we know more and let you know when they're about to go off. If you help us."

Saliva in her mouth reminded her of the feeling right before taking a hit of stimsmoke. She hadn't wanted to dose this badly since before she quit.

"I'll help you," she said, running through the names of Puros who'd be good at this job, someone clever but not so clever that he made trouble. Someone like Chico.

25

Water hides the past, covers our mistakes,
swallows dreams completely.
What a vast ocean
of cares sink
into silence.

—Ming Pearl's *Now Blossom* (1973)

30 May 1991
New Venice, The Louisiana Territories

Victor became aware of his body, feeling sore in his legs and groin. He was on his back, a red-and-black checkered surface above him, close to his face. His breath rebounded to his nose and smelled like rice.

Wonda rested a hand on his chest. "You're back. I can tell by the way you're breathing."

She was standing next to the alcove he lay in. Beyond her, a sloping wall and a window with shuttered blinds were visible.

He said thickly, "I feel like I haven't been awake for days."

"Not exactly true," she said, leaning closer. "It's been a week since I found you." She kissed the lobe of his ear.

A hard-on swelled between his legs. "Umm. Thanks," he said, shifting over, seeing he was in a bunk bed in some sort of trailer. He slid around and lowered his feet to the floor.

"I need to use the bathroom."

He tried to hide the erection tenting his pants—some type of loose synthsilk. Wonda pressed her face into his chest, reached down, and grabbed his dick.

"Don't be long," she said.

He put a hand on her shoulder, as much a gesture of affection as it was a way to push her away, and fled to a door from which the faint smell of lemon air freshener wafted. He stepped into a narrow bathroom, shutting the door behind him. He sat on the toilet cover, held his face in his hands and whispered, "What the laws," searching his memory for anything from the past few days. The last thing he remembered, and faintly at that, was sitting by a canal and Wonda taking his hand in hers.

Feeling disoriented and woozy, he shook his head. Blankness hovered nearby but held no attraction at the moment. He wanted to know what was going on. He stood, dropped his pants, and urinated, flaccid now, trying to figure out exactly how he would ask Wonda what had happened. He flushed, pulled up his pants, and stepped out.

"You're probably starving," she said, taking him by the arm. He got the feeling she was more than comfortable touching him and guiding him, almost like a duty, that if she didn't, she feared he would go wandering off into traffic. Victor followed her out a door, down a few steps, and onto a patch of synthturf shaded by an awning that hung from the top of the trailer.

She said, "We'll get us a hot meal."

Victor stopped. He had the feeling he'd left something behind. "I'm forgetting something."

Wonda said, "Tosh left this morning."

"Tosh? Left?"

"He wouldn't say where he was headed."

Wonda rubbed a hand on his back and gently ushered him forward. They walked by trailers that looked as if they hadn't moved in years. Some had decks built in front. One had a metal gangway similar to the kind used to board a boat. At the end of the street, three were lined up close almost in a semicircle, the ends chopped off and conjoined with sun rooms built between them. Further along were two trailers on opposite sides of the lane, each with a roof deck built around a central spire. A wooden suspension bridge was slung between them.

"Where are we?" Victor asked.

"Lifer Park. A little north of New Venice. Recognize that?" Wonda pointed beyond a tall barred fence, where a steep slope was marked by vertical lines that were tinged yellow by the setting sun. Ouachita Dam.

The day was almost over, yet it felt like morning, as if his circadian rhythm had been cut off as cleanly as a limb. He hoped it would come back soon; he wasn't looking forward to sleepless nights in a claustrophobic trailer.

"What's wrong?" Wonda asked.

"Nothing," he said. He told himself to stop worrying about the future and focus on what had gone on while he was blank.

"You're safe here," she said. "You know that, right?"

He took stock internally. He looked around at a place he'd never seen with his conscious mind. He did feel safe. "I guess I'm surprised how quickly this place is starting to feel like home," he said.

Wonda grinned and took his hand, walking faster, almost skipping now. As they passed more trailers, Victor noticed how each one was decorated and modified as painstakingly as a New Year's tree. Up ahead, a gate marked the edge of the district. Next to it, a squat little guard's hut.

They turned before they reached the gate and approached a simple structure: iron girders supporting an aluminum roof with walls made of gauzy fabric. Picnic tables were visible beyond as if through a haze.

"You should remember the dining hall," Wonda said. "You've eaten here enough. Remember?" Her voice, normally so open and melodic, carried a twinge of nervousness, a sliver of urgent curiosity. Victor guessed that her trepidation was about what, if anything, he remembered about the last few days.

"It smells great," he said, catching a whiff of something fried, maybe fish.

Wonda smiled, her anxiety seemingly forgotten or maybe tucked safely away for later. "I'm starving." She let go of his hand, pulled back one of the gauzy sheets, and held it open for Victor. "Hurry," she said, "We want to keep out the bugs."

He moved inside, the sheet falling from her hand and brushing his backside. They moved forward together into the Lifers' dining hall as her hand found his and gripped it tight.

Human Lifers love barbecue, Victor learned. The smell of grilled chicken, lamb, beef, and pork—sweet, smoky, and peppery—wafted from one side of the tented area where a line of people moved past the banquet table, filling their plates. Another long table held many bowls of various salads—pasta, cucumber, fingerling potatoes. Diners were piling big scoops of food on their plates.

Victor felt strangely nauseated. The thought of eating made his stomach shrink. He accompanied Wonda to the grills, waited for their turn in front of a large man whose limbs wouldn't look out of place roasting above the coals, and asked for and accepted a seasoned chicken thigh and a round slice of pork tenderloin. Looking down at his plate, he realized something was wrong. He held up the line, ignoring the cook's incredulous expression. What was it? Then it struck him—he needed two. "Another thigh, please," he said. The cook obliged and Victor plopped down at a table with Del and Wonda. *Two is the best, forget the rest*, ran through his head like a mantra.

Del clasped his hands, elbows on the table, and soon everyone who sat near them followed suit, Victor included—it was too much effort to go his own way, no one would glorify his protest, and he'd rather sit and observe, mute, without a thought in his head.

"Pure is our food, pure are our souls. May the path of purity lead us true," Del said.

"Pure is pure," each person echoed.

Victor nodded, didn't say anything. *Pure sure is pure*, he thought, and the barest smile rose up.

Whiteness cleared from Victor's vision. He watched the drapes around the eating pavilion flap gently, rippled by a breeze.

Only a moment had passed. Wonda's plate was still full. Del appeared to be cutting into his first slice of beef. Victor caught each of their gazes. They were smiling. He got the sense that everyone at the table was waiting for him to speak—about what he didn't know.

Wonda picked up a little ceramic jar with a spout like a pouty lower lip. She bent over her plate, paused, then offered him the jar. "Do you want some sauce for your meat?" she asked.

"Thanks." He took the jar, tilted it, watched a brown gravy thickly glop onto his chicken, and gave it back to her. The sauce smelled sweet, perhaps a bit spicy, and his stomach gurgled, though it didn't feel as if it were a part of him.

Victor looked at Del. "What am I doing here?"

Del cocked his head. "We decided that we needed to be a bit more lenient about the seeker's path. And a bit more hands-on in your case."

"Those hands being Wonda's?" he asked.

"And Tosh's," she whispered, so quietly he wasn't sure if she'd intended for him to hear. She looked away. Victor could almost feel heat rising from her skin, and a pink aura glowed around her.

He wasn't angry or ashamed, more incredulous than anything else. Had his disgust for Tosh been so superficial that he let himself be manhandled while blank? Had he really welcomed it?

Victor's memory returned to that one day in high school, coming out of blankness naked, deeply ashamed at the students laughing at him as he covered his crotch with his hands and searched for his clothes. He felt none of that panicked anxiousness now.

That's new, he thought. He'd always assumed it would take years of persistent and patient effort to overcome the shame of his blank actions. Now it seemed to have been discarded as easily as a used tissue.

"We know you've struggled," Del said, apparently willing to overlook the more primitive aspects of his flock's behavior. "We want to help stop the Classification Act. It's rare I see anything on the Mesh that's worth paying attention to. Your renouncement of medication has inspired us all. You are on the path of purity. Your cause is our calling. For some, it will be their greatest test." Del looked at Wonda, then at the others at the table. They watched him attentively. "You have to forgive their silence, Victor. We usually don't discuss politics at the dinner table."

The men and women at the table were all around Victor's age. Their eyes were bright, wide open, and adoring, making him feel appreciated and safe. Wonda squeezed his hand beneath the table, and he didn't shy away. Her touch was welcome, supportive. He'd kissed her in Pond Park in the middle of near-blankness, and now, it seemed, they were comfortably intimate. How had he lost his aversion to being touched so quickly? It was as if he'd come back from blankspace a different person. Could other aspects of his personality be that malleable? What would that mean?

A young man with a shaved head and nonexistent eyebrows raised his hand. "Del," he said, lowering his hand, "could I ask Victor a question? It's about my calling."

"Go ahead, Meric." Del wiped his mouth primly, using a corner of his white napkin to dab away brown sauce lingering near his lips.

"Are you going to see Samuel Miller again?" Meric asked Victor. His eyes betrayed no hint of anxiety or disgust.

Victor blinked. They knew Samuel had killed hundreds of people, didn't they? It was still so disorienting to see someone say his name without crossing themselves or doing something to ward off his evil. Victor had only ever gone to see Samuel because he needed him to get the data egg open.

A shiver ran down his back. He wouldn't think about the data egg. He'd buried it to avoid its unwelcome truths. He didn't have to see Samuel ever again.

"I'm sorry if you don't want to talk about it," Meric said. "We're concerned is all. The last MeshNews interview—we'd seen him before, he was talkative. The life in his eyes was shining, but during this last one, it was gone. We think they're dosing him again. We thought maybe now that you're—maybe now you're ready to go back and check on him."

"Check on him?"

"Make sure he's not being medicated against his will."

"I hope he's on pills!"

The unmedicated Samuel terrified Victor. His talk of voices, primals, ghosts, and crossing over were delusions as fascinating and multilayered as they were creepy. Now that Victor had gotten what he needed from Samuel, he had no intention of coming within an arm's length from him ever again. And if there was even the slightest chance his delusions were contagious—what else could explain what Granfa Jeff had said about Circe believing his deranged ideas?—then everyone would be better off with a medicated Samuel.

Wonda put a hand on the back of his neck. It was warm, soft. "What Victor means is that the path to purity isn't always a straight line, is it?"

Victor relaxed his shoulders. Her hand felt good, calming—amazing. He didn't mind that she was putting words in his mouth. She could say all she wanted on his behalf. He would stay mute, unthinking.

"Why don't we leave this talk for later," Del said. "There's something else I know the potentiate is eager to learn about. You know, purity isn't the end goal for us. Not like the Puros. They're focused on the physical world. We've a greater goal in mind that we're working toward. The path of purity, we say, is the only way to truth. As seekers, we're striving to reach our highest place in the universe. To achieve unity, if you will. Now, given that, it should be no surprise, Victor, that there's lots of curiosity about blankspace. Wonda has shared the details of some of your visions. Would you mind describing what they're all about?"

26

> Technology isn't inherently disruptive. Innovation yoked to the status quo is a stable system even as it leads to stagnation.
>
> Imagination is the great disruptor. The cynic asks, what could be different? and expects no answer. Everything can change, I believe, if we first believe we are free.
>
> —Osirus Smythe's "Data Isn't Free," an unpublished term paper

31 May 1991
Amarillo, The Republic of Texas

Elena's thumbprint marked the glass screen with a swirly pattern of dirt and oil. No matter how often she washed her hands, the dry and dusty climate of Amarillo clung to her. Bacteria as well. Her own personal biofilm. Knowledge she would rather not have gained via Mesh personal hygiene alerts, little use it was to her.

The realtor, in his burgundy, threadbare jacket and gray chevroned tie, fidgeted. This was a big sale, and his business had been slow. She'd followed him for days. It never hurt to know the person you were going to do business with. The realtor had showed a few clients into the town home, and judging by the way he moped afterward and the lack of foot or any other kind of traffic at the properties he was hawking, income was something he would be very, very excited to receive.

She rubbed her hands on her pants while they waited for her thumbprint to be processed in a clearinghouse somewhere—who knew exactly where. The Mesh in America was a sparsely clustered nether realm of data and algorithms that she'd never really understood. There would be a criminal background check when her fingerprints went through. They would find nothing. Despite a few years hanging with the Puros, a group labeled by the Republic of Texas as a terrorist organization, Elena's record lacked any smudges and was part of the reason she was so valuable to them. The apartment would be her reward.

She stood in the kitchen, wanting to rub her hands over the stone tiles of the floor but holding back. It wouldn't feel as good as it had on stims. Nothing did.

The realtor looked up with a grin that seemed decades younger than the puffy skin below his eyes. "Clear," he said.

She couldn't help but smile too. It was hers. Two floors with two bedrooms, a living room, a den, and a balcony overlooking a quiet, lush courtyard. The most insanely over-the-top bathroom adjoined the master bedroom. Elena would have to remember to bring towels the next time she came over so she could luxuriate in the walk-in shower and then soak in the bubbletub.

She could almost forgive the landlord of the last place she'd lived, the one she'd shared with Victor, for repossessing it and much of her belongings when they left so that she could go to rehab.

She stopped herself. The past was the past. Right now, she needed to start planning. With any luck, she could have all her stuff moved in less than two days. She'd need help from the Puros, of course, but she had no doubt she could get it.

I'll have to be sly though, she thought. *I don't want them thinking they've got an open invitation. That means no Xavi, definitely not Davinth. Maybe Chico. It could be nice to have him around, and naked.* Then she could casually let him know that she had a problem that needed taking care of, and was he a dog person?

Getting him hired at the kennel might be tricky. Maybe there was a contractor with onsite access. That could be Chico's way in. Or there was always the option to run it as a surveillance op. Whatever it took, she'd get it done.

The realtor presented her with the keys, still grinning, his teeth straight, if a little yellowed. For a moment, she felt a gentle lustful tug between her legs, but she dismissed it, confident it had more to do with her feeling of accomplishment and progress at landing an apartment than with his sex appeal. She did give him a quick hug, though, before she took the keys and ushered him out the door.

A little black rain cloud of doom tried to intrude on her thoughts—the image of Victor in a room with Samuel Miller—but she ignored it. His decision. His problems. She kept repeating those four words as a mantra to absolve herself. His decision. His problems. I've wasted years of my life on him. Not another second.

Elena's stomach rumbled. She was halfway to the chiller to take out a snack when she remembered it was empty, as were the cupboards and drawers. The type-pad on the side of the chiller confirmed that it wasn't even powered. She turned it on, locked the apartment, drove to the plaza in the center of town, and got a parking space along the main road.

The Puro grocers at the market were packing up, returning vegetables and fruits to their StayFresh containers. Elena bought onions, garlic, tomatoes, and squash. She would run to the store for sausage and bread later. The farmer-owners behind the stall's table, an older married couple who had wrinkled faces and most of their teeth, tried to undercharge her. The man winked at her.

She said, "I'm happy to pay full price."

"You'll pay all right," a voice said from behind her.

The husband froze and stared over Elena's shoulder. The wife hastened to pack the remaining produce.

Elena turned and stared up into the harsh expression of a man wearing a full suit of black combat armor. A Corp. His buddies, also armored and wearing utility belts to carry their weapons and tech gear, stood nearby, scowling.

Stupid, stupid, stupid, she told herself. She'd left her shockstick in the car.

An uncomfortable silence lengthened. The grocers hustled, stacking boxes. Their movements were panicked. They finished loading everything onto a cart. All that remained was to collapse the tent so they could take that as well.

"We'll take care of that," the lead Corp said when the husband moved to the tent crank. "You can leave your trash too." The Corp nodded at boxes on the cart.

People around the plaza began to approach. The non-Puro sellers had all cleared out. A few Puros—farm folk, not Elena's armed compatriots—returned from their vans, having loaded their goods already. Onlookers drifted closer.

Elena watched a crowd gather with a sinking feeling in her stomach. There wasn't much sympathy on their faces.

"Don't know if you've heard about Houston," the lead Corp said loud enough for the crowd to hear. "Puros set fire to the Emporium. Ten bodies recovered so far."

The husband and wife were standing close, arms wrapped around each other, trembling. Elena stood stone still, no idea what to do. Houston was hundreds of kilometers away. She wouldn't worry about it, normally.

"Sorry to hear it," Elena said. "Let's hope it ends there."

The lead Corp said, "Not a chance." He turned to his crew. "Light it up."

A Corp with a toothy smile stepped forward, pulled something off his belt, and squirted a viscous liquid on the produce boxes.

Elena had seen enough. She grabbed the husband and wife roughly and pulled them along with her. "Get out while you can," she whispered. They started jogging but were stopped short by more Corps.

"Make them watch!" someone shouted.

Elena felt a hot blast on her back. She turned, checking to make sure her hair wasn't aflame, and saw boxes of produce and the tent blazing. Small fireballs leapt into the air. Whatever flammable gel the Corp had used seemed designed to be a crowd pleaser—the fire changed color, blue and green flames licking skyward.

"That's two weeks of our crop gone," the husband said.

"We'll make it right," Elena said.

The wife asked, "What did he say about Houston?"

"Just a sec." Elena checked her MeshBit for the news. It was the first story in her feed. Puros protesting products laced with stims had set fire to the Emporium while there were people inside. She told the grocers what happened, adding, "I don't believe it. They wouldn't have done that. There's got to be more to the story."

People watching the fire started chanting, "Puro, Puro, no, no, no. Puro, Puro, go, go, go!"

Great, Elena thought, now we're a spectacle, which is pretty much a death sentence. Time to beg Tosh and the Diamond King for a reprieve.

27

> Overlooking the clock-face city in the desert, he said, "Money and power, that's all there is."
>
> —Muriel Stein's *The Diamond King: Portrait of a Myth*

31 May 1991
New Venice, The Louisiana Territories

After dinner, Del led a group of six potentiates, including Wonda, on a walk through the camp. Victor trailed behind. He needed some silence. Cool moist air smelled of green grass and hints of lilac. Highway traffic created a low whoosh like an unending wave retreating from the shore.

Despite everything that had happened to him, he felt good. It was a precarious balance, he knew. He was doing his best to keep a firewall between the shock of the data egg and the present moment—a feat Pearl would have congratulated him on. All the messiness of his life and the weird, dull, distance he felt between his mind and body aside, things could be worse.

Victor recalled the feeling he'd had leaving Amarillo, that maybe the problem wasn't so much with him as with the people around him. Maybe the Human Lifers gave him what he needed, like the sun and rain were for plants, nourishment.

His head was full of these thoughts as he walked down the lane of trailers. He didn't notice the buzzing sound growing louder around him until a red flashing light crossed his path, stopped midair, and crossed again, drawing closer. A dark whirring thing like a fat black beetle hovered in front of him, a single red LED blinking on a repeating pattern, one flash, a break, two flashes, a break, three flashes, a break, and then the pattern started over again. It was Ozie's code, an old joke about how easy some entry passcodes had been before biometric encryption became the standard for Mesh interfaces. The beetle thing darted away, stopped, came back, started moving away again. It wanted Victor to follow.

The beetle flew between two trailers, past miniature yards whose borders were marked by short, knee-high fences painted to glow in the dark. There was a narrow dirt track between the yards, a strip of wild grasses, and beyond the vegetation, a looming black fence like a line of ebony piano keys standing on end, the gaps between them too narrow for any adult to squeeze through. Victor followed the beetle along the path paralleling the fence. Its red light glowed steady, illuminating the ground. He came to a gate, which opened—no lock on it—and then he was hiking over a low hill. When he reached the top, he saw that he'd climbed over an embankment along the upper stretches of the Passage. Ouachita Dam loomed over him, its skeleton rib-bone architecture visible in the glare of security lights blaring on top of the dam.

Ozie stood silhouetted by the lights. He raised one hand in a quick wave, his robot arm.

"What are you doing out here?" Victor asked.

"Lifers told me I wasn't welcome inside. They say I'm not 100 percent human any more. I say they're 90 percent bacteria. The consensus is we keep our distance from each other. You all right?"

Victor had no idea how to answer that question.

"Pearl's coming to see you. All of them are: Karine, Circe, Mía, even Alia. 'Where's Victor? How is he?' Not that they ask me, of course, but I can read all their messages. Tosh told me about the data egg, who killed Jefferson. I'm sorry, Victor."

Tosh knows?!

"Let's talk about something else," Victor said, suddenly feeling as if he were walking a tightrope in a hurricane.

"I'm getting out of here. Going back to Las Vegas. The King knows, wants to make a plan to take out BioScan. I'm going to help him. You're factored in."

"What's that mean?"

"Means you have a part to play. I convinced him to leave it for now. You're taking one step at a time, I can tell." Ozie's voice in the dark was sympathetic, friendly—it sounded just how it had in their college days, but now everything was more complicated, and Victor didn't know what layers of meaning might be hidden within it. He didn't try to decode them.

Ozie said, "You can give me the data egg, okay?"

Victor shook his head, then wondered if Ozie could see his expression in the low light and whether he'd had anything done to his eyes to enhance them. He said, "I'm done with it."

"So give it to—"

"No." Victor didn't try to put into words how he felt about the way Granfa Jeff had ruined his life with his plans and secrets. His imaginary island beckoned—his mental retreat when he'd needed one during his years in SeCa's mire—warm sand, salty spray, and an endless shore without people. "I'm done with it. You're done with it. Everyone. It's over."

Ozie planted his hands on his hips. Victor wondered if one felt heavier than the other. "You don't get to say," Ozie complained. "We all—He asked us for help. It's a debt."

"He's gone. Debt absolved."

"You believe what he said, right? About stims. About a cure. About Circe."

"I don't want to talk about it." Victor turned and started heading down the hill.

"Victor!"

He stopped. He waited to hear what plea Ozie would use, already knowing he wouldn't comply, not that it would fall on deaf ears, only that it would pass through him, like he wasn't even there.

Ozie's feet made rustling noises in the grass as he veered from the path, circled around, and faced Victor, gently placing his hands on his shoulders. "I know this is hard, but you can't run away from it." Reflections from the lights atop the dam flashed in Ozie's glasses. The brightness was blinding.

Victor shrugged away. "It's my life. I decide what to do with it from now on." He stalked down the hill toward the Human Lifers' settlement.

Ozie yelled after him, "You can't ignore the truth!"

"I've got my own, thanks," Victor mumbled to himself. He headed to Wonda's trailer. It was empty. He lay down and found the sweet spot at the intersection of sleep, blankness, and dreams.

The next morning, loud knocking woke him. He dressed and went outside, blinking in the bright and dewy morning.

Del had gathered potentiates for an outing. He owned a catamaran that was moored at the farthest north dock on the Passage, a bit upstream from the entrance to the Grand Canal and about a kilometer from the Human Life camp. They walked along a grassy ridge—Del and Victor in the lead, Wonda and four potentiates behind them. The dirt trail followed the terrain up and down. Where it reached low marshy spots, they crossed on wooden bridges that seemed to be made of shipping pallets covered with plywood, damp and moldering. The sun hid behind heavy clouds that portended rain and possible lightning. "How wise is it to go for an outing on the water in this weather?" Victor had asked, but Del had ignored him and none of the others seemed concerned.

They filed past a guard hut, which was unmanned, and onto the slip, where a dozen boats floated stock still. The water was eerily calm behind a rock jetty, and the wind had died, though Victor had an intuition it would return soon.

Del went about readying the boat with the help of one of the potentiates, a wiry young man with dark skin and an irrepressible smile that revealed gleaming white teeth whenever he caught Victor's eye. Wonda helped the others board, gripping each one by the arm, holding them steady. The dock rocked under the shifting weight of so many bodies, while the boat sat heavy in the water, unperturbed.

Victor climbed aboard, the last besides Wonda, and helped her join him. Though she didn't seem to need it, he knew she would appreciate the gesture.

"Squat circle," Del called out. "As soon as I get us out to sea, so to speak."

The engine started up, a guttural sputtering that changed to a smooth hum once they'd cleared the dock and started heading into the Passage at speed. There were no waves in front of the boat, only shallow ripples, the vestigial echoes of the nonexistent breeze. The boat was making its own wind and trailing two wakes behind it.

Always two. Two is the best, Victor thought.

Wonda put up her hair in a pony tail to keep it from blowing in her face. Victor's curls jostled against each other.

They squatted on fine mesh fabric stretched between the catamaran's nacelles. Rigging underneath the mesh made X-shaped shadows when they passed through a sunny patch and vanished when they returned to the gloom beneath the clouds.

The Grand Canal entrance was far off to the left, and to avoid tourist traffic Del swung them around to follow the Passage's curve, staying close to the shore opposite New Venice. When they were level with the Petit Canal, the catamaran swung right, heading south toward Qaddo Lake, low muddy shores to the left and gentle grassy hills to the right.

Del cut the motor, and they slowed, drifting, until they were moving as sedately as the water around them. Victor noticed that the potentiates weren't talkative, though they didn't seem anxious. Most wore expressions of patient contentment, looking out at the scenery, occasionally reaching out to a neighbor to give an affectionate squeeze or pat. Wonda seemed lost in thought and perhaps slightly anxious; she kept smoothing her hair back from her forehead.

Del squatted and grinned. "We might as well sit for this," he said. A couple potentiates, the one with the white teeth included, flashed smiles of relief, and everybody sat, some cross-legged and some with legs splayed out wide, the way Victor did.

"Don't suppose you saw the MeshNews segment last night?" Del asked, raising his white eyebrows and looking at Victor.

"I didn't. No."

"Guess your friend was lurking around. Figured you had other things on your mind. We hope he doesn't keep harassing you. He's not welcome among us, you understand."

"I don't think Ozie is sticking around much longer," Victor said.

"Good," Del said. He didn't look exactly pleased, more as if he'd removed a splinter that had been bothering him and now wasn't sure if he'd gotten the whole thing. "We're alarmed by what we've seen on the MeshNews feeds. The Classification Act must not pass. It seems the authorities have no regard for purity."

Wonda cleared her throat loudly.

"You wish to speak?" Del asked.

"Yes," Wonda said. "Before, we saw Samuel with light in his eyes, animated, talking about starting his life again. But whatever light was in his eyes is gone now. They've started him back on the Personil."

Victor didn't care what drugs Samuel Miller was on or what BioScan did with him. It wasn't Victor's concern. He thought it was creepy how the Lifers shared a vocabulary where common words like "light" seemed to mean something different and unfamiliar.

Wonda said, "We know you feel Personil's not a good treatment. We want you to convince BioScan to stop treating him."

"They won't listen to me," Victor said, knowing that wasn't quite true. They would listen, sure, but then they'd go through the same, tired excuses he'd heard so many times. And recent experience had proved an unmedicated Samuel was not desirable.

Del nodded as if he'd known Victor's answer all along. "This is a sensitive time for the Seeking. The Louisiana Territories have been hostile to us and to our beliefs, to say the least." He looked significantly at Victor. "We've been chased out of towns over and over again. I'm hoping the local authorities here will be more tolerant, that the people will understand our principles."

Wonda made an exasperated face. "We've talked about this this, Del! Samuel Miller is the perfect example of how medication is failing humanity, and it's up to us to help him."

"Come on!" Victor said. "Samuel Miller staying on medication is a good thing. We're talking about a mass murderer. He's not like anyone else. He's not a perfect example of anything except a killer. What you've seen were highly edited vidfeeds of him on his good days."

Wonda put her hand on Victor's knee and squeezed. "We know it shouldn't fall solely on your shoulders to stop BioScan. That's why we've started looking into legal options."

Victor gazed into her eyes: light blue, hints of violet, untroubled conviction, determination, no second guessing. He admired her even as he shivered a bit inside. Untroubled conviction could take a person into myriad horrors; Samuel Miller was evidence of that. He supposed his aunt was as well—

He popped over to blankspace.

He was floating on his back, moist clouds surrounding him, feeling himself bobbing on the wind. A low thrum of energy pulsed in his groin. He was on the precipice of blankness, not fully gone, light and unburdened, balanced, buffeted.

Gritting his teeth, he returned to reality. It had only been a moment. Wonda was watching him, they all were. Del and the other potentiates wore curious expressions, like waiting for the curtain to rise before a show.

"Legal options?" Victor asked, remembering what Wonda had been saying.

"A private company should not be able to medicate someone against their wishes. That's what we'll argue. We've started canvasing for funds, and we've hired a law firm in town. They're young, just out of law school, and eager to take on BioScan. They're going to make a name for themselves. That's why they're taking our case."

"I'm not sure you can out-lawyer BioScan."

"We're not going to give up," Wonda said. "I know why this is hard for you."

Victor wondered exactly how much she knew. How many nights had she slept with him, asking him questions? How many had he answered?

"You're caught in the middle—an employee, an heir, and someone who's intimately familiar with the challenges of mirror resonance syndrome. We understand that. We're not asking you to give up everything you have. But you can talk to them directly, and we can't. They say they're all for alternative treatment. We need to hold their feet to the fire."

"It's not that simple," he said. The look on her face was one of dashed hopes and bitter disappointment. It twisted his stomach in knots. Somehow in only a few days they'd become intimately emotionally intertwined. He wasn't sure whether he wanted to extricate himself. He needed time to figure things out.

"It's not that simple," he repeated, "but I'll try to help them understand what you want." If I can figure that out for myself, he added silently.

Her face flashed white, which he momentarily assumed was his synesthesia flaring from her elated reaction, and then he noticed the potentiates looking around. One giddily pointed at the horizon. Two seconds passed. Then a rumbling crack sounded. A quieter echo reached them from the direction of Cemetery Hill.

"We're a group of storm enthusiasts, you see," Del said.

The potentiates were passing out sandwiches. Victor took one, smoked salmon on wheat bread with mustard and mayonnaise. They ate and watched the storm blow south of them, billowing rain, lighting striking, and thunder pounding like a hammer on a sheet of aluminum. Del brought out slickers from a storage locker when the rain started, and they all huddled together, wet observers on the tallest object for a kilometer. But the storm wasn't as close as Victor had thought a while ago. They were safe enough, he supposed.

Eventually, Del fired up the engine again and piloted north and west, back to the dock. They trudged through mud, hearing crickets and frogs and the occasional flapping drama from ducks chasing each other out on the water.

As they neared the main entrance to Lifer Park, Victor spotted Tosh, sitting and chatting with the potentiate who was assigned to gate duty. Tosh looked up, saw Victor, and went back to chatting, though Victor knew Tosh knew he was still being watched. When they reached the gate, Tosh squeezed the potentiate's knee, got up and walked over to Victor, sweeping him into a close, tight hug. Victor expected some sort of snarky comment whispered in his ear, but Tosh said nothing. He smelled of day-old sweat and barbecue. The embrace relaxed; Tosh leaned over and gave Wonda a peck on the cheek. How had Victor found himself with this intimate surrogate family so suddenly when his mind had decided to go dreamwalking? It was like waking up to someone else's life.

Wonda said, "Victor agreed to talk to BioScan. And I went and saw the lawyers yesterday. They're on the case."

"You don't quit, do you?" Tosh said.

"Are you going to tell us where you went?" Wonda said.

"To see a friend. And to pick up some supplies."

"What supplies?" she asked.

Tosh answered, wearing a grim smile. "Weapons."

28

We are at war. It is not a secret war. It is not a simmering conflict. It is open, unabashed, undeclared war.

How can the American Union look askance and refuse to help? OWS Corps are attacking our youth, our livelihoods, and our way of life. Survival is our goal. Intervention will be our only salvation.

—Republic of Texas senator Alberto Montero,
"A Plea for Solidarity" (1990)

1 June 1991
New Venice, The Louisiana Territories

"You're not serious," Victor said, hoping it was true. The look on Tosh's face wasn't entirely gleeful. He was making a big show of grave concern. But Victor could see right through it. Underneath, Victor could see red haze around the man's pupils. Tosh had a thirst for violence, and now he was salivating.

"We'll seek every alternative first," Tosh said in an accent that sounded just like Karine's "I'm-being-reasonable" voice. In other words, a liar's coo. "Legal strategy, fine. You try to convince your unhinged bosses—that's okay too. In the end, they're only going to listen to force."

"Can't you convince the King to back off?" Victor asked.

Tosh glanced at Wonda, then back to Victor.

"Well?" Victor said.

“The King’s just a story, isn’t he?” Wonda asked. “Though, I guess that would explain where the money came from. Del’s been asking questions.”

Victor could imagine why Del would be concerned. If Tosh was funding the Lifers with funds from the Diamond King, what would be expected in return?

Tosh turned to Wonda, smiled apologetically, linked arms with her, and leaned in, saying, “Would you mind if we had a little time to ourselves?”

Wonda seemed agreeable, nodding, walking a few steps with Tosh. She stopped. “Sure. If you have a good reason.”

“There’s something I know,” Tosh said, “that Victor knows too, and I’m pretty sure he doesn’t want you to know.”

She looked at each of them. “Know what?”

“It’s about him. His past, you could say. It’s not my place.”

Wonda looked at Victor pleadingly. “We’ll talk after?”

Victor nodded. She returned to him, kissed him hard on the lips while wrapping her arms around his lower back and pulling him close. Then she skipped lightly away with such boisterousness that Victor laughed out loud. He envied the speed of her swings toward a good mood; his always seemed to stray toward darkness.

Tosh came over, and then he was close, kissing Victor in a different way than Wonda, more urgently, more needfully. Tosh’s hands pulled on Victor’s lower back, shifted down until they were grabbing his butt cheeks. Tosh smelled of barbecue smoke and sauce. His lips parted, and his tongue darted into Victor’s mouth, rooted around, retreated. When he let go, Victor felt a palpable physical ache at the sudden loss of sensation. Was that how addicts felt when they finally kicked their habits?

“I don’t remember us doing that before,” Victor said. There were emotions rustling deep inside he didn’t know how to interpret. Not bad, per se, but definitely confused at feeling pleasure from the touch of a man he thought he loathed. Even if they’d reconciled while he was blank, he seriously doubted the durability of any detente he hadn’t been conscious enough to remember.

"It's an animal thing," Tosh said. "No regrets, Vic, they're not worth the energy. Sorry I sent her away, the three of us are a good sex pack, but you and I need to talk."

"Wonda doesn't know about Circe, does she?"

"You told me a lot of things, but I made sure she wasn't around to hear that part."

"Every time I think of what she did, I go blank."

"Because you're running, not because you can't control yourself."

"Yeah, I think you're right about that." Victor wiped his mouth, felt stubble on his cheek. He didn't think he'd looked in a mirror in days. "Tosh, I don't think we're friends, let alone whatever this is." He waved a hand toward Tosh's crotch like it was a nuisance.

A look of disappointment crossed Tosh's face, then was replaced by a smile. Not one of his big lying grins, more of a sad wise smirk. "We're more than that. We need each other. Don't have to like each other. Now, about your murdering aunt . . ."

Victor moved toward blankness, thought better of it. Who knew what Tosh would do to him while he was gone?

"You didn't go into much detail," Tosh said, taking Victor's hand and pulling him forward on the path. They walked hand in hand, Tosh's large, rough palm surrounding Victor's. He almost felt embarrassed by how comforted he felt. It reminded him of walking with Granfa Jeff all the many times he'd needed reassurance about his condition and his worth as a human being.

"Illuminate me," Tosh said. "Why'd she do it?"

Victor told him he didn't really understand why and wasn't sure he wanted to find out. He'd been close to Auntie Circe all his life, and now he didn't know what to think of her.

Tears formed as he thought about the splotches on Jefferson's face, his hair falling out, probably wanting to scream the truth at the world, but feeling guilty and not wanting to break his family members' hearts. It was ugly, as ugly as family could get, and still he'd acted with restraint.

Then, of course, Granfa Jeff had foisted it all on Victor, the person least capable of telling fact from fiction, making him responsible for cleaning up the mess, telling him to rely on people like Ozie, Tosh, and Pearl. Victor almost laughed at the absurdity.

Tosh pulled Victor into a hug. Victor didn't resist, but let his face be pressed into Tosh's jacket smelling of dust, solitude, and musty sweat. The hug went on. Victor thought of protesting. Then he felt how fierce Tosh's grip was and yet also how shaky, and he realized that Tosh was weeping, fighting to keep it inside him, and probably hadn't shared a genuine emotion with another human in who knew how long. Victor tightened his arms around Tosh's waist, and they stood, needing the comfort of each other's arms. Victor knew it would be the last time they were this close. Tosh wasn't someone he would choose to trust again.

29

> I was holding onto my MeshBit and suddenly it was part of me, another limb, like a neuron in the brain, one small piece of totality. I can't help but think of the Mesh that way, a giant brain the size of the planet. I wonder if it dreams too.
>
> —Victor Eastmore's dreambook

1 June 1991
New Venice, The Louisiana Territories

Victor walked with Tosh until they reached a trailer, a shiny black model almost as large as a city bus. It was nearly invisible in the dusk. The lights around the trailer park seemed to disappear into, rather than reflect off, its lacquer.

Tosh asked him to come inside. But Victor declined, said good night, and watched as Tosh laid his palm against the side of the trailer and leaned close as a panel lit up, presumably to scan his iris. He heard Tosh and a voice speak back and forth. Then a bright square appeared on the side of the trailer, and a previously invisible door slid quietly into the trailer's wall. Tosh entered, the door closed, and the trailer was again a featureless black lozenge.

So that's where the weapons are, Victor thought.

Wonda's trailer, where Victor had been sleeping, fucking, and blanking for the past week, was down the lane, past the back of the food pavilion, which was loud with the sound of clanking dishes, water spraying and echoing against the sides of large stainless steel sinks, and the raucous chatter of the cooks and cleaning crew, who were by far the most vivacious and loudest of the Human Lifers.

Victor entered Wonda's trailer. The lightstrips were on a dim, green-blue setting that made it seem like he was in a submarine moving through dark water. Wonda was lying on her stomach reading something on a MeshBit, one of the older models that streamed individual words across a small screen. She looked up when she heard him enter the room.

"Coming to bed?" she asked.

"Yes," he said wearily. The day—probably the first day Victor had spent the majority of conscious in the last week—seemed to have filled him with heavy fluid, weighing him down.

Victor used the bathroom, stripped, and climbed under the sheet next to Wonda, lying on his back. The trailer was old, not well insulated, and the air inside was already cool. She put down her MeshBit on a side table, standing it on end like a tube of lipstick. Then she snuggled close, face pressed into his chest the way she seemed to prefer. He could feel her breasts and the warmth of her crotch against him. It felt like medicine, a sedative, he relaxed so quickly.

"Tosh didn't want to stop by?" she asked. "You're still friends, aren't you?"

He turned on his side, and she rotated too until they were spooning, he the big one, she the little one. He could tell her everything was fine, knowing it was a lie, but it wasn't the time for big speeches and taking stands. He needed rest. He squeezed her with his arms and kissed the nape of her neck, then moved away to his side of the bed, as much as he could in the narrow space.

"We'll talk tomorrow. It's sleepy time." As he said the words, he was already drifting away, not really hearing her response, falling into a dead sleep.

He woke, having no memory of dreaming, aware that Wonda had just climbed over him and was using the bathroom. He rubbed his eyes, groggy, and the half-waking part of his brain began showing him things, flashes of his life over the past week.

He remembered being bookended by Tosh and Wonda, their lips seeking his, moving over his face, neck, and chest. Another flash of extreme pleasure, the three of them inside each other, standing, braced against either side of the trailer, sighs and groans in his ears. Though he hadn't been conscious, he'd been animated, moving with a vigorous passion, mirroring their hungry gestures and sounds.

His erection pressed against the sheets. He gripped his cock, gave it a good squeeze of acknowledgment, then shifted and made his way to standing. Slowly the blood retreated and left him flaccid. He wasn't sure what to feel about what he'd done while blank. He wasn't ashamed of it. In a very real way, it wasn't him who'd done those things. He knew he should be angry that Wonda and Tosh had taken advantage of him. But, really, they weren't to blame. He had a problem with losing consciousness. His problem, his responsibility.

Maybe what'd they done was good for him—he seemed more comfortable with touch now. Physically he felt a great release had occurred, an unclenching. Mostly though, he was grateful. Without Wonda taking him in, who knows what could have happened? He might have ended up drowned in a canal or causing a fuss on the highway when an autonomous vehicle stopped for him and signaled the authorities. Or any number of other problems. They'd saved him, and he was tempted to continue to let them save him.

But everything else about the situation was wrong: Tosh bringing weapons to New Venice, the Human Lifers beginning to talk about Samuel Miller like a person with rights rather than a monster who could never atone for his actions, and his Auntie, an assassin and zealot bringing the Classification Commission to the broader world.

It was time for him to stop hiding and do something about all this.

Victor dressed quickly while Wonda was showering. He knocked on the bathroom door and called to her, "I'm going to get some food. I'll see you later, okay?"

"Okay!" she called brightly. She began humming something.

The sun was out, and the sky was clear. He hurried to the dining hall and ate two fried eggs on a thick slice of sourdough toast, crunchy on the outside, still soft in the center. He went to Tosh's trailer, psyching himself up for a confrontation, knocked on the door, and shouted for Tosh to let him in, but there was no response. He headed back. Maybe he could find Del. He owed him a warning about Tosh.

Ahead of Victor on the path, he spotted six potentiates following Tosh in a kind of pyramid shape, the way birds flock together and follow the leader at the point position.

Victor caught up with one of the female potentiates. "Hey," he said.

The young woman, who had a small, square face and brown hair in a bob, looked at him, surprised. Then she smiled. She was pleased, he could tell, but something about her expression looked predatory.

"You're sitting with us?" she said. "That's fantastic. Tosh made me his second chief because I agree it's time to demand action."

Victor's stomach hardened. Whatever Tosh was feeding people, it was already taking effect. He was awaking a thirst for violence that no person would admit to having yet seemed to be lurking, waiting for an excuse to emerge.

At the end of the lane was a large pavilion made of white fabric. Six entrances allowed people to enter. Inside, a circle of tall white poles topped by a spiral lattice supported the synthsilk canopy.

Victor followed Tosh's posse through an entrance. Two dozen potentiates were inside already, milling about, chatting. There was an excited, nervous buzz.

Tosh's posse clustered together at first. Then Victor saw a few of them break away, darting though the crowd to talk to Lifers that might be converted to militancy. Some of them returned with apparent converts, and some, rebuffed, tried again with others.

Wonda came in, her hair dry, loose, and a bit wild. There were streaks of colored yarn braided through it. She looked around, spotted Victor, and headed over. She gave him a peck on the cheek and said, "Good morning. I'm just going to go say hi to Tosh."

Victor watched their interaction from a distance. Tosh broke away from talking intently with one of his pack when Wonda came over. They hugged. Wonda whispered something in his ear. Tosh shook his head gravely, gestured at his potentiates, and then looked pointedly toward Del at the center of the gathering, where he was smiling and chatting amiably with a small crowd clustered around him. Wonda frowned, said something. Tosh shrugged.

Del started clapping slowly, a second between each sound. The Lifers around him took up the clap, which accelerated. Everyone was moving, streaming past each other, hurrying to different parts of the tented area. Wonda came over to Victor and grabbed his hand.

"Come on," she said and started to lead him toward Del.

"Victor, wait!" a woman's voice called out. It was the potentiate who'd been excited to have Victor walk with Tosh's pack. "Stay here," she said.

Wonda dragged him away. Victor caught a glimpse of Tosh watching gravely, no hint of a smile on his lips.

The movements of the crowd grew still even as the clapping quickened into a synchronized frenzy of sharp smacks. Victor and Wonda were the last into place, standing at Del's right. Del brought up both hands, the clapping ceased, and eighty people simultaneously dropped into a squat, Wonda pulling Victor down with her so that only Del remained standing.

"We begin by welcoming new potentiates," Del said. "Donya Largoso, welcome." The young woman from Tosh's group—Tosh's second chief, she'd claimed—stood, waved, and turned, showing her face to the crowd. She squatted again, disappearing into the sea of heads.

The ritual repeated four more times, Del calling out names, each one standing. Victor stopped paying attention, instead trying to puzzle out the odd tension in the pavilion. He hoped it didn't have anything to do with him. What if they didn't like him now that he wasn't blank?

On a whim, Victor stood. All heads swiveled toward him. "Stretching my legs," he announced meekly. He watched Tosh's group as Del continued the introductions. There was something aggressive and threatening about the way Tosh's group clumped together, giving each other sly looks, jerking their heads toward whoever was standing or speaking, judging them, whispering to each other. It made Victor think of a pack of wolves scouting a flock of sheep and salivating. He squatted again, asking himself what Tosh was really after, and could he ever truly know and trust him?

"Moving on," Del said. "I want to talk about new developments in our faith. You all know our philosophy of Emergence, the journey we take together toward purity and embracing our humanity. What we don't talk about enough is the reason for this journey." He held up a book with a green cover and opened it to display yellowed, ragged pages.

About a quarter of the Lifers in attendance bowed their heads and raised their arms, fingers splayed. A hum arose, then a sound like wind as breath passed their lips. The other Lifers looked with envy and pride at their downcast brethren.

"What's going on?" Victor asked Wonda, whose hands were raised up.

"Emergence. Doctrine. An HL revelation," she said, leaving him no more enlightened than before.

Hands dropped and faces lifted as Del read from the book. "We are children of the universe, seeking to know the face of truth. We are eternal, we are unitary, we are human, and we must seek the truth."

"Truth is truth," a voice yelled. The crowd took up the chant. It was a full minute until they settled down enough for Del to continue, the book now closed and clasped to his chest.

"There are many who would embark on this journey with us, if only they could remove the veil from their eyes. In most cases, it's a question of coming to enlightenment and admitting it into your heart. However, there are those who are being held back, imprisoned in their medications, barred from their humanity, forced into animal subservience. Today, I am announcing a new article of faith. From now on, we must not turn a blind eye to those whose purity has been taken from them. This is no idle promise. The Louisiana Territories is moving closer to passing the Classification Act. We must influence the debate. You all know about a seeker in our midst, Victor Eastmore. You've heard about his visions and trances, the emerging enlightenment of purity he is experiencing. He has started on the journey."

Victor shifted in his squat. A year ago, if this many people had paid attention to him at the same time, he would have run. An angry mob taking their vengeance on a Broken Mirror was a relatively rare thing, but it was a fear he couldn't wipe away. Now the expressions on the faces around him were a mixture of awe and admiration. For what? Going blank? They didn't know anything about it.

"If I may," Wonda said as she stood.

Del squatted, yielding the floor.

"Our aid is needed right now, here in New Venice," Wonda said. "I'm talking about Samuel Miller."

Victor felt a wave of revulsion rise from his gut, and he was grateful he'd eaten lightly. Otherwise, he might have puked on the person in front of him.

"Samuel Miller is a killer," Wonda said, "a victim of delusions. Yet he was on the path to wellness before BioScan returned to medicating him against his will, stifling his humanity."

Victor couldn't believe what he was hearing. This myopic, twisted version of the truth felt like a needle in his ear.

"We've hired lawyers to demand a halt to his treatment. In addition, our gatherings in town will now include a call for his humane treatment. It is our number one demand. I know some of you will feel uncomfortable with this. How can we advocate for someone guilty of his crimes? I'll say only this. We do not defend his actions. We defend his humanity. We do not get to bend our principles to remain comfortable. We do what our conscience demands. If it were any of you who were force-fed drugs"—Wonda laid a hand on Victor's head—"we would not hesitate to help; we could not choose to ignore it. Nor can we now."

There was a murmur from the crowd that Victor couldn't interpret. Were they all ready to go along with this? It was absurd. Taking Samuel Miller off medication was like letting a lion out of its cage.

Wonda said, "We must also prepare to help the stim addicts whose numbers seem to be growing by the day. This will be their sanctuary." She smiled and then squatted.

Del stood and thanked her. "Does anyone else wish to speak?"

Tosh rose. "I do," he said from the periphery of the pavilion, from where, though far from Del, it was clear that he was the taller man.

The crowd's murmurs grew silent. Victor felt he was in the midst of a hive that suddenly had two queens.

"I yield," Del said. He squatted, looking toward Tosh.

"Del and Wonda have set us noble challenges. The question is: Are we up for them? Do we have the strength of will and fortitude to press our claims? We've been called to court and to parade through the streets. To provide refuge. Are these enough? Do we wait for fortune to honor us? Or do we stand tall and seek our victory?

"I know there are doubters among you. How can you seek and crawl? We cannot bend to an implacable enemy. BioScan is controlled by the Eastmore family, it's true, but they are not honorable. They enfeebled one of their own. We are hosting Victor because his family has not stood up for him—they've failed him. When it was easier to allow Broken Mirrors to be locked up, they locked them up. When it was easier to spin lies about mirror resonance syndrome, they lied through their teeth. Now they bring their lies and their prisons to the Louisiana Territories and beyond. We will not allow their fascism to continue. We who've lived on this land know what can be done to suppress a people's spirit, but it cannot be broken. We will not quietly say no. We will resist."

Victor stood up. A murmur that had been running through the crowd disappeared. The only sound was the flapping of the tent canvas in the breeze and a crow making weird clicking sounds.

"Can I say something?" Victor asked. "You're all talking about Samuel Miller like he's the only person with skin in the game. Well, I'm right here. I should be able to have my say too, right?"

Tosh stared at Victor, then squatted.

"I'm not going to tell any of you what to do or what to think. I'm not certain of anything. That's what life is like with MRS. I never know if I can trust what I'm seeing and hearing, what I'm thinking. If I can't trust myself, how can I trust anyone else?

"I was diagnosed when I was twelve. You all have probably never been to Semiautonomous California, most of you," Victor gave Tosh a significant look, then continued. "In SeCa, people with MRS are called Broken Mirrors. We're feared; we're looked down on; we're put into prisons, effectively. Very few are given the privilege of living free, walking on eggshells, waiting to be reclassified and sent away. I'd say the day I was diagnosed was the worst day of my life, but I'd be lying. Because I was four years old in Carmichael when Samuel Miller used vehicles to run people down in the streets. He gassed them to unconsciousness, then woke them up so he could shock them dead with a shockstick. He wanted them to be conscious for it so they could 'cross over.' He planted explosives on dozens of houses, including my own. I lived through Carmichael. I still have nightmares. The man who killed hundreds of people while believing he was helping them cross over to another world is here in New Venice, and you're talking about his rights. It's difficult for me to grasp."

Victor glanced at Wonda. She was looking up at him, her eyes glistening. She mouthed, "Keep going," and nodded. Tosh had a curled fist pressed to his mouth.

"I'm lucky to be alive," Victor said. "I'm lucky to be free. And I'm lucky to be sane, for the most part. I've had years of professional help in dealing with MRS, more than any other person alive, Samuel included, and still I struggle with it every day. You want to take Personil away from everyone with MRS? You want to save stim addicts? Fine, but you have to be ready to deal with the consequences. How are you going to redirect delusional thinking? How do you treat withdrawal? How are you going to deal with the emotional extremes? There are going to be manic episodes. There are going to be psychotic breaks. What kind of care are you going to provide when that happens? I'm not talking about Samuel Miller. You're starting something here much bigger than him. I can see that."

"Tell us!" someone shouted.

"What do you see when you're blank?" It was a woman's voice—Wonda's.

It was absurd the things they expected of him. They had no idea what kind of mess they were getting into by trying to decipher delusions.

"You want to know the future?" he asked. "I can see it. Not just in my dreams—I can see it waking. You're going to take in all the Broken Mirrors? You think they'll flee SeCa for this refuge? You think every stim addict in the AU will come to you begging for help?" Sarcasm gave his voice an unfamiliar, biting edge. Wonda frowned. Del was shaking his head. Good. He was getting through to them. They needed to hear how ridiculous their ideas sounded. "You'll fill up the HL camp with a bunch of mental patients and addicts who aren't used to freedom, who've never been here before, and you're going to tell them they're human, they're pure, and not to worry about the stuff in their heads. Good luck with that."

Tosh stood. He gestured that his potentiates should stand with him, and they rose to their feet. "We'll tell them that they're human," he said. A red-haired male potentiate next to him repeated his words, adding a subtle melody to them. "We'll tell them they're human."

The chant began to take hold throughout the gathered crowd. "We'll tell them they're human. We'll tell them they're human."

Victor dropped down to his butt, holding his forehead, rocking a bit. The blankness crackled in his ears.

Del crouched next to him. "Look what you've done, Victor," he said. His mouth was a taut line. "You took over a movement. I hope you're ready to lead."

Victor opened his mouth to demur when the chanting ceased and several shouts rang out.

"Stranger!"

"Visitor!"

"Is Victor here?" a familiar woman's voice asked.

He rose. At the edge of the pavilion, visible only because the Lifers had parted, her brown hair loose and wild, uncharacteristically natural, was Auntie Circe.

She said, looking straight at him, "You're coming home now."

30

A clenched hand unfurls
promises not kept
part of me flies away in the breeze

—Ming Pearl's *Now Blossom* (1973)

2 June 1991
New Venice, The Louisiana Territories

Victor stared at Auntie Circe. How could she stand there and tell him what to do? Why didn't she drop dead of existential guilt from killing her own father? Then again, people likely to feel guilt weren't the ones who could plan and follow through on murder. What was she that she didn't feel what a human should?

Wonda rushed to Victor's side and gripped his hand. "Don't go with her!" she whispered in his ear.

"We need you to come home, Victor," Auntie Circe said. She moved her gaze to members of the crowd, connecting with an individual, moving on to the next, working the crowd expertly as she was known to do. How had he not seen how manipulative she was from the start?

"Thank you for taking care of him," Auntie Circe said as she approached Del, who seemed unsure of himself, hands fluttering across his robes. He and Circe were shorter than the other adults. The two of them together formed a scene in miniature, standing close, the rest of the crowd watching from a distance. Victor noticed the pavilion's fabric walls rustling, like layers of blankspace waiting to enfold him.

"Victor is always welcome here," Del said, "and he can stay as long as he likes."

"Thank you," Circe said. She put a hand on Del's arm. The gesture was familiar, intimate, and didn't appear to be unwelcome. "It's good to see you again. The work you're doing is important, and BioScan is willing to support it. We need alternatives. The stim epidemic is too widespread for any one organization to cope with."

"You want to give them support?" Victor asked. "They don't believe in medicine!"

She was silent a moment, ear cocked, and then she said, "Of course we're on the same side. Stims are the real threat."

The crowd murmured, a slightly agitated mumble. Circe looked around, taking note, then said in a loud voice, "Victor is the future of the Eastmore line, more precious than my own son. You all know how special he is."

Robbie's going to flip when I tell him that, Victor thought. And then he felt ashamed—praise from a murderer shouldn't feel good.

"You're aware how special he is," Circe continued. "I wonder, though, if you truly understand his gifts. We're only beginning to explore them. Emergence, I'd say, is not yet underway, and it's important that we don't interfere. We need to allow him room to grow into his full self, to find his potential. To ask too much too soon would be disastrous. I know you understand my meaning." She patted Del's shoulder as if he were a housecat and stepped toward Victor.

How did she know what to say to put the Lifers at ease? How did she know how to seem like one of them herself?

"Victor, we need to get you back to BioScan," she said. "The concussion you suffered requires monitoring. There's a possibility your brain is hemorrhaging."

"That's one explanation for why I've been going blank recently. Want to hear the other?" he said.

Auntie Circe smiled sadly and looked around at the gathered Lifers, watching them. "You should know that everything in this life is a gift. Especially the difficult moments. Believe me, I know your struggle."

"I know where the polonium on the data egg came from," he said in a low voice, wondering as soon as the words were out of his mouth why he didn't shout them as loud as he could.

He tried to capture a filament of guilt or doubt running through her words, some glimmer in her eyes that she would turn back time if she could and resolve her dispute with Jefferson some other way. There was nothing.

"The King," she said, nodding. "It's so unfortunate the lengths Jefferson was willing to go to manipulate you."

Victor stood dumbfounded. After all he'd learned, she was still going to deny the truth? Then again, why should she confess? It would be difficult to press a case against her—the Diamond King would have to get involved, there was the question of jurisdiction, she had virtually limitless resources, and who would believe someone like Victor?

"I can guess what you're thinking, Victor. But remember, Father wasn't blameless. Ask yourself why he went through all this trouble. The guilt nearly destroyed him. I wish he could have been saved. But it's too late. We have to focus on the future. We can talk more about this if you come with me. Let us help you."

Her dark eyes implored him. Guilty or not, he didn't care. He'd buried the egg to buy himself some time. Now he wasn't sure if he'd ever dig it up. He wanted nothing to do with Jefferson's version of the past or Circe's version of the future. He wasn't going to be a pawn in anyone's game anymore.

"I'll be fine here," he said.

"I hope you change your mind," she said, and hugged him.

Victor froze, relaxed, and assumed a posture of blankness, letting himself hover on the edge, just enough to remain aware of his surroundings but seemingly blank to everyone around him.

Circe peered at him, nodded, turned away. "Keep him safe," she said. "He has untold revelations to share." She shook Del's hand, hugged Wonda, and recited pleasantries to a few Lifers who came up to her, curious and thrilled to meet another Eastmore. Victor watched on the edge of blankness, as she said her good-byes, feeling that home was now lost to him forever.

31

An ecosystem represents interdependence, chaotic flows, and creative dynamism. These are the principles that govern the company. Charges of profiteering misconceive everything we're working toward.

—Circe Eastmore's *Race to the Top* (1991)

2 June 1991
New Venice, The Louisiana Territories

The crowd filtered out of the pavilion while Del, Tosh, and Wonda gathered near Victor. Del commenced a squat talk, and Wonda gently pulled Victor down to join them.

"She's on our side," Wonda said. "I believe her."

"Bullshit," Tosh said. "She runs the largest health care company in the American Union. She's playing you."

Del said, "We shouldn't talk about sides. Ours is a path of seeking. Truth may come from unexpected directions, and we have to remain open to it. Who would have guessed a prophet like Victor would find his way to us?"

"I'm here—I'm not blank," Victor said, "and I'm not a prophet. Neither is Samuel Miller. Don't forget that."

"A rose by any other name," Wonda said, looking reverently at Victor.

"Circe smells like shit," Tosh said. "Lying, dirty, infectious shit. You can't listen to her."

"Tosh!" Del warned. "That kind of hostility is not welcome here."

Tosh smirked. "If a monster wants to tear off your face and eat your guts, you can call it whatever you like, but it'll still kill you."

"She's not violent," Victor said.

Tosh responded, "Tell that to Jefferson."

"Gentlemen," Del said. "Let's focus please and try to elevate our discussion. Ms. Eastmore seemed to appreciate our message. We can at the very least discuss with her how BioScan can mold itself to fit the future face of things."

Del had a tight grip on the green book he'd shown to the crowd earlier, and Victor caught a glimpse of the cover, which read, *Theories of Emergence* by Estrella Burgos. He'd never heard of it.

"You're as delusional as Victor if you think you're going to win a pinch of change by talking," Tosh said.

"How delusional am I?" Victor said. "What have I believed that didn't turn out to be true?"

Tosh had no response. He glowered and shifted in his squat, the fabric of his pants bunching around his knees.

"I believe you predicted the future," Wonda said softly. She squeezed his hand. "When you were younger, you saw Carmichael before it happened."

Revulsion like bile climbed his throat. He'd told her his most embarrassing and deepest secret while blank. He jumped to his feet. "I'm done with all of this. You do whatever you want. It's not my problem."

Tosh followed. "You inherited this mess. You've got to fix it."

Victor spun around. "No! I didn't inherit a mess; I inherited a crazy family that's playing out some sick revenge drama using me, their mentally ill relative. This situation—all this nuts talk of religion—that's a load of shit too, and you're a shit, and this whole town is shitty. I'm done. This time, don't come after me!"

Victor went to Wonda's trailer. Not having much, if anything, to pack, a short while later he stepped out of the trailer, nerves jangling. Just being in this place was making him nuts. It made everyone nuts.

The idea of psychic infections was ludicrous, so what else could explain the Human Lifers accepting radical changes in their philosophy? Was it hero worship that made them blindly follow Del, or Tosh, or whoever crowed loudest? Maybe Victor had set himself up to be the leader of lunatics, but he was getting out, so it didn't matter. When people looked at him and smiled, there was something feral, hungry, and desperate in their expressions. He wouldn't have to see that anymore.

Still, the question of what was really going on gnawed at him. Maybe their blend of faith and cult worship primed them for transformations, and they had finally found what would take them forward on their path. It didn't feel like a step forward to him, though. It felt like running into a brick wall.

"Ow!" he shouted at a pain in his ankle. He heard a whirring of motors, and when he looked down he saw a flat hexagon of metal the size of a small cat with treads like a tank on each side.

Ozie's voice came out of a cigar-shaped MeshBit strapped to the hexagon. "Pick me up."

A few Human Lifers strolling by looked at him. They'd heard his yelp. He waved until they'd passed by and then said in a lowered voice, "Go away, Ozie."

"You have to get out of there. Right now." The hexagon robot drove over his foot. "It's about to get crazy in New Venice. Come meet me in Las Vegas."

"Stop bothering me, Ozie," Victor said. "Let me live my life."

The hexagon backed up a meter, revved its little motor, and zoomed forward into Victor's ankle. The pain was a sharp thwack. He kicked the robot hard and sent it skittering across the ground. It became wedged under a trailer tire.

He walked on, then stopped when he heard a shrieking baby's cry erupt from the robot's speaker, amazingly loud. A Lifer emerged from her trailer, a woman with long unbound hair, found the hexagon, and bent over. The baby's crying stopped, and Victor heard Ozie say something to her through the hexagon's speakers. The woman dislodged the robot, set it squarely on its treads, and went back inside, unconcerned.

Victor hurried away, and the little robot followed, Ozie's voice shouting after him, a message on repeat, "The wise owl listens and leaves before it's too late," over and over.

Victor left the camp through the main gate, hoping the gravel road would prove too difficult for the little robot, but it kept up with him. He left the road, hiking over marshy ground toward the dock. The robot couldn't navigate the terrain. It pushed into the reeds, couldn't make any headway, and didn't seem too smart about it. Maybe Ozie was no longer controlling it.

The kayak Victor chose was a slender black model and a bit unsteady in the water. He had to be careful not to pull too hard with the paddle or it might overturn. Even turning his head was risky. It didn't matter. His arms added to the current's flux, and soon the kayak was turning toward the Grand Canal and passing under the cantilevered arch of the Welcome to New Venice sign.

Victor was alone for the moment, but it was an illusion. Every day held a new demand or obligation, someone demanding he do this or that, see the reality of the situation, think about the consequences, do something, don't do something. He'd had enough. The Human Life camp was no longer a refuge for him. He couldn't go blank anymore, not now that he knew what they might do to him. The sex wasn't what he was worried about. He pictured a scene where he woke up from blankspace and found dozens of Human Lifers worshipping him like a live totem. Chanting, prayers, idolatry. He wished they would go back to their silly rituals of throwing away their possessions, which seemed so quaint and innocent compared to what they'd become—and so quickly.

There were very few watercraft today. Victor counted two gondolas and three paddleboats. Maybe it was a shopping day. Or maybe there was a festival down by the entertainment district. Perhaps he should check it out and then leave town for somewhere east, the Southeastern Confederacy or the Greater Ohio Constitutional League.

Victor ditched the kayak at a dock near the main plaza. If he was headed out of town, he would need to pick up snacks and clothes. As he climbed the steps, he heard a man's amplified voice. Were some of the Lifers protesting? He could detour, but it would take him blocks out of his way.

When he reached the top, he saw he didn't have anything to worry about. It wasn't the Lifers. A man on a stage flanked by the flags of New Venice, the Louisiana Territories, and the American Union spoke to a crowd of at least a hundred people seated in neat rows, fanning themselves while they listened.

Victor caught the final words of the man's speech—something generic about sticking together through tough times. Polite applause followed. Victor was nearing the perimeter of the plaza when he heard the man say he would answer questions.

"What are you going to do about the Lifers? They're clogging up the works."

Victor turned back. A sign low on the ground that had previously been blocked by the crowd read: Torsten Lund, Solutions for Everyone. Victor strayed closer. He spotted Alia sitting in the front row, looking up at her fiancé. Victor looked at the man again. He was handsome, but a bit too light-skinned for Victor's taste, with a square face, strong jawline, and wise but pretty eyes. He and Alia would make gorgeous babies if they planned to raise a family.

"It's an important question. New Venice has always been a place that welcomes visitors. I don't see that changing. You know I'm a believer in bringing people together to find solutions to common problems, so I think—"

"They don't want solutions," the man who asked the question interrupted.

A woman in the front row jumped up and said teasingly to Torsten, "Why don't you ask old Flo what we should do?"

The crowd laughed and let out a whoop of surprise. Torsten hung his head for a moment as if he were embarrassed and then raised it again, smiling broadly. "Because I don't want to get my ear chewed off," he said. There were a few chuckles.

A man in the back row just a few meters from Victor said, "We got an Eastmore right here. Maybe he's got something to say about it." Heads in the crowd turned. The man pointed at him. "Cleaning up after your friends' protest cost me a couple hundred dollars. I expect to be reimbursed."

Sweat trickled down Victor's back. The crowd seemed to expect a response.

Torsten stared at him with a territorial scowl for a few seconds; then his expression transformed into a smile as he said, "You all know we owe a great debt to the Eastmores, so of course we thank them as always." Heads were beginning to turn back toward the stage. Victor had the feeling he'd been let off the hook. Torsten continued, "I pledge to all of you to work on behalf of all the interests at stake and come up with a solution that keeps commerce freely flowing in New Venice. We can all agree that's our number one priority."

"You have to do something about the stim heads!" A woman with short-cropped salt-and-pepper hair stood in the front row. Her hands, holding a synthleather purse, twisted and squeezed as if she were trying to strangle it. "Two of them busted the window of my shop," she complained.

Two is good. You shouldn't worry about two, Victor thought. He laughed out loud. His brain was capable of the silliest things. A few of the townspeople looked at him and shook their heads.

Torsten leaned over, one foot on the stage, arms resting on his thigh, a pose Victor thought of as sexual—only clothes kept the man's genitals from dangling and his buttocks rearing up. He chuckled to himself picturing Alia's fiancé naked like that.

"Will you be quiet!" someone hissed at him.

"There's no doubt," Torsten said, "that we face a problem—"

"You bet it's a problem! They're sleeping in the park. I see a body on the ground, I'm going to check whether they're still breathing." The woman in front paused, her voice hoarse, choking on emotion. "Think of the children."

Victor covered his mouth and snickered. It wasn't right to laugh, but the woman was being so . . .

Alia stood, went over to the woman, and hugged her. Torsten pressed the sonocap on his lapel, and when he spoke, Victor couldn't hear the words, though he appeared to be asking Alia something. He pressed the button and said, "My fiancée would like to say a few words. Alia Effendi, everyone, my best lady, please give her a round of applause."

The crowd clapped as Alia ascended the stage. "We do face challenges with stims. I want to say a few words on behalf of BioScan. As many of you know . . ." Alia continued, describing plans to treat stim addicts and conduct research to help stem the epidemic. Victor listened more to the sound of her voice than the words. Everything she said was cogently persuasive. Yet words couldn't do justice to the melody she used, the variations in rhythm, slow, pensive elaborations quickening to staccato imperatives.

"We all have a responsibility," she said. "Whether it's providing shelter, donating your time or money, we need all the help we can get. There's no action too small, except to turn away and ignore the problem." Alia pinned her gaze on Victor when she said this.

He feared she'd read his mind. Why look at him at that moment? Then he realized it was his guilt crafting a delusion. Yes, he wanted to run away, to get as far from New Venice as he could. But she didn't know that.

And yet, delusion or not, she was calling on him to do something.

There's nothing I can do, he wanted to say. The Lifers have to figure out their own way.

Only they didn't seem competent any more. Their seeking seemed more like flailing for meaning, casting about for any belief that would sustain them until the next one. Intellectual vampire bats sucking faith dry.

Victor had influence. He knew their thinking, what they were planning. And they still respected him, still listened when he spoke, still wanted him to tell them the truth about blankspace.

There was no action too small.

Victor hurried to the edge of the plaza. He wouldn't leave town. Maybe Del could somehow regain control. Or maybe Tosh could be convinced to fade into the background. Or Wonda could work her magic and get the Lifers to redirect their energies toward helping stim addicts rather than Samuel Miller.

Victor was a block away when he heard a man's voice call, "Will you look at that!" He was standing and pointing to the sky.

A thrumming sound, like the beating wings of a hummingbird, grew. Victor craned his neck.

"There's hundreds of them!" the man shouted.

A crowd had started to gather along the railing. The sound of whirring blades filled the air.

Formations of dark black birds appeared to be moving across the clouded sky. He squinted. Drones. Hundreds of them, little copters shaped like hexagons.

Victor raced along the ledge, took a set of stairs up to the foot of one of the bridges over the Grand Canal, and crossed north. The copters were headed toward the Lifers' camp.

32

The only cure for misinformation is a savvy brain.

—BrAiNhAcKeR Collective

2 June 1991
New Venice, The Louisiana Territories

Victor watched along with other New Venetians as the swarm of drone copters veered in the direction of the Lifers' camp. He hailed an autocab, jumped in, punched the manual button, and placed his hands on the steering disk. He gunned the engine, but the car didn't move. Red lights on the dash flashed, and a voice intoned, "Hazard warning. Manual mode disengaged. Please enter a destination."

He banged his hands on the dash, breathed for a moment, and then spoke: "Lifers' camp."

"I do not know that location."

"Just take me to the foot of Ouachita Dam."

"Plotting a route. Please secure your safety belt."

"Argh!" Victor jammed the buckle in and pulled the belt tight.

"Beginning journey. Please sit back, relax, and enjoy the sights of New Venice."

"Hurry!" Victor shouted. The autocab didn't reply as it accelerated smoothly and slowly away from the curb.

Five minutes later, as soon as the autocab pulled over and stopped, Victor was out and slamming the door behind him. He jogged up the road, reached the gate to the Lifers' compound, which was open, and rushed inside. There didn't seem to be much hustle and bustle. The Lifers must be having post-lunch naps in their trailers. He headed to Wonda's. She never napped.

Yelling began somewhere near the pavilion. Victor changed direction, heading that way, but stopped when he saw a Lifer banging on a trailer and shouting, "It passed. The Classification Act passed. Head over to Pond Park. We're going to demonstrate." Lifers emerged from their trailers. Many carried little black backpacks that made Victor think of Tosh and tech from Las Vegas. One of the potentiates spotted Victor and veered toward him.

"Come on," she said. "It's time to make our voices heard."

"The Act passed? I thought they weren't even going to start discussions for a few weeks."

"That's what we thought. And then we saw the news." She handed him a MeshBit with a screen big enough to scroll through a few sentences at a time. At the top, in capital letters, was a tagline that didn't scroll. "MESH NEWS EDITOR ACCESS LEVEL DIAMOND," it read. Below was an official notice from the Louisiana Territories legislature describing the new Classification System going into effect at the end of the month. Victor's head swam as he read. The details didn't matter. He'd lost. He couldn't believe it.

"Where did you get this?" Victor asked.

"The drones. About a hundred of them dropped into camp and started wailing. They wouldn't stop until they were picked up, and then we saw the news. The politicians lied to us. They were never going to have a real debate about the Act. They planned on passing it all along."

"I don't think so," Victor said. The meetings at BioScan, the ones where Mía was trying so hard to change the outcome, those weren't just for show. "Something's not right."

"I'll say. Come on."

Victor let her lead him toward where the Lifers were assembling.

"What's going on?" Del was asking a few potentiates as they walked by. But no one would stop rushing around.

"Assemble at the pavilion!" Tosh's second chief Donya called. "We leave in ten minutes."

"Leave for where?" Del wondered aloud. He seemed out of breath, lost.

Victor joined the rush of bodies jogging down the lane.

Inside the pavilion, a buzz of angry words swirled like bees around a bear. The Lifers sounded ready to riot.

Victor arrived in the pavilion as one of the potentiates was describing the strategy for the demonstration. He listened in grim silence. There would be two prongs to the operation: a ground wing and a water wing.

The ground group would occupy Triton's Deep Crossing, blocking any pedestrians from using the bridge. Tourists from out of town would have to detour a whole kilometer to reach other bridges to the main part of town, or take buses to the smaller depot at the mouth of the Grand Canal, which would mean a long walk to the entertainment and shopping districts. Townies would be furious on behalf of their customers, Victor was sure.

The water group would assemble a flotilla underneath the bridge so that no watercraft could access the Pond. They would also blockade where the Petit and Grand Canals met. Diverted traffic would clog the smaller canals throughout town. It would be chaos.

Victor didn't think New Venetians would care much about the Lifers' demands for purity—"What does that really mean?" he'd heard more than a few townies ask—when their daily life was so fundamentally disrupted. Blocking access to one of their civic treasures was sure to get attention, most of it negative.

Within twenty minutes, the "marines," led by Tosh, were hiking to the upper Passage marina, where they would climb into kayaks and make their way to the Grand Canal. The "bridgers" group, led by Donya, assembled near the gate, waiting for a few of the Lifer vehicles to caravan in.

The Lifers chanted during the ride to the park. Victor, seated on a bench in the van, bent over with his face in his knees and hugged his shins. Anxiety rummaged in his bowels, and he sought calm by listening to the Lifers' cheerful, excited voices.

The plan for the demonstration was enacted in the space of five minutes—without Victor's participation. Victor watched from a park bench as, on both sides of the bridge, small groups of tourists or townspeople gathered, puzzled looks on their faces, pointing fingers and scratching heads as they tried to figure out how to reach their destinations.

Lisabella arrived and began talking to the Lifers standing guard at the foot of Triton's Deep Crossing. She recorded footage of New Venice falling under siege. Victor wondered how much her superiors at MeshNews would allow her to broadcast. He fed the ducks some bread he bought from a vendor.

Ten minutes later he spotted Mía and Pearl, both wearing purple-gray pantsuits, striding along Petit Canal's east embankment. They were leading a group of patients from the clinic wearing sad gowns the color of frozen salmon. Mía said something to Pearl, who corralled the group of patients, and then Mía approached Lisabella. The conversation grew heated; Mia pointed and stamped her foot. Several times Lisabella turned away, only to turn back seconds later to shout something.

Victor grew curious, took out his Handy 1000, and brought up a menu to display devices in his proximity. He found a few with the MN prefix, figuring those would be MeshNews and hoping Ozie's preloaded hacks could access them. Victor selected the first one and got a vidfeed of one of the Lifers. Lisabella was interviewing Wonda. Victor selected the next device on the list. The Handy 1000 went blank, and for a moment Victor wondered if it was the result of a counterhack. Then he heard Wonda's voice.

"We think it's time for purity to be considered a fundamental right," Wonda said.

Mía, in a slightly fainter voice, said, "You cannot present this fringe group as representative of what people want here. Look, we have here half a dozen recovering addicts who are benefiting from treatment at BioScan. Their stories are stories of recovery, of resilience, of—"

"Look, Ms. Barrias," Lisabella said, "I get it. Yes, I'd love to talk with them some other time. Look around you. This is the story. Adherents of a new ideology flexing their muscles. And a town torn apart by a madman whose horrific crimes they seem to have forgiven."

Victor turned off the Handy 1000 feed. They could discuss lunacy as much as they wanted. He wanted to put things right, but this was too big, too chaotic. What could he do? Nothing. He wasn't going to get involved.

Spoke too soon, he thought, as Mía headed over to him. He shouldn't have strayed from the group, he realized. It made him an easy target. Pearl followed behind. Their patients sat down on the grass nearby and watched the Lifers on the bridge.

"Make them stop," Mía demanded. "Hardliners in the LT Legislative Council will use this as an excuse to drop the amendments we proposed and pass a Classification Act identical to SeCa's. Go. They'll listen to you."

Victor gulped. He'd missed a lot by fleeing into blankness for a week, and now it was catching up to him.

He looked at the protesters, wishing he could hide in the crowd. There would be no room for his kayak with the marines, and the bridge was full of Lifer potentiates sitting and squatting, clogging it up. To join now, he'd have to get past Lisabella, and he sure didn't want to be all over the Mesh feeds.

"They're not harming anyone," Victor said. Not yet, he added silently. Tosh wasn't going to give up on his angle just because Victor called for restraint. Donya and the rest of his band of troublemakers patrolled the cityside embankment, making sure no one could get close to the bridge. He hoped the townies and tourists had enough sense not to mess with them. Otherwise there could be violence.

Mía fumed. "It's a spectacle. The MeshNews woman is going to catch the attention of the national government."

"Isn't that good?" Victor asked. "Don't you want the spotlight on MRS? To build support for Classification?"

"Not like this. We had an agreement with MeshNews, a plan. Now that's out the window because they'll be reporting real news."

"As opposed to the news you planned to manufacture together," Victor said. "Good riddance."

The wind changed directions. The chanting marines' voices could be heard echoing off the bridge's stone underbelly. "Hey hey ho ho, compulsory meds have got to go."

"People are laughing at them," Pearl noted, "saying they're crazy for worshipping a killer."

"They're not worshipping him," Victor explained. "He's a test of their faith. If they can mobilize for him, it's a sign of their righteousness."

Mía asked, "How can you be on their side?"

"I'm just telling you what I understand about them," he said. "I'm not on anyone's side."

"Little owl," Pearl said, "If you—"

"Stop, okay? I've had enough of people telling me what to do."

"We tried," Mía said to Pearl. "I'll go tell Circe it's time for Plan B."

"Right. I'll see you in a bit," Pearl said.

Mía left them. Victor wondered if she would be shaking her head all the way back to the administration building.

Pearl sat down next to Victor.

"You don't have to look after me," he said.

"Maybe I enjoy spending time with you. There's so little time in the end." Her tone was somehow wistful and grim at the same time. "Tosh told me what Jefferson told you."

She looked at him. He could feel her gaze like a cloying fragrance trying to drag him by the nose to face her. He stared at the ducks jostling each other, swarming bread bits, not wanting to get too close to the hand that fed them.

"What I want you to know," Pearl said, speaking clearly and crisply for a change, "is that life is not binary. You don't have to choose between this and that, right and wrong, allegiance to one side or another. You don't have to struggle with not knowing whether to believe Jefferson or your aunt. You can accept the doubt. You can be at peace in the now, the beautiful, complicated, blossoming now. You understand?"

He noticed the lines on her face, countless folds around her mouth and eyes. Her hair was grayer than he remembered, and her eyes were bright behind big, round, amber-tinted glasses. Ember-red warmth radiated from her and maybe also blue-tinged resignation.

"I want to believe it's not my fight," he said flatly. "That none of this is."

Pearl patted his knee. "Perhaps not. I just thought it might help you to see it my way." She stood, theatrically brushing her sleeves. There was a dignity to her short stature, he decided, that most tall people lacked. She said, "I'll be going now."

"Where to?" he asked.

"I have a cottage in Carmichael. I think it's time to put it on the market. And then I'll see. Good-bye, Victor."

Pearl walked through the crowd of ducks, her shuffling steps causing them to clear a path, and headed toward the bridge. Victor watched as she slowly picked her way through the crowd of seated Lifers, stopping to chat several times as she made the ascent and then vanished from view.

He should be sitting with the Lifers. His influence over them was already fading. It wasn't helping that he was a spectator today rather than a participant. But he couldn't bring himself to sit in the midst of a crowd chanting to help Samuel Miller. The thought sent a shiver up his spine. If only there was a way to get them to pursue a more worthy goal.

A black van with "Sheriff" emblazoned on the side in gold block letters pulled into the parking lot along with several white vans. Men and women in riot gear began to emerge. They stood around, drank coffee, threw their cups on the ground, hoisted equipment over their shoulders and into their utility belt pouches—face shields, heavy looking air cannons, and canisters of sleeping gas. More vans arrived. The enforcers' numbers swelled past fifty, outnumbering the Lifers, but not by much.

Victor was running through things he could say to the Lifers when Del walked up and jabbed a finger into Victor's chest. His whole body was shaking.

"You did this!" he said. "You and your blank face. We were a calm congregation before you arrived."

"I didn't say anything important," Victor replied. The man's anger was visceral, sharp, as if spikes grew from his skin and clothes, and when he shook, he bristled like a porcupine.

"'I didn't say. I didn't do,'" Del said, mocking Victor's voice. "A curse on you! I'll have nothing more to do with this buffoonery."

Del stared down the Lifers who were listening to the discussion, some wearing concerned expressions, others looking amused.

Victor said, "I met you protesting. How is this any different?"

"You watch!" Del said, his voice oozing scorn. "We held peaceful gatherings. We stayed true to our beliefs. They'll follow you over the edge of a cliff, and I can only thank the laws I've come to my senses before everyone jumps."

He stalked away, kicking up a trail of dust as he went.

The operation to remove the Lifers began with the bridge wing, higher ground being most important to any battle. Victor knew that much from Ozie's many rants about the history of warfare. Gravity itself turned out to be a weapon that losing forces often failed to anticipate and wield.

Ten at a time, enforcers approached the foot of the bridge on the east side of Pond Park. There would be a scuffle as the Lifers linked arms and attempted to stop the enforcers from removing the seated protesters. The enforcers would pry one or two protestors from the group, handle them roughly, bind their ankles and wrists, and haul them through the park to one of the vans. The spectacle repeated itself over and over again, slowly eating away at the fringes of the sit-in.

It all appeared to be going smoothly, a raucous affair if not a violent one.

Then the Lifers from higher up on the bridge began to throw things at the enforcers, nothing too heavy or damaging, pill bottles mostly, all the while jeering "Fascist!" and "Freedom dies when speech falls silent!"

One of the escorted Lifers, a woman, screamed, "Pure is power!" over and over again. When she got closer, Victor saw it was one of Tosh's faction, Donya, the one who'd been so concerned about where Victor sat in the pavilion. As they passed by, she turned toward him, screaming the same mantra. Blood streamed down from the top of her shaved head, coating half her face.

As dusk set in, light towers turned on, humming, the sound mostly lost in the din of protesters' shouts of "Free Samuel Miller!" and "Stop the Classification Act!"

A group of New Venetians on the opposite side of the canals, the city side, were singing a tune Victor recognized from childhood, the city anthem, about water feeling like home. He supposed it was a counterprotest by the native gentry who understood how important BioScan was to the region's economy and who didn't really care one way or the other about a mass murderer's medical treatment.

A flurry of movement on the bridge caught Victor's attention. The Lifers were standing, putting on masks with exaggerated features, long noses, pointy chins, mouths agape in silent screaming mirth, an old Venetian design. "For purity!" someone called, and Victor thought he recognized Tosh's hoarse shout.

The Lifers rushed down the tri-bridge, in three groups, one toward town and one toward each side of Pond Park. The marine wing's flotilla started breaking up, their kayaks dislodging from one another, maneuvering to escape up the Grand Canal.

Several dozen Lifers charged the enforcers and knocked them down, freeing two of their own. Surging through the park, the Lifers had the enforcers on the defensive.

Several potentiates broke away, sprinted to Victor, hauled him to standing, and then he was jogging with them along the north side of the Grand Canal. "Don't forget you're human!" they shouted. "Free is free! No human left behind."

Someone screamed, a long wailing sob. "Let me go," a woman said over and over.

Victor turned and saw the Lifers that had descended toward town being surrounded by members of the counter-protest. They outnumbered the Lifers three to one. Townies shouted at them, grabbed their robes and shook them, reminding Victor of sheets on a line flapping in the wind. The crowd took hold of a man, pale skin whitened to almost match his robe, and tossed him into the canal. The splash seemed to ignite the townies' imaginations. Robed figures were hauled up Triton's Deep and tossed over the side. Lifers in kayaks paddled out of the way.

Victor broke free of the Lifers trying to haul him away from the scene and descended the embankment. He found an emergency box, one of the bins located every hundred meters alongside the canal that held first aid kits, floating foam rings, and rope. He took a foam ring, tied on one end of the rope, and jogged to where Lifers were flailing in the water, trying to stay afloat and struggling to overcome the weight of their drenched robes. He flung the ring in a high arc as far out into the canal as he could and tightened his grip on the rope, ready to pull.

"Grab on," he yelled.

For a moment, he felt out of body, watching himself from above—the rope, the figures in the water—and then he felt a tug in his hands as one of the Lifers grabbed onto the floating ring, and he began to pull, one hand at a time, the rope digging into his palms, his feet pressing into the cobblestones. He watched the rope moving between his hands. He didn't dare make eye contact with whomever he was saving. The panic, fear, and relief in the Lifer's eyes would shunt Victor toward blankspace in no time, and he couldn't afford to go there right now. A few other Lifers saw what Victor was doing and found more floating rings and rope.

The enforcers, having regained control of the situation, had reached the bridge and were descending townside. No more bodies were tossed in the water. It looked as if both Lifers and townies were being shackled.

Time to go, Victor thought, pulling the last person from the water. Somehow Wonda was already at his side. She grabbed his hand, and they jogged up the embankment, past the botanical garden, only slowing when they were screened by trees and bushes that stood indifferent to the chaos bordering the park.

"They're arresting everyone!" Wonda said. She didn't sound angry, only surprised and perhaps impressed.

Victor remained silent as they hiked back to the Lifer camp. The Lifers had to see that Samuel wasn't worth fighting for, and it was up to Victor to show them.

33

The 1935 Reykjavik Declaration ended the war between Europe on one side and the United States of America, the Nordic League, and Russia on the other. The terms of the peace agreement included reparations that soon drained the U.S. Treasury and caused the country to default on its international debt obligations.

Over the next few election cycles, an opposition movement came into power that demanded a devolution of powers to the states. Territories that had long been denied statehood, including lands stretching from the Rocky Mountains to the Pacific, asserted their right to self-determination. Those cries for local autonomy were echoed across the South and Midwest.

A grand bargain was proposed to repartition existing states and territories and to transfer most powers and lands from the federal government to nine new nations of the American Union. The new AU constitution and those of the nine nations were ratified in 1939.

—"The Grand Bargain: Repartition" (MeshKnows article)

9 June 1991

New Venice, The Louisiana Territories

Lifers at the end of the lane were dismantling a fence. Two within Victor's earshot discussed which piece of land outside the camp they'd claim as their own. More trailers would arrive soon. It was a boom time in the Lifer camp, thanks to the agreement reached between the Lifers, BioScan, and the New Venetian Consultative Body for Residents and Merchants.

When the sheriff's enforcer vans showed up two days ago, there had been a tense moment. The Lifers seemed ready to call for weapons. Then the van doors opened, and the protesters who'd been arrested emerged free people—another concession. The vans departed, and the whole camp celebrated.

Torsten Lund had negotiated the detente. "Peace and prosperity for all are our touchstones," he said. BioScan—in desperate need of space to house patients and addicts and eager to calm tensions and not at all reluctant to co-opt a grassroots movement—would pay Lifers to expand their camp and play host to addicts. Lifers wouldn't protest anywhere except Pond Park and wouldn't interfere with tourists in transit. The residents and merchants could return to business as usual. Everybody won.

But when word spread that their last protest was based on faulty information conveyed by Ozie's air-dropped MeshBits—the Classification Act had not been passed; in fact, there had not yet been a vote—the Lifers were disillusioned. They felt duped. Their fellows had been arrested for nothing, Samuel Miller remained medicated, and the truce began to look more like a buyout.

Wonda defended the truce, saying it was a step forward on the path to purity. She worked hard to get their hearts back in the fight, holding three well-attended readings per day from *Theories of Emergence* by Estrella Burgos. Everyone could see that Wonda had emerged as the leader of a faction that was gaining strength by stealing members from both Del's do-nothing conservatives and Tosh's armed radicals.

The philosophy she espoused boiled down to "Let's treat each day like a fresh start," but that folksy, we're-all-in-this-together rhetoric masked a zeal for being in charge. Victor could see it in the way her eyes shone whenever she laid down a new tenet of faith, the latest being that dreams and blankspace pronouncements all amounted to the spirit of the universe speaking to us.

Victor had started to wish he had a mute button, both for the spirit and for Wonda.

He still thought about leaving town, but Circe had come to him and begged him to stay and help keep the peace. "I'll tell you everything," she'd said, "once we pass through the crucible." He knew he shouldn't believe her promises, shouldn't let himself be manipulated by her. He should get as far away as possible. But the thought of finally putting the mystery of Granfa's death to rest was too attractive to pass up, and he couldn't just walk away. Part of him felt responsible for what was going on with the Lifers. He'd begun to suspect that he was the source of a psychic infection, causing them to subscribe to ridiculous beliefs, that he'd unlocked some deep vulnerability in their minds. He knew consciously such an idea was utterly delusional. And yet . . .

He was rousted from his thoughts by Wonda's excited voice. "They've seen our power, and they know they can't ignore us anymore."

"What about the Classification Act and Samuel Miller?" a young male Lifer complained. "There's nothing about them in the agreement."

"We're not giving up," Wonda said. "He's still our priority number one. Right, Tosh?"

Tosh nodded, the small gesture carrying outsized weight. His group trailed hers in numbers, but it dwarfed Del's, who only commanded a handful of old timers. What Tosh's group lacked in numbers, though, it made up for in aggression.

Victor watched the Lifers with their hammers, saws, cement mixers, and welders, expanding their little village at the foot of the Oauchita Dam. Why would people choose to live in these makeshift accommodations? Was their prior situation so bad that this seemed like an improvement? It didn't make sense to Victor.

He'd spoken with a man yesterday, a stocky bald guy with a beard and a hairy chest—he never seemed to wear a shirt. He described his hundred-square-meter home in Oklahoma City—"four bedrooms, four bathrooms, and a pool!"—the decent salary he'd earned as a court administrator, and his active sports life as a catch-and-carry captain. Then the man's wife discovered stims and left him for an addict.

Victor thought about telling the man to go track down his wife, get her some help, and rebuild his life. But the man seemed happy. He'd wanted a new start for years, he said. This was his chance to begin again, focus on the things that mattered, do something real. He was sharing a trailer with Donya, and it was great, he said, though he wasn't a gynophile—he was a duo. He put a hand on Victor's hip and winked.

Now the hairy shirtless man was helping dismantle the fence. They would reuse the material, reconfigure the borders, and create a bigger Lifer camp with more room for refugees from the materialist fantasy world, as the man called it. We're living in tune with the spirits now, he said.

And people said Victor had delusions.

Each of the Lifers seemed to be living in a bubble of hot illogical air of their own creation. It was up to Victor to find a way to pop them all at the same time.

Victor had left twenty minutes of messages full of curses for Ozie. The feeds on the MeshBits dropped by the drones had been clever distortions of the truth, enough fact to appear plausible—the legislative summary of the Classification Act was real, but it hadn't been passed yet. The Lifers weren't going to trust anything on MeshNews now, so Victor's access to Lisabella was worthless. He couldn't change their minds that way. Besides, Wonda's word was the law of the land. The Lifers didn't seem to care about Victor's opinions any more. They only wanted to talk about Samuel.

Victor sent a message to Karine: *I have an idea to stop the Lifers.*

She replied with an address and instructions: *Meet me in ten minutes.*

Soon Victor spotted Karine in front of a four-story stone building near the main shopping area that looked like a medieval castle. He rushed over and said to her, "We film Samuel at his craziest."

She frowned, puckering her lips the way she did when considering new ideas. "I'll want to hear more after."

"After what?"

The front door of the building swung open. A tall man in a crimson velour vest peeked out, saw Karine and Victor, and smiled. "Welcome," he said. "I'll give you the tour."

As the proprietor let Victor and Karine inside, all three had to duck their heads to avoid the low stone-arched doorways. "We'll have to pad those," Karine said under her breath. Further in, the interior didn't look much cheerier. Lightstrips affixed to the ceiling didn't quite exorcise the gloom that came with narrow corridors and small rooms. The proprietor said it had been designed with tourists in mind who wanted a taste of ancient living.

"What are you doing here?" Victor whispered.

"We need an option in case our deal with the Lifers falls through."

As soon as construction was finished on campus, there would be ample housing. Until then, they had to make use of what was available. The Qaddo tribe declined to help—though they had ample land, they had ill will toward the Eastmores. "Maybe in another hundred years they will have forgiven us," Circe had said cryptically. They were left with in-town housing as the only backup.

"But why are *you* looking into it?"

Karine looked around. The proprietor had left the room. "Circe is driving me batty," she said quietly. "I thought she'd be back in Cologne by now, but she won't leave until the Lifer problem is resolved. I needed fresh air." Her face was flushed with embarrassment. She was being honest, and the look on her face wasn't unfamiliar. How much of Victor's dislike of her had been from his misplaced suspicion?

The proprietor returned, and after he showed them several more identically stuffy rooms, he smiled broadly and said, "What do you think?"

Karine said the accommodations would be sufficient, on a temporary basis, and asked for the lease documents.

The proprietor nodded and said, "I'm glad to do business with the Eastmores. I have no hard feelings about it, but . . ."

Victor sensed that Karine was restraining herself from rolling her eyes.

"Let me guess," Karine said. "The rental will put you in a difficult situation. Is it the Lifers or—"

"I don't give a rat's ass about a lunatic cult. Sorry, son," he said with a quick apologetic glance at Victor, who wasn't sure exactly what the man was sorry about, but he understood facing difficult choices. "It's the merchants. They're afraid of insufficient rooming capacity in town. Word is BioScan is taking so many buildings off the market, there'll be nowhere for coin-spending visitors to stay."

"It's a temporary measure," Karine said.

"I understand that. And people will put up with a lot of grief if they can see a light at the end of the tunnel. But folks are afraid this is going to hit them in their pocketbooks. Things tend to get a bit feisty around here when it comes to money."

"You said this isn't necessarily your concern?" Karine used a light-hearted tone Victor associated with her at her most cunning and cold-blooded.

The proprietor smiled, and for a moment Victor hallucinated that he had a shining gold tooth, which had to be the funniest trick his brain had played in a long time. He grinned back.

"I'm sure I'll do just fine," the proprietor said. "I appreciate you visiting in person. It seems BioScan can afford to be generous. I'd be happy to speak up in its defense at the next merchant council meeting. How about I send over the documents to you this afternoon?"

"We'd appreciate it," Karine said, with a falsely cheering enthusiasm.

When Victor and Karine had said their good-byes, left the building, and rounded a corner to look out onto the Grand Canal and its colorful traffic of kayaks and casino boats, he finally let out the laughter he'd been stifling.

"What's so amusing?" Karine asked.

"Something Granma Cynthia always says. 'Money can't make you friends, but it sure can make people friendly.'"

Karine didn't quite smile, though the corner of her mouth ticked up. "Making people friendly is going to cost the company more than we budgeted for. My father used to tell me a fool and his money are soon parted. Let's try to put a lid on our collective foolishness."

"You ask me," Victor said, "I don't think we should spend a dime on the Lifers."

"For once, Victor, I agree with you, but the decision has been made. Now, you wanted to tell me about a plan for Samuel?"

As they crossed Triton's Deep and walked along the Petit Canal, Victor told her his plan, using a low voice so passersby wouldn't overhear. "They're obsessed with the idea of us forcibly medicating Samuel. What if we let them see what's he like off the meds? I think ranting and raving Samuel might be too much for them."

"An interesting idea. You said something about filming him?"

"Yes. We've been putting out those sanitized bits of him via MeshNews when he's calm and lucid. We need to flip the script. Show him at his worst."

She stopped under the shade of a tree. "I don't like what happened last time we reduced his dosage."

"Me neither, believe me. It would only be temporary. He's secure in the drug hut. I don't believe in any psychic infection."

Her eyebrows arched. "Don't take this the wrong way, but you impress me, Victor. I don't think I've ever seen you this grounded."

Victor blushed. "Thank you. I—I'm sorry for everything that's happened."

"There's no sense dwelling on it. Come on." She began walking toward BioScan. "The sooner we start, the sooner it'll be over."

34

Looking back, we can see the path we walked by our footsteps in the sand. We remember the feeling of our toes digging in, wet and squishy, pedestrian.

What would we be without memory? Without sight? Perhaps a bird that has never known flight.

Emergence asks us to be present and to experience the "now," but what must we give up for that privilege and how?

—Estrella Burgos's *Theories of Emergence* (1906)

13 June 1991
New Venice, The Louisiana Territories

"They put me in chains. I'm not entirely sober," Samuel said. He held up his hands, which were now manacled together.

"You're not an addict," Victor replied. "You're on medication."

Samuel was being given mild doses of Personil, about half of the hammer-down mind-wiping dose he'd been taking when he first arrived in New Venice, but more than the nothing and herbs that had brought back his delusions.

Victor set the Handy 1000 on the table, where he could view the feed. A vidcapper mounted on a short tripod pointed toward Samuel. The resolution was decent. The zoom provided a close-up view. The Lifers would be able to see the various illogic tics and emotional earthquakes passing over Samuel's face. They needed to understand the depths of Samuel's passion for killing so they could disavow him and make more reasonable demands. Victor would show them the interview personally, one by one if necessary.

Barring that? If that didn't persuade them? Then the Lifers would need to be neutralized some other way.

"You need your medication, don't you?" Victor said to Samuel. The sonobulb captured his voice, but he was staying out of the vidcapper's viewfield. He had no desire to costar in anything with Samuel.

"It doesn't stop the voices," Samuel said. "I see the primals now no matter what. Thanks to you. The veil is thin. Why can't we cross over?" His voice sounded like a plaintive, deranged song, the kind that would make parents hustle their kids across the street to avoid the person singing it.

"Why do you want to cross over?" Victor asked.

"Why do you want to stay? We're in purgatory! This isn't real." Samuel fidgeted on the couch, twisting his fingers, clapping his knees together, trapping his hands, moving in fits and jerks. "We're in the ghost world. I've explained it before. Our bodies are disconnected. We're meat bags, ghosts without our primals. They're what's real!"

"The dose of Personil you're receiving is about half of the recommended amount for someone with your severity of symptoms. BioScan is under pressure to stop prescribing Personil completely. Is that what you want?"

Samuel looked at Victor, eyes narrowed, silently.

"Do you want to be on Personil?" Victor demanded.

"No, I don't want to be on Personil. I want to cross over."

"Tell me how to cross over."

Samuel's eyes lit up. "The wave function collapses," he said, his voice a reasonable approximation of a teacher excited to share some terribly interesting fact with students. "You set up a stun stick, lethal force, with a quantum trigger. The wave function collapses, or it doesn't. It collapses here, but not there. You live on there. In the primals' world."

Murder by gadgetry. This interview was going well.

"I can show you." Samuel grinned. He probably thought he was being coy. Victor shuddered. The look on Samuel's face—this same look—was the last thing some people had seen.

"Like you showed the people in Carmichael? Hundreds died."

"They crossed over."

"All of them?"

Samuel looked down, bit his lip, and shook his head slowly. "That was the price. I planned and planned to achieve the optimal ratio." He looked up at Victor, a kind a pleading puppy beg.

Victor looked away.

"In any kind of chaos, there are more variables than can be managed. I built as many quantum triggers as I could. The gas incapacitated the majority, giving me time with the shockstick. But I couldn't afford anyone escaping, so I reprogrammed the autocabs. The crossover target rate was 60 percent. It was the best I could do."

Victor had long abhorred the twisted logic that fueled the Carmichael Massacre. He'd tried to avoid reading the voluminous SeCa MeshNews reports that circulated every year on the anniversary, but people spoke eagerly of the macabre details, especially as time went on and the raw wound of Carmichael crusted over.

Victor cleared his throat. "Do you want to help me cross over?" he asked.

"You told me to do it. You did! It was your voice." Samuel whipped his head around, snarling, and lunged. The manacles around his feet stretched taut as he tripped and fell.

That delusion again. Putting the blame on someone else. Classic psychosis.

"Will you help me cross over, Samuel?" Victor asked.

"I'll kill you!"

Victor stopped the recording. "Good," he said. "Now tell me again how to make a shockstick lethal."

"You see?" Victor asked.

He looked around to make sure the Lifers gathered in the pavilion were viewing the vidscreen, an older model with a stylized plastic frame that looked like bamboo.

The sonofeed was muted as the vidscreen showed Samuel pacing in front of his drawings, gesturing frantically to a vortex of colors, and spouting nonsense about crossing over.

Victor said, "He doesn't understand the difference between life and death."

"We understand that he's sick," Wonda said. She stood at the front of the group. "I want to find the right path forward. This is a test. Remember what Del told us about tests."

Victor had no idea what Del had said about tests. Del hadn't left his trailer in two days. He seemed to be opting out of whatever the Lifers were becoming.

"It's not about Samuel," Wonda said, pointing to the vidscreen. "It's about whether we have the courage to help people like him despite our misgivings."

"The courage to stand around and talk? Or the courage to take action?" This came from Donya, who now had a bandage on her head.

"That's not the point," Victor said, looking at Donya and then at Wonda. "If you want to build support for the Lifer movement, you have to put on a better face. This"—he pointed at a still-frame pic of Samuel's snarling face—"isn't going to cut it. The Classification Act—the horrible punitive SeCa version without amendments—is going to pass unless you can get the public on your side. I'll help you, but only if you stop insisting that Samuel doesn't need meds."

Wonda closed her eyes for a moment, no doubt seeking guidance on her path and how to navigate its twists and turns. Victor wondered what voices she heard and if they were anything like the ones that drove Samuel to madness.

"We want to talk to him," Wonda said. "That's the only way to know what he needs, what's really going on. Then we'll pool our knowledge. We'll find a creative solution."

"What if the solution doesn't make anyone happy?" Victor asked.

She smiled at him. "Someone always wins, and failure can be as illuminating as victory."

Wonda seemed able to turn any setback into a victory with a gush of enthusiasm. If they could hook her to a generator, she'd probably put out more power than Ouachita Dam. What could he do to stop her?

Victor set the feed on auto-replay, spiked the volume, and left the pavilion, taking the controller with him. If they wanted to turn off the feed, they'd have to smash the display to pieces.

35

> We should not blame our adversaries for resisting change. They are the fuel on which our engines run.
>
> —Jefferson Eastmore's *The Wheel of Progress* (1989)

15 June 1991
New Venice, The Louisiana Territories

"There's no truce," Victor said.

He stood with Alia a few steps inside Karine's office, where Circe had commandeered the high-backed ripe-strawberry-red synthleather chair behind the desk. Karine, meanwhile, leaned against the wall, biting her lips, looking as if she'd rather be anywhere else.

"You gave them hope," he said. "I don't know what they're planning, but they're not going to stop."

Karine made a fingerburst near her ear. "Then we'll withhold the payments we agreed to make in exchange for housing stimheads. We have the leverage now."

"Money isn't everything in this case," Circe said. "They have faith."

"I hope they choke on it," Karine said.

Victor said, "If we can show the Lifers how unworkable their demands are, maybe they'll find a different cause. They want to talk to Samuel. Some of them are gearing up for a fight. Some want nothing to do with any of this. *I* want nothing to do with this."

"I do think it would be best if we took the lead from here, Victor. It would be better if you stayed out of it," Karine said.

Circe appeared to consider this, her head cocking as if listening to something—music? her gut, maybe? voices?—then she shook her head. "I disagree. There's still a chance Victor can help divert their attention." She looked pointedly at Karine. "We should never have brought Samuel here. That was a poor choice."

There was a moment when Victor thought Karine's head might explode; then her mouth opened and closed like pressure releasing from a valve. She appeared to regain her composure and folded her arms across her chest, a wry smile on her lips. She said, "Who could have predicted he would become someone's messiah?"

"They do seem taken with him. And with Victor," Alia added. She'd been silent, observing. How much of the tense blame-shifting relationship between Circe and Karine was obvious to her? "Torsten said Victor swayed them more than once during the negotiations."

"Indeed," Circe said, her expression inscrutable.

"If we could be done talking about me . . ." Victor said.

Alia continued, "A few of them are less rigid about the prohibitions against medicine. Especially when someone falls ill. I hear a lot of them struggling to reconcile their faith with their conscience. From what I understand, a lot of them simply want things to settle down. It seems that it really is the question of what to do with Samuel Miller that is tearing this town apart."

"That's power," Circe mused. Karine and Alia exchanged alarmed looks. Circe didn't seem to notice. "Everyone is so concerned about him, and here we are grappling with what to do . . ."

"Can we send him back to SeCa?" Victor asked. A lump formed in his throat, remembering how his family had often discussed what to do with Victor after he was diagnosed, as if he were a burden they'd be happy to pass on.

"I'm afraid there's no appetite for that in the governor-general's office. Besides, it would make us all look like fools," Karine said.

"What about the OWS?" Victor suggested. "Make a deal with the King."

Circe looked at Victor, eyes narrowed, but when she spoke, there were hints of admiration in her voice. "That's not a bad suggestion."

Karine examined her fingernails. "I can't imagine what would be done with him."

"It's not our concern," Victor said. "Alia, what do you think?"

"It's wrong," she said immediately, forcefully. "The King has been responsible for hundreds of disappearances over the last thirty years. No one even really knows what he looks like. But it might be our only option."

"Let's explore that option," Circe said. It wasn't a suggestion, Victor could tell; it was a command. "In the meantime, let's set up this meeting with Samuel the Lifers are asking for. The facts are on our side in this case. Let's use them to our advantage."

Mía knocked on the open door. Her neck was flushed. "Good news," she said, holding up a sheaf of papers. "The prime councilor of the Louisiana Territories agreed to the two-speed Classification rules."

"What are those?" Victor asked.

Karine rolled her eyes and said, "Excuse me, this company won't run itself." She breezed past Mía, saying, "Nice work."

"We went back to the drawing board," Circe said, "on how we would identify potential patients. Mía can explain. If you don't mind?" She raised her eyebrows, and it was clear to Victor she meant, *Mía can explain elsewhere; I've got work to do.*

Alia returned to her rounds, and Victor was left standing with Mía in the hallway. "How about some fresh air?" she said.

They left the administration building and walked to Little Lock, where the Petit Canal emptied into the Passage. A group of paddleboats and kayaks waited as the water drained. The lock gates swung open, and they headed into the open water.

"Two-speed Classification rules?" Victor prompted.

Mía said, "A new set of amendments. We never really came to grips with what the stim epidemic meant for the

Classification System in SeCa. We're working on that now, and your aunt is trying to start out on a better foot in the LTs. First, there aren't going to be multiple classes. People are either Classified or not. Those with the mirror resonance syndrome genetic marker may receive therapy and medication, voluntarily. They will only be Classified—i.e., be admitted to the clinic—if they pose a reasonable danger to themselves or others, that is, if they show severe symptoms. Once they're Classified, they'll be our patients until they're deemed fit to leave. The other way someone will be classified is if they test positive for stims. They'll be enrolled in the substance abuse program and released when they're done. So that's it, two speeds for two distinct, though related, problems."

Two again, Victor thought, *the number that returns with the regularity of a metronome, tick tock, one two.*

"Huh," Victor said, trying to sort through the implications of a two-speed system in his own mind. "The way you describe it, Classification sounds temporary, like—"

"Like any other medical malady requiring treatment. Yes, I know. It's a huge improvement. The Lifers should be happy."

A red-hot flash coursed through Victor's body, heating his cheeks. "I don't think the Lifers will see this as much of an improvement, but I don't care. Shock them. It's a better approach. Thank you."

Mía's eyes fluttered and moistened. She nodded. "It means a lot to hear you say that. I wanted to make sure . . . You know how I feel about what happened in SeCa."

"I know," he said. "We're trying to do better here." He took her hand and held it, while they watched the lock cycle, water filling up, water draining, not as majestic or as instantly gratifying as ocean waves rolling ashore, but good enough, all things considered.

"The Act will pass soon," Mía said. "But the facilities here won't be completed for eighteen months. We need to keep the Lifers on board—we need their land and their silence, or, at least, their compliance. You have to stop them from focusing on Samuel Miller. If you have any pull with them left, now is the time to use it."

36

The Mesh's strength is redundancy, multiple possible paths for transmitting information. Unlike a network, which is only as secure as its weakest link, knocking out a Mesh node has little effect.

To control a mesh you have to have a pervasive, invisible architecture of surveillance that controls content and dynamically determines user access privileges. Why do you think most people don't buy MeshBits with cameras? The limiting factor isn't technology. It's fear of surveillance.

—Osirus Smythe's "Data Isn't Free," an unpublished term paper

15 June 1991
New Venice, The Louisiana Territories

Victor was called to the administration building by an urgent message on his Handy 1000. A mix of people outside were holding signs and chanting. The group in front wore white Lifer robes. They were followed by townies in normal working clothes, complaining loudly about Lifers straying from their designated protest area in Pond Park. Stragglers were visible crossing the bridge over the Petit Canal.

Victor quickly spotted Wonda at the front and went over to her. He said, "This was supposed to be a meeting, not a rally."

"I know!" she said. Her eyes were round as she surveyed the crowd. "We decided to walk through town, in case—I don't know. We thought there might be a few people interested in participating. I wasn't expecting this!"

"You brought signs," Victor said. "It looks like a protest."

A voice called out from nearby: "Exactly! They agreed to stop the protests!"

"Free Samuel Miller!"

"Shock Samuel Miller!"

The crowd traded jeers.

"Please!" Wonda shouted, climbing onto a bench. "We're here to speak with BioScan and to find a resolution. We need everyone to remain calm and be patient. Thank you!" She smiled her big, excited, naive smile, and it actually seemed to work. The crowd quieted. Then the clinic doors opened, and the crowd's chanting immediately resumed. "Human Life!" was the current refrain.

Alia emerged from the administration building and stood at the top of the steps. "We would like to speak with you, but please lower your voices. This is a clinic, and there are patients in treatment here. *Please*."

The chanting continued and seemed ready to continue into the afternoon when another voice leapt from the crowd: "Let her speak."

"Let's hear what she has to say," Wonda said, still smiling.

A tall, blond woman with a piercing voice yelled, "Let's hear her response to our demands."

"What demands?"

Confusion broke out among the crowd. Many members seemed to be unsure what the demands were and which negotiating tactics they were meant to be supporting.

Alia shouted, "While I want to move our conversation forward, we must respect the needs of patients who rely on the clinic for their health. Is there anyone who needs to proceed inside?"

Two hands went up in the back as a young couple began to move forward. Their immediate neighbors in the crowd shrank back and made way. A middle-aged woman standing toward the side also raised her hand and moved toward Alia, who beckoned her to come.

An old woman said, "First time I've ever had to wait to be seen." The crowd made way. Victor recognized his great-grandmother Florence Eastmore being supported by her caretaker, Charlene. "Surprised I haven't keeled over dead just listening to all this prattle. Can someone save my life, or do I have to do it myself?"

One of the nurses, aided by Charlene, led Florence inside. She seemed to be concentrating on each step and didn't see Victor when she passed him.

Alia continued in a more pleasant tone, "Now, we have scheduled an open house for this Saturday, and you are all welcome to attend. We will be happy to discuss our research projects and any concerns related to them or to our health services. You are free to stay here and continue demonstrating, as long as you don't harass any patients or staff, but please know this: I hear you. I do. I understand. I've worked at this clinic for the past five years, and I know everyone who works here shares the same respect and passion for helping people. Thank you."

There were a few claps of appreciation as she hopped down from the bench and approached Victor. "The Lifers can bring twelve people to the meeting. We'll escort them through the clinic when they're ready." She went inside.

Several BioScan staff members came outside and passed out flyers and pamphlets, enthusiastically inviting members of the crowd, including those with robes, to come to the community meeting. The Human Life die-hards had regrouped and lined up on either side of the steps, not protesting but making their presence known. They began singing. Victor caught snippets of lyrics about nature and souls. They seemed determined to push their luck, and he wondered when Circe and the townies would stop making concessions.

Victor told Wonda, "Choose eleven people to come with you and meet me at the entrance." He started toward the building.

Tosh rushed over and blocked his way. "I'm coming," he said.

Victor shrugged. “You two and ten others. We talk to Samuel Miller, and everyone gets what they want, okay?” he said, not believing a word of it.

37

> Look at the lilies,
> how water buoys them, or
> how the lilies feast on the pond.
> Belief is a weapon that vanquishes truth.
>
> —Ming Pearl's *Now Blossom* (1973)

15 June 1991
New Venice, The Louisiana Territories

The drug hut was stuffed with BioScan staff and Lifers. Karine, Alia, Marilyn, Blair, and Mía, in their executive-cut clothes, looked like mannequins in a shop for drab people compared to the white-robed uniforms of the Lifers, who resembled the hospice workers who'd sometimes showed up at Oak Knoll to whisk away the most hopeless patients.

Velasquez and Perry were stationed in front of the door to Samuel's bedroom. Another guard stood on the balcony. Two more guards were outside the front door. Karine was afraid the remaining Lifers were going to mob the drug hut to try to free Samuel. Victor worried that the building's stilts would crack and send them all tumbling down the hill.

The bodies in the room created a greenhouse-like heat. Tosh had gone around opening all the windows, muttering something about midday sweats, to little effect.

Velasquez and Perry brought Samuel into the room and cleared a space for him to sit on the couch. He appeared unwell, his gaze jumping from person to person, manic and at the end of his tether.

Circe wedged a fingernail between her teeth and stared at the floor.

Karine asked her, "Do you want to say something?"

Circe shook her head. "Let this play out," she said in a low voice.

"Well, I guess we're all here," Victor said, his voice booming in the small room. He was nearing the end of his own tether. He had half a mind to walk out the door, flee New Venice, and find his way to an island somewhere that hadn't yet discovered religion.

"Let's get started," Victor said to Wonda. "You're leading this séance for the dead—Oops! I meant, the crossed-over."

"Victor, hush!" Circe snapped. "Wonda, why don't you ask Samuel what you came here to ask him."

Wonda went down on her knees in front of the couch. Samuel looked at her the way one might regard a serpent that found its way into the house.

"Samuel, I'm Wonda. I'm here with other members of the Human Life movement. We believe in the purity of the human soul and that it's possible to seek truth on earth through clean living and the pursuit of justice."

"You're a ghost," Samuel said flatly. "You won't find what you're looking for in this world."

Wonda caught her breath, looked at Victor with concern. He shrugged. Did she expect Samuel to say everything she wanted to hear? She would be lucky if he didn't try to help her cross over in front of all these people. The thought made him break out in a cold sweat. He went over to Velasquez, who had remained by Samuel's bedroom door.

"Get closer," Victor told him. "If he tries anything, it's up to you to stop him." Velasquez pushed his way to one end of the couch and gestured for Perry to move to the other side, which the man did. They looked like bookends. Tosh moved to stand directly behind the couch.

"We're here to ask you if you want to be here," Wonda said. "We want to help you if you want to leave."

Samuel looked at her with suspicion. "You want to help me cross over?"

Wonda gasped. "No! Oh, laws, that's not what I meant. I meant here at BioScan. They're medicating you. Is that what you want?"

"Are you thick? Are you stupid? Of course I don't want to be here. I want to cross over. You're all ghosts!" he shouted at everyone. "Your bodies are without souls. Your primals cry out in the other world to be reunited. You think this is real life? This is purgatory!"

He began to rock forward and back, moaning.

Mía's face ran wet with tears, and an ugly sneer curled her lips.

Victor looked for Karine, caught her eye at the back of the room, and mouthed, "Fumewort." Turning back to the couch, he said, "Samuel, do you want a tincture? It might help."

"You promised to help me," he said, with a stare that hollowed Victor's chest.

Karine handed Victor a vial. It was glass, fragile. If broken, it would be dangerous.

"This will help a little. Tilt your head back," he said.

Samuel clasped his hands between his knees, and leaned back, his head against the sofa, his eyes locked on Victor. A shiver ran down Victor's spine. *Grip the vial; hold it tight; if he leaps, don't let go.*

Victor poured the tincture, and Samuel gulped it down.

"Fire," Samuel said. "Burning."

Victor tucked the empty vial in his pocket. On second thought, he took it out and gave it to Velasquez, who took it, nodded grimly, and stowed it in one of his many pockets.

Turning to Samuel, Victor said, "Okay, good. Be calm, okay? Remember, calm? 'Calm' is the word today."

"I remember your voice."

Victor said, "Wonda, can we get through this? The direct route, please."

She reached out as if she were going to grasp Samuel's hands, seemed to think better of it, and clasped her own instead. "Samuel, do you want to stop taking Personil?"

"Yes," he said. "I want clarity. I want purity. I want to find the truth. I'm a seeker too. Can you take me away from here?"

"A seeker?" Wonda brightened, smiling. "Yes, of course, we'll help you. You won't have to take Personil anymore."

Karine said, "This is unbelievable. Give him a knife, and he would cut out your heart. You can't take him with you."

Circe tapped Karine on the shoulder, whispered something in her ear, and pointed out a few of the Lifers in the room. Victor looked at them. They appeared concerned, anxious, and uncomfortable. Maybe Wonda didn't speak for them.

"What do you think?" Victor asked a middle-aged potentiate with jowls and flushed cheeks. "Want to take him back to the camp? Want to sleep in the same trailer with him?"

The man looked at Samuel with wide eyes and shook his head.

"How about you?" Victor asked a young woman who might have been fresh out of school.

She looked around uncertainly, saying, "Maybe . . . If Wonda thinks it will be okay."

"It will. We'll take every precaution," Wonda said, standing. "This is a tremendous responsibility, one we don't accept lightly."

"You're in awe of your own power," Victor said, scoffing.

Wonda's mouth opened in surprise. That was her talent, Victor thought, to be perpetually delighted, taken aback, shocked, and unexpectedly bemused. To her, the world held infinite surprises, and just because something was expected in advance didn't mean anything was lost when it finally did occur. Every moment was a multitude of emotion, and she reveled in it. She was the exact opposite of Victor.

Circe said, "Samuel's transfer is going to be complicated, legally speaking. Unless the Human Life movement is a legally recognized entity?" Circe looked at Wonda with the dead-eyed face Victor knew she used to hide what she really meant.

Wonda blinked. "I would have to ask Del about that."

"Then I think we're done here for now, don't you?"

Samuel, appearing calmer, was taken back to his room. Just before the door closed, he locked eyes with Victor and said, "Help me—you promised. I'll hold you to it."

It took several minutes for all the Lifers and BioScan staff to make their way down the hill. As they were nearing the administration building, one of the security guards rushed over.

"Chief! Karine! We have a problem."

"What is it?" Circe asked.

"We asked the demonstrators to move off the property to keep the administration building clear and accessible."

"A good idea," Circe said.

"They agreed at first, but it was just a ruse. They've occupied the construction site. They're setting up camp, chaining themselves to the equipment. What do we do?"

"We remove them," Circe said. "Call the sheriff. I'll get on the line to Oklahoma City and see what national resources we can get. Protests are one thing. I won't tolerate interference like this."

"But people will be hurt!" Wonda said.

"This can end peacefully," Tosh said. He smiled broadly, pulled out two shocksticks, pointed one in each hand at the security guards and fired.

Two bodies dropped. The rest, Victor included, wobbled a bit, residual Dirac forces scrambling the bystanders' neurons. Tosh dropped the third and last guard. He said, "It can end peacefully, but that's not how it starts."

Five Lifers crowded close and more were forming a perimeter.

"What's this?" Karine asked indignantly.

"Confinement," Tosh said. "You're not going anywhere. You're not making any calls."

"Tosh, don't do this," Victor said.

"We're not leaving without Samuel," Wonda said. She'd looked surprised by Tosh firing the shockstick, but now she seemed to be taking charge. Victor imagined her nimble mind working out a new plan second by second. "BioScan is going to agree to change how it operates. We want a signed legal agreement before we let you go."

"You planned this?" Victor asked. "That whole thing with Samuel was a show?"

"Of course not," she said, looking surprised. "It's Emergence."

Karine laughed. "We're not agreeing to anything, and everything negotiated under duress would be unenforceable anyway."

Circe spoke up, "We should at least hear what they have to say."

Victor looked at his aunt. Her face was unreadable. And that was the scariest thing of all.

38

You wouldn't tie your feet together before you run a marathon. You wouldn't close your eyes to paint a masterpiece. So why would you allow your brain to rot on Mesh feeds and propaganda and then expect democracy to deliver results?

—BrAiNhAcKeR Collective

15 June 1991
New Venice, The Louisiana Territories

Tosh confiscated electronics and issued orders to the Lifers, dictating who got tied up, locked up, or sedated. Circe cooperated, sending home most of the BioScan staff, including all the security guards who hadn't been rendered unconscious, by saying she wanted to minimize exposure to a potentially contagious pathogen, which she blamed on one of the stim addicts.

Patients who could be discharged were. A skeleton crew of nurses remained to deal with a few newly admitted stim addicts in the midst of withdrawal, a man who needed treatment for excess iron in his blood, and Florence Eastmore, who was experiencing cardiac arrhythmia. Within thirty minutes, the BioScan campus was locked down.

"We're going to settle this peacefully," Circe explained. She was leveling a hard gaze at Karine, who wasn't on the cooperation bandwagon. "*C'est de la merde*," she kept repeating. "*Le monde est fou.*"

Circe ordered Karine to cooperate. "You too," she said to Victor.

"I'm no hero," Victor said.

Tosh showed the hostages a vidfeed of the demonstration at the construction site. Judging by the high angle and wobbly frame, the vidcapper was probably a hovering drone. "Ozie is hacking MeshNews. These images are going out around the world."

Alia asked, "What are you telling the demonstrators about us? Do they know you're taking hostages?"

Tosh grimaced.

"They don't know, do they?" Alia said. "You're not being honest with them."

Wonda raised her voice so everyone could hear. "I'm going to say this once. If any of you tells anyone what we're doing here, there will be consequences, starting with Florence Eastmore."

"You can't be serious," Alia said.

"I am," Wonda replied.

"They're doing what they think is right," Tosh said. "So are we."

"Look," Alia said, turning to Tosh, "we're willing to listen to your grievances. But you have to be reasonable. Let's make a deal."

Tosh asked, "What do you have in mind?"

"If I can convince the demonstrators to leave, will you release us?" Alia was shorter than Tosh but somehow seemed the bigger one at that moment. Beautiful, principled, willing to do what was necessary.

"Are you proposing a wager?" Tosh asked, his eyebrows rising. A grin spread across his face. "This isn't a game, sweetie."

"Then you don't have to worry about losing." Alia turned and began walking up the path.

Tosh grunted, handed a shockstick to one of the Lifers wearing a Venetian mask, and told him to stay close to Alia. Three other Lifers escorted Circe and Karine to the administration building. Tosh pulled Victor by the arm toward the construction site.

"I'd recruit her in a heartbeat," Wonda said, catching up with them. There was a hungry look in her eyes as she watched Alia walking away.

"She would never join you," Victor said. "It's beneath her."

Wonda gave him a hurt look, wiped a tear—was it a real one?—and said, "I don't know why I'm still surprised how hurtful you can be."

"You're still surprised I'm not a blank puppet all the time," Victor replied. He shrugged away from Tosh and picked up his pace to walk with Alia.

They reached the lip of the foundation pit, a pair of squares etched into the hillside, open toward New Venice. There was little dirt to be seen. Enough tents had been erected to house a good chunk of New Venice's population. It reminded Victor of the slums surrounding Oakland & Bayshore but on a smaller scale. He spotted four drones hovering ten meters above the crowd.

A cheer rose up among the demonstrators. People were gathered around a makeshift stage made of wooden pallets, a flimsy and treacherous ziggurat that allowed a speaker to be seen while addressing the crowd.

"We are here to demand accountability," the man in the white robe said. He was wearing a mask that covered his eyes and gave him a long pointy nose but left his mouth free to pontificate in a voice Victor didn't recognize. "The clinic has gone far beyond its mandate to heal the sick and care for our community. We know there are genetic experiments going on right under our noses with no oversight. The work of this clinic puts our health at risk, and it defiles the purity of our bodies. It defies the natural order. It makes us into monsters."

"No more monsters!" a man in the crowd shouted.

"Except on Halloween," someone responded, and there was a round of laughter.

Victor turned to Alia, "They think this is fun?"

She shook her head. "They're not thinking about the consequences. They just want to feel empowered. I knew some people begrudged the Eastmores' control over the town, but I never thought it was this bad."

The man continued, "We demand an end to testing and treatment of the preborn. Let nature take its course. We demand an end to stem cell research. Let nature take its course. We demand an end to gene therapy and genetic engineering of all life, from humans to single-celled organisms. Let nature take its course!"

"Hooray for cancer," Alia muttered disdainfully.

On the outskirts of the tent city, a group of townies watched, grumbling to each other. Their group grew as tourists wandered by, asked what was going on, and then stayed to watch. A separate group carrying signs—"Save New Venice," "Trash Goes in the Garbage," "Lifers Out," and "Save Our Healthcare"—crossed the bridge and joined the counterprotest. Del and a few of his loyalists stood on the outskirts of the tent city, wearing normal clothing rather than Lifer robes.

The speaker continued, "We demand an end to research without accountability that threatens humanity and the sanctity of our bodies and our divine genetic code."

"Let nature take its course!" the crowd shouted. It was amazing how the man had set up a call and response pattern, Victor thought. Had they practiced or did the group-think of a hundred people suffice? They were like birds flying together that turned at the same time, spontaneously organizing. *Emergence*, he thought. *This is Emergence*. It felt like a cloud lifting from his brain, the insight was that powerful. It was all simply happening now because it couldn't have happened before. The tensions and conflicts that normally created stasis had reoriented and now pointed in the same direction. Slight predispositions and innocuous conversations had built up to a moment when everything switched into higher gear, the wheel of progress turned, and humanity surged forward in a blind race to the top.

Or perhaps the bottom, depending on how you looked at it. Ozie was beaming this footage around the world. Who knew what impact it would have?

"We are many! We are strong! This gathering is one of hundreds that will rise up throughout the American Union and the world. We will protect humanity from harmful technologies and safeguard our survival. Our demands must be met. Let nature take its course! Let nature take its course! Let nature take its course!"

Before the crowd could take up the chant and build into an unstoppable frenzy, Alia shouted from her perch, "Listen to me." There was muttering in the crowd. Alia said, "I know you don't all agree with him. I have something to say for BioScan."

"Shut her up!" someone yelled.

"Let her speak," Del countered. He and his loyalists pressed through the forest of tents to form a tight pocket of resistance in the midst of the Lifers.

Alia said, "I understand your concerns about the research conducted here. I do. However, we have procedures to ensure the ethical integrity of our work, to comply with all relevant laws and regulations, and to reach out to the community to hear their concerns. I welcome further discussions with you about our work here, which is vital to the health of the New Venice community. Let's talk about it. Let's talk—that's all I'm asking."

"Don't listen to her," a woman shouted.

"Are you mental?" someone said. "Of course we can listen. This is America. We're not afraid of words."

"We just want all this protesting and demonstrating to end," Victor heard a townie say in a tired voice.

Someone yelled, "It'll end when they're all drowned!"

Victor was growing concerned that the crowd would turn against Alia. Crowds seemed to turn more quickly than individuals. Just because there had been no violence thus far, who could say how long that would last?

"Thank you," Alia said, "The work of this clinic and others like it have saved many lives and improved the health of many people. We have developed treatments for many otherwise incurable genetically inherited diseases. We can now screen fetuses for potential problems much earlier in a pregnancy and protect the health of mothers and their pregnancies. These advancements save lives. I've seen it. We are working on compounds that slow the progress of neural degenerative diseases in old age, and someday soon, we may be able to reverse the damage and bring dignity to our parents and grandparents. We know many of you support us—"

A call rang out from a young woman in a white robe: "You are killing the human soul!"

"You're losing perspective," Alia shouted back, the first sign of annoyance slipping through her demeanor. "We treat people of all beliefs, whether they believe in souls or not. Whether they believe in God or gods or not. Our job as scientists and doctors is not to judge the beliefs of our patients or to treat one person differently than another. We heal. If we start putting boundaries on the technologies we use, we tie our own hands. I will not allow anyone to suffer or go without treatment for the sake of another person's beliefs. That is called bullying." She looked at the woman who had called out to her with a surprising ferocity. Some people in the crowd looked down at their feet.

"Are you done?" Wonda asked her.

Alia shrugged.

Wonda smiled and turned to the crowd, "Let's all talk about what she said, okay?" People looked around, seemed to regroup into small clusters, and began to converse.

Wonda said, "Let's give them some time. I want to air all perspectives. Victor, what do you think?"

"How about I go into blankspace and then you ask me? That way you get a real prophecy to work with."

"Oh, don't tease," she said in a light voice, but her eyes told a different story. She was hurt by his remark, and the growing distance between them had done more to sour her mood than anything else—he felt it.

"I think it's better not to know how things end," she said brightly. "Otherwise where's the fun?"

Victor walked with Alia, Wonda, and Tosh to the meeting room in the administration building and found Karine and Circe sitting alone at the conference table, leaning in and talking quietly. The other BioScan staff were apparently being held separately.

"We're here to solve a problem together, so let's talk it out," Wonda said in a bright voice that made Victor think fresh never tasted so foul. "Talking helps." She gave them each the look of a teacher tolerating noncooperative students.

"Thinking has also been proven to solve problems," Karine said. "You should try it sometime."

"Ugly words aren't helping," Wonda said with a tight smile.

"Why don't you and your friends crawl back to the bog you came from!" Karine yelled. She opened her eyes wide, put a hand to her breast, and smiled. "Phew, I do feel better," she said.

"We're not going anywhere," Tosh said. His gaze dared anyone to try to leave.

"We're going to take Samuel Miller out of your care," Wonda said, "but that's not all. BioScan is corrupting human life. We're going to put a stop to it."

Karine threw up her hands and rolled her eyes. She may have been second in command at BioScan, but it was clear to Victor, to everyone, that she wasn't taking responsibility for the situation.

Circe stood up and immediately assumed the mantle of the adult in the room without saying a word. It was humbling to watch. Humbling and disconcerting. Victor hated that he couldn't regain a simple love for his aunt. Every feeling he had for her was tainted and probably always would be.

He supposed that Circe, having lived in Europe for so many years, would have more experience, or at least more knowledge, about how to deal with terrorists. Though, of course, these weren't professionals or hardened radicals like the ones they had in Europe. These were average citizens who for some reason found themselves under the sway of a charismatic leader.

"We cannot appease unreasonable demands," Circe said.

Wonda's eyes flashed, apparently eager for an argument. She laid out her position: a Lifer put in charge of patient care at every BioScan facility, a ban on providing any enhancement services, no medication for mirror resonance syndrome and other mental illnesses. The list went on and on.

The two Lifers guarding the door wore proud smiles that made them look ghoulish in their Venetian masks. That was a pronouncement from Wonda—all Lifers except her, Victor, and Tosh were to keep their masks on at all times.

Victor thought there must be a gene or something in human biology or cognitive processes that made people's minds susceptible to such influence, that allowed strong men and shucksters to prey on their emotions, to manipulate them like Mesh programs: input fuzzy rhetoric; output crazed loyalty. Repeat and escalate, until taking sick people hostage no longer seemed like an insane endeavor. Victor wanted to scream. He knew it wouldn't help, but he felt pressure inside him rising. He recognized the panicked, skittering feeling of his emotions breaking from his control and poised to run amok. He had to do something.

Victor walked over to the door. "Where is everyone else?" he asked Tosh.

"You don't want a seat at the adults' table?" Tosh joked.

"This isn't my fight. Not yours either, is it?"

Tosh's eyes were like black-eyed peas gone brown and moldy. "I'll be right back," Tosh said to Wonda and the two masked Lifers at the door.

Victor's shoes squeaked on the floor as he and Tosh walked down the hall. Normally there would have been doors opening and closing, people rushing everywhere. Now it was so quiet he could hear the lightstrips gurgling. The high powered ones needed their feedstocks refreshed every month. There would be tanks nearby, little bioreactors where the waste was reprocessed into fuel. Did the Lifers want to get rid of those as well?

After a moment of walking, Victor stopped and stood eye to eye with Tosh. "Are you going to kill Circe?" he asked.

"Are you?" Tosh responded. He let out a long sigh. "If it was anyone else . . . If it had been the King or a jilted lover or some former employee with a grudge, they'd already be dead. This was family, and that's . . . That's something entirely different."

Tosh led Victor to a room that held six med bays. A few BioScan staff were treating the remaining patients. A nurse was attending to Florence, whose hand burrowed in her blouse, massaging whatever pain blossomed in her chest. He murmured quietly to her, reassuring her that everything would be fine. When he turned and saw Victor watching, an unreadable expression formed on his face.

Nearby, a young man held a sleeping infant. His eyes darted toward every sound and then the baby's face, concerned perhaps that the child would be woken.

"The rest are through there," Tosh said, prodding Victor forward with a hand on his back. "I'll check on you later."

Victor let himself be herded into a suite identical to the one he'd spent so much time recovering in after Tosh attacked him. The bed had been moved out and chairs were crammed against the walls.

Mía rushed over to him as soon as the door had shut behind him. She whispered in his ear, "I found a MeshBit and hid it under the conference table."

"Did you send any messages?" Victor asked.

"No. I—" She scratched at her throat. He noticed her eyes watering, the lines on her face deepened by shameful purple shadows. "It's difficult for me. I don't want to be the one who—"

He understood. She'd run away from Carmichael and brought militia from a nearby town. The situation was hitting too close to home for her.

Mía's tears came, and she hid her face. Victor hugged her. "It's okay," he said. Her sobs worsened; her body heaved. He ushered her to an empty chair, sat her down, and hugged her. They'd never been this close. He'd never thought of himself as someone who could give comfort. Her body was warm against his. It felt good.

"Thank you," she said. "I feel better."

“I better check on Florence, and then I’ll try to make contact.”

Florence’s bed had been moved to the far corner. A sheet was draped between an IV drip stand and a chair, providing a privacy screen. Probably she had insisted on it. Her eyes opened when he approached.

“I’m not sleeping,” Florence said. “I’m just bored with keeping my eyes open.”

“How are you feeling?” he asked.

“Not dead yet. Still waiting on my medicine. If these hooligans kill me, I’ll come back and haunt them. Tell them that.”

He checked the MeshBit around her wrist. “Your next dose is in a couple hours.”

“You run along if you’ve got somewhere to be.”

“Everything’s going to be fine,” he said. He squeezed her wrist gently and turned away.

“Most certainly is not. The Eastmores don’t do fine. We do death.”

The skin on Victor’s neck prickled. “Why do you say that?” He looked into her glassy eyes. Her wrinkled face resembled tissue paper, thin and creased. She stared back at him.

“History. Psychology. Didn’t your parents teach you anything?”

“They never talked about the bad stuff. That’s what my therapists were for.”

“Maybe they didn’t know,” Florence said. She looked at the wall for a moment. A glossy painting of flowers in a vase reflected the lightstrips’ glow.

“We lose so much to time,” Florence went on. “Memories. Truths. Sons. Daughters.” Florence closed her eyes. Breath heaved in her chest, slowly, evenly. Victor thought she’d fallen asleep.

He left the semiprivacy of her corner, pausing to see where the Lifers were. Behind him, Florence said, “Don’t forgive Circe, Victor. She chose to kill him. No one made her do it.”

Sweat broke out in Victor’s armpits. “What did you say?” he asked, turning.

Florence looked asleep. Her words hadn't been in his head, had they?

He squeezed her hand. "Florence, wake up. What did you say?"

Her body trembled. The MeshBit around her wrist chimed an alarm.

"Someone get Alia in here now!"

An hour later, Victor walked back out to the patient area. Alia had stabilized Florence, though she remained unconscious.

"We can't allow them to dictate what meds we can use," Alia said, louder than necessary. She wanted to be heard. "If we do, people will die."

The Lifers at the door to the hall appeared exhausted, uncertain, as if at any minute they might tire of the poorly written drama and walk off the stage entirely.

There were some medications in a tub that one of the Lifers had collected for disposal. *What a waste. What a stupid, ill-meaning mess of religious doctrine*, Victor thought.

He realized the Lifers didn't care about these people. They only cared about their principles, which they adopted and jettisoned like trying on clothing. No one could meet their demands. Maybe that was the point. Maybe they didn't want to be satisfied; they just wanted to be denied. Maybe that felt human to them.

If the Lifers expected to get what they wanted through the threat of violence, then that was the best proof yet of their collective insanity. *Change doesn't happen that way*, Victor thought, *at least not the kind of change they're looking for*.

Victor wanted to shout these things at the Lifers guarding the door. Instead he chewed his lips.

Victor had read the Carmichael testimony. He understood how Samuel's paranoia had twisted logic, where fantasy had intruded on reality, and the horrific consequences. One mind had done that. Here in New Venice, equally bizarre beliefs had solidified into a covenant among the cult's members and a prescription for nonmembers that would be delivered by force. What if there was a connection?, he mused. What if MRS was a contagion now spreading through a new host population? It was a frustratingly persistent and plausible delusion.

Victor gathered up supplies: mainly medications, but also patches, syringes, and tubes. He found packets of nutritional supplements and food pastes in a cabinet in the corner and added those, putting everything in a blue translucent box. He wanted to make sure at least some rudimentary supplies didn't get confiscated.

A few of the Lifers eyed him curiously. He could tell they wanted to confront him, but they were holding off. Maybe they felt guilty. Maybe now that they'd gone so far down the radical path, they wanted to leave it. He wanted to tell them it was too late. Their participation, passive as it may seem, implicated them irrevocably, fully. It was their fault that the patients would suffer.

Victor handed off the supplies to Nancy, a recovering stim addict who had come in to detox. She seemed a bit thin and slack underneath her skin. She could carry the lighter tub of medicines.

An overlarge man who most likely suffered from a metabolic disorder gestured to the box Victor carried.

"I can take that," he said. Victor wasn't sure if he could handle the extra weight and hesitated. "There's muscle under here too. Otherwise I wouldn't be able to get around." He smiled sadly.

"Okay," Victor said. It sounded insufficient, though, so he added, "Let me know if you need help."

Victor wished Elena were here. She had a way of calming people down, making them see why her way was the right way. She was practical, a problem solver. She didn't need to analyze what was right; she just knew. An ability like that would be helpful right now.

He tried channeling her wisdom, trying to figure out what she would do in this situation, but he didn't think it was clear-cut. Sure, she was practical, but she was also fiercely loyal to the Puros, to the point where she might not care about what happened to anyone else. She might look at the patients and think, "Not my problem." Or maybe not—she wasn't that callous. Much of what Victor had learned about empathy came from her. When he'd had trouble making sense of his therapy sessions, he'd gone to her to enlighten him. She usually threw his questions back at him. "What's the situation? Who's involved? What will happen if you don't do anything? Now, what's the right thing to do?"

But this was far more complicated. Any action might trigger serious, unintended consequences. "Do no harm" was an appropriate oath in controlled circumstances. Or when everyone had the proper training and skills, when they were up for the challenge.

Nancy, the large man, and Victor waited, not quite huddled together, sitting on rolling chairs near the door. Nancy was rolling her stress ball on a table, back and forth, pressing her palm down on it, occasionally flexing her fingers over it the way a spider pins its prey. Her fingertips disappeared into the red material. She pulsed her hand. It was strange. Normally, she moved, twitched. Her body was constantly in motion. When she played with the stress ball, however, the rest of her stilled, only her hand and forearm activated, as if those parts of her were a conduit for all the mental and physical energy generated by anxiety.

Nancy held the ball up, smiling. "I can't be without it for a minute," she said loudly. "It beats stims. Reusable too."

Two of the Lifers turned their heads and masks so they could see each other's eyes. Victor thought he saw a question pass between them, perhaps, and then a slight nod from the one whose breasts pushed the fabric of the robe forward into a single wide mound. The effect of the costume made her look like a bulky cartoon cloud. She bent on one knee in front of Nancy. Her words were low and quiet. Still, Victor had no trouble making them out.

The cloud-robed woman said, "Many of us have struggled to be pure."

Nancy flushed. She looked as if she might leap at the cloud and try to pull it apart. "I'm not tainted," she said.

The cloud woman half stood, though she remained bending forward.

Nancy sighed. "It would be nice to talk. You all may have some good ideas for me."

The cloud woman nodded. "I think we can help." Her voice reminded Victor of Dr. Tammet. A bit softer than the doctor's, happier. "We're here to help."

Nancy cocked her head at the cloud woman. "Thank you," she said. It might have been genuine or a menacing curse; Victor couldn't tell.

The cloud woman sniffed and walked back to the nearest robed man. Nancy squeezed her ball rhythmically while the large man's chest hitched as he tried to stop laughing and coughing at the same time. "We're here to help," he mocked. "Laws save us all."

Tosh returned and looked around the room. He noticed the supplies piled near the door and the Lifers eyeing the bins uncertainly. "Let them gather whatever they want for now. We'll take a closer look later."

There were some tentative glances between the Lifers. Maybe they saw Tosh's command as a lapse of doctrine.

Victor called out, "Can I speak with you?"

"Watch them," Tosh said and pointed for the three Lifers to take care of the remaining half dozen hostages. Then he gestured for Victor to follow him to the hall.

The building was quiet. Sunlight filtered through the windows and doors, illuminating patches of the floor.

"End this," Victor said. "There's no point. You don't care about the Lifers."

"It doesn't matter whether I do. They're here now, and they need someone to keep them on track."

"But what do you want?" Victor asked.

"When your enemy loses the advantage, you don't question it. You press yours."

"You don't know, do you? You're just figuring it out as you go. That's . . . I can't even say how stupid that is. Does the King even know what's going on?" Victor asked.

Tosh held up a MeshBit that looked like a round gray river stone. "We talk."

"Let me talk to him."

Tosh started to put the MeshBit away.

"Please! I just want to find a way out of this."

"I'll see what I can do," Tosh said. He started to push Victor back to the room with the hostages.

"Wait," Victor said, "I think I can help them negotiate now. I wasn't calm before. I understand Wonda. We spent a lot of time together, remember?" He squeezed Tosh's shoulder hard.

Tosh smiled. "I do."

"Let me try."

Tosh escorted Victor back to the conference room. "Any progress?" he asked.

"What she's asking for isn't possible," Circe said. Her tone was matter-of-fact, assertive. As much as he despised what she'd done, Victor wished he had her poise and patience. Karine was worse off: she seethed visibly and seemed about to blow herself to pieces.

Wonda said, "'The realm of the possible has a tendency to expand with an exertion of imagination over time.' Those are your words. We've been thinking of ways forward, and we believe this is workable. Perhaps you need time to consider our demands."

"You are a ridiculous person," Karine said. "The longer you keep us here, the harder the enforcers will come down on you." Her eyes bored into Tosh. Victor was almost surprised when Tosh didn't evaporate under her hot glare.

"I want an amicable resolution to this situation," Circe said. "My patience, however, can only be stretched so far. You have to work out a more reasonable set of demands, or I will alert the police to this situation."

"You'll do no such thing. We control the timeline," Tosh said. "We're going to move you to the drug huts. You'll be more comfortable there."

"This is outrageous," Karine said. "You can't keep us overnight."

Tosh's hand dropped to the shockstick at his side, reminding her of the painful wages their disobedience would earn. "In case it wasn't clear. We're keeping you indefinitely."

Karine laughed loudly. Victor couldn't believe she was so bold. Had she forgotten that Tosh had been ready to kill her in Amarillo?

She said, "You've just sealed your own fate, *mal chien*."

Tosh ignored her insult. "Take them," he instructed a follower.

As she was ushered out the door, Circe turned to Victor. "Do what you can to convince them to back off."

Circe and Karine were led away.

Victor eyed Tosh. He knew how to manipulate him: show him attention; activate his lust.

Wonda looked at Victor with an unidentifiable emotion. It might have been suspicion. "I'm willing to be reasonable."

"You're asking them to go out of business. How is that reasonable?"

"It'll take time to change minds. I accept that. In the interim, we can take pleasure in the present. Tonight, I'm making a new proclamation. We're amending the prohibition against medication."

"It's about time," Victor said. "I'll give Florence her pills."

Wonda shook her head. "That's not what I meant. We're making an exception only for those medicines that help treat communicable diseases. Human life is sacred. Bugs are not. We can celebrate tonight." She winked and left them.

Victor stepped toward the window. His shoulder nearly brushed Tosh's.

They looked out together at the water. A few boats edged far into the Passage, while more waited for the Little Lock to open. One paddleboat had started the journey across the water after embarking from the opposite shore. Victor wished he was outside, feeling the wind, alone somewhere near the water.

"She's crazier than I ever was," Victor said.

Tosh scratched the hair poking around his chin. There were a few small grey patches that made him look older than he was.

"You might not be wrong about that."

"Tosh, it's just a matter of time before there's a fight, a real one. People will get hurt. You will get hurt." Victor put a hand on his shoulder. The words of his coach, Dr. Tammet, sounded in his ears. *Show empathy. Try to connect. Feel what they're feeling.* "Any minute now Karine is going to lose control and try to peel your face off with her bare hands."

Tosh grunted and smiled. "I'd like to see her try."

"All their demands. I know you can see how pointless, how utterly effing illogical they are. Circe would never agree to anything they're asking for. So why keep their pipe dreams alive?"

"You heard the woman. They'll stay until they achieve something tangible. Samuel Miller's release would go a long way toward that. Maybe if that happens, they'll let go of the rest."

"He's not safe if he leaves BioScan. *No one* is safe if he leaves BioScan," Victor said.

"They see it as a matter of principle."

"How do you see it? Aren't you in charge?"

"That's debatable. Come on, I'll walk you myself."

"Wait." Victor gulped, flirting with blankspace. "I need . . . I need a few minutes. Please? With everything . . ."

"I get it. I'll be back after we move the others." Tosh left Victor alone.

Victor found the MeshBit under the conference table.

He had to send a message, but to whom? The sheriff? That could lead to violence. Lisabella? Media attention wouldn't do anything to de-escalate the situation.

Ozie?

Ozie had resources. He would probably cooperate. Victor just had to figure out what to ask him to do.

39

How changed are we by the crucible? How harden our hearts?

—Ming Pearl's *Now Blossom* (1973)

15 June 1991
New Venice, The Louisiana Territories

Victor sat with Florence in a bedroom of one of the drug huts. She'd regained consciousness and complained in a breathy voice of feeling weak.

"This is the end," she whispered.

"It's not the end," Victor said. He held her cool hand to his cheek. "You'll make it through this."

The masked Lifers standing by the door spoke to each other in quiet voices. They avoided his stare and acted as if they weren't slowly killing her.

Wonda had come in three separate times to announce new dictates. Enforcements, she called them. Hostages must be escorted by a Lifer at all times. Hostages could not speak to each other. Hostages could not speak to Lifers unless they were addressed first. Infractions would be punished.

Enforcements didn't apply to Victor. Wonda called him the "Avatar."

"The Avatar walks his own path," she said.

Part of him felt grateful to be able to move around. The other part felt ashamed of being singled out, and he was embarrassed for her. With the hostages increasingly controlled, it fell more squarely on his shoulders to fix the situation.

He made the rounds between the drug huts, checking on the other hostages. In the hut at the end of the lane, a crisis was brewing. The bedridden male patient moaned and whimpered. The scent of urine wafted through the room. Victor watched as Alia and a nurse conferred, an infraction, according to Wonda's rules.

"His iron levels are becoming toxic," the nurse said. "If we don't give him chelaters soon, the damage to his organs will kill him. There's only so much blood we can take—"

"I know that!" Alia snapped. She wiped tears off her cheeks and glared at the Lifers. "You! Get over here."

One stayed by the door glowering while the other sheepishly approached her. Wonda's enforcement hadn't yet become unbreakable. Victor wondered how long the hostages could count on that.

Alia spoke calmly and insistently to the Lifer. "This man is suffering from severe hemachromatosis. He's going to die unless we give him medicine."

"I can't do anything about it," the Lifer said. "Wonda—"

"Bring her here. She has to listen to reason."

The Lifer left and returned a few minutes later with Wonda, Tosh, and two larger, burlier, masked Lifers. Wonda walked up to Alia, grabbed her arm, and hauled her to the door. Alia began to protest, and Wonda smacked her hard in the mouth. She instructed the Lifers to lock her away.

"What are you doing?" Victor said.

"Establishing boundaries," Wonda said. "Everybody out except him." She pointed at the man with hemochromatosis.

"Tosh, you can't let her do this!" Victor said.

Tosh walked over to the patient. He put a hand on his forehead and whispered something. It looked like a benediction.

"Tosh, please," Victor said.

"Wonda decides questions of doctrine. It's out of my hands."

Victor caught a snippet of Wonda's instructions as she stood outside the room with the sick man. "No one goes in there without my permission under any circumstances. Resist impure temptations. This is going to be a test for all of us."

Later, after a walk through the gardens to avoid Wonda, Victor returned to the drug hut where Florence was being kept and sat with her while she slept.

Someone tapped on the window. It was Mía. He went over and opened it.

"Why haven't you contacted anyone?" she asked.

He looked down, failing to think of an excuse that would make sense to her.

"Give me the MeshBit," she said.

Victor shook his head. "You don't understand how dangerous Tosh is. If he's cornered, there's no telling what he'll do. People will get hurt. I'll think of something."

"I can't say I'm reassured," she said coldly.

A guard outside shouted at her and hauled her away.

Victor looked at Florence, hoping she was too weary to understand what was going on. Her eyes were open now, pale blue.

"I need to tell you something, Victor. In case I don't get another chance."

"You're going to be fine. I'll get your medication, even if I have to take out Wonda to do it."

"I wouldn't mind sticking around to see that," Florence said with a hollow cough that might have been a chuckle. "It's about Circe, something you need to know."

Victor pulled up a stool and leaned his elbows on the edge of her bed.

"She's always wanted more from life that it could offer. Ever since she was very young and she heard the story of Zoë Eastmore."

"Who?" asked Victor.

"Zoë was my husband's older sister. His other sister was Albinia. When Zoë was twelve years old, Albinia was six. One day their school took a trip to visit the Qaddo reservation. This was before the turn of the century. It was a dry year, during the summer, so the kids had the treat of a real rain dance."

Florence's breath wheezed and smelled musty, like a closet that hasn't been opened for a year.

"At some point, they lost track of Albinia. She wandered off or became separated. The whole town looked for her. They still hadn't found her when the sun set. Some thought they should start again in the morning when they had more light, but plenty of folk kept looking in the dark, carrying torches.

"One of the search party lost his grip on the torch. When the flames hit the forest floor, the dry grasses lit up. They beat the fire with their shirts, trying to put it out, but it spread. The wind blew it around the top of the mountain. This was before the canals, so there were a few shacks on the mountain that were lost, but luckily they held the line at the crest of the main road, and the town was spared. The fire put itself out in about a day.

"Zoë found Albinia the next day floating in a hot spring. Whether she was driven there by the fire or fell on her own we don't know. Sulfur. Boiling hot. She had no chance of getting out."

Victor imagined Albinia surrounded by fire, lost, confused. He'd had dreams like that. He'd felt fire burn him to a crisp. The dream-memory of boiling alive came back too. He gripped the cool steel railing of the hospital bed. "That's horrible," he said.

"Zoë was haunted by Albinia for the rest of her life, or so she believed. She fled to Asia and got caught up in a mess there. I don't know the gory details. Something about a massacre when some dynasty or another fell and Zoë was there in the thick of things. Some say she caused it. One cult called her a monster, tracked her for decades in exile. Another started to worship her. Why would someone exalt someone like that, I ask you?"

"I don't know," Victor said, feeling as if his feet were on fire.

"Here's a final piece of crazy. The Lifers here are talking about Emergence. They're even walking around with that book by Estrella Burgos. That was Zoë Eastmore's pen name, you know. Circe must have read it a hundred times. She carried it everywhere. If there's one thing she believes, it's that she has a destiny as spectacular as Zoë's. I fear for anyone who counters her. She's patient, cunning, and utterly mad. I said it before, Victor: Eastmores attract more than their share of pain. But we always deserve it. Now run along," she said. "I need to rest up for the final sleep."

The drug hut seemed to tilt as if it were sliding down the hill. He sat on the floor and took off his shoes. The wooden floor soothed him.

Burnt by fire and boiled alive. One Eastmore's death, the other's dreams. It was a coincidence. Dreams were just dreams, weren't they?

40

The twists and turns of fate remain knotted until you become the knife.

—Estrella Burgos's *Theories of Emergence* (1906)

17 June 1991
New Venice, The Louisiana Territories

Two days of arguing left everyone in a foul mood, Tosh included, but the rest of the Lifers had the benefit of nightly orgies to keep their spirits up. The couplings took place in the gardens outside the drug huts and had a desperate feel to them, more pain than pleasure, more spectacle than intimacy. Tosh declined to participate. He watched a couple fucking in the dirt long enough to get himself off, spattering the shrubs with his semen. Then he made the rounds of the drug huts to keep tabs on security arrangements for the hostages.

In the morning, the MeshNews feeds showed that drones carrying explosive charges had settled on Ouachita Dam. No demands had been made, it was reported.

Tosh knew that the drones were Ozie's, sent on orders from the Diamond King. Their sole purpose was to distract. The authorities would be so focused on the drones they would miss what else was going on right under their noses. Like a hostage crisis at BioScan.

Tosh reassured the nervous Lifers there was nothing to worry about, and they trusted his assessment. They had no idea how tenuous the situation was becoming. Ozie reported that a European special forces team was inbound to try to neutralize the drones. If they should turn their attention to the BioScan campus . . .

Time to create another layer of protection. Another layer of lies.

"You have to create a counternarrative," Ozie told him, "that explains why the hostages—sorry, definitely don't use that word, that would give it away—why the patients and staff—especially the staff—why they're not leaving the clinic. The simplest explanation is the best, the most believable: quarantine."

"Circe told that to the staff when she dismissed them," Tosh replied.

"That's great," Ozie said. "You have to keep elaborating. A drip feed of plausible lies will do the trick."

Tosh set up a vidcapper in front of a conference table. One at a time, the hostages were brought into the room and made to record messages to their loved ones or friends wondering what was going on at the shuttered BioScan facility. To those familiar with the company, it would look like a repeat of what had happened at Oak Knoll Hospital, and they would be more right than wrong. Tosh had rigged sleeping gas bombs in the air ducts of every building, including the drug huts, which he controlled with a biometrically locked MeshBit. He was in charge, no matter how much he let Wonda think she was.

Beyond a window, the waters of the Passage and Qaddo Lake gleamed. Trees lining the levees of the western shore bordered ordered squares of farms. The Qaddo mudflats on the eastern side baked in the sun.

Tosh's robe was starting to itch. He'd taken to wearing fewer clothes underneath. It had helped at first, but then he started to notice the scratchiness of the fabric. Worse, when he did scratch somewhere, the robe acted like sandpaper. When he checked his arms during a break from filming, he found red spots multiplying on his skin. Not that his discomfort was of any consequence, but it was a nagging distraction when he needed to be focused on enforcing obedience.

He didn't want to be here. The Lifers were a bunch of trippy loonies looking for the meaning of life in superficial edicts and the faux righteousness of community. He'd seen it all before on the Qaddo reservation. When the real things that mattered were stripped from you—history, heritage, dignity, the communal spirit—everything else was a pale reconstruction. The Lifers wanted to matter so badly because they didn't. Science and medicine were too useful, too fundamental to be done away with. A lot of Lifers probably knew that, deep down, but they were too busy anointing leaders and following charlatans to think too much about what they were doing and why.

Tosh had no illusions about his role. He was a pawn serving the Diamond King, helping him entrap the other players. Having established an unshakeable grip over the Organized Western States, the Diamond King now amused himself by destabilizing the other nations of the American Union, no doubt planning to one day extend his influence over them.

If the LT council dared to pass the Classification Act, there would soon be thousands of citizens opposing it, inspired by the Lifers. Riots would spread, as they had in the ROT over stims, and demand for the Diamond King's Corps security forces would rise. Or, if the Act didn't pass, then the stim epidemic would continue to spread, and the Diamond King would profit from the drug trade. The plan ensured that no matter the outcome, the King secured a share of the spoils. Pure genius.

Tosh took credit for a job well done, at least thus far. He had the chief and the second chief of BioScan confined, unable to do much of anything, let alone run the company. The clinic operations were paralyzed, and construction had ground to a halt.

All thanks to Tosh's ability to radicalize the Lifers, who apparently had nothing better to do than take a stand for a vague cause of humanness. So earnest these fools were, Wonda chief among them.

He felt bad that Victor had been so helplessly caught up in the scheme. Every time Tosh looked at Victor, he felt a weird rush of attraction, confusion, loyalty, dismay, and the protective instinct that makes you hurt someone to toughen them up. Victor was strong in some ways and squishy soft in others. He had none of Jefferson's certainty or drive, though that was probably a good thing, considering how far Jefferson had gone astray.

That was no reason for Jefferson's daughter to go and off him, if that was what had happened. Tosh was 80 percent sure it was. Still, he wanted to hear her side of it before snapping her neck.

Circe didn't know Tosh's history with Jefferson. Victor hadn't told her. That might be an advantage, but an advantage that could be wiped out by a slip of the tongue was nothing to set plans by.

Enough trophy gazing, he told himself—focus on advancing the ball. He wished keeping hostages was as simple as winning a catch-and-carry game. First things first: he needed to assuage any fears and doubts that might be blossoming among the hostages' friends and family. Law enforcement too.

It was a gamble, but it wasn't his money on the table. It would be the Lifers who would suffer in the long run. At best they'd be seen as opportunists taking advantage of a difficult situation—that's if people believed the quarantine rumor. More likely, once the truth came out, they would be despised for their actions. Wonda was smart to make them wear masks.

The first few vidcaps went as expected. After several takes, coaching from the Lifers, and wearing down the hostages' reluctance, he coaxed out some good material. Once the first few messages were sent, Tosh started feeling optimistic.

Then Alia refused to cooperate. That was dangerous, given who her fiancé was. He told the Lifers who'd escorted her in to leave. They filed out.

Tosh thought Alia was pretty, smart, and willful. A strong adversary. He had to break her down.

"As soon as Torsten suspects something is wrong, your whole plan will fall apart," she said.

"Your fiancé is running for office, right?" he asked.

Her eyes narrowed. "Which means he has a platform to completely eviscerate this movement."

"Platforms can be unstable. Is Torsten a friend of BioScan?"

"He's a good man." Alia crossed her arms and turned to look out the window, but not before eyeing him up and down.

"Good or bad, like beauty, is in the eye of the beholder. Look, I understand we're making your job a bit difficult, but it's in your best interest to cooperate. We're taking good care of everyone here. The best thing you can do to help Torsten is to keep him out of our way. Sure, there's a small, a very small chance that he could ride to the rescue and come out on top. But there's so many ways for this to end badly. A botched rescue attempt. The public siding with us. Controversy over his ties to the Eastmores."

"They're not fools."

"The Eastmores? They're an odd bunch, but they're not fools, no."

"No, I mean the public. You can't attack people, sick people, and expect to get away with it."

"We're not attacking anyone."

"You're holding us hostage!"

"We're keeping you safe from the protesters, for your own protection!" Tosh smiled. It felt like playing a role—the tired arguments, the solipsistic thinking, everyone getting so agitated over a situation they didn't really understand. This wasn't about Lifers versus BioScan. The Lifers were a convenient cover. This was about a revenge so drawn out, so meticulously crafted, that he could retire on it, confident he'd never achieve anything as worthwhile again. Circe and her company would go down in flames. This was just laying the groundwork. The one tricky thing Tosh hadn't quite figured out yet was how to extricate Victor so he didn't crash and burn with the rest of the Eastmores.

He said, "You should think of me as an ally. I can protect you from Wonda. Regardless of our difference of opinion, it really is important that you cooperate."

"Go fuck yourself."

Tosh reached into his pocket and pulled a small pill container out. He held it up, with the label facing Alia. She refused to look at first, but he held it steady, waiting for her with a patience only the truly committed know. As he knew she would, after a minute or so, she relented and read the label. Digitalis.

"We know a certain patient who by now is missing her treatment."

Alia looked as if she wanted to come at him with her nails out and scratch his face off. Good. She would be easier to manipulate when she was angry.

Tosh's voice was soft, gentle. Still, she seemed to flinch when he said, "Record the message, and you can give this to Florence Eastmore."

"No."

Alia stared at him with wide, innocent, begging-to-be-bleeding-for-justice eyes. She had no idea how violent Tosh could be, how his mood could turn on a dime from charmer to sadist, how quickly the wolf shed his disguise.

"You should know how far Wonda is willing to take this. The other patient is dead."

Alia blinked. Her eyes welled with tears.

"I grew up here, you know," Tosh said. He pointed to the Qaddo mudflats.

She looked at him with malice. "You disgrace your tribe."

"Wrong. I share their disgrace. A man without pride has no boundaries. Remember that."

She looked at him with chin raised, defiant.

"Look," he said, "I don't want anyone to get hurt. I wouldn't have to resort to threats if you would cooperate. It's your decision. You decide whether Florence suffers. This is very difficult for me. I love the Eastmores. I think you do too."

She wouldn't look at him. Probably from shame, being forced to choose between her principles. Hesitation—that was the sign of a weak moral system. Tosh pressed the button to start the recording.

"Tell Torsten that you're fine, you miss him, you just have to keep working on some cases with unfamiliar symptoms. Short and simple."

Alia glared at him. Then she sighed, looked down at the table and wiped her cheeks. Her weariness was apparent.

Eventually she looked up at the recorder. "Hi, sweetie. Sorry I didn't call earlier. There's a case . . . We've got some patients here that aren't doing well. I need to stay with them. It's really touch and go. And I—I miss you." Her voice cracked. She took a moment to compose herself. "I'll be home as soon as I can."

"Do it again," Tosh said.

Alia repeated the message. He made her do it twice more. He'd have to splice sections together and share only the audio feed, but it would sound genuine. Alia left the room with the small bottle of pills in her hand. An escort would take her to Florence.

Tosh ran his palms over his face. He hadn't slept much the last two nights. It was like a chess game, mentally grueling, a patient man's game, but with no clear terms of victory, without the turn taking, and with the pieces behaving unpredictably.

Tosh was pretty sure it would all come crashing down any moment. No matter. He knew how he would escape. This was his old stomping ground after all.

It wasn't time to give up yet. The same strategies he'd learned in Mexico applied here, he told himself. It's all about projecting force and avoiding threats.

The biggest threats: someone escaping and convincing authorities to investigate the clinic, the Lifers losing their nerve and walking away, one of the Eastmores—Victor or Circe—marshaling resources to retake the clinic by force. The prospect of a violent hostage revolt was minimal. Few of them had a fighting spirit. Those who did were being dosed with mind-clouding drugs, one of the few exceptions to the Lifers' coda. They'd accepted his reasoning for it; sometimes people have to overdose on the hegemony to see the need to escape it. Wonda had loved that. "We're showing them the broken system they live in. Afterward, they'll beg us to take them in."

It gave Tosh chills to hear her speak impossibilities with such certainty, but he had to admit, she had the tenacity and ruthlessness to get results. She was fascinating, frustrating, and full of surprises—a firecracker in a cherubic package.

Later, word came down from the Diamond King: *Time to release the beast.*

Laws help us all, Tosh thought, *Wonda is going to get what she wants. Here's hoping it doesn't kill her.*

41

I'm guilty of the same sin as Jefferson: believing my words would help. I found my voice and damned us all.

—Victor Eastmore's *Apology*

18 June 1991
New Venice, The Louisiana Territories

The practice of solitary confinement expanded. Alia remained separated. Mía was put under guard and not allowed to talk to fellow hostages after she lost control and slapped Wonda. The daily negotiations were dragging on, but Victor sensed something different about Tosh, who watched Wonda carefully. A sly trickster sheen of green glistened on his face, betraying his otherwise stoic expression. Victor could tell he was planning something.

"Can you imagine," Circe said, "the legal liability for BioScan if we begin denying treatments based on your advice? It would open the door to countless lawsuits."

Wonda replied, "We're only asking for seats on your policy board."

"Would you commit to making all decisions based on the latest medical science?"

"Of course. We're open to deliberation as long as we control a majority of the seats."

Karine shouted, "Circe! You can't trust them."

"I agree," Circe said. "I was testing their position."

Victor looked at Circe and Karine. They were a tight pair. Victor wasn't like them, not really. Could he ever become part of the BioScan family in New Venice? Could he coexist with their kind of callous, calculating, and self-centered mindset?

Circe stared at Wonda. "Here's where any rational person is going to part ways with you. If a technology saves lives, if it improves the quality of someone's life, the basis of that technology—be it genetic, pharmaceutical, or whatever—is irrelevant. What matters is what works. I respect religious beliefs. I have to. I lead a company that operates in over fifty different countries. But I'm not going to make policy decisions on any basis except science. No deal."

"We're not asking you to change your beliefs. We're asking you to respect ours, to respect human nature, to avoid contaminating our bodies and those of our children."

Karine spoke up. "What do you know about respect? The people you've imprisoned here will remember how you've treated them. I'll remember. You won't be able to hide the bodies for long."

Wonda marched over to Karine and bent over. Their faces were almost touching. "You act like everything you do here is for some higher purpose. Medicine. Science. Helping people. How much do you profit from that? How much? How much of your revenue comes from unnecessary treatments? From enhancements? You can't have it both ways. You can't enjoy the privileges of being a medical institution and make the profits of a human body shop."

Victor tried to ease the tension, saying in a smooth voice, "They're just asking for transparency."

Karine looked past Wonda and threw him a withering look. "I forget sometimes how naive you can be. You think they'll stop there? If we open our books, they'll never stop needling us, criticizing our investment decisions, trying to redline our activities. They'll make it impossible to run our business."

Wonda straightened and backed off a few steps. "We're drawing lines in the sand, not trying to run your business. We simply want to preserve our humanity."

"Perhaps we should take Samuel Miller and go," Tosh said.

Wonda spun around and gaped at him. "How can you say that?"

"They're not budging. Maybe we need to count our victories while we're winning."

"That doesn't sound like you," she said. "What happened?"

Tosh reached up and rubbed his neck. *He's trying and failing to look casual about what he's proposing,* Victor realized. *What's his angle?*

"I'm just saying that if you want to transform BioScan, it's going to take more than a discussion here in private. Demonstrations like the one outside are what's really going to make a difference. We should take Samuel Miller and go."

"There's wisdom in his words," Circe said.

Victor felt he could see the wheels turning in Circe's mind. As soon as the Lifers left, she'd make a big announcement about how the BioScan staff had been held captive and Samuel Miller had been freed. The Lifers would get all the blame. Whatever damage he caused would be their responsibility.

"What if he kills someone?" Victor asked. "He's clever, in case you've forgotten. I wouldn't trust him with a tincture vial, let alone a MeshBit. BioScan will be blamed."

Wonda's face flushed. Then she looked at Circe with contempt. "You don't understand the world we live in. People will flock to our cause. You think you're tricking me? You're tricking yourself."

"Fine, it sounds like we're all agreed," Karine said. "Take the rope to hang yourselves and be gone."

"No!" Victor banged his fist on the table. "If Samuel Miller goes on another rampage, people will want a more restrictive Classification System."

"Our responsibility right now is to our patients. We can't help them while we're under siege," Circe said. "Think of Florence. She doesn't have long."

Wonda seemed uncertain for the first time Victor could remember. She walked onto the deck and looked out at the demonstrators. Enforcers had surrounded the construction site over night. No one could get in or out. Law enforcement on BioScan's doorstep, unaware of the hostage situation right next to them. How long could it last?

Victor realized a sad irony—he wanted negotiations to go on longer, if only to keep Samuel Miller from walking free. He had to do something to convince everyone it was the wrong course of action. But he'd tried everything already.

Two Lifers rushed into the drug hut and looked around. One of them said to Wonda, "We have a problem."

The other, Donya, Tosh's second, said, "Some of the protesters broke through the enforcers lines, but they were injured. There's lots of blood downstairs." She still wore the bandage from the wound she'd received during the blockage of Triton's Deep.

"Downstairs?!" Wonda said, alarmed.

"Lifers let them in the admin building. They were injured. We can treat injuries, right? And they're our compatriots."

"Did the enforcers see them?" Tosh asked.

"I don't know," Donya said.

"Come on," Tosh said, gesturing to Wonda. "We need to see what we're dealing with. You stay here and watch them," he said to Donya.

Tosh's robe fluttered as he sped out of the room.

When they were gone, the three of them, Victor, Karine, and Circe, looked at each other and laughed. It was funny. It was horrifying. How do you reason with someone who believes in feelings and intuitions, not facts? How had we ever built civilizations when so much of our mental machinery was vulnerable to emotional hacking?

"Quiet!" Donya shouted. She gave him a hostile look, and then her gaze flicked to Karine and Circe.

Victor looked down at his shaking hands. He crossed his arms and repeated the owl mantra quietly. His body was primed to fight. Outside, grey clouds sucked color out of the day. The greens of the grasses and plants were muted; flowers seemed dim.

This was Victor's chance. He slipped under the dinner table.

"Get up from there," Donya ordered.

"The Avatar deserves a moment."

"Victor, what are you doing?" Circe asked.

"No talking!" Donya shouted.

Victor pictured the look on Auntie's face. Perhaps she was sharing a knowing glance with Karine. "Why do we suffer these fools?" he was sure she wanted to say, and "Poor Victor, the trouble he has to go to stay sane."

He had one chance to redirect the situation. They might all be comfortable with Samuel Miller in the Lifers hands, but Victor couldn't be. He'd seen how easily their beliefs twisted and contorted. How long before they became believers in ghosts and primals? Wonda had been willing to let someone die by neglect. Victor had no reason to believe she couldn't kill for her faith too.

We're not so different after all, he thought.

"I said get up," Donya shouted. He could see her feet from under the table.

"Leave him be," Circe said. "This has been taxing on all of us."

"Don't speak unless I demand it."

"And if we don't obey your silly rules?" Karine countered.

Victor took out the MeshBit and sent a message to Ozie asking him to send a Dirac shockstick, a power supply modification kit, and a quantum trigger.

The reply came back almost instantly: *for you?!?!*

No, Victor replied, *send them to the drug hut, Samuel's. Can you take care of the guards?*

Will do. It's about time. Drone incoming ETA fifteen minutes.

"Don't let her muzzle you, Auntie," Victor said. "You're better than that."

"Thank you, Victor, but I'm all right—you just focus on yourself."

"Last warning," Donya said.

He heard the sound of a shockstick powering up.

"Karine, remember Amarillo?" Victor asked. "We need some of that right now!"

He lunged from under the table into Donya's legs. She toppled on top of him. The shockstick wasn't in her hands.

"Grab her!" Circe shouted.

Victor pawed at Donya, but she was kicking and twisting. A knee smashed into his cheek, and he rolled away. Karine dropped to her knees and put Donya in a headlock. Victor spotted the shockstick near the wall and elbow-crawled to it, just as Donya slipped out of the headlock. Victor turned and fired. Both Donya and Karine were hit by a shimmering wave, and they slumped down. Victor rose and walked to the door.

"Wait," Circe said. "Where are you going?"

"I'm stopping this."

She approached him with her hands reaching out. "You need to rethink—"

"Stop," he said, raising the shockstick at her face. "You're not coming with me."

She pleaded, "Victor—"

"Don't," he said, shutting the door. "Don't come after me."

He heard her call through the door: "What are you going to do?"

42

> People turn away from me in public. I am a shadow of what we've all been through. A fossil of death. That day in Carmichael, I became a ghost of the fallen.
>
> —Interview with Mía Barrias in *Five Years After Carmichael* (1976)

18 June 1991
New Venice, The Louisiana Territories

Victor entered Samuel's drug hut. A sleeping gas haze was visible but had mostly cleared out. A Lifer lay slumped over the couch, a MeshBit in his hand. Victor hoped he hadn't had time to contact anyone. Another was sprawled in the doorway to the deck. Victor stepped gingerly over him and found Ozie's drone beneath a hole in the transplastic guardwrap. Strapped to the drone was a standard shockstick, a modified energy pack, a set of pliers, and a tiny gray box, the quantum trigger. Victor pried off the shockstick's cap and removed a discharge impeder, which looked like a semitranslucent glass cylinder. He swapped out the energy pack, inserted the quantum trigger, and reattached the cap.

So that was what it looked like. A lethal shockstick. Indistinguishable from a normal one except in its effects.

When Victor stepped into Samuel's room, he was sitting in a chair, waiting, expressionless except for a tiny twitch at the corner of his mouth. He said, "Welcome to the sick ward. In the event of smoke, hold your breath and pray. Nobody said BioScan was humane."

"The Lifers can't stop talking about you. They want to take you with them."

Samuel's voice changed. "I have a different way out of here," he said. Victor's ears burned when he used that tone.

Samuel recrossed his legs. A shadow covered his face. It was as if the light didn't reach him, as if there were another body behind his body and his actual self had slipped backward somehow, nestled in shadows.

Victor shivered. Double vision, lateral thinking—an episode was coming on. Every time he was around Samuel, the fantastical part of his imagination ran wild, nightmares took a stroll in the daylight, and his logical mind threw up its arms in surrender.

"Samuel, do you regret what you did in Carmichael?" Victor asked.

"I don't know." Samuel's eyes glinted with mirth. He smiled, and his goofball incisors crowded out his other teeth. "Did it happen on this world or the other?"

Victor massaged his forehead. His other hand gripped the shockstick. The situation was unraveling. He had to hurry.

"I remember now how they fought over me," Samuel said. "Jefferson wanted me to recant. She wanted to know about my 'visions.'"

Victor looked up. Samuel was tracing a finger around one of the primal drawings, a hazy red halo around a blue figure that was shorter than the others.

A sly look crossed Samuel's face. "The nice thing about a background in physics is that you don't have to believe in magical nonsense. She, on the other hand, listened to every word I said about the ghosts. I'm not sure she understood."

"Who did?"

"The one in charge."

"Circe?"

"She wishes she could see them." Samuel backed up to the wall, arranged his arms in a way that mirrored his primal drawing. "You know that we're the ghosts. You feel it. That's why you return to blankspace again and again. That's why we need to cross over."

Victor felt his ears burning. Did Samuel really know any of what Circe was thinking? Then again, what, if anything, did Samuel really know that wasn't a delusion?

Samuel watched him. "You feel it, don't you? You hear them?"

Victor imagined the Carmichael dead calling out for justice while he spoke calmly to their killer. The world wasn't right, true, but Samuel couldn't be the key to understanding it. He couldn't.

"How's it going out there?" Samuel asked. "Minds are meant to intermingle. What's the function for the exponential spread of a contagion through a population? Unit of time to the power of the rate of transmission?"

"I'm not here to talk about an infection."

"Aren't you? You're the vortex, you know. Patient naught, patient zed, patient zero. I wouldn't be here without you. My conscience is clean now, even if I did kill those people. I didn't understand until I heard your voice. Not your kid voice, not your voice at school. Your adult voice, like now but older maybe. I heard it in Carmichael. 'Cross over,' you said. I believed you."

"That's impossible."

"Is it?" Samuel's long face seemed to shine. Victor saw that he was crying. "You're going to help me," he said. "Now."

"We might be able to cure you someday."

"No. Help me. Do it."

Blankness was near, a wave in Victor's brain, cascading outward. His head felt cottony, insubstantial. Blankness was coming for him fast.

Victor raised the shockstick, one hand gripping the quantum trigger. He could fire or not.

Samuel rushed forward, the shockstick pressed between them.

"It's time," Samuel said, exultant.

Victor tried to tear himself away before they both felt the blast.

43

"Cross over," a whispering voice said out of the foggy white blankness surrounding Victor. "You need to see the shape of the world. Understand the echoes of your future. I've said it plainly so many times, I don't know how else to express it, but I'll try. Cross over. There are infinite worlds, so many possible paths."

It wasn't clear who was speaking. Victor could barely make out the words. He tried walking, but he couldn't feel his legs or any other part of himself.

Home, he thought, a command to get him out of this place. He tried to unblank, to get back to a feeling of gravity, of groundedness, of being unmistakably him, in his body, in a real place. *Unblank*, he prayed.

The white ether surrounding him swirled, cleared. He was no longer in a drug hut in New Venice. Walls made of stone blocks surrounded him. There were two figures huddled on the floor, embracing, intertwined with rubble fallen from the ceiling. Their features and shapes were partially obscured by thick brown robes, blankets, and fractured stone.

Unblank.

The scene vanished. Victor was in a tunnel now, again without a body, only a consciousness and a view of the things around him. Wires and pipes ran along a brightly lit tunnel. Thrumming filled the air. High-voltage signs hung on the walls. "Warning: Radiation. Do Not Enter" marked a nearby door with the message repeated in German, Breton, Occitan, Romansh, and a few other languages.

A voice boomed inside his head—except he had no head, so how was he hearing? "The shape of the future," it said. "Cross over."

"I am over," Victor grumbled, without a voicebox to vocalize.

And then he was back. In a drug hut, holding a shockstick, standing over Samuel's prone body. The limbs made a circle, hands meeting above the head, eyes open and glazed. Red foam leaked from the lips, formed a trail down the cheek.

Samuel was dead, and Victor had killed him.

Victor had fired the shockstick and then went blank. Or he went blank and fired the shockstick. Samuel had made him do it. Or had he?

Victor glanced around the room. He had the feeling there was another body. Always two. Two was the best. Two was the answer. He looked again. There was only one body on the ground: Samuel's. He paced the room. Why did it feel as if there were two?

He'd seen two bodies in the blankness, but that was a dream or a vision or whatever. The room had been different. That couldn't be what was bothering him.

Victor stood there, looking at the body, trying to make one equal two, not sure what to do. He looked down. His hand, still holding the shockstick, felt numb, like an alien body part grafted onto his arm.

Shocks. The word ran through his head again and again. *Shocks. Shocks.*

What now?

He left the room. The guards were still unconscious.

Time, which seemed to be oozing along at a snail's pace, began to accelerate. His heartbeats jammed together. His breath sped up. He had little time to make things right before he was swept up in the consequences of his action.

Start with the shockstick. He disconnected the quantum trigger and shoved it in his pocket. He replaced the discharge impeder and swapped the high-powered energy cell for the standard one. Finally, he put the shockstick inside his shirt, tucked the shirt into his pants, and went outside.

Think. Think!, he told himself. His mind was sludge.

The drug hut next door housed Florence. Beyond it was the one where Alia was being kept under guard. With leaden steps, he walked toward it. A plan began to take shape. He knocked and entered. The female Lifer with the cloud-like bosom sat on the living room couch, hands clasped, praying. A male Lifer was out on the balcony staring at the Qaddo mudflats. They both looked over when Victor walked in.

"It's over," he said. His voice, when it came out, was surprisingly calm. The female Lifer closed her eyes and whispered something.

The male one stepped inside. "What do you mean?" he asked.

"I'm the Avatar, right? I say it's over now. Go home."

"What does Wonda say?" the woman asked.

"I haven't told her yet." Victor raised his hands, the way he'd seen them do it in the pavilion when listening to Estrella Burgos's writings—his great great great aunt's writings, that is. "You are the first. The witnesses. Hear me: Samuel Miller crossed over."

Both of the Lifers looked at him, stunned.

"It's your job to spread the word. Tell everyone. Samuel is gone, and it's time to leave."

The female Lifer picked up a book from the table, swept her gaze around the living room, and started toward the door. The male Lifer moved to follow, then stopped. "What about—er, the Effendi woman is in there. Should I—"

"I'll take care of it," Victor said. "Find Wonda and Tosh and tell them to meet me in the administration building with Circe and Karine. Mía too. Tell them, 'A solution has emerged.' I'll be there soon."

The man looked at the door to the room where Alia was kept. He seemed torn between his duty and Victor's orders.

Victor put a hand on the man's shoulder and said, "Don't stand in the way of Emergence. Let it happen."

The man bit his lip, nodded again, unlocked the door to the room where Alia was by typing his code, and then went outside, where the cloud-bosom Lifer woman waited.

Victor opened the door. Alia, sitting on the couch, looked up at Victor and jumped to her feet. "Are you getting me out of here?" she said.

"Yes, you've got to hurry and get help. Find your way out of here without being seen. Use the path above the construction site maybe." He reached into his pocket and put the quantum trigger and energy pack in her hands. "Dump these in the first canal you find."

"What are—"

"There's no time," he said as he took her arm and walked her outside.

"Get rid of those, and go get help. The Lifers are assembling at the admin building. I think you can make it."

She looked down at the gadgets in her hands, questions pursing her lips.

"Please," he said. "This is almost over."

Without a word, she stuffed the gadgets in her pockets, turned, and headed upslope toward a dirt track that wound around the BioScan campus and ended in Pond Park. Victor watched her until she disappeared behind a stand of trees, and then he headed downhill.

Back at the administration building, the Lifer guarding the door saw Victor approaching and let him inside.

"You can go if you want," Victor said. "This is over."

The Lifer snorted. "I'm not going anywhere until Wonda says so."

"Fine. Come listen to what she has to say."

Victor walked to the center of the atrium, where Wonda stood flanked by Tosh and Donya. Mía, Circe, and Karine were off to the side, guarded by four Lifers with their shocksticks out.

In the polished floor he saw two shadows reflected, but they vanished as he approached. Two shadows. Two bodies, curled together, crushed. He had seen Samuel's body, alone in the drug hut, missing its other half. *Why two?*

Wonda ran across the atrium, her shoes clacking on smooth gray synthstone. "What happened?" she asked. "Is it true?"

Victor announced the news in a loud voice: "Samuel Miller is dead."

Wonda's mouth fell open. "No!"

Karine and Circe exchanged a glance, and then both looked at Victor with unreadable expressions. He knew they would have questions for him before long.

"In the drug huts," Victor started to explain, "I found him—"

Found him and killed him. Not on purpose. The blankness made me do it. Victor knew better than to let the truth pass his lips. He took a breath and began again. "It looks like he killed himself," he said, a half-truth that would make his family proud. "There was a drone but no weapon."

"Oh, laws," Wonda said. "Oh, life. No! We were going to get him out of here."

"It's too late," Victor said. "You can tell everyone he crossed over."

Wonda looked at him. "You sound relieved. How can you be so cruel?"

"He got what he wanted. This is over," Victor said. "Everyone is going home."

Wonda looked at him with naked hate. "It's not over. Not until I say."

"The authorities are on their way," Victor told her. He noticed Tosh's stance harden. He said to Tosh, "You know this has to end now."

"They can't touch us," Wonda said. She gestured at the shocksticks in the hands of the Lifers. One of them had taken off his Venetian mask and dropped it on the ground. The man's face was lined with weariness, the bags under his eyes heavy.

"Think, Wonda!" Victor said. "What does a fight get you? The only way this ends well for you is if you leave now. I'm willing to make you a deal."

Circe gazed at Victor with cold fury in her eyes. "We will never agree to their demands." She looked at Wonda. "You have nothing to win. Leave."

"No!" Wonda fired back.

"If you leave now," Victor said, "we'll never speak of the care our hemochromatosis patient received. The kind of care that could constitute a felony."

Wonda licked and then chewed her lips.

"And," Victor added, "you can have Samuel's body."

Wonda furrowed her brow, confused.

Tosh stepped forward, put a hand to her ear, and whispered something that Victor barely caught, something about a "continuing ritual."

A spark lit Wonda's eyes, and her mouth curled the way it did when she was about to make a pronouncement. She closed her eyes, brought her fingers to her lips, kissed the tips, and blew on them.

"We need to pay our respects," she said.

Victor felt a nauseating mixture of disgust and admiration. The way her brain worked terrified him, yet there was still sweetness there, a gentleness that came into flower when she let it, when she wasn't fighting for some ephemeral sense of honor stronger than any logic he could wield. He held out his hand, met her round-eyed gaze, and wrapped his arms around her.

Tosh watched them embrace and then rushed out the front door.

Karine looked relieved, while Circe looked inscrutable as always. They were safe in their power, now that the Lifers had no reason to stay.

The Lifers gathered at the new harbor. A group had run up to the Pond along the same track Alia had taken and brought down a flotilla of kayaks. Mía watched stonily as they laid Samuel's body in a kayak and covered him with clothes. Wonda pushed the kayak away from the dock. It rocked on the waves, losing momentum. In death Samuel was lingering far too languidly for Victor's taste.

Enforcers were arresting the protesters at the construction site. They had been waiting for Circe to file a complaint. "Next time I see you or any Lifers on this campus, I'll have you arrested, your homes repossessed. I'll have you shipped to the ROT and let the Corps do what they will," she'd told the crowd.

The Lifers boarded their kayaks and set off downstream. They'd appeared sad but grateful that the siege was over.

It was then Victor realized he hadn't really thought things through. The Lifers had gained a totem. Wonda could no doubt spin a new thread of crazy focused on Samuel's discarded husk.

In any case, the sheriff was going to be asking a lot of questions.

44

Comparative advantage leads inevitably to conflict. In an economic context, this means wasted effort and money down the drain. Symbiosis requires a different approach—mutualism, openness, and integrity—but the rewards are much greater.

—Circe Eastmore's *Race to the Top* (1991)

1 August 1991
New Venice, The Louisiana Territories

Concrete sludge laced with StoneStrong microbes surged through pipes big enough for a person to stand inside. The gray material, like thick unappealing porridge, filled gaps between wooden frames and rebar lattices, rising quickly, a flood of foundation, soon to dry and harden. Piles of steel beams waited to be assembled into spindly fingers reaching toward the sky, the skeleton of the BioScan towers. Construction was on schedule. The future would arrive soon.

The LT Council blamed recent troubles on foreign meddling—without naming the Diamond King explicitly—and refused to alter their plans. They passed Mía's two-speed Classification Act and cracked down on the resultant protests in New Venice and elsewhere.

Neither Karine nor Circe had confronted Victor about Samuel's death. He thought that was far more disturbing than if they had. Maybe it had something to do with the sheriff's inquiry, which had yet to solicit any statements from the hostages and seemed to face repeated delays thanks to BioScan lawyers.

The drug huts were being torn down to build proper inpatient facilities. The Human Lifers' settlement had been repossessed, part of the two-speed Classification Act's largesse. The addicts would live there, side by side with MRS patients. Mesh IDs would be fused to their bones. Legal wrangling over adjacent parcels continued. The whole complex would expand to a footprint ten times its original size.

Wonda had sent Victor a message. The Lifers were squatting on Qaddo mudflats downstream. She wanted him to see how they were living, what he'd accomplished by betraying them. He didn't respond. There were too many urgent pleas from people who needed help. He'd never imagined a sanctuary to be such a busy place.

Victor tried to keep up with the deluge of tasks needing to be assigned, new staff asking where they should get started, and an endless stream of complaints, prayers, bribes, and invective from Broken Mirrors and their legal custodians hoping to be transferred to New Venice.

The cramped BioScan administration building—though its expansion was complete with new office wings, an expanded emergency room, and a cavernous, glass-encased atrium—didn't have enough room for all the functions that were due to move into the towers. The hallways were jammed, the rooms were jammed, Victor conducted business from a desk crammed into an alcove, everyone had to make do with hardships, and there simply wasn't enough space.

Victor's Handy 1000 chimed. Time for the staff meeting. He downed a fumewort tincture, as much out of habit as anything else. Something had changed in his head: the resonant episodes still came on suddenly, but he was better able to manage them and never went blank—unless he wanted to. He tried not to think about crossing over.

Mía grunted a greeting when he walked through the door. She sat next to Karine, who was wearing emerald green glasses. Idiot Blair the finance guy pecked at a MeshBit, oblivious to anything else. Marilyn paced in a corner. Alia smiled at Victor and pulled out a chair for him. He sat down.

The meeting proceeded at a blistering pace. Questions, answers, commands, and requests bounced back and forth faster than a pro ping-pong ball match. No talk of Samuel. No mention of the Lifers. Everyone was getting on with the business of helping people, not looking back.

Tosh had left town, but he'd be back. Victor was certain.

They were close to wrapping up when a young man with a shaved head and chunky black glasses came into the room. He apologized, "So sorry," made a half bow, and searched out Victor with his gaze. "Could you please come with me, Mr. Eastmore? So sorry to bother you."

"What is it?" Victor asked, rising from his seat.

"Sorry to interrupt. There's a woman and a—patient downstairs who are asking to speak with you."

"Why me? We have protocols for—"

"I'm sorry, I didn't think I should—"

"Let's talk in the hallway," Victor said. He turned to Karine and the others. "I'm sorry about this. I'll take care of whatever it is."

"We've already paused," Karine said, "and I'm curious." She raised her voice, directing it at the young man: "Why have you interrupted our meeting?"

His eyes went wide behind his glasses, looking like a vidscreen magnification. "It's the young woman. She says her name is Elena Morales, and the man with her—he looks bad. Some kind of jaundice and fever." He looked at Victor. "She says it's your fault. Something to do with a kennel?"

Victor gulped, feeling as if he'd swallowed a hot slug of lead. He glanced at Karine. She nodded toward the door.

"Come on," Victor said, taking the young man by the elbow.

"I'm coming, too," Alia called behind him and joined them in the hall.

Downstairs, before they'd rounded the corner to the main reception, he heard Elena shouting. "I don't care. Get him in a stretcher. Put on a fucking space suit if you don't want to touch him—just get me some help."

In the waiting area, Elena was holding up Chico as best she could. His face looked drained of blood, replaced by some combination of mustard and sulfur. His neck flushed red. Victor and Alia rushed over and helped support him by the arms.

"Finally!" Elena said. She was sniffling, wiping tears off her cheeks. Relieved of Chico's weight, she walked around randomly, almost a birdlike wandering. "We were in the car for eight hours. I was so worried he'd stop breathing and I'd be—"

"What's wrong with him?" Victor asked.

She stopped, put her hands on her hips. "You tell me! He was working in the kennel. I barely saw him for days on end. I went away for a day and a half and came back, and he was like this. He's on fire!"

Alia had already put on gloves. "We have to treat him. Now."

Two attendants arrived with a stretcher. Their arms flexed as they hefted Chico up and onto it. His eyes, which had been half-open and heavy-lidded, closed as soon as he was lying down.

Alia led the attendants toward the emergency room.

Victor approached Elena and put a hand on her arm gently. "We need to take a look at you too. Just in case."

"It's Jefferson," she said. "Whatever he did to those dogs, it's happening to people now too."

Victor blanched. He could almost feel the color run out of his face. Jefferson had used the Lone Star Kennel in Amarillo as a bioreservoir for something, "a tool," he'd said in his message.

"Come on," he said. "Let's go figure out what we're dealing with."

"Fucking Eastmores," Elena said as Victor led her toward the emergency room.

TO BE CONTINUED

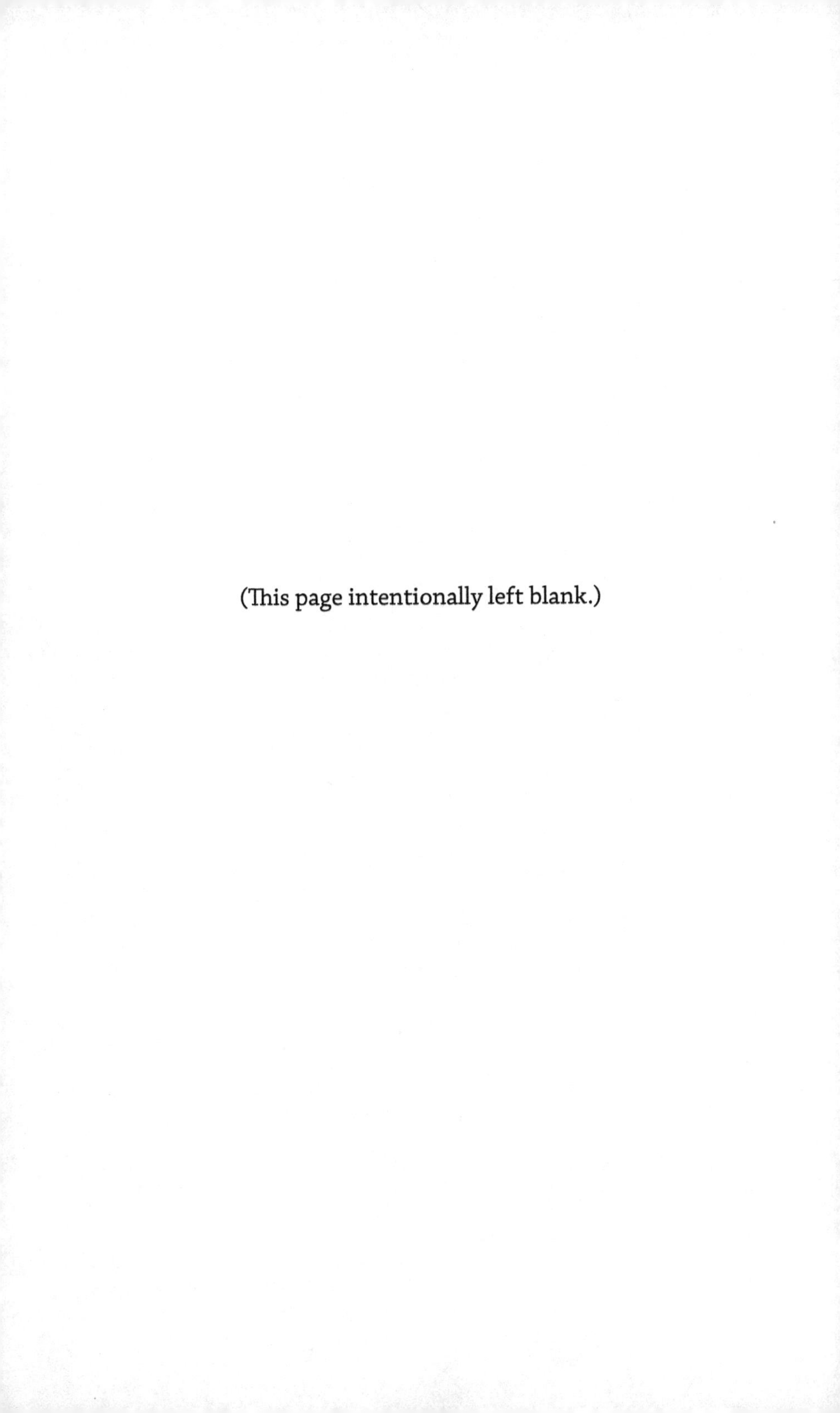

(This page intentionally left blank.)

Afterword

Thank you for reading *Tortured Echoes*. I'd love to hear your thoughts on the book. Head on over to Goodreads or to the retailer's page online to leave a review.

This novel was written throughout 2016, and much of the latter half of the book took shape in the final stages of the U.S. presidential election. Readers might recognize the toxic blends of fact and fiction, belief and rhetoric, stated purposes and secret plans that run through New Venice as disturbingly familiar. I never intended the world of Resonant Earth to be utopic; the problems facing Victor and his fellow seekers aren't easily resolved. But, in a time of geopolitical uncertainty and realignment, a world without guns, where "skin is skin," and there is no risk of nuclear war, it seems readers might want to escape to Resonant Earth for as long as they can.

The third book in the series promises to be darker, to show more of the American Union and beyond, to explore the frontiers of blankspace, and to ask the question: how far will Victor go to get what he wants?

About the Author

Cody Sisco is the author of speculative fiction that straddles the divide between plausible and extraordinary and sit in the "uncanny valley"—discomfortingly odd yet familiar, where morality is not clear-cut, technology bestows blessings and curses, and outsiders struggle to find their niche. He lives in Los Angeles.

Acknowledgments

I continue to be deeply grateful to my family, friends, and writing colleagues, and, of course, the readers I've had the privilege of meeting since the release of *Broken Mirror*.

My thanks to Lindsey Alexander and Beth Wright for again helping me through the editing process.

Thank you to Derek Jentzsch, Jessica Barnett, Nate Cardin, Holly McHugh, Richard Merrill, and Susan Sisco for their feedback on early drafts. And my thanks to the members of the Northeast Los Angeles Writers Group, especially my co-organizers, Mike Radice and Gabi Lorino.

Jay Fennelly, you are an inspiration, always proving that truth-seeking and hard work are the bedrock of loving, supportive relationships. You are precious to me.

Finally, thank you to all the countless indie authors who are bucking the odds and finding ways to share their stories with the world. Keep writing. The world needs you.

Connect

You can read more about the events that set Victor's journey in motion in "Believe and Live," a short story set during the Carmichael massacre. Subscribe to my newsletter for a free copy at codysisco.com/contact/.

Indie authors depend on word of mouth. Please consider leaving a review at the retailer where you purchased Broken Mirror, Goodreads, or other platforms. You can find links on my website at codysisco.com/books/#Broken-Mirror.

www.ingramcontent.com/pod-product-compliance
Lightning Source LLC
Chambersburg PA
CBHW031139120726
47905CB00006B/1739
* 9 7 8 0 9 9 7 0 3 4 8 4 4 *